2/-00

D1580262

Everyman, I will go with thee, and be thy guide,
In thy most need to go by thy side.

This is No. 954 of Everyman's Library. A
list of authors and their works in this series
will be found at the end of this volume. The
publishers will be pleased to send freely to all
applicants a separate, annotated list of the
Library.

J. M. DENT & SONS LIMITED
10–13 BEDFORD STREET LONDON W.C.2

E. P. DUTTON & CO. INC.
286–302 FOURTH AVENUE
NEW YORK

EVERYMAN'S LIBRARY
EDITED BY ERNEST RHYS

FICTION

MODERN SHORT STORIES
EDITED BY JOHN HADFIELD

MODERN SHORT STORIES

EDITED BY JOHN HADFIELD

LONDON: J. M. DENT & SONS LTD

All rights reserved
Made in Great Britain
at The Temple Press Letchworth
and decorated by Eric Ravilious
for
J. M. Dent & Sons Ltd
Aldine House Bedford St London
This Collection First Published 1939

INTRODUCTION

THE short story is one of the oldest forms of literature—perhaps the oldest of all. It probably originated around primitive camp fires, when hunters described, with unconscious art and imaginative emphasis, their deeds of the day. It found more formal expression in the classical fables and in some of the tales of the Old Testament and Apocrypha. In the Middle Ages it flowered in many different pastures. Later, the Renaissance gave birth to the *novella*, which is exemplified by the *Decameron* of Boccaccio. From this model came the French *conte*, and such collections of stories in English as William Painter's *The Palace of Pleasure.*

During the last fifty years, however, the short story has developed in scope and variety more rapidly than during the preceding five centuries. There is no other form of imaginative writing in which the twentieth century has discovered so many new possibilities of art, interpretation of life, and entertainment.

Some of the reasons for this sudden development of the short story are bound up with the development of fiction in general. The vast expansion of the reading public and the rise of the circulating library have caused so many minds—and so many more pens—to grapple with the technique of the novel that fiction has discovered a hundred and one new tricks and methods. All of these have become part of the equipment of the short-story writer.

The short story, however, has also made rapid growth in its own particular territory. During the eighteenth century it was not a popular form of writing, and in the earlier part of the nineteenth century it was regarded primarily as an abbreviated novel—as something for a novelist to toy with when not engaged on full-scale work. At the end of the nineteenth century, however, writers of talent and enterprise began to realize that the short story presented problems of story-telling and composition that were quite different from, and often more difficult or more satisfying than, those of the full-length novel. The short story became a distinct literary form.

At the same time the demand for short stories increased. The last fifty years have seen a phenomenal growth in the production and circulation of newspapers and magazines. To cater for the requirements of this new and extensive market short stories were a necessary commodity. Inevitably, the majority of these stories were—and are—machine-made, ephemeral things. But literature is seldom the product of ivory towers; in all ages good writers as well as bad writers have to serve the public that is available to them. 'No form of art,' writes W. Somerset Maugham, 'is produced unless there is a demand for it, and if newspapers and magazines did not publish short stories they would not be written. All short stories are magazine stories or newspaper stories. The writers must accept certain (but constantly changing) conditions; it has never been known yet that a good writer was unable to write his best owing to the conditions under which alone he could gain a public for his work.'

By the beginning of the twentieth century, therefore, commercial opportunity and the development of fictional technique had conspired to give exceptional encouragement to the short-story writer. During the twentieth century other influences have furthered the growth of the short story in the English-speaking countries. Culturally we have always learnt much from France; and the stories of Guy de Maupassant probably had an even greater influence upon English writers than upon the French. Later, with the vogue for Russian literature, came the stories and sketches of Tchekhov—another stimulus to English short-story writers. Then again, with the gradual decline in public appreciation of poetry, many would-be poets found themselves without an audience. The short story, in many cases, provided them with the most sympathetic and effective alternative medium.

In recent years there have been many critical dissertations on the art of the short story. There have also been many attempts to define the short story as distinct from the novel. In introducing this collection of short stories

I would avoid such definitions. A short story is a story that is not long; that would seem to be a sufficient, if inexact, rule of thumb by which to work. For the rest, I would emphasize the variety of the stories rather than their adherence to any critical formulae. 'I have never from the first had the slightest interest in plots,' writes H. E. Bates. To O. Henry, on the other hand, plots were almost everything. Tchekhov said that a story should have neither beginning nor end. Obviously this is a theory that would not have commended itself to Kipling or Stacy Aumonier.

Perhaps there are two guiding principles only that need influence an editor in compiling an anthology of this kind. One is expressed in the words of John Galsworthy: 'The first essential in a short-story writer is the power of interesting sentence by sentence.' Unlike the novelist, the short-story writer cannot rely on the cumulative effect of chapter after chapter. His writing, for this reason, must be more taut, highly charged, and rigorously controlled. The other principle has been voiced by Somerset Maugham. 'To my mind,' he writes in the preface to *Cosmopolitans*, 'it is not enough when the writer gives you the plain facts seen through his own eyes (which means, of course, that they are not plain facts, but facts distorted by his own idiosyncrasy); I think he should impose upon them a design.'

. . . . . .

The present selection is intended to be a companion to the earlier volume of *English Short Stories* (No. 743) in Everyman's Library, which traced the growth of the short story in England from 'The Green Knight,' of Arthurian legend, to the twentieth century. Several modern writers, such as Thomas Hardy, John Galsworthy, Sir Arthur Quiller-Couch, and Sir Hugh Walpole, are represented in *English Short Stories*, and have therefore been omitted from this further volume. Nor are the short stories of G. K. Chesterton, Walter de la Mare, and Aldous Huxley represented here, for separate miscellanies of their work have already appeared in Everyman's Library. Writers of ghost stories have been excluded too, since Everyman has a separate collection of them (No. 952), to which such masters as M. R. James and Algernon Blackwood contribute.

With these exceptions, however, the present volume aims at giving a representative selection of short stories by authors who have lived and written in the twentieth century.

The collection begins on one side of the Atlantic with Joseph Conrad and Rudyard Kipling, two masters of the craft, whose methods and models have inspired two schools of younger writers, and on the other side of the Atlantic with O. Henry, whose 'Jeff Peters as a Personal Magnet' is a perfect example of the tale with an unexpected ending. As a literary exemplar, Stephen Crane should stand beside O. Henry, but his greatest story, 'The Open Boat,' is already reprinted in several anthologies, and as he died in 1900 he is not strictly eligible for this book.

America has contributed much to the golden age of the short story. Some of the best of the early American work in this medium will be found in *American Short Stories of the Nineteenth Century* (No. 840 in Everyman's Library). For the twentieth-century selection two writers of successive generations have been chosen to follow O. Henry. Sherwood Anderson, whose influence has been much greater than his own fame, reveals in 'I 'm a Fool' the poetry and poignancy of emotion that can be experienced by an inarticulate sensibility in a commonplace situation. William Saroyan, the youngest writer in the book, shows the development of short-story technique to an almost acrobatic virtuosity.

Fantasy has been a favourite element in modern short stories, and has inevitably inspired much whimsical and undisciplined writing. It is represented here in its more restrained forms, with Saki's urbane and matter-of-fact 'Tobermory,' with T. F. Powys's bucolic fable about 'Mr Pim and the Holy Crumb,' and with Richard Hughes's 'The Ghost.' Fantasy also hovers over E. M. Forster's 'Story of the Siren,' though this finely balanced tale never crosses the margin of the unseen.

It is not possible to do justice with only one choice to the varied work of W. Somerset Maugham; but 'Louise' is one of the most skilful of his shorter tales, and demonstrates that command of social comedy which is evident in his plays and in such novels as *Cakes and Ale* (which is also to be found in Everyman's Library). Comedy is

the essence, too, of Stacy Aumonier's 'Miss Bracegirdle.'
This story, Gerald Bullett's sardonic little comedy 'Wax,'
and V. S. Pritchett's wry 'Sense of Humour,' effectively
show how modern story-tellers can pierce a tragic
situation with shafts of irony. They effectively answer
the complaint that modern short stories are preoccupied
with gloom.

The more sombre undertones of life, it is true, are echoed
in some of the finest modern stories. Three notable
examples are James Joyce's 'Clay,' the slight but disturbing piece by D. H. Lawrence, 'Second Best,' and Katherine
Mansfield's deeply moving story, 'The Garden Party.'

Any close study of the outstanding short-story tellers of
our time reveals again and again their remarkable diversity.
There are hosts of imitators of temporarily fashionable
moods and methods; but amongst the true artists the
predominant characteristic is individuality. That sly and
devastatingly simple tale, 'The Green Drake,' for example,
bears in every line the unmistakable imprint of A. E.
Coppard. That pathetic, yet strangely comic study of
racial distinctions, 'The Desert Islander,' has the characteristic signature of Stella Benson.

Another element, which will be found in at least three-
quarters of the tales in this book, is poetry. As I have
already suggested, it is arguable that in an earlier age
many of the writers represented here would have written
in verse, lyrical or satirical. In our era, however, the
short story has been so developed and perfected that it can
provide the medium for poetry no less than narrative.
There is a lovely lyrical perception running through
H. E. Bates's narrative of a child's day, 'Alexander';
and strange though it may seem, P. G. Wodehouse's 'The
Fiery Wooing of Mordred' ends on a note which may be
ludicrous, but is sheerly lyrical in its humour.

Humour and poetry, narrative excitement and character,
fun, fantasy, satire, and philosophy—all these can be
expressed in that compact and versatile medium, the
modern story. All can be found amongst the twenty
stories in this book.

                                            J. H.

1939.

ACKNOWLEDGMENTS

Thanks are due to the following authors and publishers for permission to include stories:

Mrs Aumonier for 'Miss Bracegirdle does her Duty' from *Ups and Downs* by Stacy Aumonier; Ernest Benn, Ltd, and the Trustees of the Conrad Estate for 'The Lagoon' from *Tales of Unrest* by Joseph Conrad; Mr Gerald Bullett for 'Wax' from *Twenty-Four Tales*; Jonathan Cape, Ltd, for 'Alexander' from *Thirty Tales* by H. E. Bates, 'The Green Drake' from *Nixey's Harlequin* by A. E. Coppard, and 'Clay' from *Dubliners* by James Joyce; Chatto & Windus for 'The Ghost' from *A Moment of Time* by Richard Hughes, 'Mr Pim and the Holy Crumb' from *No Painted Plumage* by T. F. Powys, and 'Sense of Humour' from *You make your own Life* by V. S. Pritchett; Constable & Co., Ltd, and Mr Middleton Murry for 'The Garden Party' from *The Garden Party and Other Stories* by Katherine Mansfield; Doubleday, Doran & Co., Inc., for 'Jeff Peters as a Personal Magnet' by O. Henry; Faber & Faber, Ltd, Modern Age Books, Inc., and Mr Saroyan for 'Ever fall in Love with a Midget?' from *Love, here is my Hat*; William Heinemann, Ltd, for 'Louise' from *Cosmopolitans* by Somerset Maugham; Herbert Jenkins, Ltd, and Mr P. G. Wodehouse for 'The Fiery Wooing of Mordred' from *Young Men in Spats*; John Lane, The Bodley Head, Ltd, for 'Tobermory' from *The Complete Stories of 'Saki'*; The Executors of the late D. H. Lawrence for 'Second Best' from *The Tales of D. H. Lawrence*; Macmillan & Co., Ltd, and the Executors of the late Stella Benson for 'The Desert Islander'; Macmillan & Co., Ltd, and Mrs Kipling for 'The Miracle of Purun Bhagat' from *The Second Jungle Book* by Rudyard Kipling; Sidgwick & Jackson, Ltd, and Mr E. M. Forster for 'The Story of the Siren' from *The Eternal Moment*; and The Viking Press for 'I 'm a Fool' from *Horses and Men* by Sherwood Anderson.

CONTENTS

THE LAGOON

BY JOSEPH CONRAD

THE white man, leaning with both arms over the roof of the little house in the stern of the boat, said to the steersman:

'We will pass the night in Arsat's clearing. It is late.'

The Malay only grunted, and went on looking fixedly at the river. The white man rested his chin on his crossed arms and gazed at the wake of the boat. At the end of the straight avenue of forests cut by the intense glitter of the river, the sun appeared unclouded and dazzling, poised low over the water that shone smoothly like a band of metal. The forests, sombre and dull, stood motionless and silent on each side of the broad stream. At the foot of big, towering trees, trunkless nipa palms rose from the mud of the bank, in bunches of leaves enormous and heavy, that hung unstirring over the brown swirl of eddies. In the stillness of the air every tree, every leaf, every bough, every tendril of creeper and every petal of minute blossoms seemed to have been bewitched into an immobility perfect and final. Nothing moved on the river but the eight paddles that rose flashing regularly, dipped together with a single splash; while the steersman swept right and left with a periodic and sudden flourish of his blade describing a glinting semicircle above his head. The churned-up water frothed alongside with a confused murmur. And the white man's canoe, advancing upstream in the short-lived disturbance of its own making, seemed to enter the portals of a land from which the very memory of motion had for ever departed.

The white man, turning his back upon the setting sun, looked along the empty and broad expanse of the sea-reach. For the last three miles of its course the wandering, hesitating river, as if enticed irresistibly by the freedom of an open horizon, flows straight into the sea, flows straight to the east—to the east that harbours both light and darkness. Astern of the boat the repeated call of some bird, a cry discordant and feeble, skipped along over the smooth water and lost itself, before it could reach the other shore, in the breathless silence of the world.

The steersman dug his paddle into the stream, and held hard with stiffened arms, his body thrown forward. The water gurgled aloud; and suddenly the long straight reach seemed to pivot on its centre, the forests swung in a semicircle, and the slanting beams of sunset touched the broadside of the canoe with a fiery glow, throwing the slender and distorted shadows of its crew upon the streaked glitter of the river. The white man turned to look ahead. The course of the boat had been altered at right-angles to the stream, and the carved dragon-head of its prow was pointing now at a gap in the fringing bushes of the bank. It glided through, brushing the overhanging twigs, and disappeared from the river like some slim and amphibious creature leaving the water for its lair in the forests.

The narrow creek was like a ditch: tortuous, fabulously deep; filled with gloom under the thin strip of pure and shining blue of the heaven. Immense trees soared up, invisible behind the festooned draperies of creepers. Here and there, near the glistening blackness of the water, a twisted root of some tall tree showed amongst the tracery of small ferns, black and dull, writhing and motionless, like an arrested snake. The short words of the paddlers reverberated loudly between the thick and sombre walls of vegetation. Darkness oozed out from between the trees, through the tangled maze of the creepers, from behind the great fantastic and unstirring leaves; the darkness, mysterious and invincible; the darkness scented and poisonous of impenetrable forests.

The men poled in the shoaling water. The creek broadened, opening out into a wide sweep of a stagnant lagoon. The forests receded from the marshy bank, leaving a level strip of bright green, reedy grass to frame the reflected blueness of the sky. A fleecy pink cloud drifted high above, trailing the delicate colouring of its image under the floating leaves and the silvery blossoms of the lotus. A little house, perched on high piles, appeared black in the distance. Near it, two tall nibong palms, that seemed to have come out of the forests in the background, leaned slightly over the ragged roof, with a suggestion of sad tenderness and care in the droop of their leafy and soaring heads.

The steersman, pointing with his paddle, said, 'Arsat is there. I see his canoe fast between the piles.'

The polers ran along the sides of the boat glancing over their shoulders at the end of the day's journey. They would have preferred to spend the night somewhere else than on this lagoon of weird aspect and ghostly reputation. Moreover, they disliked Arsat, first as a stranger, and also because he who repairs a ruined house, and dwells in it, proclaims that he is not afraid to live amongst the spirits that haunt the places abandoned by mankind. Such a man can disturb the course of fate by glances or words; while his familiar ghosts are not easy to propitiate by casual wayfarers upon whom they long to wreak the malice of their human master. White men care not for such things, being unbelievers and in league with the Father of Evil, who leads them unharmed through the invisible dangers of this world. To the warnings of the righteous they oppose an offensive pretence of disbelief. What is there to be done?

So they thought, throwing their weight on the end of their long poles. The big canoe glided on swiftly, noiselessly, and smoothly, towards Arsat's clearing, till, in a great rattling of poles thrown down, and the loud murmurs of 'Allah be praised!' it came with a gentle knock against the crooked piles below the house.

The boatmen with uplifted faces shouted discordantly, 'Arsat! O Arsat!' Nobody came. The white man began to climb the rude ladder giving access to the bamboo platform before the house. The juragan of the boat said sulkily, 'We will cook in the sampan, and sleep on the water.'

'Pass my blankets and the basket,' said the white man, curtly.

He knelt on the edge of the platform to receive the bundle. Then the boat shoved off, and the white man, standing up, confronted Arsat, who had come out through the low door of his hut. He was a man young, powerful, with broad chest and muscular arms. He had nothing on but his sarong. His head was bare. His big, soft eyes stared eagerly at the white man, but his voice and demeanour were composed as he asked, without any words of greeting:

'Have you medicine, Tuan?'

'No,' said the visitor in a startled tone. 'No. Why? Is there sickness in the house?'

'Enter and see,' replied Arsat, in the same calm manner, and turning short round, passed again through the small doorway. The white man, dropping his bundles, followed.

In the dim light of the dwelling he made out on a couch of bamboos a woman stretched on her back under a broad sheet of red cotton cloth. She lay still, as if dead; but her big eyes, wide open, glittered in the gloom, staring upwards at the slender rafters, motionless and unseeing. She was in a high fever, and evidently unconscious. Her cheeks were sunk slightly, her lips were partly open, and on the young face there was the ominous and fixed expression— the absorbed, contemplating expression of the unconscious who are going to die. The two men stood looking down at her in silence.

'Has she been long ill?' asked the traveller.

'I have not slept for five nights,' answered the Malay, in a deliberate tone. 'At first she heard voices calling her from the water and struggled against me who held her. But since the sun of to-day rose she hears nothing—she hears not me. She sees nothing. She sees not me—me!'

He remained silent for a minute, then asked softly:

'Tuan, will she die?'

'I fear so,' said the white man, sorrowfully. He had known Arsat years ago, in a far country in times of trouble and danger, when no friendship is to be despised. And since his Malay friend had come unexpectedly to dwell in the hut on the lagoon with a strange woman, he had slept many times there, in his journeys up and down the river. He liked the man who knew how to keep faith in council and how to fight without fear by the side of his white friend. He liked him—not so much perhaps as a man likes his favourite dog—but still he liked him well enough to help and ask no questions, to think sometimes vaguely and hazily in the midst of his own pursuits, about the lonely man and the long-haired woman with audacious face and triumphant eyes, who lived together hidden by the forests—alone and feared.

The white man came out of the hut in time to see the enormous conflagration of sunset put out by the swift and stealthy shadows that, rising like a black and impalpable vapour above the tree-tops, spread over the heaven, extinguishing the crimson glow of floating clouds and the red brilliance of departing daylight. In a few moments all the stars come out above the intense blackness of the earth and the great lagoon gleaming suddenly with reflected lights resembled an oval patch of night sky flung down into the hopeless and abysmal night of the wilderness. The white man had some supper out of the basket, then collecting a few sticks that lay about the platform, made up a small fire, not for warmth, but for the sake of the smoke, which would keep off the mosquitoes. He wrapped himself in the blankets and sat with his back against the reed wall of the house, smoking thoughtfully.

Arsat came through the doorway with noiseless steps and squatted down by the fire. The white man moved his outstretched legs a little.

'She breathes,' said Arsat in a low voice, anticipating the expected question. 'She breathes and burns as if with a great fire. She speaks not; she hears not—and burns!'

He paused for a moment, then asked in a quiet, incurious tone:

'Tuan . . . will she die?'

The white man moved his shoulders uneasily and muttered in a hesitating manner:

'If such is her fate.'

'No, Tuan,' said Arsat, calmly. 'If such is my fate. I hear, I see, I wait. I remember . . . Tuan, do you remember the old days? Do you remember my brother?'

'Yes,' said the white man. The Malay rose suddenly and went in. The other, sitting still outside, could hear the voice in the hut. Arsat said: 'Hear me! Speak!' His words were succeeded by a complete silence. 'O Diamelen!' he cried, suddenly. After that cry there was a deep sigh. Arsat came out and sank down again in his old place.

They sat in silence before the fire. There was no sound within the house, there was no sound near them; but far away on the lagoon they could hear the

voices of the boatmen ringing fitful and distinct on
the calm water. The fire in the bows of the sampan
shone faintly in the distance with a hazy red glow.
Then it died out. The voices ceased. The land and
the water slept invisible, unstirring and mute. It
was as though there had been nothing left in the
world but the glitter of stars streaming, ceaseless and
vain, through the black stillness of the night.

The white man gazed straight before him into
the darkness with wide-open eyes. The fear and
fascination, the inspiration and the wonder of death
—of death near, unavoidable, and unseen, soothed
the unrest of his race and stirred the most indistinct,
the most intimate of his thoughts. The ever-ready
suspicion of evil, the gnawing suspicion that lurks in
our hearts, flowed out into the stillness round him—
into the stillness profound and dumb, and made it
appear untrustworthy and infamous, like the placid
and impenetrable mask of an unjustifiable violence.
In that fleeting and powerful disturbance of his being
the earth enfolded in the starlight peace became a
shadowy country of inhuman strife, a battle-field of
phantoms terrible and charming, august or ignoble,
struggling ardently for the possession of our helpless
hearts. An unquiet and mysterious country of
inextinguishable desires and fears.

A plaintive murmur rose in the night; a murmur
saddening and startling, as if the great solitudes of
surrounding woods had tried to whisper into his ear
the wisdom of their immense and lofty indifference.
Sounds hesitating and vague floated in the air round
him, shaped themselves slowly into words; and at
last flowed on gently in a murmuring stream of soft

and monotonous sentences. He stirred like a man waking up and changed his position slightly. Arsat, motionless and shadowy, sitting with bowed head under the stars, was speaking in a low and dreamy tone:

'. . . for where can we lay down the heaviness of our trouble but in a friend's heart? A man must speak of war and of love. You, Tuan, know what war is, and you have seen me in time of danger seek death as other men seek life! A writing may be lost; a lie may be written; but what the eye has seen is truth and remains in the mind!'

'I remember,' said the white man, quietly. Arsat went on with mournful composure:

'Therefore I shall speak to you of love. Speak in the night. Speak before both night and love are gone—and the eye of day looks upon my sorrow and my shame; upon my blackened face; upon my burnt-up heart.'

A sigh, short and faint, marked an almost imperceptible pause, and then his words flowed on, without a stir, without a gesture.

'After the time of trouble and war was over and you went away from my country in the pursuit of your desires, which we, men of the islands, cannot understand, I and my brother became again, as we had been before, the sword-bearers of the Ruler. You know we were men of family, belonging to a ruling race, and more fit than any to carry on our right shoulder the emblem of power. And in the time of prosperity Si Dendring showed us favour, as we, in time of sorrow, had showed to him the faithfulness of our courage. It was a time of peace. A

time of deer-hunts and cock-fights; of idle talks
and foolish squabbles between men whose bellies
are full and weapons are rusty. But the sower
watched the young rice-shoots grow up without fear,
and the traders came and went, departed lean and
returned fat into the river of peace. They brought
news, too. Brought lies and truth mixed together,
so that no man knew when to rejoice and when to be
sorry. We heard from them about you also. They
had seen you here and had seen you there. And I
was glad to hear, for I remembered the stirring times,
and I always remembered you, Tuan, till the time
came when my eyes could see nothing in the past,
because they had looked upon the one who is dying
there—in the house.'

He stopped to exclaim in an intense whisper, 'O
Mara bahia! O Calamity!' then went on speaking
a little louder:

'There's no worse enemy and no better friend than
a brother, Tuan, for one brother knows another, and
in perfect knowledge is strength for good or evil. I
loved my brother. I went to him and told him that
I could see nothing but one face, hear nothing but
one voice. He told me: "Open your heart so that
she can see what is in it—and wait. Patience is
wisdom. Inchi Midah may die or our Ruler may
throw off his fear of a woman!" . . . . I waited!
. . . . You remember the lady with the veiled face,
Tuan, and the fear of our Ruler before her cunning
and temper. And if she wanted her servant, what
could I do? But I fed the hunger of my heart on
short glances and stealthy words. I loitered on the
path to the bath-houses in the daytime, and when the

sun had fallen behind the forest I crept along the jasmine hedges of the women's courtyard. Unseeing, we spoke to one another through the scent of flowers, through the veil of leaves, through the blades of long grass that stood still before our lips; so great was our prudence, so faint was the murmur of our great longing. The time passed swiftly . . . and there were whispers amongst women—and our enemies watched—my brother was gloomy, and I began to think of killing and of a fierce death. . . . We are of a people who take what they want—like you whites. There is a time when a man should forget loyalty and respect. Might and authority are given to rulers, but to all men is given love and strength and courage. My brother said, "You shall take her from their midst. We are two who are like one." And I answered, "Let it be soon, for I find no warmth in sunlight that does not shine upon her." Our time came when the Ruler and all the great people went to the mouth of the river to fish by torchlight. There were hundreds of boats, and on the white sand, between the water and the forests, dwellings of leaves were built for the households of the Rajahs. The smoke of cooking-fires was like a blue mist of the evening, and many voices rang in it joyfully. While they were making the boats ready to beat up the fish, my brother came to me and said, "To-night!" I looked to my weapons, and when the time came our canoe took its place in the circle of boats carrying the torches. The lights blazed on the water, but behind the boats there was darkness. When the shouting began and the excitement made them like mad we dropped out. The water swallowed our fire, and we floated back to the shore that was dark with only here and there the glimmer of embers. We could hear the talk of slave-girls amongst the sheds. Then we found a place deserted and silent. We waited there. She came. She came running along the shore, rapid and leaving no trace, like a leaf driven by the wind into the sea. My brother said gloomily, "Go and take her; carry her into our boat." I lifted her in my arms. She panted. Her heart was beating against my breast. I said, "I take you from those people. You came to the cry of my heart, but my arms take you into my boat against the will of the great!" "It is right," said my brother. "We are men who take what we want and can hold it against many. We should have taken her in daylight." I said, "Let us be off"; for since she was in my boat I began to think of our Ruler's many men. "Yes. Let us be off," said my brother. "We are cast out and this boat is our country now— and the sea is our refuge." He lingered with his foot on the shore, and I entreated him to hasten, for I remembered the strokes of her heart against my breast and thought that two men cannot withstand a hundred. We left, paddling down-stream close to the bank; and as we passed by the creek where they were fishing, the great shouting had ceased, but the murmur of voices was loud like the humming of insects flying at noonday. The boats floated, clustered together, in the red light of torches, under a black roof of smoke; and men talked of their sport. Men that boasted, and praised, and jeered—men that would have been our friends in the morning, but on that night were already our enemies. We

paddled swiftly past. We had no more friends in
the country of our birth. She sat in the middle of
the canoe with covered face; silent as she is now;
unseeing as she is now—and I had no regret at what
I was leaving because I could hear her breathing
close to me—as I can hear her now.'

He paused, listened with his ear turned to the doorway, then shook his head and went on:

'My brother wanted to shout the cry of challenge—
one cry only—to let the people know we were free-
born robbers who trusted our arms and the great sea.
And again I begged him in the name of our love to be
silent. Could I not hear her breathing close to me?
I knew the pursuit would come quick enough. My
brother loved me. He dipped his paddle without a
splash. He only said, "There is half a man in you
now—the other half is in that woman. I can wait.
When you are a whole man again, you will come back
with me here to shout defiance. We are sons of the
same mother." I made no answer. All my strength
and all my spirit were in my hands that held the
paddle—for I longed to be with her in a safe place
beyond the reach of men's anger and of women's
spite. My love was so great, that I thought it
could guide me to a country where death was unknown, if I could only escape from Inchi Midah's fury
and from our Ruler's sword. We paddled with
haste, breathing through our teeth. The blades bit
deep into the smooth water. We passed out of the
river; we flew in clear channels amongst the shallows.
We skirted the black coast; we skirted the sand
beaches where the sea speaks in whispers to the land;
and the gleam of white sand flashed back past our

boat, so swiftly she ran upon the water. We spoke
not. Only once I said, "Sleep, Diamelen, for soon
you may want all your strength." I heard the
sweetness of her voice, but I never turned my head.
The sun rose and still we went on. Water fell from
my face like rain from a cloud. We flew in the light
and heat. I never looked back, but I knew that
my brother's eyes, behind me, were looking steadily
ahead, for the boat went as straight as a bushman's
dart, when it leaves the end of the sumpitan. There
was no better paddler, no better steersman than my
brother. Many times, together, we had won races
in that canoe. But we never had put out our
strength as we did then—then, when for the last
time we paddled together! There was no braver or
stronger man in our country than my brother. I
could not spare the strength to turn my head and
look at him, but every moment I heard the hiss of his
breath getting louder behind me. Still he did not
speak. The sun was high. The heat clung to my
back like a flame of fire. My ribs were ready to
burst, but I could no longer get enough air into my
chest. And then I felt I must cry out with my last
breath, "Let us rest!" . . . "Good!" he answered;
and his voice was firm. He was strong. He was
brave. He knew not fear and no fatigue . . . My
brother!'

A murmur powerful and gentle, a murmur vast and
faint; the murmur of trembling leaves, of stirring
boughs, ran through the tangled depths of the forests,
ran over the starry smoothness of the lagoon, and the
water between the piles lapped the slimy timber once
with a sudden splash. A breath of warm air touched

the two men's faces and passed on with a mournful sound—a breath loud and short like an uneasy sigh of the dreaming earth.

Arsat went on in an even, low voice.

'We ran our canoe on the white beach of a little bay close to a long tongue of land that seemed to bar our road; a long wooded cape going far into the sea. My brother knew that place. Beyond the cape a river has its entrance, and through the jungle of that land there is a narrow path. We made a fire and cooked rice. Then we lay down to sleep on the soft sand in the shade of our canoe, while she watched. No sooner had I closed my eyes than I heard her cry of alarm. We leaped up. The sun was half-way down the sky already, and coming in sight in the opening of the bay we saw a prau manned by many paddlers. We knew it at once; it was one of our Rajah's praus. They were watching the shore, and saw us. They beat the gong, and turned the head of the prau into the bay. I felt my heart become weak within my breast. Diamelen sat on the sand and covered her face. There was no escape by sea. My brother laughed. He had the gun you had given him, Tuan, before you went away, but there was only a handful of powder. He spoke to me quickly: "Run with her along the path. I shall keep them back, for they have no firearms, and landing in the face of a man with a gun is certain death for some. Run with her. On the other side of that wood there is a fisherman's house—and a canoe. When I have fired all the shots I will follow. I am a great runner, and before they can come up we shall be gone. I will hold out as long as I can, for she is but a woman

—that can neither run nor fight, but she has your heart in her weak hands." He dropped behind the canoe. The prau was coming. She and I ran, and as we rushed along the path I heard shots. My brother fired—once—twice—and the booming of the gong ceased. There was silence behind us. That neck of land is narrow. Before I heard my brother fire the third shot I saw the shelving shore, and I saw the water again; the mouth of a broad river. We crossed a grassy glade. We ran down to the water. I saw a low hut above the black mud, and a small canoe hauled up. I heard another shot behind me. I thought, "That is his last charge." We rushed down to the canoe; a man came running from the hut, but I leaped on him, and we rolled together in the mud. Then I got up, and he lay still at my feet. I don't know whether I had killed him or not. I and Diamelen pushed the canoe afloat. I heard yells behind me, and I saw my brother run across the glade. Many men were bounding after him; I took her in my arms and threw her into the boat, then leaped in myself. When I looked back I saw that my brother had fallen. He fell and was up again, but the men were closing round him. He shouted, "I am coming!" The men were close to him. I looked. Many men. Then I looked at her. Tuan, I pushed the canoe! I pushed it into deep water. She was kneeling forward looking at me, and I said, "Take your paddle," while I struck the water with mine. Tuan, I heard him cry. I heard him cry my name twice; and I heard voices shouting, "Kill! Strike!" I never turned back. I heard him calling my name again with a great shriek, as when life is

going out together with the voice—and I never
turned my head. My own name! . . . My brother!
Three times he called—but I was not afraid of life.
Was she not there in that canoe? And could I not
with her find a country where death is forgotten—
where death is unknown!'

The white man sat up. Arsat rose and stood, an
indistinct and silent figure above the dying embers of
the fire. Over the lagoon a mist drifting and low
had crept, erasing slowly the glittering images of the
stars. And now a great expanse of white vapour
covered the land: it flowed cold and grey in the
darkness, eddied in noiseless whirls round the tree-
trunks and about the platform of the house, which
seemed to float upon a restless and impalpable
illusion of a sea. Only far away the tops of the trees
stood outlined on the twinkle of heaven, like a
sombre and forbidding shore—a coast deceptive,
pitiless and black.

Arsat's voice vibrated loudly in the profound
peace.

'I had her there! I had her! To get her I
would have faced all mankind. But I had her
—and——'

His words went out ringing into the empty
distances. He paused, and seemed to listen to them
dying away very far—beyond help and beyond recall.
Then he said quietly:

'Tuan, I loved my brother.'

A breath of wind made him shiver. High above
his head, high above the silent sea of mist, the drooping leaves of the palms rattled together with a
mournful and expiring sound. The white man

stretched his legs. His chin rested on his chest, and he murmured sadly without lifting his head:

'We all love our brothers.'

Arsat burst out with an intense whispering violence:

'What did I care who died? I wanted peace in my own heart.'

He seemed to hear a stir in the house—listened—then stepped in noiselessly. The white man stood up. A breeze was coming in fitful puffs. The stars shone paler as if they had retreated into the frozen depths of immense space. After a chill gust of wind there were a few seconds of perfect calm and absolute silence. Then from behind the black and wavy line of the forests a column of golden light shot up into the heavens and spread over the semicircle of the eastern horizon. The sun had risen. The mist lifted, broke into drifting patches, vanished into thin flying wreaths; and the unveiled lagoon lay, polished and black, in the heavy shadows at the foot of the wall of trees. A white eagle rose over it with a slanting and ponderous flight, reached the clear sunshine and appeared dazzlingly brilliant for a moment, then soaring higher, became a dark and motionless speck before it vanished into the blue as if it had left the earth for ever. The white man, standing gazing upwards before the doorway, heard in the hut a confused and broken murmur of distracted words ending with a loud groan. Suddenly Arsat stumbled out with outstretched hands, shivered, and stood still for some time with fixed eyes. Then he said:

'She burns no more.'

Before his face the sun showed its edge above the
tree-tops, rising steadily. The breeze freshened; a
great brilliance burst upon the lagoon, sparkled on
the rippling water. The forests came out of the clear
shadows of the morning, became distinct, as if they
had rushed nearer—to stop short in a great stir of
leaves, of nodding boughs, of swaying branches. In
the merciless sunshine the whisper of unconscious
life grew louder, speaking in an incomprehensible
voice round the dumb darkness of that human
sorrow. Arsat's eyes wandered slowly, then stared
at the rising sun.

'I can see nothing,' he said half aloud to himself.

'There is nothing,' said the white man, moving to
the edge of the platform and waving his hand to his
boat. A shout came faintly over the lagoon and the
sampan began to glide towards the abode of the
friend of ghosts.

'If you want to come with me, I will wait all the
morning,' said the white man, looking away upon the
water.

'No, Tuan,' said Arsat, softly. 'I shall not eat or
sleep in this house, but I must first see my road.
Now I can see nothing—see nothing! There is no
light and no peace in the world; but there is death—
death for many. We were sons of the same mother—
and I left him in the midst of enemies; but I am
going back now.'

He drew a long breath and went on in a dreamy
tone:

'In a little while I shall see clear enough to strike—
to strike. But she has died, and . . . now . . .
darkness.'

B 954

He flung his arms wide open, let them fall along his body, then stood still with unmoved face and stony eyes, staring at the sun. The white man got down into his canoe. The polers ran smartly along the sides of the boat, looking over their shoulders at the beginning of a weary journey. High in the stern, his head muffled up in white rags, the juragan sat moody, letting his paddle trail in the water. The white man, leaning with both arms over the grass roof of the little cabin, looked back at the shining ripple of the boat's wake. Before the sampan passed out of the lagoon into the creek he lifted his eyes. Arsat had not moved. He stood lonely in the searching sunshine; and he looked beyond the great light of a cloudless day into the darkness of a world of illusions.

THE MIRACLE OF PURUN BHAGAT

By Rudyard Kipling

The night we felt the earth would move
  We stole and plucked him by the hand,
Because we loved him with the love
  That knows but cannot understand.

And when the roaring hillside broke,
  And all our world fell down in rain,
We saved him, we the Little Folk;
  But lo! he does not come again!

Mourn now, we saved him for the sake
  Of such poor love as wild ones may.
Mourn ye! Our brother will not wake,
  And his own kind drive us away!

Dirge of the Langurs.

THERE was once a man in India who was Prime
Minister of one of the semi-independent native
States in the north-western part of the country.
He was a Brahmin, so high-caste that caste ceased
to have any particular meaning for him; and his
father had been an important official in the gay-
coloured tag-rag and bobtail of an old-fashioned
Hindu Court. But as Purun Dass grew up he felt
that the old order of things was changing, and that
if any one wished to get on in the world he must
stand well with the English, and imitate all that
the English believed to be good. At the same time
a native official must keep his own master's favour.

This was a difficult game, but the quiet, close-mouthed young Brahmin, helped by a good English education at a Bombay University, played it coolly, and rose, step by step, to be Prime Minister of the kingdom. That is to say, he held more real power than his master the Maharajah.

When the old king—who was suspicious of the English, their railways and telegraphs—died, Purun Dass stood high with his young successor, who had been tutored by an Englishman; and between them, though he always took care that his master should have the credit, they established schools for little girls, made roads, and started State dispensaries and shows of agricultural implements, and published a yearly blue-book on the 'Moral and Material Progress of the State,' and the Foreign Office and the Government of India were delighted. Very few native States take up English progress altogether, for they will not believe, as Purun Dass showed he did, that what was good for the Englishman must be twice as good for the Asiatic. The Prime Minister became the honoured friend of Viceroys, and Governors, and Lieutenant-Governors, and medical missionaries, and common missionaries, and hard-riding English officers who came to shoot in the State preserves, as well as of whole hosts of tourists who travelled up and down India in the cold weather, showing how things ought to be managed. In his spare time he would endow scholarships for the study of medicine and manu-factures on strictly English lines, and write letters to the *Pioneer*, the greatest Indian daily paper, explaining his master's aims and objects.

At last he went to England on a visit, and had to pay enormous sums to the priests when he came back; for even so high-caste a Brahmin as Purun Dass lost caste by crossing the black sea. In London he met and talked with every one worth knowing—men whose names go all over the world —and saw a great deal more than he said. He was given honorary degrees by learned universities, and he made speeches and talked of Hindu social reform to English ladies in evening dress, till all London cried, 'This is the most fascinating man we have ever met at dinner since cloths were first laid.'

When he returned to India there was a blaze of glory, for the Viceroy himself made a special visit to confer upon the Maharajah the Grand Cross of the Star of India—all diamonds and ribbons and enamel; and at the same ceremony, while the cannon boomed, Purun Dass was made a Knight Commander of the Order of the Indian Empire; so that his name stood Sir Purun Dass, K.C.I.E.

That evening, at dinner in the big Viceregal tent, he stood up with the badge and the collar of the Order on his breast, and replying to the toast of his master's health, made a speech few Englishment could have bettered.

Next month, when the city had returned to its sun-baked quiet, he did a thing no Englishman would have dreamed of doing; for, so far as the world's affairs went, he died. The jewelled order of his knighthood went back to the Indian Government, and a new Prime Minister was appointed to the charge of affairs, and a great game of General

Post began in all the subordinate appointments. The priests knew what had happened, and the people guessed; but India is the one place in the world where a man can do as he pleases and nobody asks why; and the fact that Dewan Sir Purun Dass, K.C.I.E., had resigned position, palace, and power, and taken up the begging-bowl and ochre-coloured dress of a Sunnyasi, or holy man, was considered nothing extraordinary. He had been, as the Old Law recommends, twenty years a youth, twenty years a fighter—though he had never carried a weapon in his life—and twenty years head of a household. He had used his wealth and his power for what he knew both to be worth; he had taken honour when it came his way; he had seen men and cities far and near, and men and cities had stood up and honoured him. Now he would let those things go, as a man drops the cloak he no longer needs.

Behind him, as he walked through the city gates, an antelope skin and brass-handled crutch under his arm, and a begging-bowl of polished brown *coco-de-mer* in his hand, barefoot, alone, with eyes cast on the ground—behind him they were firing salutes from the bastions in honour of his happy successor. Purun Dass nodded. All that life was ended; and he bore it no more ill-will or good-will than a man bears to a colourless dream of the night. He was a Sunnyasi—a houseless, wandering mendicant, depending on his neighbours for his daily bread; and so long as there is a morsel to divide in India, neither priest nor beggar starves. He had never in his life tasted meat, and very seldom eaten even fish. A five-pound note would have covered his personal expenses for food through any one of the many years in which he had been absolute master of millions of money. Even when he was being lionized in London he had held before him his dream of peace and quiet—the long, white, dusty Indian road, printed all over with bare feet, the incessant, slow-moving traffic, and the sharp-smelling wood smoke curling up under the fig-trees in the twilight, where the wayfarers sit at their evening meal.

When the time came to make that dream true the Prime Minister took the proper steps, and in three days you might more easily have found a bubble in the trough of the long Atlantic seas than Purun Dass among the roving, gathering, separating millions of India.

At night his antelope skin was spread where the darkness overtook him—sometimes in a Sunnyasi monastery by the roadside; sometimes by a mud-pillar shrine of Kala Pir, where the Jogis, who are another misty division of holy men, would receive him as they do those who know what castes and divisions are worth; sometimes on the outskirts of a little Hindu village, where the children would steal up with the food their parents had prepared; and sometimes on the pitch of the bare grazing-grounds, where the flame of his stick fire waked the drowsy camels. It was all one to Purun Dass— or Purun Bhagat, as he called himself now. Earth, people, and food were all one. But unconsciously his feet drew him away northward and eastward; from the south to Rohtak; from Rohtak to Kurnool; from Kurnool to ruined Samanah, and then upstream along the dried bed of the Gugger river that fills only when the rain falls in the hills, till one day he saw the far line of the great Himalayas.

Then Purun Bhagat smiled, for he remembered that his mother was of Rajput Brahmin birth, from Kulu way—a Hill-woman, always home-sick for the snows—and that the least touch of Hill blood draws a man in the end back to where he belongs.

'Yonder,' said Purun Bhagat, breasting the lower slopes of the Sewaliks, where the cacti stand up like seven - branched candlesticks — 'yonder I shall sit down and get knowledge'; and the cool wind of the Himalayas whistled about his ears as he trod the road that led to Simla.

The last time he had come that way it had been in state, with a clattering cavalry escort, to visit the gentlest and most affable of Viceroys; and the two had talked for an hour together about mutual friends in London, and what the Indian common folk really thought of things. This time Purun Bhagat paid no calls, but leaned on the rail of the Mall, watching that glorious view of the Plains spread out forty miles below, till a native Mohammedan policeman told him he was obstructing traffic; and Purun Bhagat salaamed reverently to the Law, because he knew the value of it, and was seeking for a Law of his own. Then he moved on, and slept that night in an empty hut at Chota Simla, which looks like the very last end of the earth, but it was only the beginning of his journey.

He followed the Himalaya-Thibet road, the little ten-foot track that is blasted out of solid rock, or strutted out on timbers over gulfs a thousand feet

deep; that dips into warm, wet, shut-in valleys, and
climbs out across bare, grassy hill-shoulders where
the sun strikes like a burning-glass; or turns through
dripping, dark forests where the tree-ferns dress
the trunks from head to heel, and the pheasant calls
to his mate. And he met Thibetan herdsmen with
their dogs and flocks of sheep, each sheep with a
little bag of borax on his back, and wandering
wood-cutters, and cloaked and blanketed Lamas
from Thibet, coming into India on pilgrimage, and
envoys of little solitary Hill-states, posting furiously
on ring-streaked and piebald ponies, or the cavalcade
of a Rajah paying a visit; or else for a long, clear
day he would see nothing more than a black bear
grunting and rooting below in the valley. When
he first started, the roar of the world he had left
still rang in his ears, as the roar of a tunnel rings
long after the train has passed through; but when
he had put the Mutteeanee Pass behind him that
was all done, and Purun Bhagat was alone with
himself, walking, wondering, and thinking, his eyes
on the ground, and his thoughts with the clouds.

One evening he crossed the highest pass he had
met till then—it had been a two-day's climb—and
came out on a line of snow-peaks that banded all
the horizon — mountains from fifteen to twenty
thousand feet high, looking almost near enough to
hit with a stone, though they were fifty or sixty
miles away. The pass was crowned with dense,
dark forest—deodar, walnut, wild cherry, wild olive,
and wild pear, but mostly deodar, which is the
Himalayan cedar; and under the shadow of the
deodars stood a deserted shrine to Kali—who is

Durga, who is Sitala, who is sometimes worshipped against the smallpox.

Purun Dass swept the stone floor clean, smiled at the grinning statue, made himself a little mud fireplace at the back of the shrine, spread his ante-lope skin on a bed of fresh pine-needles, tucked his *bairagi*—his brass-handled crutch—under his arm-pit, and sat down to rest.

Immediately below him the hillside fell away, clean and cleared for fifteen hundred feet, where a little village of stone-walled houses, with roofs of beaten earth, clung to the steep tilt. All round it the tiny terraced fields lay out like aprons of patchwork on the knees of the mountain, and cows no bigger than beetles grazed between the smooth stone circles of the threshing-floors. Looking across the valley, the eye was deceived by the size of things, and could not at first realize that what seemed to be low scrub, on the opposite mountain-flank, was in truth a forest of hundred-foot pines. Purun Bhagat saw an eagle swoop across the gigantic hollow, but the great bird dwindled to a dot ere it was half-way over. A few bands of scattered clouds strung up and down the valley, catching on a shoul-der of the hills, or rising up and dying out when they were level with the head of the pass. And 'Here shall I find peace,' said Purun Bhagat.

Now, a Hill-man makes nothing of a few hundred feet up or down, and as soon as the villagers saw the smoke in the deserted shrine, the village priest climbed up the terraced hillside to welcome the stranger.

When he met Purun Bhagat's eyes—the eyes of

a man used to control thousands—he bowed to
the earth, took the begging-bowl without a word,
and returned to the village, saying, 'We have at
last a holy man. Never have I seen such a man.
He is of the Plains—but pale-coloured—a Brahmin
of the Brahmins.' Then all the housewives of the
village said, 'Think you he will stay with us?' and
each did her best to cook the most savoury meal
for the Bhagat. Hill-food is very simple, but with
buckwheat and Indian corn, and rice and red pep-
per, and little fish out of the stream in the valley,
and honey from the flue-like hives built in the stone
walls, and dried apricots, and turmeric, and wild
ginger, and bannocks of flour, a devout woman can
make good things, and it was a full bowl that the
priest carried to the Bhagat. Was he going to stay?
asked the priest. Would he need a *chela*—a disciple—to beg for him? Had he a blanket against
the cold weather? Was the food good?

Purun Bhagat ate, and thanked the giver. It
was in his mind to stay. That was sufficient, said
the priest. Let the begging-bowl be placed outside the shrine, in the hollow made by those two
twisted roots, and daily should the Bhagat be fed;
for the village felt honoured that such a man—he
looked timidly into the Bhagat's face—should tarry
among them.

That day saw the end of Purun Bhagat's wander-
ings. He had come to the place appointed for him
—the silence and the space. After this, time stopped,
and he, sitting at the mouth of the shrine, could not
tell whether he were alive or dead; a man with
control of his limbs, or a part of the hills, and the

clouds, and the shifting rain and sunlight. He would repeat a Name softly to himself a hundred hundred times, till, at each repetition, he seemed to move more and more out of his body, sweeping up to the doors of some tremendous discovery; but, just as the door was opening, his body would drag him back, and, with grief, he felt he was locked up again in the flesh and bones of Purun Bhagat.

Every morning the filled begging-bowl was laid silently in the crutch of the roots outside the shrine. Sometimes the priest brought it; sometimes a Ladakhi trader, lodging in the village, and anxious to get merit, trudged up the path; but, more often, it was the woman who had cooked the meal over-night; and she would murmur, hardly above her breath: 'Speak for me before the gods, Bhagat. Speak for such a one, the wife of so-and-so!' Now and then some bold child would be allowed the honour, and Purun Bhagat would hear him drop the bowl and run as fast as his little legs could carry him, but the Bhagat never came down to the village. It was laid out like a map at his feet. He could see the evening gatherings, held on the circle of the threshing-floors, because that was the only level ground; could see the wonderful unnamed green of the young rice, the indigo blues of the Indian corn, the dock-like patches of buckwheat, and, in its season, the red bloom of the amaranth, whose tiny seeds, being neither grain nor pulse, make a food that can be lawfully eaten by Hindus in time of fasts.

When the year turned, the roofs of the huts were all little squares of purest gold, for it was on the roots that they laid out their cobs of the corn to dry. Hiving and harvest, rice-sowing and husking, passed before his eyes, all embroidered down there on the many-sided plots of fields, and he thought of them all, and wondered what they all led to at the long last.

Even in populated India a man cannot a day sit still before the wild things run over him as though he were a rock; and in that wilderness very soon the wild things, who knew Kali's shrine well, came back to look at the intruder. The *langurs*, the big grey-whiskered monkeys of the Himalayas, were, naturally, the first, for they are alive with curiosity; and when they had upset the begging-bowl, and rolled it round the floor, and tried their teeth on the brass-handled crutch, and made faces at the antelope skin, they decided that the human being who sat so still was harmless. At evening, they would leap down from the pines, and beg with their hands for things to eat, and then swing off in graceful curves. They liked the warmth of the fire, too, and huddled round it till Purun Bhagat had to push them aside to throw on more fuel; and in the morning, as often as not, he would find a furry ape sharing his blanket. All day long, one or other of the tribe would sit by his side, staring out at the snows, crooning and looking unspeakably wise and sorrowful.

After the monkeys came the *barasingh*, that big deer which is like our red deer, but stronger. He wished to rub off the velvet of his horns against the cold stones of Kali's statue, and stamped his feet when he saw the man at the shrine. But Purun

Bhagat never moved, and, little by little, the royal
stag edged up and nuzzled his shoulder. Purun
Bhagat slid one cool hand along the hot antlers, and
the touch soothed the fretted beast, who bowed his
head, and Purun Bhagat very softly rubbed and
ravelled off the velvet. Afterward, the *barasingh*
brought his doe and fawn—gentle things that
mumbled on the holy man's blanket—or would
come alone at night, his eyes green in the fire-
flicker, to take his share of fresh walnuts. At
last, the musk-deer, the shyest and almost the
smallest of the deerlets, came, too, her big rabbity
ears erect; even brindled, silent *mushick-nabha*
must needs find out what the light in the shrine
meant, and drop her moose-like nose into Purun
Bhagat's lap, coming and going with the shadows
of the fire. Purun Bhagat called them all 'my
brothers,' and his low call of '*Bhai! Bhai!*' would
draw them from the forest at noon if they were
within earshot. The Himalayan black bear, moody
and suspicious—Sona, who has the V-shaped white
mark under his chin—passed that way more than
once; and since the Bhagat showed no fear, Sona
showed no anger, but watched him, and came
closer, and begged a share of the caresses, and a
dole of bread or wild berries. Often, in the still
dawns, when the Bhagat would climb to the very
crest of the pass to watch the red day walking along
the peaks of the snows, he would find Sona shuffling
and grunting at his heels, thrusting a curious fore-
paw under fallen trunks, and bringing it away with
a *whoof* of impatience; or his early steps would wake
Sona where he lay curled up, and the great brute,

rising erect, would think to fight, till he heard the Bhagat's voice and knew his best friend.

Nearly all hermits and holy men who live apart from the big cities have the reputation of being able to work miracles with the wild things, but all the miracle lies in keeping still, in never making a hasty movement, and, for a long time, at least, in never looking directly at a visitor. The villagers saw the outline of the *barasingh* stalking like a shadow through the dark forest behind the shrine; saw the *minaul*, the Himalayan pheasant, blazing in her best colours before Kali's statue; and the *langurs* on their haunches, inside, playing with the walnut shells. Some of the children, too, had heard Sona singing to himself, bear-fashion, behind the fallen rocks, and the Bhagat's reputation as miracle-worker stood firm.

Yet nothing was farther from his mind than miracles. He believed that all things were one big Miracle, and when a man knows that much he knows something to go upon. He knew for a certainty that there was nothing great and nothing little in this world: and day and night he strove to think out his way into the heart of things, back to the place whence his soul had come.

So thinking, his untrimmed hair fell down about his shoulders, the stone slab at the side of the antelope skin was dented into a little hole by the foot of his brass-handled crutch, and the place between the tree-trunks, where the begging-bowl rested day after day, sunk and wore into a hollow almost as smooth as the brown shell itself; and each beast knew his exact place at the fire. The fields changed their colours with the seasons; the threshing-floors filled and emptied, and filled again and again; and again and again, when winter came, the *langurs* frisked among the branches feathered with light snow, till the mother-monkeys brought their sad-eyed little babies up from the warmer valleys with the spring. There were few changes in the village. The priest was older, and many of the little children who used to come with the begging-dish sent their own children now; and when you asked of the villagers how long their holy man had lived in Kali's Shrine at the head of the pass, they answered, 'Always.'

Then came such summer rains as had not been known in the Hills for many seasons. Through three good months the valley was wrapped in cloud and soaking mist — steady, unrelenting downfall, breaking off into thunder - shower after thunder-shower. Kali's Shrine stood above the clouds, for the most part, and there was a whole month in which the Bhagat never caught a glimpse of his village. It was packed away under a white floor of cloud that swayed and shifted and rolled on itself and bulged upward, but never broke from its piers—the streaming flanks of the valley.

All that time he heard nothing but the sound of a million little waters, overhead from the trees, and underfoot along the ground, soaking through the pine-needles, dripping from the tongues of draggled fern, and spouting in newly-torn muddy channels down the slopes. Then the sun came out, and drew forth the good incense of the deodars and the rhododendrons, and that far-off, clean smell which the Hill people call 'the smell of the snows.'

The hot sunshine lasted for a week, and then the rains gathered together for their last downpour, and the water fell in sheets that flayed off the skin of the ground and leaped back in mud. Purun Bhagat heaped his fire high that night, for he was sure his brothers would need warmth; but never a beast came to the shrine, though he called and called till he dropped asleep, wondering what had happened in the woods.

It was in the black heart of the night, the rain drumming like a thousand drums, that he was roused by a plucking at his blanket, and, stretching out, felt the little hand of a *langur*. 'It is better here than in the trees,' he said sleepily, loosening a fold of blanket; 'take it and be warm.' The monkey caught his hand and pulled hard. 'Is it food, then?' said Purun Bhagat. 'Wait awhile, and I will prepare some.' As he kneeled to throw fuel on the fire the *langur* ran to the door of the shrine, crooned and ran back again, plucking at the man's knee.

'What is it? What is thy trouble, Brother?' said Purun Bhagat, for the *langur's* eyes were full of things that he could not tell. 'Unless one of thy caste be in a trap—and none set traps here— I will not go into that weather. Look, Brother, even the *barasingh* comes for shelter!'

The deer's antlers clashed as he strode into the shrine, clashed against the grinning statue of Kali. He lowered them into Purun Bhagat's direction and stamped uneasily, hissing through his half-shut nostrils.

'Hai! Hai! Hai!' said the Bhagat, snapping his fingers. 'Is *this* payment for a night's lodging?' But the deer pushed him toward the door, and as

he did so Purun Bhagat heard the sound of something opening with a sigh, and saw two slabs of the
floor draw away from each other, while the sticky
earth below smacked its lips.

'Now I see,' said Purun Bhagat. 'No blame
to my brothers that they did not sit by the fire
to-night. The mountain is falling. And yet—why
should I go?' His eye fell on the empty begging-
bowl, and his face changed. 'They have given me
good food daily since—since I came, and, if I am
not swift, to-morrow there will not be one mouth in
the valley. Indeed, I must go and warn them below.
Back there, Brother! Let me get to the fire.'

The *barasingh* backed unwillingly as Purun
Bhagat drove a pine torch deep into the flame,
twirling it till it was well lit. 'Ah! ye came to
warn me,' he said, rising. 'Better than that we
shall do; better than that. Out, now, and lend
me thy neck, Brother, for I have but two feet.'

He clutched the bristling withers of the *barasingh* with his right hand, held the torch away with
his left, and stepped out of the shrine into the
desperate night. There was no breath of wind,
but the rain nearly drowned the flare as the great
deer hurried down the slope, sliding on his haunches.
As soon as they were clear of the forest more of the
Bhagat's brothers joined them. He heard, though
he could not see, the *langurs* pressing about him,
and behind them the *uhh! uhh!* of Sona. The rain
matted his long white hair into ropes; the water
splashed beneath his bare feet, and his yellow robe
clung to his frail old body, but he stepped down
steadily, leaning against the *barasingh*. He was no

longer a holy man, but Sir Purun Dass, K.C.I.E.,
Prime Minister of no small State, a man accustomed
to command, going out to save life. Down the
steep, plashy path they poured all together, the
Bhagat and his brothers, down and down till the
deer's feet clicked and stumbled on the wall of a
threshing-floor, and he snorted because he smelt
Man. Now they were at the head of the one
crooked village street, and the Bhagat beat with
his crutch on the barred windows of the blacksmith's house, as his torch blazed up in the shelter
of the eaves. 'Up and out!' cried Purun Bhagat;
and he did not know his own voice, for it was years
since he had spoken aloud to a man. 'The hill falls!
The hill is falling! Up and out, oh, you within!'

'It is our Bhagat,' cried the blacksmith's wife.
'He stands among his beasts. Gather the little ones
and give the call.'

It ran from house to house, while the beasts,
cramped in the narrow way, surged and huddled
round the Bhagat, and Sona puffed impatiently.

The people hurried into the street—they were
no more than seventy souls all told—and in the glare
of the torches they saw their Bhagat holding back
the terrified *barasingh*, while the monkeys plucked
piteously at his skirts, and Sona sat on his haunches
and roared.

'Across the valley and up the next hill!' shouted
Purun Bhagat. 'Leave none behind! We follow!'

Then the people ran as only Hill folk can run,
for they knew that in a landslip you must climb
for the highest ground across the valley. They
fled, splashing through the little river at the bottom,

and panted up the terraced fields on the far side, while the Bhagat and his brethren followed. Up and up the opposite mountain they climbed, calling to each other by name—the roll-call of the village—and at their heels toiled the big *barasingh*, weighted by the failing strength of Purun Bhagat. At last the deer stopped in the shadow of a deep pine-wood, five hundred feet up the hillside. His instinct, that had warned him of the coming slide, told him he would be safe here.

Purun Bhagat dropped fainting by his side, for the chill of the rain and that fierce climb were killing him; but first he called to the scattered torches ahead, 'Stay and count your numbers'; then, whispering to the deer as he saw the lights gather in a cluster: 'Stay with me, Brother. Stay —till—I—go!'

There was a sigh in the air that grew to a mutter, and a mutter that grew to a roar, and a roar that passed all sense of hearing, and the hillside on which the villagers stood was hit in the darkness, and rocked to the blow. Then a note as steady, deep, and true as the deep C of the organ drowned everything for perhaps five minutes, while the very roots of the pines quivered to it. It died away, and the sound of the rain falling on miles of hard ground and grass changed to the muffled drum of water on soft earth. That told its own tale.

Never a villager—not even the priest—was bold enough to speak to the Bhagat who had saved their lives. They crouched under the pines and waited till the day. When it came they looked across the valley and saw that what had been forest, and terraced fields, and track-threaded grazing-ground was

one raw, red, fan-shaped smear, with a few trees
flung head-down on the scarp. That red ran high
up the hill of their refuge, damming back the little
river, which had begun to spread into a brick-
coloured lake. Of the village, of the road to the
shrine itself, and the forest behind, there was no
trace. For one mile in width and two thousand
feet in sheer depth the mountain-side had come
away bodily, planed clean from head to heel.

And the villagers, one by one, crept through the
wood to pray before their Bhagat. They saw the
barasingh standing over him, who fled when they
came near, and they heard the *langurs* wailing in
the branches, and Sona moaning up the hill; but
their Bhagat was dead, sitting cross-legged, his
back against a tree, his crutch under his armpit,
and his face turned to the north-east.

The priest said: ' Behold a miracle after a miracle,
for in this very attitude must all Sunnyasis be buried!
Therefore where he now is we will build the temple
to our holy man.'

They built the temple before a year was ended—
a little stone-and-earth shrine—and they called the
hill the Bhagat's hill, and they worship there with
lights and flowers and offerings to this day. But
they do not know that the saint of their worship
is the late Sir Purun Dass, K.C.I.E., D.C.L., Ph.D.,
etc., once Prime Minister of the progressive and
enlightened State of Mohiniwala, and honorary or
corresponding member of more learned and scientific
societies than will ever do any good in this world or
the next.

JEFF PETERS AS A PERSONAL MAGNET

By O. Henry (William Sydney Porter)

JEFF PETERS has been engaged in as many schemes for making money as there are recipes for cooking rice in Charleston, S.C.

Best of all I like to hear him tell of his earlier days when he sold liniments and cough cures on street corners, living hand to mouth, heart to heart, with the people, throwing heads or tails with fortune for his last coin.

'I struck Fisher Hill, Arkansaw,' said he, 'in a buckskin suit, moccasins, long hair, and a thirty-carat diamond ring that I got from an actor in Texarkana. I don't know what he ever did with the pocket-knife I swapped him for it.

'I was Dr Waugh-hoo, the celebrated Indian medicine man. I carried only one best bet just then, and that was Resurrection Bitters. It was made of life-giving plants and herbs accidentally discovered by Ta-qua-la, the beautiful wife of the chief of the Choctaw Nation, while gathering truck to garnish a platter of boiled dog for the annual corn dance.

'Business hadn't been good at the last town, so I only had five dollars. I went to the Fisher Hill druggist and he credited me for half a gross of eight-ounce bottles and corks. I had the labels and ingredients in my valise, left over from the last town.

Life began to look rosy again after I got in my hotel room with the water running from the tap, and the Resurrection Bitters lining up on the table by the dozen.

'Fake? No, sir. There was two dollars' worth of fluid extract of cinchona and a dime's worth of aniline in that half-gross of bitters. I've gone through towns years afterwards and had folks ask for 'em again.

'I hired a wagon that night and commenced selling the bitters on Main Street. Fisher Hill was a low, malarial town; and a compound hypothetical pneumocardiac anti-scorbutic tonic was just what I diagnosed the crowd as needing. The bitters started off like sweetbreads-on-toast at a vegetarian dinner. I had sold two dozen at fifty cents apiece when I felt somebody pull my coat tail. I knew what that meant; so I climbed down and sneaked a five-dollar bill into the hand of a man with a German silver star on his lapel.

'"Constable," says I, "it's a fine night."

'"Have you got a city licence," he asks, "to sell this illegitimate essence of spooju that you flatter by the name of medicine?"

'"I have not," says I. "I didn't know you had a city. If I can find it to-morrow I'll take one out if it's necessary."

'"I'll have to close you up till you do," says the constable.

'I quit selling and went back to the hotel. I was talking to the landlord about it.

'"Oh, you won't stand no show in Fisher Hill," says he. "Dr Hoskins, the only doctor here, is a brother-in-law of the Mayor, and they won't allow no fake doctor to practise in town."

'"I don't practise medicine," says I, "I 've got a State pedlar's licence, and I take out a city one wherever they demand it."

'I went to the Mayor's office the next morning and they told me he hadn't showed up yet. They didn't know when he 'd be down. So Doc Waugh-hoo hunches down again in a hotel chair and lights a jimpson-weed regalia, and waits.

'By and by a young man in a blue neck-tie slips into the chair next to me and asks the time.

'"Half-past ten," says I, "and you are Andy Tucker. I 've seen you work. Wasn't it you that put up the Great Cupid Combination package on the Southern States? Let's see, it was a Chilian diamond engagement ring, a wedding-ring, a potato masher, a bottle of soothing syrup, and Dorothy Vernon—all for fifty cents."

'Andy was pleased to hear that I remembered him. He was a good street man; and he was more than that—he respected his profession, and he was satisfied with 300 per cent profit. He had plenty of offers to go into the illegitimate drug and garden seed business; but he was never to be tempted off of the straight path.

'I wanted a partner; so Andy and me agreed to go out together. I told him about the situation in Fisher Hill and how finances was low on account of the local mixture of politics and jalap. Andy had just got in on the train that morning. He was pretty low himself, and was going to canvass the town for a few dollars to build a new battleship by popular subscription at Eureka Springs. So we went out and sat on the porch and talked it over.

'The next morning at eleven o'clock, when I was sitting there alone, an Uncle Tom shuffles into the hotel and asked for the doctor to come and see Judge Banks, who, it seems, was the mayor and a mighty sick man.

'"I 'm no doctor," says I. "Why don't you go and get the doctor?"

'"Boss," says he, "Doc Hoskins am done gone twenty miles in de country to see some sick persons. He 's de only doctor in de town, and Massa Banks am powerful bad off. He sent me to ax you to please, suh, come."

'"As man to man," says I, "I 'll go and look him over." So I put a bottle of Resurrection Bitters in my pocket and goes up on the hill to the Mayor's mansion, the finest house in town, with a mansard roof and two cast-iron dogs on the lawn.

'This Mayor Banks was in bed all but his whiskers and feet. He was making internal noises that would have had everybody in San Francisco hiking for the parks. A young man was standing by the bed holding a cup of water.

'"Doc," says the Mayor, "I 'm awful sick. I 'm about to die. Can't you do nothing for me?"

'"Mr Mayor," says I, "I 'm not a regular pre-ordained disciple of S. Q. Lapius. I never took a course in a medical college," says I, "I 've just come as a fellow-man to see if I could be of assistance."

'"I 'm deeply obliged," says he. "Doc Waugh-hoo, this is my nephew, Mr Biddle. He has tried to alleviate my distress, but without success. Oh, Lordy! Ow-ow-ow!!" he sings out.

'I nods at Mr Biddle and sets down by the bed and feels the Mayor's pulse. "Let me see your liver—your tongue, I mean," says I. Then I turns up the lids of his eyes and looks close at the pupils of 'em.

'"How long have you been sick?" I asked.

'I was taken down—ow-ouch—last night," says the Mayor. "Gimme something for it, doc, won't you?"

'"Mr Fiddle," says I, "raise the window shade a bit, will you?"

'"Biddle," says the young man. "Do you feel like you could eat some ham and eggs, Uncle James?"

'"Mr Mayor," says I, after laying my ear to his right shoulder-blade and listening, "you 've got a bad attack of super-inflammation of the right clavicle of the harpsichord!"

'"Good Lord!" says he, with a groan. "Can't you rub something on it, or set it or anything?"

'I picks up my hat and starts for the door.

'"You ain't going, doc?" says the Mayor with a howl. "You ain't going away and leave me to die with this—superfluity of the clapboards, are you?"

'"Common humanity, Dr Whoa-ha," says Mr Biddle, "ought to prevent your deserting a fellow-human in distress."

'"Dr Waugh-hoo, when you get through ploughing," says I. And then I walks back to the bed and throws back my long hair.

'"Mr Mayor," says I, "there is only one hope for you. Drugs will do you no good. But there is another power higher yet, although drugs are high enough," says I.

"'And what is that?" says he.

"'Scientific demonstrations," says I. "The triumph of mind over sarsaparilla. The belief that there is no pain and sickness except what is produced when we ain't feeling well. Declare yourself in arrears. Demonstrate."

"'What is this paraphernalia you speak of, doc?" says the Mayor. "You ain't a Socialist, are you?"

"'I am speaking," says I, "of the great doctrine of psychic financiering—of the enlightened school of long-distance, subconscientious treatment of fallacies and meningitis—of that wonderful indoor sport known as personal magnetism."

"'Can you work it, doc?" asks the Mayor.

"'I 'm one of the Sole Sanhedrims and Ostensible Hooplas of the Inner Pulpit," says I. "The lame talk and the blind rubber whenever I make a pass at 'em. I am a medium, a coloratura hypnotist and a spirituous control. It was only through me at the recent séances at Ann Arbor that the late president of the Vinegar Bitters Company could revisit the earth to communicate with his sister Jane. You see me peddling medicine on the streets," says I, "to the poor. I don't practise personal magnetism on them. I do not drag it in the dust," says I, "because they haven't got the dust."

"'Will you treat my case?" asks the Mayor.

"'Listen," says I. "I 've had a good deal of trouble with medical societies everywhere I 've been. I don't practise medicine. But, to save your life,

I 'll give you the pyschic treatment if you 'll agree as mayor not to push the licence question.''

'"Of course I will," says he. "And now get to work, doc, for them pains are coming on again."

'"My fee will be $250.00, cure guaranteed in two treatments," says I.

'"All right," says the Mayor. "I 'll pay it. I guess my life's worth that much."

'I sat down by the bed and looked him straight in the eye.

'"Now," says I, "get your mind off the disease. You ain't sick. You haven't got a heart or a clavicle or a funny-bone or brains or anything. You haven't got any pain. Declare error. Now you feel the pain that you didn't have leaving, don't you?"

'"I do feel some little better, doc," says the Mayor, "darned if I don't. Now state a few lies about my not having this swelling in my left side, and I think I could be propped up and have some sausage and buckwheat cakes."

'I made a few passes with my hands.

'"Now," says I, "the inflammation's gone. The right lobe of the perihelion has subsided. You 're getting sleepy. You can't hold your eyes open any longer. For the present the disease is checked. Now, you are asleep."

'The Mayor shut his eyes slowly and began to snore.

'"You observe, Mr Tiddle," says I, "the wonders of modern science."

'"Biddle," says he. "When will you give uncle the rest of the treatment, Dr Pooh-pooh?"

'"Waugh-hoo," says I. "I'll come back at eleven to-morrow. When he wakes up give him eight drops of turpentine and three pounds of steak. Good morning."

'The next morning I went back on time. "Well, Mr Riddle," says I, when he opened the bedroom door, "and how is uncle this morning?"

'"He seems much better," says the young man.

'The Mayor's colour and pulse was fine. I gave him another treatment, and he said the last of the pain left him.

'"Now," says I, "you'd better stay in bed for a day or two, and you'll be all right. It's a good thing I happened to be in Fisher Hill, Mr Mayor," says I, "for all the remedies in the cornucopia that the regular schools of medicine use couldn't have saved you. And now that error has flew and pain proved a perjurer, let's allude to a cheerfuller subject —say the fee of $250. No cheques, please; I hate to write my name on the back of a cheque almost as bad as I do on the front."

'"I've got the cash here," says the Mayor, pulling a pocket-book from under his pillow.

'He counts out five fifty-dollar notes and holds 'em in his hand.

'"Bring the receipt," he says to Biddle.

'I signed the receipt and the Mayor handed me the money. I put it in my inside pocket careful.

'"Now do your duty, officer," says the Mayor, grinning much unlike a sick man.

'Mr Biddle lays his hand on my arm.

'"You're under arrest, Dr Waugh-hoo, alias

Peters," says he, "for practising medicine without authority under the State law."

"'Who are you?'" I asks.

"'I'll tell you who he is," says Mr Mayor, sitting up in bed. "He's a detective employed by the State Medical Society. He's been following you over five counties. He came to me yesterday and we fixed up this scheme to catch you. I guess you won't do any more doctoring around these parts, Mr Faker. What was it you said I had, doc?" the Mayor laughs, "compound—well it wasn't softening of the brain, I guess, anyway."

"'A detective,'" says I.

"'Correct,'" says Biddle. "I'll have to turn you over to the sheriff."

"'Let's see you do it,'" says I, and I grabs Biddle by the throat and half throws him out of the window, but he pulls a gun and sticks it under my chin, and I stand still. Then he puts handcuffs on me, and takes the money out of my pocket.

"'I witness,'" says he, "that they're the same bills that you and I marked, Judge Banks. I'll turn them over to the sheriff when we get to his office, and he'll send you a receipt. They'll have to be used as evidence in the case."

"'All right, Mr Biddle,'" says the Mayor. "And now, Doc Waugh-hoo," he goes on, "why don't you demonstrate? Can't you pull the cork out of your magnetism with your teeth and hocus-pocus them handcuffs off?"

"'Come on, officer,'" says I, dignified. "I may as well make the best of it." And then I turns to old Banks and rattles my chains.

'"Mr Mayor," says I, "the time will come soon when you 'll believe that personal magnetism is a success. And you 'll be sure that it succeeded in this case, too."

'And I guess it did.

'When we got nearly to the gate, I says: "We might meet somebody now, Andy. I reckon you better take 'em off, and——" Hey? Why, of course it was Andy Tucker. That was his scheme; and that 's how we got the capital to go into business together."'

TOBERMORY

By Saki (H. H. Munro)

It was a chill, rain-washed afternoon of a late August day, that indefinite season when partridges are still in security or cold storage, and there is nothing to hunt—unless one is bounded on the north by the Bristol Channel, in which case one may lawfully gallop after fat red stags. Lady Blemley's house-party was not bounded on the north by the Bristol Channel, hence there was a full gathering of her guests round the tea-table on this particular afternoon. And, in spite of the blankness of the season and the triteness of the occasion, there was no trace in the company of that fatigued restlessness which means a dread of the pianola and a subdued hankering for auction bridge. The undisguised, open-mouthed attention of the entire party was fixed on the homely negative personality of Mr Cornelius Appin. Of all her guests, he was the one who had come to Lady Blemley with the vaguest reputation. Someone had said he was 'clever,' and he had got his invitation in the moderate expectation, on the part of his hostess, that some portion at least of his cleverness would be contributed to the general entertainment. Until tea-time that day she had been unable to discover in what direction, if any, his cleverness lay. He was neither a wit nor a croquet champion, a hypnotic force nor a begetter of amateur theatricals. Neither did his exterior suggest the sort of man in

whom women are willing to pardon a generous
measure of mental deficiency. He had subsided
into mere Mr Appin, and the Cornelius seemed a
piece of transparent baptismal bluff. And now he
was claiming to have launched on the world a discovery beside which the invention of gunpowder, of
the printing-press, and of steam locomotion were
inconsiderable trifles. Science had made bewilder-
ing strides in many directions during recent decades,
but this thing seemed to belong to the domain of
miracle rather than to scientific achievement.

'And do you really ask us to believe,' Sir Wilfrid
was saying, 'that you have discovered a means for
instructing animals in the art of human speech, and
that dear old Tobermory has proved your first
successful pupil?'

'It is a problem at which I have worked for the
last seventeen years,' said Mr Appin, 'but only
during the last eight or nine months have I been
rewarded with glimmerings of success. Of course
I have experimented with thousands of animals,
but latterly only with cats, those wonderful creatures which have assimilated themselves so mar-
vellously with our civilization while retaining all
their highly developed feral instincts. Here and
there among cats one comes across an outstanding
superior intellect, just as one does among the ruck
of human beings, and when I made the acquaintance
of Tobermory a week ago I saw at once that I was
in contact with a "Beyond-cat" of extraordinary
intelligence. I had gone far along the road to
success in recent experiments; with Tobermory, as
you call him, I have reached the goal.'

Mr Appin concluded his remarkable statement in a voice which he strove to divest of a triumphant inflection. No one said 'Rats,' though Clovis's lips moved in a monosyllabic contortion which probably invoked those rodents of disbelief.

'And do you mean to say,' asked Miss Resker, after a slight pause, 'that you have taught Tobermory to say and understand easy sentences of one syllable?'

'My dear Miss Resker,' said the wonder-worker patiently, 'one teaches little children and savages and backward adults in that piecemeal fashion; when one has once solved the problem of making a beginning with an animal of highly developed intelligence one has no need for those halting methods. Tobermory can speak our language with perfect correctness.'

This time Clovis very distinctly said, 'Beyond-rats!' Sir Wilfrid was more polite, but equally sceptical.

'Hadn't we better have the cat in and judge for ourselves?' suggested Lady Blemley.

Sir Wilfrid went in search of the animal, and the company settled themselves down to the languid expectation of witnessing some more or less adroit drawing-room ventriloquism.

In a minute Sir Wilfrid was back in the room, his face white beneath its tan and his eyes dilated with excitement.

'By Gad, it's true!'

His agitation was unmistakably genuine, and his hearers started forward in a thrill of awakened interest.

Collapsing into an armchair he continued breath
lessly: 'I found him dozing in the smoking-room,
and called out to him to come for his tea. He
blinked at me in his usual way, and I said, "Come
on, Toby; don't keep us waiting"; and, by Gad!
he drawled out in a most horribly natural voice
that he'd come when he dashed well pleased! I
nearly jumped out of my skin!'

Appin had preached to absolutely incredulous
hearers; Sir Wilfrid's statement carried instant
conviction. A Babel-like chorus of startled exclamation arose, amid which the scientist sat mutely
enjoying the first fruit of his stupendous discovery.

In the midst of the clamour Tobermory entered
the room and made his way with velvet tread and
studied unconcern across to the group seated round
the tea-table.

A sudden hush of awkwardness and constraint
fell on the company. Somehow there seemed an
element of embarrassment in addressing on equal
terms a domestic cat of acknowledged dental ability.

'Will you have some milk, Tobermory?' asked
Lady Blemley in a rather strained voice.

'I don't mind if I do,' was the response, couched
in a tone of even indifference. A shiver of sup-
pressed excitement went through the listeners, and
Lady Blemley might be excused for pouring out
the saucerful of milk rather unsteadily.

'I'm afraid I've spilt a good deal of it,' she said
apologetically.

'After all, it's not my Axminster,' was Tobermory's rejoinder.

Another silence fell on the group, and then Miss

Resker, in her best district-visitor manner, asked if the human language had been difficult to learn. Tobermory looked squarely at her for a moment and then fixed his gaze serenely on the middle distance. It was obvious that boring questions lay outside his scheme of life.

'What do you think of human intelligence?' asked Mavis Pellington lamely.

'Of whose intelligence in particular?' asked Tobermory coldly.

'Oh, well, mine, for instance,' said Mavis, with a feeble laugh.

'You put me in an embarrassing position,' said Tobermory, whose tone and attitude certainly did not suggest a shred of embarrassment. 'When your inclusion in this house-party was suggested Sir Wilfrid protested that you were the most brainless woman of his acquaintance, and that there was a wide distinction between hospitality and the care of the feeble-minded. Lady Blemley replied that your lack of brain-power was the precise quality which had earned you your invitation, as you were the only person she could think of who might be idiotic enough to buy their old car. You know, the one they call "The Envy of Sisyphus," because it goes quite nicely up-hill if you push it.'

Lady Blemley's protestations would have had greater effect if she had not casually suggested to Mavis only that morning that the car in question would be just the thing for her down at her Devonshire home.

Major Barfield plunged in heavily to effect a diversion.

'How about your carryings-on with the tortoise-shell puss up at the stables, eh?'

The moment he had said it every one realized the blunder.

'One does not usually discuss these matters in public,' said Tobermory frigidly. 'From a slight observation of your ways since you've been in this house I should imagine you'd find it inconvenient if I were to shift the conversation on to your own little affairs.'

The panic which ensued was not confined to the Major.

'Would you like to go and see if cook has got your dinner ready?' suggested Lady Blemley hurriedly, affecting to ignore the fact that it wanted at least two hours to Tobermory's dinner-time.

'Thanks,' said Tobermory, 'not quite so soon after my tea. I don't want to die of indigestion.'

'Cats have nine lives, you know,' said Sir Wilfrid heartily.

'Possibly,' answered Tobermory; 'but only one liver.'

'Adelaide!' said Mrs Cornett, 'do you mean to encourage that cat to go out and gossip about us in the servants' hall?'

The panic had indeed become general. A narrow ornamental balustrade ran in front of most of the bedroom windows at the Towers, and it was recalled with dismay that this had formed a favourite promenade for Tobermory at all hours, whence he could watch the pigeons—and heaven knew what else besides. If he intended to become reminiscent in his present outspoken strain the effect would be something more than disconcerting.

Mrs Cornett, who spent much time at her toilet table, and whose complexion was reputed to be of a nomadic though punctual disposition, looked as ill at ease as the Major. Miss Scrawen, who wrote fiercely sensuous poetry and led a blameless life, merely displayed irritation; if you are methodical and virtuous in private you don't necessarily want every one to know it. Bertie van Tahn, who was so depraved at seventeen that he had long ago given up trying to be any worse, turned a dull shade of gardenia white, but he did not commit the error of dashing out of the room like Odo Finsberry, a young gentleman who was understood to be reading for the Church and who was possibly disturbed at the thought of scandals he might hear concerning other people. Clovis had the presence of mind to maintain a composed exterior; privately he was calculating how long it would take to procure a box of fancy mice through the agency of the *Exchange and Mart* as a species of hush-money.

Even in a delicate situation like the present, Agnes Resker could not endure to remain too long in the background.

'Why did I ever come down here?' she asked dramatically.

Tobermory immediately accepted the opening.

'Judging by what you said to Mrs Cornett on the croquet-lawn yesterday, you were out for food. You described the Blemleys as the dullest people to stay with that you knew, but said they were clever enough to employ a first-rate cook; otherwise they'd find it difficult to get any one to come down a second time.'

'There's not a word of truth in it! I appeal to Mrs Cornett——' exclaimed the discomfited Agnes.

'Mrs Cornett repeated your remark afterwards to Bertie van Tahn,' continued Tobermory, 'and said, "That woman is a regular Hunger Marcher; she'd go anywhere for four square meals a day," and Bertie van Tahn said——'

At this point the chronicle mercifully ceased. Tobermory had caught a glimpse of the big yellow Tom from the Rectory working his way through the shrubbery towards the stable wing. In a flash he had vanished through the open French window.

With the disappearance of his too brilliant pupil Cornelius Appin found himself beset by a hurricane of bitter upbraiding, anxious inquiry, and frightened entreaty. The responsibility for the situation lay with him, and he must prevent matters from becoming worse. Could Tobermory impart his dangerous gift to other cats? was the first question he had to answer. It was possible, he replied, that he might have initiated his intimate friend the stable puss into his new accomplishment, but it was unlikely that his teaching could have taken a wider range as yet.

'Then,' said Mrs Cornett, 'Tobermory may be a valuable cat and a great pet; but I'm sure you'll agree, Adelaide, that both he and the stable cat must be done away with without delay.'

'You don't suppose I've enjoyed the last quarter of an hour, do you?' said Lady Blemley bitterly. 'My husband and I are very fond of Tobermory— at least, we were before this horrible accomplishment was infused into him; but now, of course, the only thing is to have him destroyed as soon as possible.'

'We can put some strychnine in the scraps he always gets at dinner-time,' said Sir Wilfrid, 'and I will go and drown the stable cat myself. The coach-man will be very sore at losing his pet, but I'll say a very catching form of mange has broken out in both cats and we're afraid of it spreading to the kennels.'

'But my great discovery!' expostulated Mr Appin; 'after all my years of research and experiment——'

'You can go and experiment on the shorthorns at the farm, who are under proper control,' said Mrs Cornett, 'or the elephants at the Zoological Gardens. They're said to be highly intelligent, and they have this recommendation, that they don't come creeping about our bedrooms and under chairs, and so forth.'

An archangel ecstatically proclaiming the Millen-nium, and then finding that it clashed unpardonably with Henley and would have to be definitely post-poned, could hardly have felt more crestfallen than Cornelius Appin at the reception of his wonderful achievement. Public opinion, however, was against him—in fact, had the general voice been consulted on the subject it is probable that a strong minority vote would have been in favour of including him in the strychnine diet.

Defective train arrangements and a nervous desire to see matters brought to a finish prevented an immediate dispersal of the party, but dinner that evening was not a social success. Sir Wilfrid had had rather a trying time with the stable cat and subsequently with the coachman. Agnes Resker

ostentatiously limited her repast to a morsel of dry
toast, which she bit as though it were a personal
enemy; while Mavis Pellington maintained a vindic-
tive silence throughout the meal. Lady Blemley
kept up a flow of what she hoped was conversation,
but her attention was fixed on the doorway. A
plateful of carefully dosed fish scraps was in readiness on the sideboard, but sweets and savoury and
dessert went their way, and no Tobermory appeared
either in the dining-room or kitchen.

The sepulchral dinner was cheerful compared with
the subsequent vigil in the smoking-room. Eating
and drinking had at least supplied a distraction
and cloak to the prevailing embarrassment. Bridge
was out of the question in the general tension of
nerves and tempers, and after Odo Finsberry had
given a lugubrious rendering of *Mélisande in the
Wood* to a frigid audience, music was tacitly
avoided. At eleven the servants went to bed,
announcing that the small window in the pantry
had been left open as usual for Tobermory's private
use. The guests read steadily through the current
batch of magazines, and fell back gradually on the
'Badminton Library' and bound volumes of *Punch*.
Lady Blemley made periodic visits to the pantry,
returning each time with an expression of listless
depression which forestalled questioning.

At two o'clock Clovis broke the dominating silence.

'He won't turn up to-night. He's probably in
the local newspaper office at the present moment,
dictating the first instalment of his reminiscences.
Lady What's-her-name's book won't be in it. It
will be the event of the day.'

* C 954

Having made this contribution to the general cheerfulness, Clovis went to bed. At long intervals the various members of the house-party followed his example.

The servants taking round the early tea made a uniform announcement in reply to a uniform question. Tobermory had not returned.

Breakfast was, if anything, a more unpleasant function than dinner had been, but before its conclusion the situation was relieved. Tobermory's corpse was brought in from the shrubbery, where a gardener had just discovered it. From the bites on his throat and the yellow fur which coated his claws it was evident that he had fallen in unequal combat with the big Tom from the Rectory.

By midday most of the guests had quitted The Towers, and after lunch Lady Blemley had sufficiently recovered her spirits to write an extremely nasty letter to the Rectory about the loss of her valuable pet.

Tobermory had been Appin's one successful pupil, and he was destined to have no successor. A few weeks later an elephant in the Dresden Zoological Garden, which had shown no previous signs of irritability, broke loose and killed an Englishman who had apparently been teasing it. The victim's name was variously reported in the papers as Oppin and Eppelin, but his front name was faithfully rendered Cornelius.

'If he was trying German irregular verbs on the poor beast,' said Clovis, 'he deserved all he got.'

LOUISE

By W. Somerset Maugham

I COULD never understand why Louise bothered
with me. She disliked me and I knew that behind
behind my back, in that gentle way of hers, she
seldom lost the opportunity of saying a disagreeable
thing about me. She had too much delicacy ever
to make a direct statement, but with a hint and a
sigh and a little flutter of her beautiful hands she
was able to make her meaning plain. She was a
mistress of cold praise. It was true that we had
known one another almost intimately, for five-and-
twenty years, but it was impossible for me to believe
that she could be affected by the claims of old asso-
ciation. She thought me a coarse, brutal, cynical,
and vulgar fellow. I was puzzled at her not taking the obvious course and dropping me. She did
nothing of the kind; indeed, she would not leave me
alone; she was constantly asking me to lunch and
dine with her and once or twice a year invited me to
spend a week-end at her house in the country. At
last I thought that I had discovered her motive.
She had an uneasy suspicion that I did not believe
in her; and if that was why she did not like me, it
was also why she sought my acquaintance: it galled
her that I alone should look upon her as a comic
figure and she could not rest till I acknowledged
myself mistaken and defeated. Perhaps she had an

inkling that I saw the face behind the mask and because I alone held out was determined that sooner or later I too should take the mask for the face. I was never quite certain that she was a complete humbug. I wondered whether she fooled herself as thoroughly as she fooled the world or whether there was some spark of humour at the bottom of her heart. If there was it might be that she was attracted to me, as a pair of crooks might be attracted to one another, by the knowledge that we shared a secret that was hidden from everybody else.

I knew Louise before she married. She was then a frail, delicate girl with large and melancholy eyes. Her father and mother worshipped her with an anxious adoration, for some illness, scarlet fever I think, left her with a weak heart and she had to take the greatest care of herself. When Tom Maitland proposed to her they were dismayed, for they were convinced that she was much too delicate for the strenuous state of marriage. But they were not too well off and Tom Maitland was rich. He promised to do everything in the world for Louise and finally they entrusted her to him as a sacred charge. Tom Maitland was a big, husky fellow, very good-looking, and a fine athlete. He doted on Louise. With her weak heart he could not hope to keep her with him long and he made up his mind to do everything he could to make her few years on earth happy. He gave up the games he excelled in, not because she wished him to, she was glad that he should play golf and hunt, but because by a coincidence she had a heart attack whenever he proposed to leave her for a day. If they had a difference of opinion she gave in to him at once, for she was the most submissive wife a man could have, but her heart failed her and she would be laid up, sweet and uncomplaining, for a week. He could not be such a brute as to cross her. Then they would have a quiet little tussle about which should yield and it was only with difficulty that at last he persuaded her to have her own way. On one occasion seeing her walk eight miles on an expedition that she particularly wanted to make, I suggested to Tom Maitland that she was stronger than one would have thought. He shook his head and sighed.

'No, no, she's dreadfully delicate. She's been to all the best heart specialists in the world, and they all say that her life hangs on a thread. But she has an unconquerable spirit.'

He told her that I had remarked on her endurance.

'I shall pay for it to-morrow,' she said to me in her plaintive way. 'I shall be at death's door.'

'I sometimes think that you're quite strong enough to do the things you want to,' I murmured.

I had noticed that if a party was amusing she could dance till five in the morning, but if it was dull she felt very poorly and Tom had to take her home early. I am afraid she did not like my reply, for though she gave me a pathetic little smile I saw no amusement in her large blue eyes.

'You can't very well expect me to fall down dead just to please you,' she answered.

Louise outlived her husband. He caught his death of cold one day when they were sailing and Louise needed all the rugs there were to keep her warm. He left her a comfortable fortune and a daughter. Louise was inconsolable. It was wonderful that she managed to survive the shock. Her friends expected her speedily to follow poor Tom Maitland to the grave. Indeed they already felt dreadfully sorry for Iris, her daughter, who would be left an orphan. They redoubled their attentions towards Louise. They would not let her stir a finger; they insisted on doing everything in the world to save her trouble. They had to, because if she was called upon to do anything tiresome or inconvenient her heart went back on her and there she was at death's door. She was entirely lost without a man to take care of her, she said, and she did not know how, with her delicate health, she was going to bring up her dear Iris. Her friends asked why she did not marry again. Oh, with her heart it was out of the question, though of course she knew that dear Tom would have wished her to, and perhaps it would be the best thing for Iris if she did; but who would want to be bothered with a wretched invalid like herself? Oddly enough more than one young man showed himself quite ready to undertake the charge and a year after Tom's death she allowed George Hobhouse to lead her to the altar. He was a fine, upstanding fellow, and he was not at all badly off. I never saw any one so grateful as he for the privilege of being allowed to take care of this frail little thing.

'I shan't live to trouble you long,' she said.

He was a soldier and an ambitious one, but he resigned his commission. Louise's health forced her to spend the winter at Monte Carlo and the summer at Deauville. He hesitated a little at throwing up his career, and Louise at first would not hear of it; but at last she yielded as she always yielded, and he prepared to make his wife's last few years as happy as might be.

'It can't be very long now,' she said. 'I'll try not to be troublesome.'

For the next two or three years Louise managed, notwithstanding her weak heart, to go beautifully dressed to all the most lively parties, to gamble very heavily, to dance and even to flirt with tall, slim young men. But George Hobhouse had not the stamina of Louise's first husband and he had to brace himself now and then with a stiff drink for his day's work as Louise's second husband. It is possible that the habit would have grown on him, which Louise would not have liked at all, but very fortunately (for her) the war broke out. He rejoined his regiment and three months later was killed. It was a great shock to Louise. She felt, however, that in such a crisis she must not give way to a private grief; and if she had a heart attack nobody heard of it. In order to distract her mind, she turned her villa at Monte Carlo into a hospital for convalescent officers. Her friends told her that she would never survive the strain.

'Of course it will kill me,' she said, 'I know that. But what does it matter? I must do my bit.'

It didn't kill her. She had the time of her life. There was no convalescent home in France that was more popular. I met her by chance in Paris. She was lunching at the Ritz with a tall and very handsome Frenchman. She explained that she was there on business connected with the hospital. She told me that the officers were too charming to her. They knew how delicate she was and they wouldn't let her do a single thing. They took care of her, well—as though they were all her husbands. She sighed.

'Poor George, who would ever have thought that I, with my heart, should survive him?'

'And poor Tom!' I said.

I don't know why she didn't like my saying that. She gave me her plaintive smile and her beautiful eyes filled with tears.

'You always speak as though you grudged me the few years that I can expect to live.'

'By the way, your heart's much better, isn't it?'

'It'll never be better. I saw a specialist this morning and he said I must be prepared for the worst.'

'Oh, well, you've been prepared for that for nearly twenty years now, haven't you?'

When the war came to an end Louise settled in London. She was now a woman of over forty, thin and frail still, with large eyes and pale cheeks, but she did not look a day more than twenty-five. Iris, who had been at school and was now grown up, came to live with her.

'She'll take care of me,' said Louise. 'Of course it'll be hard on her to live with such a great invalid as I am, but it can only be for such a little while, I'm sure she won't mind.'

Iris was a nice girl. She had been brought up with the knowledge that her mother's health was precarious. As a child she had never been allowed to make a noise. She had always realized that her mother must on no account be upset. And though Louise told her now that she would not hear of her sacrificing herself for a tiresome old woman the girl simply would not listen. It wasn't a question of sacrificing herself, it was a happiness to do what she could for her poor dear mother. With a sigh her mother let her do a great deal.

'It pleases the child to think she's making herself useful,' she said.

'Don't you think she ought to go out and about more?' I asked.

'That's what I'm always telling her. I can't get her to enjoy herself. Heaven knows, I never want any one to put themselves out on my account.'

And Iris, when I remonstrated with her, said: 'Poor dear mother, she wants me to go and stay with friends and go to parties, but the moment I start off anywhere she has one of her heart attacks, so I much prefer to stay at home.'

But presently she fell in love. A young friend of mine, a very good lad, asked her to marry him and she consented. I liked the child and was glad that she was to be given the chance to lead a life of her own. She had never seemed to suspect that such a thing was possible. But one day the young man came to me in great distress and told me that his marriage was indefinitely postponed. Iris felt that she could not desert her mother. Of course it was really no business of mine, but I made the opportunity to go and see Louise. She was always glad to receive her friends at tea-time and now that she was older she cultivated the society of painters and writers.

'Well, I hear that Iris isn't going to be married,' I said after a while.

'I don't know about that. She's not going to be married quite as soon as I could have wished. I've begged her on my bended knees not to consider me, but she absolutely refuses to leave me.'

'Don't you think it's rather hard on her?'

'Dreadfully. Of course it can only be for a few months, but I hate the thought of any one sacrificing themselves for me.'

'My dear Louise, you've buried two husbands, I can't see the least reason why you shouldn't bury at least two more.'

'Do you think that's funny?' she asked me in a tone that she made as offensive as she could.

'I suppose it's never struck you as strange that you're always strong enough to do anything you want to and that your weak heart only prevents you from doing things that bore you?'

'Oh, I know, I know what you've always thought of me. You've never believed that I had anything the matter with me, have you?'

I looked at her full and square.

'Never. I think you've carried out for twenty-five years a stupendous bluff. I think you're the most selfish and monstrous woman I have ever known. You ruined the lives of those two wretched men you married and now you're going to ruin the life of your daughter.'

I should not have been surprised if Louise had had a heart attack then. I fully expected her to fly into a passion. She merely gave me a gentle smile.

'My poor friend, one of these days you 'll be so dreadfully sorry you said this to me.'

'Have you quite determined that Iris shall not marry this boy?'

'I 've begged her to marry him. I know it 'll kill me, but I don't mind. Nobody cares for me. I 'm just a burden to everybody.'

'Did you tell her it would kill you?'

'She made me.'

'As if any one ever made you do anything that you were not yourself quite determined to do.'

'She can marry her young man to-morrow if she likes. If it kills me, it kills me.'

'Well, let 's risk it, shall we?'

'Haven't you got any compassion for me?'

'One can't pity any one who amuses one as much as you amuse me,' I answered.

A faint spot of colour appeared on Louise's pale cheeks and though she smiled still her eyes were hard and angry.

'Iris shall marry in a month's time,' she said, 'and if anything happens to me I hope you and she will be able to forgive yourselves.'

Louise was as good as her word. A date was fixed, a trousseau of great magnificence was ordered, and invitations were issued. Iris and the very good lad were radiant. On the wedding-day, at ten o'clock in the morning, Louise, that devilish woman, had one of her heart attacks—and died. She died gently forgiving Iris for having killed her.

MR PIM AND THE HOLY CRUMB

By T. F. Powys

THE Holy Communion was about to be celebrated one winter's morning at the church of St Nicholas in the village of Madder.

The event was of very little importance to any one, save perhaps to the clergyman, to Pim the church clerk, and to a little mouse who lived under the altar.

Pim was obliged to rise early when the celebration was to take place, and to use his best endeavour to light the church fire, leaving his own bed at an hour when he liked most to remain in it. What the ceremony really meant, Pim had never had the least idea.

Though clerk of the church, he had never yet received the sacrament, for it had ever been his habit, after collecting the alms, to take his cap from his pew and retire on tiptoe from the church.

But this Christmas morning was to prove an exception, for Mr Thomas Tucker, the clergyman, had caught Pim at a disadvantage, got him into a corner of the vestry, and compelled his attention. Then it was that Mr Tucker told to Pim so strange a tale of the holy feast that the clerk, having an inquisitive mind, promised his master that this once he would partake of the elements.

When Mr Tucker had explained to him the meaning of the rite, Pim made the necessary preparations. He found the church cold, for the fire he had lit earlier with so many pains was gone out, and Pim was glad to exercise himself a little by returning to the vestry and pulling at the bell-rope.

After ringing himself warm, Pim, while Mr Tucker rested upon a chair, stepped out of the church to see what was doing abroad. The heavy tranquil weather, with its still silence, informed Pim as he looked around him that it was going to snow. He looked this way and that, with his hands placed behind his coat-tails, and as if in answer to his thoughts a large snowflake fluttered down, remained upon the path for a moment, and then melted into water.

Pim, looking up from the vanished flake, beheld Miss Jarrett and Mrs Patch, two old women who chattered like crows, coming his way. He was full of the strange story that Mr Tucker had told him in the vestry, for, shake his head as he might, he could not rid himself of it. The snowflake that he had thought to confer with had gone too soon, but the two old women appeared more likely to remain and listen.

Pim was not the man to keep anything to himself. If he heard any surprising news he would always tell it to the first person he met, whether the news was a maiden ill-treated, a nest of eggs stolen from Farmer Told, or a fire in London.

'Mr Tucker do tell I,' said Pim, addressing himself to Miss Jarrett, 'that the Lord God, the Creator of the world, who be named Christ by drunken folk when pub do close, do change 'Isself into they scrimpy bites of Mr Johnson's bread that thee do take and eat up at church railings.'

Miss Jarrett hurriedly placed her muff before her mouth to stop her laughter, while Mrs Patch winked expressively as if she knew all about such wonderful doings, though her repeated winks told Pim that the particular moment wasn't a proper one for her to explain them.

Miss Jarrett, who could hardly contain her mirth, now put her finger to her lips and passed by the clerk together with Mrs Patch, bidding him in a whisper to beware what he said, for Miss Pettifer was coming.

Pim stood to one side as the lady from the Manor walked by with her little silver bag. He touched his hat respectfully and informed Miss Pettifer that he believed it would snow before the night came.

'Can't you see,' said Miss Pettifer, a little rudely, 'that it snows now, Pim?'

Pim looked in another direction, for he once had a friend whose name was John Toole. It had always been the custom of these two, when John was alive, to meet of an evening by the village green, exchange remarks about the weather, and then walk slowly and thoughtfully to the inn. Once there, but having little money to spend, they would share a pot of beer so that their order might sound large.

John Toole hanged himself, and now Pim shook his head at his grave.

As Miss Pettifer, however late she came, had always to be allowed time to adjust her veil, sprinkle a little scent upon her handkerchief, and kneel down, Pim had no need to hurry back to the church. With his hands still behind his back, he bent over the grave.

'John,' said Pim, 'I 've a-heard something that must make 'ee laugh—'tis that God Almighty in our little church do change 'Isself into a bite of stale bread.'

'That be a tale,' replied a muffled voice from the ground; 'but what be weather doing up above?'

'There be snowflakes a-falling as large as feathers,' replied Pim, showing no surprise because his friend spoke so lowlily, 'as large as feathers, but they do melt on ground.'

'So I did fancy,' replied the buried John; 'but now I 've somewhat to ask of 'ee that bain't about the weather.'

'Ask away, Johnnie,' replied Pim.

'If 'ee do happen,' said the muffled voice, 'to get a word wi' thik crumb of bread that be the Lord on High, ask 'E to be kind enough to look over Johnnie Toole at the last day, for I be well content to bide where I be now. There bain't no work to do here and all be ease and comfort, and many a merry story do we bones tell together.'

Pim sighed. He nodded twice at the grave, turned, and walked to the church. Mr Tucker was standing ready robed in the vestry, Miss Pettifer was kneeling with her black fur stole covering her shoulders.

Pim solemnly tolled the last bell; he proceeded to the back pew and knelt down. The wonderful story that he had heard of—the transformation of God into the Holy Bread—made him fearful, but yet he wished to ask John Toole's question.

Another matter troubled him too. He remembered that only the evening before his wife Jane had blamed Mr Johnson's bread for giving her a pain in her chest. What if God should pain him too? Pim looked gloomy.

When his turn came Pim knelt at the altar rail next to Mrs Patch. He trembled exceedingly. He was so fearful of the consequences of the act of eating, that when he was going to put the bread into his mouth he let a large crumb fall upon the floor.

As soon as the service was over and Mr Tucker was gone out, Pim returned in a slow and fearful manner to the altar again. To have eaten so much of Mr Johnson's bread, as well as so much of his Maker, seemed a dreadful thing, but to have dropped a crumb of Him upon the floor seemed a worse.

After he had eaten God, Pim wondered what God was like. He supposed that God would very much resemble the landlord at the village inn. Mr Hookes, the landlord, looked like a judge, and indeed he might well have been the creator of all men.

''E did draw I out of 'Is great barrel into a little cup,' said Pim aloud, 'and when I die 'E do but empty I again into the dirt from whence I came. They be 'Is notions. But if I do eat 'E, between meals, and become as lordly as 'Isself, all me happiness be gone.

'And 'tis likely,' continued Pim, eyeing in a cautious manner the crumb upon the floor, ''E won't be pleased wi' Pim for dropping 'E upon church carpet so carelessly. 'Tain't proper for a Holy Crumb to be so fallen. And what be I? Only a small worm of the earth, while 'E it were who did make the round world, the seas, and wold

Madder hill. 'Twouldn't do for Pim to go to heaven no more than for Johnnie Toole. Maybe 'E 'll let we bide a merry family. Some do fall of a sudden, some bent and tottering like wold Barker do tarry long, but all do go to dust.

'I be sorry,' said Pim, addressing himself to the crumb, 'that I did swallow t'other half of 'Ee.'

'Mr Pim!'

The clerk of St Nicholas looked into the pulpit, he looked down the church aisle, but could see no one.

'Mr Pim!'

His name was spoken very near to him.

'If thik little crumb be changed into God, mayhap 'tis 'E who do speak,' observed Pim.

'And why not?' said the Holy Crumb; 'surely I have as good a right to speak as any other person.'

'Why, so Thee have,' exclaimed Pim, 'and now that I 've found 'Ee so talkative, perhaps Thee 'll listen to what I do say and maybe Thee 'll grant Johnnie and I our one desire.'

'Speak on,' said the Crumb.

'John Toole and I,' remarked Pim, '—'tis 'e who do lie along by yew tree where no sun don't shine—do ask Thee to let we two bide in ground at last day.'

'But you 're not dead yet.'

'I do owe God a death,' said the clerk. The Crumb smiled. 'A well-dug grave be good and a coffin be pretty, but I haven't a fancy for neither heaven nor hell. I 've a mind to bide where I be put same as Johnnie, while above, in village, days will pass and be gone, will return again and be gone. Thik grey stone that do bide out in field will still be there, and maybe Mr Told's barn will bide about too. Johnnie and I don't want to go to no new place, we'd sooner be dry bones in Madder—for 'tis our home—than lords in heaven.'

'Alas!' said the Crumb.

'Thee do know for a truth,' continued Pim, 'that I bain't a proper companion for the risen gentry; they'd only laugh at me.'

'Why, so they would,' answered the Crumb, 'of course they would.'

'I bain't dissatisfied with the world,' observed Pim. 'My life has pleased me well. Before I were clerk to church and rabbit-trapper, I were ploughman to Mr Told. I do like to sit down at night-time and talk of folk that be gone. Soon I will go too, and I don't want, no more than Johnnie, to be disturbed by no trumpet.'

'But every one else wants to rise again,' remarked the Crumb, 'even the clergy.'

'Clergymen,' observed Pim, 'bain't easily satisfied. They do keep servants, and often a little dog. They do eat mutton and rice pudding, stretch out their legs before the fire, and listen to music being played.'

'Say,' inquired the Crumb, 'do people ever talk about me here? Do they name me at all?'

'Thee's name be useful,' murmured Pim.

'For what?' asked the Crumb.

'Shepherd do shout Thee's name to 'is dog, Carter Beer do damn wold Boxer wi' Thee, and Mr Tucker do say Thee bain't no liar.'

'And yet I made the green grass, Mr Pim!'

''Tis plain Pim with the clergy,' remarked the clerk.

'Mr Pim!'

'Yes, Holy Crumb.'

'Mr Pim, I am disappointed with you. I hoped you would have wished to dwell with me, for, to tell you a truth, I made heaven glorious for you and for John Toole.'

'But Thee made the earth too, and the sweet mould for our bed, and Thee 'll have Miss Pettifer in heaven, who be a lady.'

'But you, Mr Pim, who have never eaten of the tree of knowledge: I had a mind to be happy with you for all eternity.'

'Ha! ha! ha!' laughed Pim, 'I do see the fix Thee be in, but bain't 'Ee God?'

'Yes, alas so!'

'Then do 'Ee come and be a rotted bone by John and I. But allsame Thee needn't hurry I there. I have a mind to eat a spring cabbage at Easter.'

'Mr Pim, Mr Pim, you are exactly what I meant myself to be. When I consider the troubles I have caused,' said the Holy Crumb in a low voice, 'I almost wish I had entered into a mouse instead of a man.'

'Hist! hist!' whispered Pim, 'Thee may do thik now, for a mouse do live under altar table, who do creep out when all 's quiet.'

Pim moved to the front pew, winked at the Crumb and remained silent. A little mouse, with a pert, prying look, crept out from under the altar and devoured the Holy Crumb.

I'M A FOOL

BY SHERWOOD ANDERSON

IT was a hard jolt for me, one of the bitterest I ever had to face. And it all came about through my own foolishness, too. Even yet sometimes, when I think of it, I want to cry or swear or kick myself. Perhaps, even now, after all this time, there will be a kind of satisfaction in making myself look cheap by telling of it.

It began at three o'clock one October afternoon as I sat in the grand-stand at the fall trotting-and-pacing meet at Sandusky, Ohio.

To tell the truth, I felt a little foolish that I should be sitting in the grand-stand at all. During the summer before I had left my home town with Harry Whitehead and, with a nigger named Burt, had taken a job as swipe with one of the two horses Harry was campaigning through the fall race-meets that year. Mother cried and my sister Mildred, who wanted to get a job as a school-teacher in our town that fall, stormed and scolded about the house all during the week before I left. They both thought it something disgraceful that one of our family should take a place as a swipe with race-horses. I've an idea Mildred thought my taking the place would stand in the way of her getting the job she'd been working so long for.

But after all I had to work, and there was no other work to be got. A big lumbering fellow of nineteen couldn't just hang around the house and I had got too big to mow people's lawns and sell newspapers. Little chaps who could get next to people's sympathies by their sizes were always getting jobs away from me. There was one fellow who kept saying to every one who wanted a lawn mowed or a cistern cleaned, that he was saving money to work his way through college, and I used to lay awake nights thinking up ways to injure him without being found out. I kept thinking of wagons running over him and bricks falling on his head as he walked along the street. But never mind him.

I got the place with Harry and I liked Burt fine. We got along splendid together. He was a big nigger with a lazy sprawling body and soft, kind eyes, and when it came to a fight he could hit like Jack Johnson. He had Bucephalus, a big black pacing stallion that could do 2·09 or 2·10, if he had to, and I had a little gelding named Doctor Fritz that never lost a race all fall when Harry wanted him to win.

We set out from home late in July in a box car with the two horses, and after that, until late November, we kept moving along to the race-meets and the fairs. It was a peachy time for me, I 'll say that. Sometimes now I think that boys who are raised regular in houses, and never have a fine nigger like Burt for best friend, and go to high schools and college, and never steal anything, or get drunk a little, or learn to swear from fellows who know how, or come walking up in front of a grand-stand in their shirt sleeves and with dirty horsy pants on when the races are going on and the grand-stand is full of people all dressed up—— What 's the use of talking about it? Such fellows don't know nothing at all. They 've never had no opportunity.

But I did. Burt taught me how to rub down a horse and put the bandages on after a race and steam a horse out and a lot of valuable things for any man to know. He could wrap a bandage on a horse's leg so smooth that if it had been the same colour you would think it was his skin, and I guess he 'd have been a big driver, too, and got to the top like Murphy and Walter Cox and the others if he hadn't been black.

Gee whizz! it was fun. You got to a county seat town, maybe say on a Saturday or Sunday, and the fair began the next Tuesday and lasted until Friday afternoon. Doctor Fritz would be, say in the 2·25 trot on Tuesday afternoon, and on Thursday afternoon Bucephalus would knock 'em cold in the 'free-for-all' pace. It left you a lot of time to hang around and listen to horse talk, and see Burt knock some yap cold that got too gay, and you 'd find out about horses and men and pick up a lot of stuff you could use all the rest of your life, if you had some sense and salted down what you heard and felt and saw.

And then at the end of the week when the race-meet was over, and Harry had run home to tend up to his livery-stables business, you and Burt hitched the two horses to carts and drove slow and steady across country, to the place for the next meeting, so as to not overheat the horses, etc. etc., you know.

Gee whizz! Gosh a'mighty! the nice hickory-nut and beech-nut and oaks and other kinds of trees along the roads, all brown and red, and the good smells, and Burt singing a song that was called *Deep*

River, and the country girls at the windows of houses and everything. You can stick your colleges up your nose for all me. I guess I know where I got my education.

Why, one of those little burgs of towns you come to on the way, say now on a Saturday afternoon, and Burt says, 'Let's lay up here.' And you did.

And you took the horses to a livery stable and fed them, and you got your good clothes out of a box and put them on.

And the town was full of farmers gaping, because they could see you were race-horse people, and the kids maybe never see a nigger before and was afraid and run away when the two of us walked down their main street.

And that was before prohibition and all that foolishness, and so you went into a saloon, the two of you, and all the yaps come and stood around, and there was always someone pretended he was horsy and knew things and spoke up and began asking questions, and all you did was to lie and lie all you could about what horses you had, and I said I owned them, and then some fellow said 'Will you have a drink of whisky?' and Burt knocked his eye out the way he could say, off-hand like, 'Oh well, all right, I 'm agreeable to a little nip. I 'll split a quart with you.' Gee whizz!

But that isn't what I want to tell my story about. We got home late in November and I promised mother I 'd quit the race-horses for good. There's a lot of things you 've got to promise a mother because she don't know any better.

And so, there not being any work in our town any more than when I left there to go to the races, I went on to Sandusky and got a pretty good place taking care of horses for a man who owned a teaming and delivery and storage and coal and real-estate business there. It was a pretty good place with good eats, and a day off each week, and sleeping on a cot in a big barn, and mostly just shovelling in hay and oats to a lot of big good-enough skates of horses, that couldn't have trotted a race with a toad. I wasn't dissatisfied and I could send money home.

And then, as I started to tell you, the fall races come to Sandusky and I got the day off and I went. I left the job at noon and had on my good clothes and my new brown derby hat, I'd just bought the Saturday before, and a stand-up collar.

First of all I went down town and walked about with the dudes. I've always thought to myself, 'Put up a good front,' and so I did it. I had forty dollars in my pocket, and so I went into the West House, a big hotel, and walked up to the cigar-stand. 'Give me three twenty-five cent cigars,' I said. There was a lot of horsemen and strangers and dressed-up people from other towns standing around in the lobby and in the bar, and I mingled amongst them. In the bar there was a fellow with a cane and a Windsor tie on, that it made me sick to look at him. I like a man to be a man and dress up, but not to go put on that kind of airs. So I pushed him aside, kind of rough, and had me a drink of whisky. And then he looked at me, as though he thought maybe he'd get gay, but he changed his mind and didn't say anything. And then I had another drink of whisky, just to show him something, and went out and had a hack out to the races, all to myself, and when I got there I bought myself the best seat I could get up in the grand-stand, but didn't go in for any of these boxes. That 's putting on too many airs.

And so there I was, sitting up in the grand-stand as gay as you please and looking down on the swipes coming out with their horses, and with their dirty horsy pants on and the horse blankets swung over their shoulders, same as I had been doing all the year before. I liked one thing about the same as the other, sitting up there and feeling grand and being down there and looking up at the yaps and feeling grander and more important, too. One thing 's about as good as another, if you take it just right. I 've often said that.

Well, right in front of me, in the grand-stand that day, there was a fellow with a couple of girls and they was about my age. The young fellow was a nice guy all right. He was the kind maybe that goes to college and then comes to be a lawyer or maybe a newspaper editor or something like that, but he wasn't struck on himself. There are some of that kind are all right and he was one of the ones.

He had his sister with him and another girl and the sister looked around over his shoulder, accidental at first, not intending to start anything — she wasn't that kind—and her eyes and mine happened to meet.

You know how it is. Gee, she was a peach! She had on a soft dress, kind of a blue stuff and it looked carelessly made, but was well sewed and made and everything. I knew that much. I blushed when

D 954

she looked right at me and so did she. She was the nicest girl I 've ever seen in my life. She wasn't struck on herself and she could talk proper grammar without being like a school-teacher or something like that. What I mean is, she was O.K. I think maybe her father was well-to-do, but not rich to make her chesty because she was his daughter, as some are. Maybe he owned a drugstore or a dry-goods store in their home town, or something like that. She never told me and I never asked.

My own people are all O.K., too, when you come to that. My grandfather was Welsh and over in the old country, in Wales he was—— But never mind that.

The first heat of the first race come off and the young fellow sitting there with the two girls left them and went down to make a bet. I knew what he was up to, but he didn't talk big and noisy and let every one around know he was a sport, as some do. He wasn't that kind. Well, he come back and I heard him tell the two girls what horse he 'd bet on, and when the heat was trotted they all half got their feet and acted in the excited, sweaty way people do when they 've got money down on a race, and the horse they bet on is up there pretty close at the end, and they think maybe he 'll come on with a rush, but he never does because he hasn't got the old juice in him, come right down to it.

And then, pretty soon, the horses came out for the 2·18 pace and there was a horse in it I knew. He was a horse Bob French had in his string, but Bob didn't own him. He was a horse owned by a Mr Mathers down at Marietta, Ohio.

This Mr Mathers had a lot of money and owned some coal mines or something, and he had a swell place out in the country, and he was struck on race-horses, but was a Presbyterian or something, and I think more than likely his wife was one, too, maybe a stiffer one than himself. So he never raced his horses hisself, and the story round the Ohio race-tracks was that when one of his horses got ready to go to the races he turned him over to Bob French and pretended to his wife he was sold.

So Bob had the horses and he did pretty much as he pleased and you can't blame Bob, at least, I never did. Sometimes he was out to win and sometimes he wasn't. I never cared much about that when I was swiping a horse. What I did want to know was that my horse had the speed and could go out in front, if you wanted him to.

And, as I 'm telling you, there was Bob in this race with one of Mr Mathers's horses, which was named 'About Ben Ahem' or something like that, and was fast as a streak. He was a gelding and had a mark of 2·21, but could step in ·08 or ·09.

Because when Burt and I were out, as I 've told you, the year before, there was a nigger, Burt knew, worked for Mr Mathers and we went out there one day when we didn't have no race on at the Marietta Fair and our boss Harry was gone home.

And so every one was gone to the fair but just this one nigger and he took us all through Mr Mathers's swell house and he and Burt tapped a bottle of wine Mr Mathers had hid in his bedroom, back in a closet, without his wife knowing, and he showed us this Ahem horse. Burt was always struck on being a driver but didn't have much chance to get to the top, being a nigger, and he and the other nigger gulped that whole bottle of wine and Burt got a little lit up.

So the nigger let Burt take this About Ben Ahem and step him a mile in a track Mr Mathers had all to himself, right there on the farm. And Mr Mathers had one child, a daughter, kinda sick and not very good looking, and she came home and we had to hustle and get About Ben Ahem stuck back in the barn.

I 'm only telling you to get everything straight. At Sandusky, that afternoon I was at the fair, this young fellow with the two girls was fussed, being with the girls and losing his bet. You know how a fellow is that way. One of them was his girl and the other his sister. I had figured that out.

'Gee whizz!' I says to myself, 'I 'm going to give him the dope.'

He was mighty nice when I touched him on the shoulder. He and the girls were nice to me right from the start and clear to the end. I 'm not blaming them.

And so he leaned back and I give him the dope on About Ben Ahem. 'Don't bet a cent on this first heat because he 'll go like an oxen hitched to a plough, but when the first heat is over go right down and lay on your pile.' That 's what I told him.

Well, I never saw a fellow treat any one sweller. There was a fat man sitting beside the little girl, that had looked at me twice by this time, and I at her, and both blushing, and what did he do but have the nerve to turn back and ask the fat man to get up and change places with me so I could sit with his crowd.

Gee whizz, craps a'mighty! There I was. What a chump I was to go and get gay up there in the West House bar, and just because that dude was standing there with a cane and that kind of a necktie on, to go and get all balled up and drink that whisky, just to show off.

Of course she would know, me sitting right beside her and letting her smell of my breath. I could have kicked myself right down out of that grand-stand and all around that race-track and made a faster record than most of the skates of horses they had there that year.

Because that girl wasn't any mutt of a girl. What wouldn't I have give right then for a stick of chewing-gum to chew, or a lozenger, or some liquorice, or most anything. I was glad I had those twenty-five-cent cigars in my pocket and right away I give that fellow one and lit one myself. Then that fat man got up and we changed places and there I was, plunked right down beside her.

They introduced themselves and the fellow's best girl, he had with him, was named Miss Elinor Woodbury, and her father was a manufacturer of barrels from a place called Tiffin, Ohio. And the fellow himself was named Wilbur Wessen and his sister was Miss Lucy Wessen.

I suppose it was their having such swell names got me off my trolly. A fellow, just because he has been a swipe with a race-horse, and works taking care of horses for a man in the teaming, delivery, and storage business, isn't any better or worse than any one else. I 've often thought that, and said it, too.

But you know how a fellow is. There 's something in that kind of nice clothes, and the kind of nice eyes she had, and the way she had looked at me, awhile before, over her brother's shoulder, and me looking back at her, and both of us blushing.

I couldn't show her up for a boob, could I?

I made a fool of myself, that 's what I did. I said my name was Walter Mathers from Marietta, Ohio, and then I told all three of them the smashingest lie you ever heard. What I said was that my father owned the horse About Ben Ahem and that he had let him out to this Bob French for racing purposes, because our family was proud and had never gone into racing that way, in our own name, I mean. Then I had got started and they were all leaning over and listening, and Miss Lucy Wessen's eyes were shining, and I went the whole hog.

I told about our place down at Marietta, and about the big stables and the grand brick house we had on a hill, up above the Ohio River, but I knew enough not to do it in no bragging way. What I did was to start things and then let them drag the rest out of me. I acted just as reluctant to tell as I could. Our family hasn't got any barrel factory, and, since I 've known us, we 've always been pretty poor, but not asking anything of any one at that, and my grandfather, over in Wales—— But never mind that.

We sat there talking like we had known each other for years and years, and I went and told them that my father had been expecting maybe this Bob French wasn't on the square, and had sent me up to Sandusky on the sly to find out what I could.

And I bluffed it through I had found out all about

the 2 18 pace, in which About Ben Ahem was to start.

I said he would lose the first heat by pacing like a lame cow and then he would come back and skin 'em alive after that. And to back up what I said I took thirty dollars out of my pocket and handed it to Mr Wilbur Wessen and asked him, would he mind, after the first heat, to go down and place it on About Ben Ahem for whatever odds he could get. What I said was that I didn't want Bob French to see me and none of the swipes.

Sure enough the first heat come off and About Ben Ahem went off his stride, up the back stretch, and looked like a wooden horse or a sick one, and come in to be last. Then this Wilbur Wessen went down to the betting-place under the grand-stand and there I was with the two girls, and when that Miss Woodbury was looking the other way once, Lucy Wessen kinda, with her shoulder you know, kinda touched me. Not just tucking down, I don't mean. You know how a woman can do. They get close, but not getting gay either. You know what they do. Gee whizz!

And then they give me a jolt. What they had done, when I didn't know, was to get together, and they had decided Wilbur Wessen would bet fifty dollars, and the two girls had gone and put in ten dollars each, of their own money, too. I was sick then, but I was sicker later.

About the gelding, About Ben Ahem, and their winning their money, I wasn't worried a lot about that. It come out O.K. Ahem stepped the next three heats like a bushel of spoiled eggs going to market before they could be found out, and Wilbur Wessen had got nine to two for the money. There was something else eating at me.

Because Wilbur come back, after he had bet the money, and after that he spent most of his time talking to that Miss Woodbury, and Lucy Wessen and I was left alone together like on a desert island. Gee, if I 'd only been on the square, or if there had been any way of getting myself on the square. There ain't any Walter Mathers, like I said to her and them, and there hasn't ever been one, but if there was I bet I 'd go to Marietta, Ohio, and shoot him to-morrow.

There I was, big boob that I am. Pretty soon the race was over, and Wilbur had gone down and collected our money, and we had a hack down-town, and he stood us a swell supper at the West House, and a bottle of champagne beside.

And I was with that girl and she wasn't saying much, and I wasn't saying much either. One thing I know. She wasn't struck on me because of the lie about my father being rich and all that. There 's a way you know. . . . Craps a'mighty! There 's a kind of girl, you see just once in your life, and if you don't get busy and make hay, then you 're gone for good and all, and might as well go jump off a bridge. They give you a look from inside of them somewhere, and it ain't no vamping, and what it means is—you want that girl to be your wife, and you want nice things around her like flowers and swell clothes, and you want her to have the kids you 're going to have, and you want good music played and no ragtime. Gee whizz!

There 's a place over near Sandusky, across a
kind of bay, and it 's called Cedar Point. And
after we had supper we went over to it in a launch,
all by ourselves. Wilbur and Miss Lucy and that
Miss Woodbury had to catch a ten o'clock train back
to Tiffin, Ohio, because, when you 're out with
girls like that, you can't get careless and miss any
trains and stay out all night, like you can with some
some kinds of Janes.

And Wilbur blowed himself to the launch, and it
cost him fifteen cold plunks, but I wouldn't never
have knew if I hadn't listened. He wasn't no tin-
horn kind of a sport.

Over at the Cedar Point place, we didn't stay
around where there was a gang of common kind of
cattle at all.

There was big dance-halls and dining-places for
yaps, and there was a beach you could walk along
and get where it was dark, and we went there.

She didn't talk hardly at all and neither did I, and
I was thinking how glad I was my mother was all
right, and always made us kids learn to eat with a
fork at table, and not swill soup, and not be noisy
and rough like a gang you see around a race-track
that way.

Then Wilbur and his girl went away up the beach
and Lucy and I sat down in a dark place, where there
was some roots of old trees the water had washed up,
and after that the time, till we had to go back in the
launch and they had to catch their trains, wasn't
nothing at all. It went like winking your eye.

Here 's how it was. The place we were sitting in
was dark, like I said, and there was the roots from

* D 954

that old stump sticking up like arms, and there was a
watery smell, and the night was like—as if you could
put your hand out and feel it—so warm and soft and
dark and sweet like an orange.

I 'most cried and I 'most swore and I 'most
jumped up and danced, I was so mad and happy and
sad.

When Wilbur come back from being alone with
his girl, and she saw him coming, Lucy she says,
'We got to go to the train now,' and she was 'most
crying, too, but she never knew nothing I knew,
and she couldn't be so all busted up. And then,
before Wilbur and Miss Woodbury got up to where
we was, she put her face up and kissed me quick and
put her head up against me and she was all quivering
and—— Gee whizz!

Sometimes I hope I have cancer and die. I guess
you know what I mean. We went in the launch
across the bay to the train like that, and it was dark,
too. She whispered and said it was like she and I
could get out of the boat and walk on the water, and
it sounded foolish, but I knew what she meant.

And then quick we were right at the depot, and
there was a big gang of yaps, the kind that goes to
the fairs, and crowded and milling around like cattle,
and how could I tell her? 'It won't be long because
you 'll write and I 'll write to you.' That 's all she
said.

I got a chance like a hay-barn afire. A swell
chance I got.

And maybe she would write me, down at Marietta
that way, and the letter would come back, and

stamped on the front of it by the U.S.A., 'There ain't any such guy,' or something like that, whatever they stamp on a letter that way.

And me trying to pass myself off for a big bug and a swell—to her, as decent a little body as God ever made. Craps a'mighty—a swell chance I got!

And then the train come in, and she got on it, and Wilbur Wessen he come and shook hands with me, and that Miss Woodbury was nice, too, and bowed to me, and I at her, and the train went and I busted out and cried like a kid.

Gee, I could have run after that train and made Dan Patch look like a freight train after a wreck but, socks a'mighty, what was the use? Did you ever see such a fool?

I 'll bet you what—if I had an arm broke right now or a train had run over my foot—I wouldn't go to no doctor at all. I 'd go sit down and let her hurt and hurt—that 's what I 'd do.

I 'll bet you what—if I hadn't a drunk that booze I 'd a never been such a boob as to go tell such a lie— that couldn't never be made straight to a lady like her.

I wish I had that fellow right here that had on a Windsor tie and carried a cane. I 'd smash him for fair. Gosh darn his eyes. He 's a big fool—that 's what he is.

And if I 'm not another you just go find me one and I 'll quit working and be a bum and give him my job. I don't care nothing for working, and earning money, and saving it for no such boob as myself.

THE GREEN DRAKE

By A. E. Coppard

In the village of So-and-so lived an old woman, Rebecca Cracknell, who had a dog with an odd eye and the name of Jack, a kitten with an odd tail and the name of Jack, and a green drake with odd ambitions that was called Jack. The old woman's only son was young Jack, and her husband, long since dead, had been known as old Jack. They began by having different names, every one of them, but the forces of habit were so strong in the good old woman that she always called everything and everybody by that one name. The drake was a middle-aged duck, cooped up in a yard as dry as the deserts of Egypt. Sometimes it tried to go sporting out into the great wet world of gutters and puddles and pools, but Rebecca could not bear to see it behaving so untidily so she confined it, and there in the dry yard it pined and lived.

One day her son Jack tucked the drake under his arm.

'Jacky, my lad, I do believe to-day is your birth-day!' And off he went with the drake under his arm for a mile or more until he came to a field with a barn in it and a pond beside, whose grassy banks so moist and green sloped gently into the water. The water itself was only a dark bronze liquid that stank, but there were three or four chestnut trees close by just casting their pure blooms into it. How bright the day! And how the wind blew!

Into this pond the young man Jack threw Jack
the drake, and the drake became demented with
joy. It heaved the water up with its beak and cast
it over its back. It trod and danced, or flew skim-
ming the pond from shore to shore. It tried to
bury itself in the waters, to burst down through them
into that duck paradise that lies at the bottom of all
ponds, but half of him—and the worst half—always
remained quivering in the common world above.

The lad Jack said he would leave him there to
enjoy himself, because it was his birthday, and he
would come again and fetch him before nightfall.
So the drake was left alone on the pond, and swam
about quacking incessantly in his pride and excitement. How bright the day and how the wind blew,
dashing among the chestnut trees until their heavy
foliage seemed a burden to them and they snowed
their white petals upon the bosom of the pond!
A crow came chattering in the trees, to scoff
at the buffoonery and bad manners of the drake.
Intoxicated it was!

Later on a man in the prime of life with a brown
face and a weather-coloured hat came passing by.
He'd a moleskin suit on with the breeches belted
below the knees, and a wicker bag slung across his
shoulder. He had drunk ale in the sweetness of
the morning. One hand rested in the broad belt
round his belly, with the other he took out his pipe
—and spat fulsomely.

'Hey, my cocky!' he cried when he saw the drake,
and he stood viewing its antics with meditative
eyes.

The drake replied, 'Quack.'

'Quack to me!' cried the man in surly tones. 'Where's your manners?'

So the drake knew he was not conversing with a common creature, but one who might be a god or a gentleman, and he answered him then with care and addressed him with respect.

'Hey, my hearty!' the man exclaimed, 'you's as fine a young feller of a duck as ever I see.'

It was—the drake informed him—his birthday.

'Hi up!' cried the man, and at once he squatted down upon a hump on the bank of the pond, a great castle of a place that some ants had built— ants are such ambitious creatures.

'Hi up!' repeated the man, and he said it was his birthday too. 'Allecapantho!' Now wasn't that curious?

'So I stops me at home this morning,' he continued, 'but my old woman kept growling and groaning until I had to ask her, very civil-like: Whatever's come over you?—I asks her—on my birthday? You're like a dog with a sore nose— I says—and I can't do with you and I can't stand your company, not on my birthday. You're naught but a bag o' mutton—I says—you go and pick the fleas out of your tail—I told her—and I went off to my allotment and cultivated a few chain of the earth. And now my neck's as stiff as a crust of beeswax. Cold winds and sweat, I suppose. Misfortune was ever following me, I tell you. Misfortune was my downfall, and so it is, I can tell you. If you wants to know my history I can tell you: I was born honest, so I shall die poor.'

The drake snoozed upon the water, blinking with

affability and deep enjoyment. Never had anybody taken so much notice of him before, or flattered him with so much kindly attention. And here he was now! The man sat on the ant-hill dividing his attention in three parts: by puffing at a cold pipe, by trying to light it again, by talking genially to the duck on the pond.

'You's as pretty a little duck as ever I seed, I couldn't say no fairer if I'd a mind to.'

'But,' the drake sorrowfully sighed, 'I am only an orphan.'

'Pooh! What about it? Any one can be an orphan if they like. Any one. 'Cept royalty. You mustn't run away with any funny notions, young feller,' the bluff man declared. 'What part are you from?'

The drake told him that he came from the village of So-and-so.

The man knew the place very well. 'Hi up! yes,' he said, 'but there's not a mortal thing in that village to attract a sunny soul, neither bliss nor blessing. There's not a man of that sort nor a woman of that sort; there's not a house of that sort, nor an inn of that sort, not a child, pony, hog, dog or hen of that sort. All poor bred-uns they be.'

The drake confessed that life there was very dull, yes; often it had desired to change its habitation.

'Dull!' roared the other. 'Why, I could not bear to live in that hole, not if the streets was paved with crystal and there was gold on every floor. No, I live in a better place nor that.'

'Pardon me, sir,' said the polite little drake. 'I do not know your name, or where you dwell.'

'Ha, ha! Allecapantho!' returned the man.

'Appercrampus! You would like to know my
pedigree? There 's a touch of Muscovy about you,
I should say, with a brush of Indian blood. Oh, I
can see it, you 're a good bred-un. So am I;
there 's few can trace their ancestors back to history
like me, not straight forward they can't. That 's
sound truth, speak it or be shamed. Two stones in
Barclay Buttle churchyard—d' ye know it? No!
Two stones in Shimp churchyard—d' ye know it?
No! There used to be four in Shimp but two on
'em fell over (or was pushed over, if truth be known),
and Fiddler Kinch stole 'em for his hog-pen, but he
never had no more luck with a pig till the day he
died after it. Bolted his food, he did. It 's true;
every one can tell you truth as knows it, but if it ain't
known it can't be revealed. Two stones in Shimp,
two stones in Barclay Buttle, brass plate with a
skull's head on it in Tooby chancel. What 's amiss
in that for pedigree? Tooby, Shimp, and Barclay
Buttle? Came over with the king of the Busbys
and we 're still hereabouts. William Busby.' Here
the man smote his bosom with pride, and thus the
duck learned that his friend's name was W. Busby,
and not allecapantho or appercrampus.

'When Fiddler died the reverend Saxby discovered they stones where they were—course he 'd
known all along. Parson took 'em up in the dead
a night and transferred them. If you want to see
they stones you just lift up the cloth and you 'll see
'em on top of the altar in Shimp church, all fixed and
fast and consecrated upside down. What 's amiss
with our tribe? You never hear nothing against
the family of Busby—not as a family. I could

show you the stone now, if you had the time, of the
Busby twins, Hezekiah and Joseph, who met un-
timely ends (just what it says) from the sting of
a viper coming from church after being confirmed,
1766. Hi up! God bless us, I remember my old
great-grandfather as used to tell me about William
the Conqueror, all about that man he told me, every
word. The Busbys are a great nation of chaps,
they're everywhere, high up and well-breeched,
please God. I heard a one up in the county of
Nottinghamshire as owns a row of houses with a
shaving-shop at one end and a coastguard station
at the other! And all belongs, all belongs—a
master man, ye know. He used to stuff birds and
fishes and one thing and another, could stuff 'em
well, life-like. Used to stuff for the Duke of Whatever's-the-name-of-the-feller, and for royalty. Years
and years—rows of houses—till his eyes give out
and he got old and his spirits sunk. Kidneys, I
shouldn't wonder; I be troubled the same myself.
Master man! They've got it up here.'

With his finger Busby indicated a position in the
middle of his forehead, and then appeared to swallow
something. 'Appercrampus!' he added mystically.

The little drake smiled, and quacked his delight
at the conversation of Mr Busby who now stood up,
surveyed the surrounding field with deliberation,
and then sat down upon the ant-hill again, drawing
a tobacco-box from his pocket. A pipe was filled
and ignited, and for a while Mr Busby puffed and
gazed dreamily at the pond and the drake, and
listened to the wind threshing in the chestnut trees.
Ah, a lovely day!

'Who do you live with in So-and-so?' the man inquired.

'I live with Jack Cracknell,' answered the gentle duck, 'do you know him?'

'Know him! Allecapantho! I knew his father; we were at school together. He always said he was younger than me, but I can't understand how that could be because he left school afore I did and went and drove plough for the sleepy girl's husband. I kept on at school for another six months, and then I became a thatcher. All the Busbys be master men. They got it up here.' The man took his pipe from his mouth and pointed with it to his forehead again, and then spat richly over his shoulder to defeat the play of the wind.

The drake asked him another question: 'Who was the sleepy girl?'

'Eli Sadler's daughter,' continued Busby. 'She dropped off to sleep one day and she slept so 's they couldn't rouse her no more. There were two girls and Eli and their mother. Of course Eli died, and there was Mary and there was this Annie. Mary was in service at the squire's, but Annie went to sleep and didn't wake up for seven years. She lay in her bed for seven unconscious years, and she didn't wake up and she didn't die. People came from all parts of the world to look at her and stick pins in her —dukes and schoolmasters and members of Parliament—but they could not wake her up, nobody couldn't. Seven years is a long time, ye know. Mystery. Her mother made a fortune a money out a that girl, a fortune. Sacks of it. But of course the mother died, and every one said to Mary: 'Mary,

you 'll have to come home and look arter your sleepy
sister.' Mary said no, she wouldn't have that caper.
'Why not?' they says to her, 'she 's your sister,'
they says, 'helpless and dependent on your care.'
'Because,' says Mary, 'I shall damn soon wake her
up.' And that's what she did do—woke her up!
And Annie went and got married and had ten children in next to no time. Never went to sleep no
more. Sleeping beauty, they called her. Huh.
She was the biggest fraud as ever stepped on England's ground, the biggest fraud within forty
thousand miles. And old Jack Cracknell began
work for the sleepy girl's husband. Well, upon my
soul, there 's all sorts a dodges for getting a living,
and if you wants a thing in this world you must get
it by force or by fudge. Force and fudge rule this
sinful world, my cocky; everything 's for someone's
selfish pleasure — never your own. D' ye know
what my advice is to you? My advice to you, sir, is
this: if your pleasure brings more harm to another
than it brings in joy to you—and it very often will
—then you must do the best you can with your
pleasure. If '—Busby pointed with his pipe straight
at the attentive little duck—'if so be you are the
sort as don't stop to think, you won't know of the
harm you do, and you won't pause, and you won't
care. Mind you, if you are of the other sort, the
sort that *do* care as man to man, my advice would
be wasted—for of course you wouldn't follow it, you
could not. Such is human nature,' Busby said, apply-
ing yet another match to his pipe, 'and such is life.'

'Yes, that is very true,' sighed the happy drake.

'And another thing,' continued the philosophizing

thatcher. 'We may not get all we asks for, but you may lay your life we 'll get all that 's coming to us, and I shan't be far away from my own funeral. Nor will you, my cocky. Force and fudge, I tell you, rule this sinful world. If you can tell the tale, grief will never be your master. Take Jack Cracknell, as worked for sleepy girl's husband: I never did trust that man Cracknell. For one thing, he 'd talk the skin off your nostrils! I never trusted any one from the village of So-and-so, I never liked 'em; poor bred-uns, all. Young Jack's the same. And my advice to you is: don't return there any more, preserve your independence now you 've got it, and don't own him, don't listen to him, don't follow him. Never let misfortune be your downfall. My lad, I like you, I will be your friend for life. There 's my hand on it.'

Busby stood up, surveyed the landscape with care, spat a good spit, rubbed his right hand upon his haunch, and went to the water's edge. So the little drake swam in to accept of his friendship.

'Hey, my cocky!' The man's hand closed tightly round the duck's neck, and the bird was snatched from the water. In a few moments its neck was limp; it fluttered no more, it spake no more, it lived no more.

'Nice li'l bird,' commented Busby, feeling its breast and back, 'beautiful bird.' And putting the body in his bag he slung the bag over his shoulder again.

'Appercrampus!' he joyously murmured as he walked away. 'Allecapantho!'

THE STORY OF THE SIREN

By E. M. Forster

FEW things could have been more beautiful than my notebook on the Deist Controversy as it fell downward through the waters of the Mediterranean. It dived, like a piece of black slate, but opened soon, disclosing leaves of pale green, which quivered into blue. Now it had vanished, now it was a piece of magical india-rubber stretching out to infinity, now it was a book again, but bigger than the book of all knowledge. It grew more fantastic as it reached the bottom, where a puff of sand welcomed it and obscured it from view. But it reappeared, quite sane though a little tremulous, lying decently open on its back, while unseen fingers fidgeted among its leaves.

'It is such pity,' said my aunt, 'that you will not finish your work in the hotel. Then you would be free to enjoy yourself and this would never have happened.'

'Nothing of it but will change into something rich and strange,' warbled the chaplain, while his sister said, 'Why, it's gone in the water!' As for the boatmen, one of them laughed, while the other, without a word of warning, stood up and began to take his clothes off.

'Holy Moses!' cried the Colonel. 'Is the fellow mad?'

'Yes, thank him, dear,' said my aunt: 'that is to say, tell him he is very kind, but perhaps another time.'

'All the same I do want my book back,' I complained. 'It's for my Fellowship Dissertation. There won't be much of it left by another time.'

'I have an idea,' said some woman or other through her parasol. 'Let us leave this child of nature to dive for the book while we go on to the other grotto. We can land him either on this rock or on the ledge inside, and he will be ready when we return.'

The idea seemed good; and I improved it by saying I would be left behind too, to lighten the boat. So the two of us were deposited outside the little grotto on a great sunlit rock that guarded the harmonies within. Let us call them blue, though they suggest rather the spirit of what is clean—cleanliness passed from the domestic to the sublime, the cleanliness of all the sea gathered together and radiating light. The Blue Grotto at Capri contains only more blue water, not bluer water. That colour and that spirit is the heritage of every cave in the Mediterranean into which the sun can shine and the sea flow.

As soon as the boat left I realized how imprudent I had been to trust myself on a sloping rock with an unknown Sicilian. With a jerk he became alive, seizing my arm and saying, 'Go to the end of the grotto, and I will show you something beautiful.'

He made me jump off the rock on to the ledge over a dazzling crack of sea; he drew me away from the light till I was standing on the tiny beach of sand which emerged like powdered turquoise at the farther end. There he left me with his clothes, and returned swiftly to the summit of the entrance rock. For a moment he stood naked in the brilliant sun, looking down at the spot where the book lay. Then he crossed himself, raised his hands above his head, and dived.

If the book was wonderful, the man is past all description. His effect was that of a silver statue, alive beneath the sea, through whom life throbbed in blue and green. Something infinitely happy, infinitely wise—but it was impossible that it should emerge from the depths sunburned and dripping, holding the notebook on the Deist Controversy between its teeth.

A gratuity is generally expected by those who bathe. Whatever I offered, he was sure to want more, and I was disinclined for an argument in a place so beautiful and also so solitary. It was a relief that he should say in conversational tones, 'In a place like this one might see the Siren.'

I was delighted with him for thus falling into the key of his surroundings. We had been left together in a magic world, apart from all the commonplaces that are called reality, a world of blue whose floor was the sea and whose walls and roof of rock trembled with the sea's reflections. Here only the fantastic would be tolerable, and it was in that spirit I echoed his words, 'One might easily see the Siren.'

He watched me curiously while he dressed. I was parting the sticky leaves of the notebook as I sat on the sand.

'Ah,' he said at last. 'You may have read the little book that was printed last year. Who would have thought that our Siren would have given the foreigners pleasure!'

(I read it afterward. Its account is, not unnaturally, incomplete, in spite of there being a woodcut of the young person, and the words of her song.)

'She comes out of this blue water, doesn't she,' I suggested, 'and sits on the rock at the entrance, combing her hair.'

I wanted to draw him out, for I was interested in his sudden gravity, and there was a suggestion of irony in his last remark that puzzled me.

'Have you ever seen her?' he asked.

'Often and often.'

'I, never.'

'But have you heard her sing?'

He put on his coat and said impatiently, 'How can she sing under the water? Who could? She sometimes tries, but nothing comes from her but great bubbles.'

'She could climb on to the rock.'

'How can she?' he cried again, quite angry. 'The priests have blessed the air, so she cannot breathe it, and blessed the rocks, so that she cannot sit on them. But the sea no man can bless, because it is too big and always changing. So she lives in the sea.'

I was silent.

At this his face took on a gentler expression. He looked at me as though something was on his mind, and going out to the entrance rock gazed at the external blue. Then returning into our twilight he said, 'As a rule only good people see the Siren.'

I made no comment. There was a pause, and he continued. 'That is a very strange thing, and the priests do not know how to account for it; for she of course is wicked. Not only those who fast and go to Mass are in danger, but even those who are merely good in daily life. No one in the village had seen her for two generations. I am not surprised. We all cross ourselves before we enter the water, but it is unnecessary. Giuseppe, we thought, was safer than most. We loved him, and many of us he loved: but that is a different thing from being good.'

I asked who Giuseppe was.

'That day—I was seventeen and my brother was twenty and a great deal stronger than I was, and it was the year when the visitors, who have brought such prosperity and so many alterations into the village, first began to come. One English lady in particular, of very high birth, came, and has written a book about the place, and it was through her that the Improvement Syndicate was formed, which is about to connect the hotels with the station by a funicular railway.'

'Don't tell me about that lady in here,' I observed.

'That day we took her and her friends to see the grottoes. As we rowed close under the cliffs I put out my hand, as one does, and caught a little crab, and having pulled off its claws offered it as a curiosity. The ladies groaned, but a gentleman was pleased, and held out money. Being inexperienced, I refused it, saying that his pleasure was sufficient reward! Giuseppe, who was rowing behind, was very angry with me and reached out his hand and hit me on the side of the mouth, so that a tooth cut my lip, and I bled. I tried to hit him back, but he always was too quick for me, and as I stretched round he kicked me under the armpit, so that for a moment I could not even row. There was a great noise among the ladies, and I heard afterwards that they were planning to take me away from my brother and train me as a waiter. That, at all events, never came to pass.

'When we reached the grotto—not here, but a larger one—the gentleman was very anxious that one of us should dive for money, and the ladies consented, as they sometimes do. Giuseppe, who had discovered how much pleasure it gives foreigners to see us in the water, refused to dive for anything but silver, and the gentleman threw in a two-lira piece.

'Just before my brother sprang off he caught sight of me holding my bruise, and crying, for I could not help it. He laughed and said, "This time, at all events, I shall not see the Siren!" and went into the water without crossing himself. But he saw her.'

He broke off and accepted a cigarette. I watched the golden entrance rock and the quivering walls and the magic water through which great bubbles constantly rose.

At last he dropped his hot ash into the ripples and turned his head away, and said, 'He came up without the coin. We pulled him into the boat, and he was so large that he seemed to fill it, and so wet that we could not dress him. I have never seen a man so wet. I and the gentleman rowed back, and we covered Giuseppe with sacking and propped him up in the stern.'

'He was drowned, then?' I murmured, supposing that to be the point.

'He was not,' he cried angrily. 'He saw the Siren. I told you.'

I was silenced again.

'We put him to bed, though he was not ill. The doctor came, and took money, and the priest came and spattered him with holy water. But it was no good. He was too big—like a piece of the sea. He kissed the thumb-bones of San Biagio and they never dried till evening.'

'What did he look like?' I ventured.

'Like any one who has seen the Siren. If you have seen her 'often and often' how is it you do not know? Unhappy, unhappy because he knew everything. Every living thing made him unhappy because he knew it would die. And all he cared to do was sleep.'

I bent over my notebook.

'He did no work, he forgot to eat, he forgot whether he had his clothes on. All the work fell on me, and my sister had to go out to service. We tried to make him into a beggar, but he was too robust to inspire pity, and as for an idiot, he had not the right look in his eyes. He would stand in the street looking at people, and the more he looked at them the more unhappy he became. When a child was born he would cover his face with his hands. If any one was married—he was terrible then, and would frighten them when they came out of church. Who would have believed he would marry himself! I caused that, I. I was reading out of the paper how a girl at Ragusa had 'gone mad through bathing in the sea.' Giuseppe got up, and in a week he and that girl came in.

'He never told me anything, but it seems that he went straight to her house, broke into her room, and carried her off. She was the daughter of a rich mineowner, so you may imagine our peril. Her father came down, with a clever lawyer, but they could do no more than I. They argued and they threatened, but at last they had to go back and we lost nothing—that is to say, no money. We took Giuseppe and Maria to the church and had them married. Ugh! that wedding! The priest made no jokes afterwards, and coming out the children threw stones. . . . I think I would have died to make her happy; but as always happens, one could do nothing.'

'Were they unhappy together, then?'

'They loved each other, but love is not happiness. We can all get love. Love is nothing. I had two people to work for now, for she was like him in everything—one never knew which of them was speaking. I had to sell our own boat and work under the bad old man you have to-day. Worst of all, people began to hate us. The children first — everything begins with them — and then the women, and last of all, the men. For the cause of every misfortune was—you will not betray me?'

I promised good faith, and immediately he burst into the frantic blasphemy of one who has escaped from supervision, cursing the priests, who had ruined his life, he said. 'Thus are we tricked!' was his cry, and he stood up and kicked at the azure ripples with his feet, till he had obscured them with a cloud of sand.

I, too, was moved. The story of Giuseppe, for all its absurdity and superstition, came nearer to reality than anything I had known before. I don't know why, but it filled me with desire to help others —the greatest of all our desires, I suppose, and the most fruitless. The desire soon passed.

'She was about to have a child. That was the end of everything. People said to me, "When will your charming nephew be born? What a cheerful, attractive child he will be, with such a father and mother!" I kept my face steady and replied, "I think he may be. Out of sadness shall come gladness"—it is one of our proverbs. And my answer frightened them very much, and they told the priests, who were frightened too. Then the whisper started that the child would be Antichrist. You need not be afraid: he was never born.

'An old witch began to prophesy, and no one stopped her. Giuseppe and the girl, she said, had silent devils, who could do little harm. But the child would always be speaking and laughing and perverting, and last of all he would go into the sea and fetch up the Siren into the air and all the world would see her and hear her sing. As soon as she sang, the Seven Vials would be opened, and the Pope

would die and Mongibello flame, and the veil of
Santa Agata would be burned. Then the boy and
the Siren would marry, and together they would
rule the world, for ever and ever.

'The whole village was in tumult, and the hotel-
keepers became alarmed, for the tourist season was
just beginning. They met together and decided
that Giuseppe and the girl must be sent inland until
the child was born, and they subscribed the money.
The night before they were to start there was a full
moon and wind from the east, and all along the
coast the sea shot up over the cliffs in silver clouds.
It is a wonderful sight, and Maria said she must see
it once more.

'"Do not go," I said. "I saw the priest go by,
and someone with him. And the hotel-keepers do
not like you to be seen, and if we displease them
also we shall starve."

'"I want to go,' she replied. "The sea is stormy,
and I may never feel it again."

'"No, he is right," said Giuseppe. "Do not go
—or let one of us go with you."

'"I want to go alone," she said; and she went
alone.

'I tied up their luggage in a piece of cloth, and
then I was so unhappy at thinking I should lose
them that I went and sat down by my brother and
put my arm round his neck, and he put his arm
round me, which he had not done for more than a
year, and we remained thus I don't remember how
long.

'Suddenly the door flew open and moonlight and
wind came in together, and a child's voice said

laughing, "They have pushed her over the cliffs into the sea."

'I stepped to the drawer where I keep my knives.

"'Sit down again," said Giuseppe—Giuseppe of all people! "If she is dead, why should others die, too?"

"'I guess who it is," I cried, "and I will kill him."

'I was almost out of the door, and he tripped me up, and kneeling upon me, took hold of both my hands and sprained my wrists; first my right one, then my left. No one but Giuseppe would have thought of such a thing. It hurt more than you would suppose, and I fainted. When I woke up, he was gone, and I never saw him again.'

But Giuseppe disgusted me.

'I told you he was wicked,' he said. 'No one would have expected him to see the Siren.'

'How do you know he did see her?'

'Because he did not see her "often and often," but once.'

'Why do you love him if he is wicked?'

He laughed for the first time. That was his only reply.

'Is that the end?' I asked.

'I never killed her murderer, for by the time my wrists were well he was in America; and one cannot kill a priest. As for Giuseppe, he went all over the world, too, looking for someone who had seen the Siren—either a man, or, better still, a woman, for then the child might still have been born. At last he came to Liverpool—is the district probable?—

and there he began to cough, and spat blood until he died.

'I do not suppose there is any one living now who has seen her. There has seldom been more than one in a generation, and never in my life will there be both a man and a woman from whom that child can be born, who will fetch up the Siren from the sea, and destroy silence, and save the world!'

'Save the world?' I cried. 'Did the prophecy end like that?'

He leaned back against the rock, breathing deep. Through all the blue-green reflections I saw him colour. I heard him say: 'Silence and loneliness cannot last for ever. It may be a hundred or a thousand years, but the sea lasts longer, and she shall come out of it and sing.' I would have asked him more, but at that moment the whole cave darkened, and there rode in through its narrow entrance the returning boat.

THE FIERY WOOING OF MORDRED

By P. G. Wodehouse

THE Pint of Lager breathed heavily through his nose.

'Silly fathead!' he said. 'Ash-trays in every nook and cranny of the room—ash-trays staring you in the eye wherever you look—and he has to go and do a fool thing like that.'

He was alluding to a young gentleman with a vacant, fish-like face who, leaving the bar-parlour of the Anglers' Rest a few moments before, had thrown his cigarette into the waste-paper basket, causing it to burst into a cheerful blaze. Not one of the little company of amateur fire-fighters but was ruffled. A Small Bass with a high blood pressure had had to have his collar loosened, and the satin-clad bosom of Miss Postlethwaite, our emotional barmaid, was still heaving.

Only Mr Mulliner seemed disposed to take a tolerant view of what had occurred.

'In fairness to the lad,' he pointed out, sipping his hot Scotch and lemon, 'we must remember that our bar-parlour contains no grand piano or priceless old walnut table, which to the younger generation are the normal and natural repositories for lighted cigarette-ends. Failing these, he, of course, selected the waste-paper basket. Like Mordred.'

'Like who?' asked a Whisky and Splash.

'Whom,' corrected Miss Postlethwaite.

The Whisky and Splash apologized.

'A nephew of mine. Mordred Mulliner, the poet.'

'Mordred,' murmured Miss Postlethwaite pensively. 'A sweet name.'

'And one,' said Mr Mulliner, 'that fitted him admirably, for he was a comely lovable sensitive youth with large, fawn-like eyes, delicately chiselled features, and excellent teeth. I mention these teeth, because it was owing to them that the train of events started which I am about to describe.'

'He bit somebody?' queried Miss Postlethwaite, groping.

'No. But if he had had no teeth he would not have gone to the dentist's that day, and if he had not gone to the dentist's he would not have met Annabelle.'

'Annabelle whom?'

'Who,' corrected Miss Postlethwaite.

'Oh, shoot,' said the Whisky and Splash.

'Annabelle Sprockett-Sprockett, the only daughter of Sir Murgatroyd and Lady Sprockett-Sprockett of Smattering Hall, Worcestershire. Impractical in many ways,' said Mr Mulliner, 'Mordred never failed to visit his dentist every six months, and on the morning on which my story opens he had just seated himself in the empty waiting-room and was turning the pages of a three-months-old copy of the *Tatler* when the door opened and there entered a girl at the sight of whom—or who, if our friend here prefers it—something seemed to explode on the left side of his chest like a bomb. The *Tatler* swam before his eyes, and when it solidified again he realized that love had come to him at last.

Most of the Mulliners have fallen in love at first sight, but few with so good an excuse as Mordred. She was a singularly beautiful girl, and for a while it was this beauty of hers that enchained my nephew's attention to the exclusion of all else. It was only after he had sat gulping for some minutes like a dog with a chicken bone in its throat that he detected the sadness in her face. He could see now that her eyes, as she listlessly perused her four-months-old copy of *Punch*, were heavy with pain.

His heart ached for her, and as there is something about the atmosphere of a dentist's waiting-room which breaks down the barriers of conventional etiquette he was emboldened to speak.

'Courage!' he said. 'It may not be so bad, after all. He may just fool about with that little mirror thing of his, and decide that there is nothing that needs to be done.'

For the first time she smiled—faintly, but with sufficient breadth to give Mordred another powerful jolt.

'I'm not worrying about the dentist,' she explained. 'My trouble is that I live miles away in the country and only get a chance of coming to London about twice a year for about a couple of hours. I was hoping that I should be able to put in a long spell of window-shopping in Bond Street, but now I've got to wait goodness knows how long I don't suppose I shall have time to do a thing. My train goes at one-fifteen.'

All the chivalry in Mordred came to the surface like a leaping trout.

'If you would care to take my place——'

'Oh, I couldn't.'

'Please. I shall enjoy waiting. It will give me an opportunity of catching up with my reading.'

'Well, if you really wouldn't mind——'

Considering that Mordred by this time was in the market to tackle dragons on her behalf or to climb the loftiest peak of the Alps to supply her with edelweiss, he was able to assure her that he did not mind. So in she went, flashing at him a shy glance of gratitude which nearly doubled him up, and he lit a cigarette and fell into a reverie. And presently she came out and he sprang to his feet, courteously throwing his cigarette into the waste-paper basket.

She uttered a cry. Mordred recovered the cigarette.

'Silly of me,' he said, with a deprecating laugh. 'I 'm always doing that. Absent-minded. I 've burned two flats already this year.'

She caught her breath.

'Burned them to the ground?'

'Well, not to the ground. They were on the top floor.'

'But you burned them?'

'Oh, yes. I burned them.'

'Well, well!' She seemed to muse. 'Well, good-bye, Mr——'

'Mulliner. Mordred Mulliner.'

'Good-bye, Mr Mulliner, and thank you so much.'

'Not at all, Miss——'

'Sprockett-Sprockett.'

'Not at all, Miss Sprockett-Sprockett. A pleasure.'

She passed from the room, and a few minutes

later he was lying back in the dentist's chair, filled with an infinite sadness. This was not due to any activity on the part of the dentist, who had just said with a rueful sigh that there didn't seem to be anything to do this time, but to the fact that his life was now a blank. He loved this beautiful girl, and he would never see her more. It was just another case of ships that pass in the waiting-room.

Conceive his astonishment, therefore, when by the afternoon post next day he received a letter which ran as follows:

'Smattering Hall,
'Lower Smattering-on-the-Wissel,
'Worcestershire.

'Dear Mr Mulliner,

'My little girl has told me how very kind you were to her at the dentist's to-day. I cannot tell you how grateful she was. She does so love to walk down Bond Street and breathe on the jewellers' windows, and but for you she would have had to go another six months without her little treat.

'I suppose you are a very busy man, like everybody in London, but if you can spare the time it would give my husband and myself so much pleasure if you could run down and stay with us for a few days—a long week-end, or even longer if you can manage it.

'With best wishes,
'Yours sincerely,
'Aurelia Sprockett-Sprockett.'

Mordred read this communication six times in a minute and a quarter and then seventeen times rather more slowly in order to savour any *nuance* of it that he might have overlooked. He took it that the girl must have got his address from the dentist's secretary on her way out, and he was doubly thrilled —first, by this evidence that one so lovely was as intelligent as she was beautiful, and secondly because the whole thing seemed to him so frightfully significant. A girl, he meant to say, does not get her mother to invite fellows to her country home for long week-ends (or even longer if they can manage it) unless such fellows have made a pretty substantial hit with her. This, he contended, stood to reason.

He hastened to the nearest post office, dispatched a telegram to Lady Sprockett-Sprockett assuring her that he would be with her on the morrow, and returned to his flat to pack his effects. His heart was singing within him. Apart from anything else, the invitation could not have come at a more fortunate moment, for what with musing on his great love while smoking cigarettes he had practically gutted his little nest on the previous evening, and while it was still habitable in a sense there was no gainsaying the fact that all those charred sofas and things struck a rather melancholy note and he would be glad to be away from it all for a few days.

It seemed to Mordred, as he travelled down on the following afternoon, that the wheels of the train, clattering over the metals, were singing 'Sprockett-Sprockett'—not 'Annabelle,' of course, for he did not yet know her name—and it was with a whispered

'Sprockett-Sprockett' on his lips that he alighted at the little station of Smattering-cum-Blimpstead-in-the-Vale, which, as his hostess's note-paper had informed him, was where you got off for the Hall. And when he perceived that the girl herself had come to meet him in a two-seater car the whisper nearly became a shout.

For perhaps three minutes, as he sat beside her, Mordred remained in this condition of ecstatic bliss. Here he was, he reflected, and here she was—here, in fact, they both were—together, and he was just about to point out how jolly this was and—if he could work it without seeming to rush things too much—to drop a hint to the effect that he could wish this state of affairs to continue through all eternity, when the girl drew up outside a tobacconist's.

'I won't be a minute,' she said. 'I promised Biffy I would bring him back some cigarettes.'

A cold hand seemed to lay itself on Mordred's heart.

'Biffy?'

'Captain Biffing, one of the men at the Hall. And Guffy wants some pipe-cleaners.'

'Guffy?'

'Jack Guffington. I expect you know his name, if you are interested in racing. He was third in last year's Grand National.'

'Is he staying at the Hall, too?'

'Yes.'

'You have a large house-party?'

'Oh, not so very. Let me see. There's Billy Biffing, Jack Guffington, Ted Prosser, Freddie Boot —he's the tennis champion of the county—Tommy

Mainprice, and—oh, yes, Algy Fripp—the big-game hunter, you know.'

The hand on Mordred's heart, now definitely iced, tightened its grip. With a lover's sanguine optimism, he had supposed that this visit of his was going to be just three days of jolly sylvan solitude with Annabelle Sprockett-Sprockett. And now it appeared that the place was unwholesomely crowded with his fellow men. And what fellow men! Big-game hunters . . . Tennis champions . . . Chaps who rode in Grand Nationals . . . He could see them in his mind's eye—lean, wiry, riding-breeched and flannel-trousered young Apollos, any one of them capable of cutting out his weight in Clark Gables.

A faint hope stirred within him.

'You have also, of course, with you Mrs Biffing, Mrs Guffigton, Mrs Prosser, Mrs Bott, Mrs Mainprice, and Mrs Algernon Fripp?'

'Oh, no, they aren't married.'

'None of them?'

'No.'

The faint hope coughed quietly and died.

'Ah,' said Mordred.

While the girl was in the shop, he remained brooding. The fact that not one of these blisters should be married filled him with an austere disapproval. If they had had the least spark of civic sense, he felt, they would have taken on the duties and responsibilities of matrimony years ago. But no. Intent upon their selfish pleasures, they had callously remained bachelors. It was this spirit of *laissez-faire*, Mordred considered, that was eating like a canker into the soul of England.

He was aware of Annabelle standing beside him.
'Eh?' he said, starting.
'I was saying: "Have you plenty of cigarettes?"'
'Plenty, thank you.'
'Good.   And of course there will be a box in your
room.   Men always like to smoke in their bedrooms,
don't they?   As a matter of fact, two boxes—
Turkish and Virginian.   Father put them there
specially.'
'Very kind of him,' said Mordred mechanically.
He relapsed into a moody silence, and they drove
off.

It would be agreeable (said Mr Mulliner) if, having
shown you my nephew so gloomy, so apprehensive,
so tortured with dark forebodings at this juncture, I
were able now to state that the hearty English
welcome of Sir Murgatroyd and Lady Sprockett-
Sprockett on his arrival at the Hall cheered him up
and put new life into him.   Nothing, too, would
give me greater pleasure than to say that he found,
on encountering the dreaded Biffies and Guffies,
that they were negligible little runts with faces in-
capable of inspiring affection in any good woman.

But I must adhere rigidly to the facts.   Genial,
even effusive, though his host and hostess showed
themselves, their cordiality left him cold.   And,
so far from his rivals being weeds, they were one and
all models of manly beauty, and the spectacle of
their obvious worship of Annabelle cut my nephew
like a knife.

And on top of all this there was Smattering Hall
itself.

E * 954

Smattering Hall destroyed Mordred's last hope. It was one of those vast edifices, so common throughout the countryside of England, whose original founders seem to have budgeted for families of twenty-five or so and a domestic staff of not less than a hundred. 'Home isn't home,' one can picture them saying to themselves, 'unless you have plenty of elbow room.' And so this huge, majestic pile had come into being. Romantic persons, confronted with it, thought of knights in armour riding forth to the Crusades. More earthy individuals felt that it must cost a packet to keep up. Mordred's reaction on passing through the front door was a sort of sick sensation, a kind of settled despair.

How, he asked himself, even assuming that by some miracle he succeeded in fighting his way to her heart through all these Biffies and Guffies, could he ever dare to take Annabelle from a home like this? He had quite satisfactory private means, of course, and would be able, when married, to give up the bachelor flat and spread himself to something on a bigger scale—possibly, if sufficiently *bijou*, even a desirable residence in the Mayfair district. But after Smattering Hall would not Annabelle feel like a sardine in the largest of London houses?

Such were the dark thoughts that raced through Mordred's brain before, during and after dinner. At eleven o'clock he pleaded fatigue after his journey, and Sir Murgatroyd accompanied him to his room, anxious, like a good host, to see that everything was comfortable.

'Very sensible of you to turn in early,' he said, in his bluff, genial way. 'So many young men ruin their health with late hours. Now you, I imagine, will just get into a dressing-gown and smoke a cigarette or two and have the light out by twelve. You have plenty of cigarettes? I told them to see that you were well supplied. I always think the bedroom smoke is the best one of the day. Nobody to disturb you, and all that. If you want to write letters or anything, there is lots of paper, and here is the waste-paper basket, which is always so necessary. Well, good night, my boy, good night.'

The door closed, and Mordred, as foreshadowed, got into a dressing-gown and lit a cigarette. But though, having done this, he made his way to the writing-table, it was not with any idea of getting abreast of his correspondence. It was his purpose to compose a poem to Annabelle Sprockett-Sprockett. He had felt it seething within him all the evening, and sleep would be impossible until it was out of his system.

Hitherto, I should mention, my nephew's poetry, for he belonged to the modern fearless school, had always been stark and rhymeless and had dealt principally with corpses and the smell of cooking cabbage. But now, with the moonlight silvering the balcony outside, he found that his mind had become full of words like 'love' and 'dove' and 'eyes' and 'summer skies.'

> *Blue eyes*, wrote Mordred . . .
>
> *Sweet lips*, wrote Mordred . . .
>
> *Oh, eyes like skies of summer blue* . . .
>
> *Oh, love* . . .
>
> *Oh, dove* . . .
>
> *Oh, lips* . . .

With a muttered ejaculation of chagrin he tore the sheet across and threw it into the waste-paper basket.

Blue eyes that burn into my soul,
  Sweet lips that smile my heart away,
Pom-pom, pom-pom, pom something whole (Goal?)
  And tiddly-iddly-umpty-ay (Gay? Say? Happy day?)

Blue eyes into my soul that burn,
  Sweet lips that smile away my heart,
Oh, something something turn or yearn
  And something something something part.

You burn into my soul, blue eyes,
  You smile my heart away, sweet lips,
Short long short long of summer skies
  And something something something trips. (Hips?
    Ships? Pips?)

He threw the sheet into the waste-paper basket and rose with a stifled oath. The waste-paper basket was nearly full now, and still his poet's sense told him that he had not achieved perfection. He thought he saw the reason for this. You can't just sit in a chair and expect inspiration to flow— you want to walk about and clutch your hair and snap your fingers. It had been his intention to pace the room, but the moonlight pouring in through the open window called to him. He went out on to the balcony. It was but a short distance to the dim, mysterious lawn. Impulsively he dropped from the stone balustrade.

The effect was magical. Stimulated by the improved conditions, his Muse gave quick service, and this time he saw at once that she had rung the bell and delivered the goods.   One turn up and down the lawn, and he was reciting as follows:

TO ANNABELLE

Oh, lips that smile! Oh, eyes that shine
  Like summer skies, or stars above!
Your beauty maddens me like wine,
  Oh, umpty-pumpty-tumty love!

And he was just wondering, for he was a severe critic of his own work, whether that last line couldn't be polished up a bit, when his eye was attracted by something that shone like summer skies or stars above and, looking more closely, he perceived that his bedroom curtains were on fire.

Now, I will not pretend that my nephew Mordred was in every respect the cool-headed man of action, but this happened to be a situation with which use had familiarized him.   He knew the procedure.

'Fire!' he shouted.

A head appeared in an upstairs window. He recognized it as that of Captain Biffing.

'Eh?' said Captain Biffing.

'Fire!'

'What?'

'Fire!' vociferated Mordred. 'F for Francis, I for Isabel . . . '

'Oh, fire?' said Captain Biffing. 'Right ho.'

And presently the house began to discharge its occupants.

In the proceedings which followed, Mordred, I fear, did not appear to the greatest advantage. This is an age of specialization, and if you take the

specialist off his own particular ground he is at a
loss. Mordred's genius, as we have seen, lay in the
direction of starting fires. Putting them out called
for quite different qualities, and these he did not
possess. On the various occasions of holocausts at
his series of flats, he had never attempted to play an
active part, contenting himself with going down-
stairs and asking the janitor to step up and see what
he could do about it. So now, though under the
bright eyes of Annabelle Sprockett-Sprockett he
would have given much to be able to dominate the
scene, the truth is that the Biffies and Guffies simply
played him off the stage.

His heart sank as he noted the hideous efficiency
of these young men. They called for buckets. They
formed a line. Freddie Boot leaped lissomely on to
the balcony, and Algy Fripp, mounted on a wheel-
barrow, handed up to him the necessary supplies.
And after Mordred, trying to do his bit, had tripped
up Jack Guffington and upset two buckets over Ted
Prosser, he was advised in set terms to withdraw into
the background and stay there.

It was a black ten minutes for the unfortunate
young man. One glance at Sir Murgatroyd's twisted
face as he watched the operations was enough to tell
him how desperately anxious the fine old man was
for the safety of his ancestral home and how bitter
would be his resentment against the person who had
endangered it. And the same applied to Lady
Sprockett-Sprockett and Annabelle. Mordred could
see the anxiety in their eyes, and the thought that ere
long those eyes must be turned accusingly on him
chilled him to the marrow.

Presently Freddie Boot emerged from the bedroom to announce that all was well.

'It's out,' he said, jumping lightly down. 'Anybody know whose room it was?'

Mordred felt a sickening qualm, but the splendid Mulliner courage sustained him. He stepped forward, white and tense.

'Mine,' he said.

He became the instant centre of attention. The six young men looked at him.

'Yours?'

'Oh, yours, was it?'

'What happened?'

'How did it start?'

'Yes, how did it start?'

'Must have started somehow, I mean,' said Captain Biffing, who was a clear thinker. 'I mean to say, must have, don't you know, what?'

Mordred mastered his voice.

'I was smoking, and I suppose I threw my cigarette into the waste-paper basket, and as it was full of paper . . .'

'Full of paper? Why was it full of paper?'

'I had been writing a poem.'

There was a stir of bewilderment.

'A what?' said Ted Prosser.

'Writing a what?' said Jack Guffington.

'Writing a *poem*?' asked Captain Biffing of Tommy Mainprice.

'That's how I got the story,' said Tommy Mainprice, plainly shaken.

'Chap was writing a poem,' Freddie Boot informed Algy Fripp.

'You mean the chap writes poems?'

'That's right. Poems.'

'Well, I'm dashed!'

'Well, I'm blowed!'

Their now unconcealed scorn was hard to bear. Mordred chafed beneath it. The word 'poem' was flitting from lip to lip, and it was only too evident that, had there been an 's' in the word, those present would have hissed it. Reason told him that these men were mere clods, Philistines, fatheads who would not recognize the rare and the beautiful if you handed it to them on a skewer, but that did not seem to make it any better. He knew that he should be scorning them, but it is not easy to go about scorning people in a dressing-gown, especially if you have no socks on and the night breeze is cool around the ankles. So, as I say, he chafed. And finally, when he saw the butler bend down with pursed lips to the ear of the cook, who was a little hard of hearing, and after a contemptuous glance in his direction speak into it, spacing his syllables carefully, something within him seemed to snap.

'I regret, Sir Murgatroyd,' he said, 'that urgent family business compels me to return to London immediately. I shall be obliged to take the first train in the morning.'

Without another word he went into the house.

In the matter of camping out in devastated areas my nephew had, of course, become by this time an old hand. It was rarely nowadays that a few ashes and cinders about the place disturbed him. But when he had returned to his bedroom one look was

enough to assure him that nothing practical in the
way of sleep was to be achieved here. Apart from the
unpleasant, acrid smell of burned poetry, the apart-
ment, thanks to the efforts of Freddie Boot, had been
converted into a kind of inland sea. The carpet was
awash, and on the bed only a duck could have made
itself at home.

And so it came about that some ten minutes later
Mordred Mulliner lay stretched upon a high-backed
couch in the library, endeavouring by means of
counting sheep jumping through a gap in a hedge to
lull himself into unconsciousness.

But sleep refused to come. Nor in his heart had
he really thought that it would. When the human
soul is on the rack, it cannot just curl up and close
its eyes and expect to get its eight hours as if nothing
had happened. It was all very well for Mordred to
count sheep, but what did this profit him when each
sheep in turn assumed the features and lineaments
of Annabelle Sprockett-Sprockett and, what was
more, gave him a reproachful glance as it drew itself
together for the spring?

Remorse gnawed him. He was tortured by a
wild regret for what might have been. He was not
saying that with all these Biffies and Guffies in the
field he had ever had more than a hundred to eight
chance of winning that lovely girl, but at least his
hat had been in the ring. Now it was definitely out.
Dreamy Mordred may have been—romantic—impractical—but he had enough sense to see that the
very worst thing you can do when you are trying to
make a favourable impression on the adored object
is to set fire to her childhood home, every stick and

stone of which she has no doubt worshipped since they put her into rompers.

He had reached this point in his meditations, and was about to send his two hundred and thirty-second sheep at the gap, when with a suddenness which affected him much as an explosion of gelignite would have done, the lights flashed on. For an instant, he lay quivering, then, cautiously poking his head round the corner of the couch, he looked to see who his visitors were.

It was a little party of three that had entered the room. First came Sir Murgatroyd, carrying a tray of sandwiches. He was followed by Lady Sprockett-Sprockett with a siphon and glasses. The rear was brought up by Annabelle, who was bearing a bottle of whisky and two dry ginger ales.

So evident was it that they were assembling here for purposes of a family council that, but for one circumstance, Mordred, to whom anything in the nature of eavesdropping was as repugnant as it has always been to all the Mulliners, would have sprung up with a polite 'Excuse me' and taken his blanket elsewhere. This circumstance was the fact that on lying down he had kicked his slippers under the couch, well out of reach. The soul of modesty, he could not affront Annabelle with the spectacle of his bare toes.

So he lay there in silence, and silence, broken only by the swishing of soda-water and the *whoosh* of opened ginger-ale bottles, reigned in the room beyond.

Then Sir Murgatroyd spoke.

'Well, that's that,' he said, bleakly.

There was a gurgle as Lady Sprockett-Sprockett

drank ginger ale. Then her quiet, well-bred voice broke the pause.

'Yes,' she said, 'it is the end.'

'The end,' agreed Sir Murgatroyd heavily. 'No good trying to struggle on against luck like ours. Here we are and here we have got to stay, mouldering on in this blasted barrack of a place which eats up every penny of my income when, but for the fussy interference of that gang of officious, ugly nitwits, there would have been nothing left of it but a pile of ashes, with a man from the Insurance Company standing on it with his fountain-pen, writing cheques. Curse those imbeciles! Did you see that young Fripp with those buckets?'

'I did, indeed,' sighed Lady Sprockett-Sprockett.

'Annabelle,' said Sir Murgatroyd sharply.

'Yes, father?'

'It has seemed to me lately, watching you with a father's eye, that you have shown signs of being attracted by Algernon Fripp. Let me tell you that if ever you allow yourself to be ensnared by his insidious wiles, or by those of William Biffing, John Guffington, Edward Prosser, Thomas Mainprice, or Frederick Boot, you will do so over my dead body. After what occurred to-night, those young men shall never darken my door again. They and their buckets! To think that we could have gone and lived in London . . .'

'In a nice little flat . . .' said Lady Sprockett-Sprockett.

'Handy for my club . . .'

'Convenient for the shops . . .'

'Within a stone's throw of the theatres . . .'

'Seeing all our friends . . .'

'Had it not been,' said Sir Murgatroyd, summing up, 'for the pestilential activities of these Guffingtons, these Biffings, these insufferable Fripps, men who ought never to be trusted near a bucket of water when a mortgaged country-house has got nicely alight. I did think,' proceeded the stricken old man, helping himself to a sandwich, 'that when Annabelle, with a ready intelligence which I cannot over-praise, realized this young Mulliner's splendid gifts and made us ask him down here, the happy ending was in sight. What Smattering Hall has needed for generations has been a man who throws his cigarette-ends into waste-paper baskets. I was convinced that here at last was the angel of mercy we required.'

'He did his best, father.'

'No man could have done more,' agreed Sir Murgatroyd cordially. 'The way he upset those buckets and kept getting entangled in people's legs. Very shrewd. It thrilled me to see him. I don't know when I 've met a young fellow I liked and respected more. And what if he is a poet? Poets are all right. Why, dash it, I 'm a poet myself. At the last dinner of the Loyal Sons of Worcestershire I composed a poem which, let me tell you, was pretty generally admired. I read it out to the boys over the port, and they cheered me to the echo. It was about a young lady of Bewdley, who sometimes behaved rather rudely . . .'

'Not before mother, father.'

'Perhaps you 're right. Well, I 'm off to bed. Come along, Aurelia. You coming, Annabelle?'

'Not yet, father. I want to stay and think.'

'Do what?'

'Think.'

'Oh, think? Well, all right.'

'But, Murgatroyd,' said Lady Sprockett-Sprockett, 'is there no hope? After all, there are plenty of cigarettes in the house, and we could always give Mr Mulliner another waste-paper basket. . . .'

'No good. You heard him say he was leaving by the first train to-morrow. When I think that we shall never see that splendid young man again . . . Why, hullo, hullo, hullo, what's this? Crying, Annabelle?'

'Oh, mother!'

'My darling, what is it?'

A choking sob escaped the girl.

'Mother, I love him! Directly I saw him in the dentist's waiting-room, something seemed to go all over me, and I knew that there could be no other man for me. And now . . .'

'Hi!' cried Mordred, popping up over the side of the couch like a jack-in-the-box.

He had listened with growing understanding to the conversation which I have related, but had shrunk from revealing his presence because, as I say, his toes were bare. But this was too much. Toes or no toes, he felt that he must be in this.

'You love me, Annabelle?' he cried.

His sudden advent had occasioned, I need scarcely say, a certain reaction in those present. Sir Murgatroyd had leaped like a jumping bean. Lady Sprockett-Sprockett had quivered like a jelly. As

for Annabelle, her lovely mouth was open to the
extent of perhaps three inches, and she was staring
like one who sees a vision.

'You really love me, Annabelle?'

'Yes, Mordred.'

Sir Murgatroyd,' said Mordred formally, 'I have
the honour to ask for your daughter's hand. I am
only a poor poet . . .'

'How poor?' asked the other, keenly.

'I was referring to my art,' explained Mordred.
'Financially, I am nicely fixed. I could support
Annabelle in modest comfort.'

'Then take her, my boy, take her. You will live,
of course'—the old man winced—'in London?'

'Yes. And so shall you.'

Sir Murgatroyd shook his head.

'No, no, that dream is ended. It is true that in
certain circumstances I had hoped to do so, for the
insurance, I may mention, amounts to as much as a
hundred thousand pounds, but I am resigned now to
spending the rest of my life in this infernal family
vault. I see no reprieve.'

'I understand,' said Mordred, nodding. 'You
mean you have no paraffin in the house?'

Sir Murgatroyd started.

'Paraffin?'

'If,' said Mordred, and his voice was very gentle
and winning, 'there had been paraffin on the
premises, I think it possible that to-night's conflagration, doubtless imperfectly quenched, might
have broken out again, this time with more serious
results. It is often this way with fires. You pour
buckets of water on them and think they are

extinguished, but all the time they have been smouldering unnoticed, to break out once more in—well, in here, for example.'

'Or the billiard-room,' said Lady Sprockett-Sprockett.

'*And* the billiard-room,' corrected Sir Murgatroyd.

'And the billiard-room,' said Mordred. 'And possibly — who knows? — in the drawing-room, dining-room, kitchen, servants' hall, butler's pantry and the usual domestic offices, as well. Still, as you say you have no paraffin . . .'

'My boy,' said Sir Murgatroyd, in a shaking voice, 'what gave you the idea that we have no paraffin? How did you fall into this odd error? We have gallons of paraffin. The cellar is full of it.'

'And Annabelle will show you the way to the cellar—in case you thought of going there,' said Lady Sprockett-Sprockett. 'Won't you, dear?'

'Of course, mother. You will like the cellar, Mordred, darling. Most picturesque. Possibly, if you are interested in paraffin, you might also care to take a look at our little store of paper and shavings, too.'

'My angel,' said Mordred, tenderly, 'you think of everything.'

He found his slippers, and hand in hand they passed down the stairs. Above them, they could see the head of Sir Murgatroyd, as he leaned over the banisters. A box of matches fell at their feet like a father's benediction.

CLAY

By James Joyce

THE matron had given her leave to go out as soon as the women's tea was over, and Maria looked forward to her evening out. The kitchen was spick and span: the cook said you could see yourself in the big copper boilers. The fire was nice and bright and on one of the side-tables were four very big barmbracks. These barmbracks seemed uncut; but if you went closer you would see that they had been cut into long thick even slices and were ready to be handed round at tea. Maria had cut them herself.

Maria was a very, very small person indeed, but she had a very long nose and a very long chin. She talked a little through her nose, always soothingly: 'Yes, my dear,' and 'No, my dear.' She was always sent for when the women quarrelled over their tubs and always succeeded in making peace. One day the matron had said to her:

'Maria, you are a veritable peace-maker!'

And the sub-matron and two of the Board ladies had heard the compliment. And Ginger Mooney was always saying what she wouldn't do to the dummy who had charge of the irons if it wasn't for Maria. Every one was so fond of Maria.

The women would have their tea at six o'clock and she would be able to get away before seven. From Ballsbridge to the Pillar, twenty minutes; from the Pillar to Drumcondra, twenty minutes; and twenty minutes to buy the things. She would be there before eight. She took out her purse with the silver clasps and read again the words 'A Present from Belfast.' She was very fond of that purse because Joe had brought it to her five years before when he and Alphy had gone to Belfast on a Whit-Monday trip. In the purse were two half-crowns and some coppers. She would have five shillings clear after paying the tram fare. What a nice evening they would have, all the children singing! Only she hoped that Joe wouldn't come in drunk. He was so different when he took any drink.

Often he had wanted her to go and live with them; but she would have felt herself in the way (though Joe's wife was ever so nice with her) and she had become accustomed to the life of the laundry. Joe was a good fellow. She had nursed him and Alphy too; and Joe used often to say:

'Mamma is mamma, but Maria is my proper mother.'

After the break-up at home the boys had got her that position in the 'Dublin by Lamplight' laundry, and she liked it. She used to have such a bad opinion of Protestants, but now she thought they were very nice people, a little quiet and serious, but still very nice people to live with. Then she had her plants in the conservatory and she liked looking after them. She had lovely ferns and wax-plants and, whenever any one came to visit her, she always gave the visitor one or two slips from her conservatory. There was one thing she didn't like and that was the tracts on the walls; but the matron was such a nice person to deal with, so genteel.

When the cook told her everything was ready she went into the women's room and began to pull the big bell. In a few minutes the women began to come in by twos and threes, wiping their steaming hands in their petticoats and pulling down the sleeves of their blouses over their red steaming arms. They settled down before their huge mugs which the cook and the dummy filled up with hot tea, already mixed with milk and sugar in huge tin cans. Maria superintended the distribution of the barmbrack and saw that every woman got her four slices. There was a great deal of laughing and joking during the meal. Lizzie Fleming said Maria was sure to get the ring and, though Fleming had said that for so many Hallow Eves, Maria had to laugh and say she didn't want any ring or man either; and when she laughed her grey-green eyes sparkled with disappointed shyness and the tip of her nose nearly met the tip of her chin. Then Ginger Mooney lifted up her mug of tea and proposed Maria's health, while all the other women clattered with their mugs on the table, and said she was sorry she hadn't a sup of porter to drink it in. And Maria laughed again till the tip of her nose nearly met the tip of her chin and till her minute body nearly shook itself asunder, because she knew that Mooney meant well, though of course she had the notions of a common woman.

But wasn't Maria glad when the women had finished their tea and the cook and the dummy had begun to clear away the tea-things! She went into her little bedroom and, remembering that the next morning was a mass morning, changed the hand of the alarm from seven to six. Then she took off

her working skirt and her house-boots and laid her
best skirt out on the bed and her tiny dress-boots
beside the foot of the bed. She changed her blouse
too and, as she stood before the mirror, she thought
of how she used to dress for mass on Sunday morning
when she was a young girl; and she looked with
quaint affection at the diminutive body which she
had so often adorned. In spite of its years she found
it a nice tidy little body.

When she got outside the streets were shining with
rain and she was glad of her old brown waterproof.
The tram was full and she had to sit on the little
stool at the end of the car, facing all the people, with
her toes barely touching the floor. She arranged in
her mind all she was going to do, and thought how
much better it was to be independent and to have
your own money in your pocket. She hoped they
would have a nice evening. She was sure they
would, but she could not help thinking what a pity it
was Alphy and Joe were not speaking. They were
always falling out now, but when they were boys
together they used to be the best of friends; but such
was life.

She got out of her tram at the Pillar and ferreted
her way quickly among the crowds. She went into
Downes's cake-shop, but the shop was so full of
people that it was a long time before she could get
herself attended to. She bought a dozen of mixed
penny cakes, and at last came out of the shop laden
with a big bag. Then she thought what else would
she buy: she wanted to buy something really nice.
They would be sure to have plenty of apples and
nuts. It was hard to know what to buy and all she

could think of was cake. She decided to buy some plumcake, but Downes's plumcake had not enough almond icing on top of it, so she went over to a shop in Henry Street. Here she was a long time in suiting herself, and the stylish young lady behind the counter, who was evidently a little annoyed by her, asked her was it wedding-cake she wanted to buy. That made Maria blush and smile at the young lady; but the young lady took it all very seriously and finally cut a thick slice of plumcake, parcelled it up, and said:

'Two-and-four, please.'

She thought she would have to stand in the Drumcondra tram because none of the young men seemed to notice her, but an elderly gentleman made room for her. He was a stout gentleman and he wore a brown hard hat; he had a square red face and a greyish moustache. Maria thought he was a colonel-looking gentleman and she reflected how much more polite he was than the young men who simply stared straight before them. The gentleman began to chat with her about Hallow Eve and the rainy weather. He supposed the bag was full of good things for the little ones and said it was only right that the youngsters should enjoy themselves while they were young. Maria agreed with him and favoured him with demure nods and hems. He was very nice with her, and when she was getting out at the Canal Bridge she thanked him and bowed, and he bowed to her and, raised his hat and smiled agreeably; and while she was going up along the terrace, bending her tiny head under the rain, she thought how easy it was to know a gentleman even when he has a drop taken.

Everybody said: 'Oh, here's Maria!' when she came to Joe's house. Joe was there, having come home from business, and all the children had their Sunday dresses on. There were two big girls in from next door and games were going on. Maria gave the bag of cakes to the eldest boy, Alphy, to divide, and Mrs Donnelly said it was too good of her to bring such a big bag of cakes, and made all the children say: 'Thanks, Maria.'

But Maria said she had brought something special for papa and mamma, something they would be sure to like, and she began to look for her plumcake. She tried in Downes's bag and then in the pockets of her waterproof and then on the hallstand, but nowhere could she find it. Then she asked all the children had any of them eaten it—by mistake, of course—but the children all said no and looked as if they did not like to eat cakes if they were to be accused of stealing. Everybody had a solution for the mystery and Mrs Donnelly said it was plain that Maria had left it behind her in the tram. Maria, remembering how confused the gentleman with the greyish moustache had made her, coloured with shame and vexation and disappointment. At the thought of the failure of her little surprise and of the two and fourpence she had thrown away for nothing she nearly cried outright.

But Joe said it didn't matter and made her sit down by the fire. He was very nice with her. He told her all that went on in his office, repeating for her a smart answer which he had made to the manager. Maria did not understand why Joe laughed so much over the answer he had made, but she said that the manager must have been a very overbearing person to deal with. Joe said he wasn't so bad when you knew how to take him, that he was a decent sort so long as you didn't rub him the wrong way. Mrs Donnelly played the piano for the children and they danced and sang. Then the two next-door girls handed round the nuts. Nobody could find the nut-crackers, and Joe was nearly getting cross over it and asked how did they expect Maria to crack nuts without a nutcracker. But Maria said she didn't like nuts and that they weren't to bother about her. Then Joe asked would she take a bottle of stout, and Mrs Donnelly said there was port wine too in the house if she would prefer that. Maria said she would rather they didn't ask her to take anything: but Joe insisted.

So Maria let him have his way and they sat by the fire talking over old times and Maria thought she would put in a good word for Alphy. But Joe cried that God might strike him stone dead if ever he spoke a word to his brother again and Maria said she was sorry she had mentioned the matter. Mrs Donnelly told her husband it was a great shame for him to speak that way of his own flesh and blood, but Joe said that Alphy was no brother of his and there was nearly being a row on the head of it. But Joe said he would not lose his temper on account of the night it was, and asked his wife to open some more stout. The two next-door girls had arranged some Hallow Eve games and soon everything was merry again. Maria was delighted to see the children so merry and Joe and his wife in such good spirits. The next-door girls put some saucers on the

table and then led the children up to the table, blindfold. One got the prayer-book and the other three
got the water; and when one of the next-door girls
got the ring Mrs Donnelly shook her finger at the
blushing girl as much as to say: ' O, I know all about
it ! ' They insisted then on blindfolding Maria and
leading her up to the table to see what she would
get; and, while they were putting on the bandage,
Maria laughed and laughed again till the tip of her
nose nearly met the tip of her chin.

They led her up to the table amid laughing and
joking, and she put her hand out in the air as she
was told to do. She moved her hand about here and
there in the air and descended on one of the saucers.
She felt a soft wet substance with her fingers and
was surprised that nobody spoke or took off her
bandage. There was a pause for a few seconds;
and then a great deal of scuffling and whispering.
Somebody said something about the garden, and at
last Mrs Donnelly said something very cross to one
of the next-door girls and told her to throw it out
at once: that was no play. Maria understood that
it was wrong that time and so she had to do it over
again: and this time she got the prayer-book.

After that Mrs Donnelly played Miss McCloud's
Reel for the children, and Joe made Maria take a
glass of wine. Soon they were all quite merry again,
and Mrs Donnelly said Maria would enter a convent
before the year was out because she had got the
prayer-book. Maria had never seen Joe so nice to
her as he was that night, so full of pleasant talk and
reminiscences. She said they were all very good to
her.

At last the children grew tired and sleepy and Joe asked Maria would she not sing some little song before she went, one of the old songs. Mrs Donnelly said ' Do, please, Maria ! ' and so Maria had to get up and stand beside the piano. Mrs Donnelly bade the children be quiet and listen to Maria's song. Then she played the prelude and said ' Now, Maria ! ' and Maria, blushing very much, began to sing in a tiny quavering voice. She sang *I dreamt that I dwelt*, and when she came to the second verse she sang again :

> ' I dreamt that I dwelt in marble halls
>   With vassals and serfs at my side,
> And of all who assembled within those walls
>   That I was the hope and the pride.

> ' I had riches too great to count, could boast
>   Of a high ancestral name,
> But I also dreamt, which pleased me most,
>   That you loved me still the same.'

But no one tried to show her her mistake; and when she had ended her song Joe was very much moved. He said that there was no time like the long ago and no music for him like poor old Balfe, whatever other people might say; and his eyes filled up so much with tears that he could not find what he was looking for and in the end he had to ask his wife to tell him where the corkscrew was.

SECOND BEST

By D. H. Lawrence

'Oh, I 'm tired!' Frances exclaimed petulantly, and in the same instant she dropped down on the turf, near the hedge-bottom. Anne stood a moment surprised, then, accustomed to the vagaries of her beloved Frances, said:

'Well, and aren't you always likely to be tired, after travelling that blessed long way from Liverpool yesterday?' and she plumped down beside her sister. Anne was a wise young body of fourteen, very buxom, brimming with common sense. Frances was much older, about twenty-three, and whimsical, spasmodic. She was the beauty and the clever child of the family. She plucked the goosegrass buttons from her dress in a nervous, desperate fashion. Her beautiful profile, looped above with black hair, warm with the dusky-and-scarlet complexion of a pear, was calm as a mask, her thin brown hand plucked nervously.

'It 's not the journey,' she said, objecting to Anne's obtuseness. Anne looked inquiringly at her darling. The young girl, in her self-confident, practical way, proceeded to reckon up this whimsical creature. But suddenly she found herself full in the eyes of Frances; felt two dark, hectic eyes flaring challenge at her, and she shrank away. Frances was peculiar for these great, exposed looks, which disconcerted people by their violence and their suddenness.

'What 's a matter, poor old duck?' asked Anne, as she folded the slight, wilful form of her sister in her arms. Frances laughed shakily, and nestled down for comfort on the budding breasts of the strong girl.

'Oh, I 'm only a bit tired,' she murmured, on the point of tears.

'Well, of course you are, what do you expect?' soothed Anne. It was a joke to Frances that Anne should play elder, almost mother to her. But then, Anne was in her unvexed teens; men were like big dogs to her: while Frances, at twenty-three, suffered a good deal.

The country was intensely morning-still. On the common everything shone beside its shadow, and the hill-side gave off heat in silence. The brown turf seemed in a low state of combustion, the leaves of the oaks were scorched brown. Among the blackish foliage in the distance shone the small red and orange of the village.

The willows in the brook-course at the foot of the common suddenly shook with a dazzling effect like diamonds. It was a puff of wind. Anne resumed her normal position. She spread her knees, and put in her lap a handful of hazel nuts, whity-green leafy things, whose one cheek was tanned between brown and pink. These she began to crack and eat. Frances, with bowed head, mused bitterly.

'Eh, you know Tom Smedley?' began the young girl, as she pulled a tight kernel out of its shell.

'I suppose so,' replied Frances sarcastically.

'Well, he gave me a wild rabbit what he 'd caught, to keep with my tame one—and it 's living.'

'That 's a good thing,' said Frances, very detached and ironic.

'Well, it *is*! He reckoned he 'd take me to Ollerton Feast, but he never did. Look here, he took a servant from the rectory; I saw him.'

'So he ought,' said Frances.

'No, he oughtn't! And I told him so. And I told him I should tell you—an' I have done.'

Click and snap went a nut between her teeth. She sorted out the kernel, and chewed complacently.

'It doesn't make much difference,' said Frances.

'Well, 'appen it doesn't; but I was mad with him all the same.'

'Why?'

'Because I was; he 's no right to go with a servant.'

'He 's a perfect right,' persisted Frances, very just and cold.

'No, he hasn't, when he 'd said he 'd take me.'

Frances burst into a laugh of amusement and relief.

'Oh, no; I 'd forgot that,' she said, adding, 'and what did he say when you promised to tell me?'

'He laughed and said, "She won't fret her fat over that."'

'And she won't,' sniffed Frances.

There was silence. The common, with its sere, blonde-headed thistles, its heaps of silent bramble, its brown-husked gorse in the glare of sunshine, seemed visionary. Across the brook began the immense pattern of agriculture, white chequering of barley stubble, brown squares of wheat, khaki patches of pasture, red stripes of fallow, with the woodland and the tiny village dark like ornaments, leading away to the distance, right to the hills, where the check-pattern grew smaller and smaller, till, in the blackish haze of heat, far off, only the tiny white squares of barley stubble showed distinct.

'Eh, I say, here's a rabbit hole!' cried Anne suddenly. 'Should we watch if one comes out? You won't have to fidget, you know.'

The two girls sat perfectly still. Frances watched certain objects in her surroundings: they had a peculiar, unfriendly look about them: the weight of greenish elderberries on their purpling stalks; the twinkling of the yellowing crab-apples that clustered high up in the hedge, against the sky: the exhausted, limp leaves of the primroses lying flat in the hedge-bottom: all looked strange to her. Then her eyes caught a movement. A mole was moving silently over the warm, red soil, nosing, shuffling hither and thither, flat, and dark as a shadow, shifting about, and as suddenly brisk, and as silent, like a very ghost of *joie de vivre*. Frances started, from habit was about to call on Anne to kill the little pest. But, to-day her lethargy of unhappiness was too much for her. She watched the little brute paddling, snuffing, touching things to discover them, running in blindness, delighted to ecstasy by the sunlight and the hot, strange things that caressed its belly and its nose. She felt a keen pity for the little creature.

'Eh, our Fran, look there! It's a mole.'

Anne was on her feet, standing watching the dark, unconscious beast. Frances frowned with anxiety.

'It doesn't run off, does it?' said the young girl softly. Then she stealthily approached the creature. The mole paddled fumblingly away. In an instant Anne put her foot upon it, not too heavily. Frances could see the struggling, swimming movement of the little pink hands of the brute, the twisting and twitching of its pointed nose, as it wrestled under the sole of the boot.

'It *does* wriggle!' said the bonny girl, knitting her brows in a frown at the eerie sensation. Then she bent down to look at her trap. Frances could now see, beyond the edge of the boot-sole, the heaving of the velvet shoulders, the pitiful turning of the sightless face, the frantic rowing of the flat, pink hands.

'Kill the thing,' she said, turning away her face.

'Oh—I'm not,' laughed Anne, shrinking. 'You can, if you like.'

'I *don't* like,' said Frances, with quiet intensity.

After several dabbing attempts, Anne succeeded in picking up the little animal by the scruff of its neck. It threw back its head, flung its long blind snout from side to side, the mouth open in a peculiar oblong, with tiny pinkish teeth at the edge. The blind, frantic mouth gaped and writhed. The body, heavy and clumsy, hung scarcely moving.

'Isn't it a snappy little thing?' observed Anne, twisting to avoid the teeth.

'What are you going to do with it?' asked Frances sharply.

'It's got to be killed—look at the damage they do. I s'll take it home and let dadda or somebody kill it. I'm not going to let it go.'

She swaddled the creature clumsily in her pocket-handkerchief and sat down beside her sister. There was an interval of silence, during which Anne combated the efforts of the mole.

'You 've not had much to say about Jimmy this time. Did you see him often in Liverpool?' Anne asked suddenly.

'Once or twice,' replied Frances, giving no sign of how the question troubled her.

'And aren't you sweet on him any more, then?'

'I should think I 'm not, seeing that he 's engaged.

'Engaged? Jimmy Barrass! Well, of all things! I never thought *he* 'd get engaged.'

'Why not? he 's as much right as anybody else,' snapped Frances.

Anne was fumbling with the mole.

''Appen so,' she said at length; 'but I never thought Jimmy would, though.'

'Why not?' snapped Frances.

'*I* don't know—this blessed mole, it 'll not keep still!—who 's he got engaged to?'

'How should I know?'

'I thought you 'd ask him; you 've known him long enough. I s'd think he thought he 'd get engaged now he 's a Doctor of Chemistry.'

Frances laughed in spite of herself.

'What 's that got to do with it?' she asked.

'I 'm sure it 's got a lot. He 'll want to feel *somebody* now, so he 's got engaged. Hey, stop it; go in!'

But at this juncture the mole almost succeeded in wriggling clear. It wrestled and twisted frantically, waved its pointed blind head, its mouth standing like a little shaft, its big, wrinkled hands spread out.

'Go in with you!' urged Anne, poking the little

creature with her forefinger, trying to get it back into the handkerchief. Suddenly the mouth turned like a spark on her finger.

'Oh!' she cried, 'he's bit me.'

She dropped him to the floor. Dazed, the blind creature fumbled round. Frances felt like shrieking. She expected him to dart away in a flash, like a mouse, and there he remained groping; she wanted to cry to him to be gone. Anne, in a sudden decision of wrath, caught up her sister's walking-cane. With one blow the mole was dead. Frances was startled and shocked. One moment the little wretch was fussing in the heat, and the next it lay like a little bag, inert and black—not a struggle, scarce a quiver.

'It is dead!' Frances said breathlessly. Anne took her finger from her mouth, looked at the tiny pinpricks, and said:

'Yes, he is, and I'm glad. They're vicious little nuisances, moles are.'

With which her wrath vanished. She picked up the dead animal.

'Hasn't it got a beautiful skin?' she mused, stroking the fur with her forefinger, then with her cheek.

'Mind,' said Frances sharply. 'You'll have the blood on your skirt!'

One ruby drop of blood hung on the small snout, ready to fall. Anne shook it off on to some harebells. Frances suddenly became calm; in that moment, grown-up.

'I suppose they have to be killed,' she said, and a certain rather dreary indifference succeeded to her grief. The twinkling crab-apples, the glitter of brilliant willows now seemed to her trifling, scarcely worth the notice. Something had died in her, so that things lost their poignancy. She was calm, indifference overlying her quiet sadness. Rising, she walked down to the brook course.

'Here, wait for me,' cried Anne, coming tumbling after.

Frances stood on the bridge, looking at the red mud trodden into pockets by the feet of cattle. There was not a drain of water left, but everything smelled green, succulent. Why did she care so little for Anne, who was so fond of her? she asked herself. Why did she care so little for any one? She did not know, but she felt a rather stubborn pride in her isolation and indifference.

They entered a field where stooks of barley stood in rows, the straight, blonde tresses of the corn streaming on to the ground. The stubble was bleached by the intense summer, so that the expanse glared white. The next field was sweet and soft with a second crop of seeds; thin, straggling clover whose little pink knobs rested prettily in the dark green. The scent was faint and sickly. The girls came up in single file, Frances leading.

Near the gate a young man was mowing with the scythe some fodder for the afternoon feed of the cattle. As he saw the girls he left off working and waited in an aimless kind of way. Frances was dressed in white muslin, and she walked with dignity, detached and forgetful. Her lack of agitation, her simple, unheeding advance made him nervous. She had loved the far-off Jimmy for five years, having had in return his half-measures. This man only affected her slightly.

Tom was of medium stature, energetic in build. His smooth, fair-skinned face was burned red, not brown, by the sun, and this ruddiness enhanced his appearance of good humour and easiness. Being a year older than Frances, he would have courted her long ago had she been so inclined. As it was, he had gone his uneventful way amiably, chatting with many a girl, but remaining unattached, free of trouble for the most part. Only he knew he wanted a woman. He hitched his trousers just a trifle self-consciously as the girls approached. Frances was a rare, delicate kind of being, whom he realized with a queer and delicious stimulation in his veins. She gave him a slight sense of suffocation. Somehow this morning she affected him more than usual. She was dressed in white. He, however, being matter-of-fact in his mind, did not realize. His feeling had never become conscious, purposive.

Frances knew what she was about. Tom was ready to love her as soon as she would show him. Now that she could not have Jimmy, she did not poignantly care. Still, she would have something. If she could not have the best—Jimmy, whom she knew to be something of a snob—she would have the second best, Tom. She advanced rather indifferently.

'You are back, then!' said Tom. She marked the touch of uncertainty in his voice.

'No,' she laughed, 'I 'm still in Liverpool,' and the undertone of intimacy made him burn.

'This isn't you, then?' he asked.

Her heart leapt up in approval. She looked in his eyes, and for a second was with him.

* F 954

'Why, what do you think?' she laughed.

He lifted his hat from his head with a distracted little gesture. She liked him, his quaint ways, his humour, his ignorance, and his slow masculinity.

'Here, look here, Tom Smedley,' broke in Anne.

'A moudiwarp! Did you find it dead?' he asked.

'No, it bit me,' said Anne.

'Oh, aye! An' that got your rag out, did it?'

'No, it didn't!' Anne scolded sharply. 'Such language!'

'Oh, what 's up wi' it?'

'I can't bear you to talk broad.'

'Can't you?'

He glanced at Frances.

'It isn't nice,' Frances said. She did not care, really. The vulgar speech jarred on her as a rule; Jimmy was a gentleman. But Tom's manner of speech did not matter to her.

'I like you to talk *nicely*,' she added.

'Do you,' he replied, tilting his hat, stirred.

'And generally you *do*, you know,' she smiled.

'I s'll have to have a try,' he said, rather tensely gallant.

'What?' she asked brightly.

'To talk nice to you,' he said. Frances coloured furiously, bent her head for a moment, then laughed gaily, as if she liked this clumsy hint.

'Eh now, you mind what you 're saying,' cried Anne, giving the young man an admonitory pat.

'You wouldn't have to give yon mole many knocks like that,' he teased, relieved to get on safe ground, rubbing his arm.

'No indeed, it died in one blow,' said Frances, with a flippancy that was hateful to her.

'You're not so good at knockin' 'em?' he said, turning to her.

'I don't know, if I'm cross,' she said decisively.

'No?' he replied, with alert attentiveness.

'I could,' she added, harder, 'if it was necessary.'

He was slow to feel her difference.

'And don't you consider it *is* necessary?' he asked, with misgiving.

'W-ell—is it?' she said, looking at him steadily, coldly.

'I reckon it is,' he replied, looking away, but standing stubborn.

She laughed quickly.

'But it isn't necessary for *me*,' she said, with slight contempt.

'Yes, that's quite true,' he answered.

She laughed in a shaky fashion.

'*I know it is*,' she said; and there was an awkward pause.

'Why, would you *like* me to kill moles then?' she asked tentatively, after a while.

'They do us a lot of damage,' he said, standing firm on his own ground, angered.

'Well, I'll see the next time I come across one,' she promised, defiantly. Their eyes met, and she sank before him, her pride troubled. He felt uneasy and triumphant and baffled, as if fate had gripped him. She smiled as she departed.

'Well,' said Anne, as the sisters went through the wheat stubble; 'I don't know what you two's been jawing about, I'm sure.'

'Don't you?' laughed Frances significantly.

'No, I don't. But, at any rate, Tom Smedley's a good deal better to my thinking than Jimmy, so there—and nicer.'

'Perhaps he is,' said Frances coldly.

And the next day, after a secret, persistent hunt, she found another mole playing in the heat. She killed it, and in the evening, when Tom came to the gate to smoke his pipe after supper, she took him the dead creature.

'Here you are then!' she said.

'Did you catch it?' he replied, taking the velvet corpse into his fingers and examining it minutely. This was to hide his trepidation.

'Did you think I couldn't?' she asked, her face very near his.

'Nay, I didn't know.'

She laughed in his face, a strange little laugh that caught her breath, all agitation, and tears, and recklessness of desire. He looked frightened and upset. She put her hand to his arm.

'Shall you go out wi' me?' he asked, in a difficult, troubled tone.

She turned her face away, with a shaky laugh. The blood came up in him, strong, overmastering. He resisted it. But it drove him down, and he was carried away. Seeing the winsome, frail nape of her neck, fierce love came upon him for her, and tenderness.

'We s'll 'ave to tell your mother,' he said. And he stood, suffering, resisting his passion for her.

'Yes,' she replied, in a dead voice. But there was a thrill of pleasure in this death.

MISS BRACEGIRDLE DOES HER DUTY

By Stacy Aumonier

'This is the room, madame.'

'Ah, thank you . . . thank you.'

'Does it appear satisfactory to madame?'

'Oh, yes, thank you . . . quite.'

'Does madame require anything further?'

'Er—if not too late, may I have a hot bath?'

'*Parfaitement*, madame. The bathroom is at the end of the passage on the left. I will go and prepare it for madame.'

'There is one thing more. . . . I have had a very long journey. I am very tired. Will you please see that I am not disturbed in the morning until I ring.'

'Certainly, madame.'

Millicent Bracegirdle was speaking the truth—she *was* tired. In the sleepy cathedral town of Easingstoke, from which she came, it was customary for every one to speak the truth. It was customary, moreover, for every one to lead simple, self-denying lives—to give up their time to good works and elevating thoughts. One had only to glance at little Miss Bracegirdle to see that in her were epitomized all the virtues and ideals of Easingstoke. Indeed, it was the pursuit of duty which had brought her to the Hôtel de l'Ouest at Bordeaux on this summer's night. She had travelled from Easingstoke to London, then without a break to Dover, crossed that horrid stretch of sea to Calais, entrained for Paris, where she of necessity had to spend four hours—a terrifying experience—and then had come on to Bordeaux, arriving at midnight. The reason of this journey being that someone had to come to Bordeaux to meet her young sister-in-law, who was arriving the next day from South America. The sister-in-law was married to a missionary in Paraguay, but the climate not agreeing with her, she was returning to England. Her dear brother, the dean, would have come himself, but the claims on his time were so extensive, the parishioners would miss him so . . . it was clearly Millicent's duty to go.

She had never been out of England before, and she had a horror of travel, and an ingrained distrust of foreigners. She spoke a little French—sufficient for the purposes of travel and for obtaining any modest necessities, but not sufficient for carrying on any kind of conversation. She did not deplore this latter fact, for she was of opinion that French people were not the kind of people that one would naturally want to have conversation with; broadly speaking, they were not quite 'nice,' in spite of their ingratiating manners.

The dear dean had given her endless advice, warning her earnestly not to enter into conversation with strangers, to obtain all information from the police, railway officials—in fact, any one in an official uniform. He deeply regretted to say that he was afraid that France was not a country for a woman to travel about in *alone*. There were loose, bad people about, always on the look-out. . . . He really thought perhaps he ought not to let her go. It was only by the utmost persuasion, in which she rather exaggerated her knowledge of the French language and character, her courage, and indifference to discomfort, that she managed to carry the day.

She unpacked her valise, placed her things about the room, tried to thrust back the little stabs of homesickness as she visualized her darling room at the deanery. How strange and hard and unfriendly seemed these foreign hotel bedrooms—heavy and depressing, no chintz and lavender and photographs of . . . all the dear family, the dean, the nephews and nieces, the interior of the cathedral during harvest festival, no samplers and needlework or coloured reproductions of the paintings by Marcus Stone. Oh dear, how foolish she was! What did she expect?

She disrobed and donned a dressing-gown; then, armed with a sponge-bag and towel, she crept timidly down the passage to the bathroom, after closing her bedroom door and turning out the light. The gay bathroom cheered her. She wallowed luxuriously in the hot water, regarding her slim legs with quiet satisfaction. And for the first time since leaving home there came to her a pleasant moment—a sense of enjoyment in her adventure. After all, it *was* rather an adventure, and her life had been peculiarly devoid of it. What queer lives some people must live, travelling about, having experiences! How old was she? Not really old—not by any means. Forty-two? Forty-three? She had shut herself up so. She hardly ever regarded the potentialities of age. As the world went, she was a well-preserved woman for her age. A life of self-abnegation, simple living, healthy walking and fresh air, had kept her younger than these hurrying, pampered city people.

Love? yes, once when she was a young girl . . . he was a schoolmaster, a most estimable kind gentleman. They were never engaged—not actually, but it was a kind of understood thing. For three years it went on, this pleasant understanding and friendship. He was so gentle, so distinguished and considerate. She would have been happy to have continued in this strain for ever. But there was something lacking. Stephen had curious restless lapses. From the physical aspect of marriage she shrunk—yes, even with Stephen, who was gentleness and kindness itself. And then one day . . . one day he went away—vanished, and never returned. They told her he had married one of the country girls—a girl who used to work in Mrs Forbes's dairy—not a very nice girl, she feared, one of these fast, pretty, foolish women. Heigho! well, she had lived that down, destructive as the blow appeared at the time. One lives everything down in time. There is always work, living for others, faith, duty. . . . At the same time she could sympathize with people who found satisfaction in unusual experiences.

There would be lots to tell the dear dean when she wrote to him on the morrow; nearly losing her spectacles on the restaurant car; the amusing remarks of an American child on the train to Paris; the curious food everywhere, nothing simple and plain; the two English ladies at the hotel in Paris who told her about the death of their uncle—the poor man being taken ill on Friday and dying on Sunday afternoon, just before tea-time; the kindness of the hotel proprietor who had sat up for her; the prettiness of the chambermaid. Oh, yes, every one was really very kind. The French people, after all, were very nice. She had seen nothing—nothing but was quite nice and decorous. There would be lots to tell the dean to-morrow.

Her body glowed with the friction of the towel. She again donned her night attire and her thick, woollen dressing-gown. She tidied up the bathroom carefully in exactly the same way she was accustomed to do at home, then once more gripping her sponge-bag and towel, and turning out the light, she crept down the passage to her room. Entering the room she switched on the light and shut the door quickly. Then one of those ridiculous things happened—just the kind of thing you would expect to happen in a foreign hotel. The handle of the door came off in her hand.

She ejaculated a quiet 'Bother!' and sought to replace it with one hand, the other being occupied with the towel and sponge-bag. In doing this she behaved foolishly, for thrusting the knob carelessly against the steel pin—without properly securing it—she only succeeded in pushing the pin farther into the door and the knob was not adjusted. She uttered another little 'Bother!' and put her sponge-bag and towel down on the floor. She then tried to recover the pin with her left hand, but it had gone in too far.

'How very foolish!' she thought, 'I shall have to ring for the chambermaid—and perhaps the poor girl has gone to bed.'

She turned and faced the room, and suddenly the

awful horror was upon her. *There was a man asleep in her bed!*

The sight of that swarthy face on the pillow, with its black tousled hair and heavy moustache, produced in her the most terrible moment of her life. Her heart nearly stopped. For some seconds she could neither think nor scream, and her first thought was: 'I mustn't scream!'

She stood there like one paralysed, staring at the man's head and the great curved hunch of his body under the clothes. When she began to think she thought very quickly, and all her thoughts worked together. The first vivid realization was that it wasn't the man's fault; it was *her* fault. *She was in the wrong room.* It was the man's room. The rooms were identical, but there were all his things about, his clothes thrown carelessly over chairs, his collar and tie on the wardrobe, his great heavy boots and the strange yellow trunk. She must get out somehow, anyhow.

She clutched once more at the door, feverishly driving her finger-nails into the hole where the elusive pin had vanished. She tried to force her fingers in the crack and open the door that way, but it was of no avail. She was to all intents and purposes locked in—locked in a bedroom in a strange hotel alone with a man . . . a foreigner . . . *a Frenchman!* She must think. She must think. . . . She switched off the light. If the light was off he might not wake up. It might give her time to think how to act. It was surprising that he had not awakened. If he *did* wake up, what would he do? How could she explain herself? He wouldn't believe her. No one would believe her. In an English hotel it would be difficult enough, but here where she wasn't known, where they were all foreigners and consequently antagonistic . . . merciful heavens!

She *must* get out. Should she wake the man? No, she couldn't do that. He might murder her. He might . . . Oh, it was too awful to contemplate! Should she scream? ring for the chambermaid? But no, it would be the same thing. People would come rushing. They would find her there in the strange man's bedroom after midnight—she, Millicent Bracegirdle, sister of the Dean of Easingstoke! Easingstoke!

Visions of Easingstoke flashed through her alarmed mind. Visions of the news arriving, women whispering around tea-tables: 'Have you heard, my dear? . . . Really no one would have imagined! Her poor brother! He will of course have to resign, you know, my dear. Have a little more cream, my love.'

Would they put her in prison? She might be in the room for the purpose of stealing or . . . She might be in the room for the purpose of breaking every one of the ten commandments. There was no explaining it away. She was a ruined woman, suddenly and irretrievably, unless she could open the door. The chimney? Should she climb up the chimney? But where would that lead to? And then she visualized the man pulling her down by her legs when she was already smothered in soot. Any moment he might wake up. . . .

She thought she heard the chambermaid going along the passage. If she had wanted to scream, she ought to have screamed before. The maid would know she had left the bathroom some minutes ago. Was she going to her room? Suddenly she remembered that she had told the chambermaid that she was not to be disturbed until she rang the next morning. That was something. Nobody would be going to her room to find out that she was not there.

An abrupt and desperate plan formed in her mind. It was already getting on for one o'clock. The man was probably a quite harmless commercial traveller or business man. He would probably get up about seven or eight o'clock, dress quickly, and go out. She would hide under his bed until he went. Only a matter of a few hours. Men don't look under their beds, although she made a religious practice of doing so herself. When he went he would be sure to open the door all right. The handle would be lying on the floor as though it had dropped off in the night. He would probably ring for the chambermaid or open it with a penknife. Men were so clever at those things. When he had gone she would creep out and steal back to her room, and then there would be no necessity to give any explanation to any one. But heavens! What an experience! Once under the white frill of that bed she would be safe till the morning. In daylight nothing seemed so terrifying.

With feline precaution she went down on her hands and knees and crept toward the bed. What a lucky thing there was that broad white frill! She lifted it at the foot of the bed and crept under. There was just sufficient depth to take her slim

body. The floor was fortunately carpeted all over,
but it seemed very close and dusty. Suppose she
coughed or sneezed! Anything might happen. Of
course . . . it would be much more difficult to
explain her presence under the bed than to explain
her presence just inside the door. She held her
breath in suspense. No sound came from above,
but under this frill it was difficult to hear anything.
It was almost more nerve-racking than hearing
everything . . . listening for signs and portents.
This temporary escape in any case would give her
time to regard the predicament detachedly. Up to
the present she had not been able to visualize the full
significance of her action. She had in truth lost her
head. She had been like a wild animal, consumed
with the sole idea of escape . . . a mouse or a cat
would do this kind of thing—take cover and lie
low. If only it hadn't all happened *abroad*! She
tried to frame sentences of explanation in French,
but French escaped her. And then—they talked
so rapidly, these people. They didn't listen. The
situation was intolerable. Would she be able to
endure a night of it?

At present she was not altogether uncomfortable,
only stuffy and . . . very, very frightened. But
she had to face six or seven or eight hours of it—
perhaps even then discovery in the end! The
minutes flashed by as she turned the matter over
and over in her head. There was no solution. She
began to wish she had screamed or awakened the
man. She saw now that that would have been the
wisest and most politic thing to do; but she had
allowed ten minutes or a quarter of an hour to

elapse from the moment when the chambermaid would know that she had left the bathroom. They would want an explanation of what she had been doing in the man's bedroom all that time. Why hadn't she screamed before?

She lifted the frill an inch or two and listened. She thought she heard the man breathing but she couldn't be sure. In any case it gave her more air. She became a little bolder, and thrust her face partly through the frill so that she could breathe freely. She tried to steady her nerves by concentrating on the fact that—well, there it was. She had done it. She must make the best of it. Perhaps it would be all right after all.

'Of course I shan't sleep,' she kept on thinking, 'I shan't be able to. In any case it will be safer not to sleep. I must be on the watch.'

She set her teeth and waited grimly. Now that she had made up her mind to see the thing through in this manner she felt a little calmer. She almost smiled as she reflected that there would certainly be something to tell the dear dean when she wrote to him to-morrow. How would he take it? Of course he would believe it—he had never doubted a single word that she had uttered in her life—but the story would sound so . . . preposterous. In Easing-stoke it would be almost impossible to envisage such an experience. She, Millicent Bracegirdle, spending a night under a strange man's bed in a foreign hotel! What would those women think? Fanny Shields and that garrulous old Mrs Rusbridger? Perhaps . . . yes, perhaps it would be advisable to tell the dear dean to let the story go no further. One could hardly expect Mrs Rushbridger to . . . not make implications . . . exaggerate.

Oh, dear! What were they all doing now? They would be all asleep, every one in Easingstoke. Her dear brother always retired at ten-fifteen. He would be sleeping calmly and placidly, the sleep of the just . . . breathing the clear sweet air of Sussex, not this—oh, it *was* stuffy! She felt a great desire to cough. She mustn't do that. Yes, at nine-thirty all the servants summoned to the library—a short service—never more than fifteen minutes, her brother didn't believe in a great deal of ritual—then at ten o'clock cocoa for every one. At ten-fifteen bed for every one. The dear sweet bedroom with the narrow white bed, by the side of which she had knelt every night as long as she could remember—even in her dear mother's day—and said her prayers.

Prayers! Yes, that was a curious thing. This was the first night in her life's experience that she had not said her prayers on retiring. The situation was certainly very peculiar . . . exceptional, one might call it. God would understand and forgive such a lapse. And yet after all, why . . . what was to prevent her saying her prayers? Of course she couldn't kneel in the proper devotional attitude, that would be a physical impossibility; nevertheless, perhaps her prayers might be just as efficacious . . . if they came from the heart. So little Miss Brace-girdle curved her body and placed her hands in a devout attitude in front of her face and quite in-audibly murmured her prayers under the strange man's bed.

'Our Father which art in heaven, Hallowed be Thy

name. Thy kingdom come. Thy will be done in earth as it is in heaven; Give us this day our daily bread. And forgive us our trespasses. . . .'

Trespasses! Yes, surely she was trespassing on this occasion, but God would understand. She had not wanted to trespass. She was an unwitting sinner. Without uttering a sound she went through her usual prayers in her heart. At the end she added fervently:

'Please God protect me from the dangers and perils of this night.'

Then she lay silent and inert, strangely soothed by the effort of praying. 'After all,' she thought, 'it isn't the attitude which matters—it is that which occurs deep down in us.'

For the first time she began to meditate—almost to question—church forms and dogma. If an attitude was not indispensable, why a building, a ritual, a church at all? Of course her dear brother couldn't be wrong, the church was so old, so very old, its root deep buried in the story of human life, it was only that . . . well, outward forms *could* be misleading. Her own present position for instance. In the eyes of the world she had, by one silly careless little action, convicted herself of being the breaker of every single one of the ten commandments.

She tried to think of one of which she could not be accused. But no—even to dishonouring her father and mother, bearing false witness, stealing, coveting her neighbour's . . . husband! That was the worst thing of all. Poor man! He might be a very pleasant honourable married gentleman with children and she—she was in a position to compromise him! Why hadn't she screamed? Too late! Too late!

It began to get very uncomfortable, stuffy, but at the same time draughty, and the floor was getting harder every minute. She changed her position stealthily and controlled her desire to cough. Her heart was beating rapidly. Over and over again recurred the vivid impression of every little incident and argument that had occurred to her from the moment she left the bathroom. This must, of course, be the room next to her own. So confusing, with perhaps twenty bedrooms all exactly alike on one side of a passage—how was one to remember whether one's number was 115 or 116?

Her mind began to wander idly off into her school-days. She was always very bad at figures. She disliked Euclid and all those subjects about angles and equations—so unimportant, not leading any-where. History she liked, and botany, and reading about strange foreign lands, although she had always been too timid to visit them. And the lives of great people, *most* fascinating—Oliver Cromwell, Lord Beaconsfield, Lincoln, Grace Darling—*there* was a heroine for you—General Booth, a great, good man, even if a little vulgar. She remembered dear old Miss Trimming talking about him one afternoon at the vicar of St. Bride's garden party. She was *so* amusing. She . . . *Good heavens!*

Almost unwittingly, Millicent Bracegirdle had emitted a violent sneeze!

It was finished! For the second time that night she was conscious of her heart nearly stopping. For the second time that night she was so paralysed with fear that her mentality went to pieces. Now she would hear the man get out of bed. He would walk across to the door, switch on the light, and then lift up the frill. She could almost see that fierce moustached face glaring at her and growling something in French. Then he would thrust out an arm and drag her out. And then? O God in heaven! What then? . . .

'I shall scream before he does it. Perhaps I had better scream now. If he drags me out he will clap his hand over my mouth. Perhaps chloroform . . .'

But somehow she could not scream. She was too frightened even for that. She lifted the frill and listened. Was he moving stealthily across the carpet? She thought—no, she couldn't be sure. Anything might be happening. He might strike her from above—with one of those heavy boots perhaps. Nothing seemed to be happening, but the suspense was intolerable. She realized now that she hadn't the power to endure a night of it. Anything would be better than this—disgrace, imprisonment, even death. She would crawl out, wake the man, and try and explain as best she could.

She would switch on the light, cough, and say: '*Monsieur!*'

Then he would start up and stare at her.

Then she would say—what should she say?

'*Pardon, monsieur, mais je——*' What on earth was the French for 'I have made a mistake.'

'*J'ai tort. C'est la chambre*—er—incorrect. *Voulez-vous*—er——'

What was the French for 'door-knob,' 'let me go'? It didn't matter. She would turn on the light, cough and trust to luck. If he got out of bed, and came toward her, she would scream the hotel down. . . .

The resolution formed, she crawled deliberately out at the foot of the bed. She scrambled hastily toward the door—a perilous journey. In a few seconds the room was flooded with light. She turned toward the bed, coughed, and cried out boldly:

'*Monsieur!*'

Then, for the third time that night, little Miss Bracegirdle's heart all but stopped. In this case the climax of the horror took longer to develop, but when it was reached, it clouded the other two experiences into insignificance.

The man on the bed was dead!

She had never beheld death before, but one does not mistake death.

She stared at him bewildered, and repeated almost in a whisper:

'*Monsieur! . . . Monsieur!*'

Then she tiptoed toward the bed. The hair and moustache looked extraordinarily black in that grey, wax-like setting. The mouth was slightly open, and the face, which in life might have been vicious and sensual, looked incredibly peaceful and far away. It was as though she were regarding the features of a man across some vast passage of time, a being who had always been completely remote from mundane preoccupations.

When the full truth came home to her, little Miss Bracegirdle buried her face in her hands and murmured:

'Poor fellow . . . poor fellow!'

For the moment her own position seemed an affair of small consequence. She was in the presence of something greater and more all-pervading. Almost instinctively she knelt by the bed and prayed.

For a few moments she seemed to be possessed by an extraordinary calmness and detachment. The burden of her hotel predicament was a gossamer trouble—a silly, trivial, almost comic episode, something that could be explained away.

But this man—he had lived his life, whatever it was like, and now he was in the presence of his Maker. What kind of man had he been?

Her meditations were broken by an abrupt sound. It was that of a pair of heavy boots being thrown down by the door outside. She started, thinking at first it was someone knocking or trying to get in. She heard the 'boots,' however, stumping away down the corridor, and the realization stabbed her with the truth of her own position. She mustn't stop there. The necessity to get out was even more urgent.

To be found in a strange man's bedroom in the night is bad enough, but to be found in a dead man's bedroom was even worse. They could accuse her of murder, perhaps. Yes, that would be it—how could she possibly explain to these foreigners? Good God! they would hang her. No, guillotine her, that's what they do in France. They would chop her head off with a great steel knife. Merciful heavens! She envisaged herself standing blindfold, by a priest and an executioner in a red cap, like that man in the Dickens story—what was his name? . . . Sydney Carton, that was it, and before he went on the scaffold he said:

'It is a far, far better thing that I do than I have ever done.'

But no, she couldn't say that. It would be a far, far worse thing that she did. What about the dear dean? Her sister-in-law arriving alone from Paraguay to-morrow? All her dear people and friends in Easingstoke? Her darling Tony, the large grey tabby cat? It was her duty not to have her head chopped off if it could possibly be avoided. She could do no good in the room. She could not recall the dead to life. Her only mission was to escape. Any minute people might arrive. The chambermaid, the boots, the manager, the gendarmes. . . . Visions of gendarmes arriving armed with swords and note-books vitalized her almost exhausted energies. She was a desperate woman. Fortunately now she had not to worry about the light. She sprang once more at the door and tried to force it open with her fingers. The result hurt her and gave her pause. If she was to escape she must *think*, and think intensely. She mustn't do anything rash and silly, she must just think and plan calmly.

She examined the lock carefully. There was no keyhole, but there was a slip-bolt, so that the hotel guest could lock the door on the inside, but it couldn't be locked on the outside. Oh, why didn't this poor dear dead man lock his door last night? Then this trouble could not have happened. She could see the end of the steel pin. It was about half an inch down the hole. If any one was passing they must surely notice the handle sticking out too far the other side! She drew a hairpin out of her hair and tried to coax the pin back, but she only succeeded in pushing it a little farther in. She felt the colour leaving her face, and a strange feeling of faintness come over her.

She was fighting for her life, she mustn't give way. She darted round the room like an animal in a trap, her mind alert for the slightest crevice of escape. The window had no balcony and there was a drop of five stories to the street below. Dawn was breaking. Soon the activities of the hotel and the city would begin. The thing must be accomplished before then.

She went back once more and stared at the lock. She stared at the dead man's property, his razors, and brushes, and writing materials, pens and pencils and rubber and sealing-wax. . . . Sealing-wax!

Necessity is truly the mother of invention. It is in any case quite certain that Millicent Bracegirdle, who had never invented a thing in her life, would never have evolved the ingenious little device she did, had she not believed that her position was utterly desperate. For in the end this is what she did. She got together a box of matches, a candle, a bar of sealing-wax, and a hairpin. She made a little pool of hot sealing-wax, into which she dipped the end of the hairpin. Collecting a small blob on the end of it she thrust it into the hole, and let it adhere to the end of the steel pin. At the seventh attempt she got the thing to move. It took her just an hour and ten minutes to get that steel pin back into the room, and when at length it came far enough through for her to grip it with her finger-nails, she burst into tears through the sheer physical tension of the strain. Very, very carefully she pulled it through, and holding it firmly with her left hand she fixed the knob with her right, then slowly turned it. The door opened!

The temptation to dash out into the corridor and scream with relief was almost irresistible, but she forbore. She listened; she peeped out. No one was about. With beating heart, she went out, closing the door inaudibly. She crept like a little mouse to the room next door, stole in and flung herself on her bed. Immediately she did so it flashed through her mind that *she had left her sponge-bag and towel in the dead man's room*!

In looking back upon her experience she always considered that that second expedition was the worst of all. She might have left the sponge-bag and towel there, only that the towel—she never used hotel towels—had neatly inscribed in the corner 'M. B.'

With furtive caution she managed to retrace her steps. She re-entered the dead man's room, re-claimed her property, and returned to her own. When this mission was accomplished she was indeed wellnigh spent. She lay on her bed and groaned feebly. At last she fell into a fevered sleep. . . .

It was eleven o'clock when she awoke and no one had been to disturb her. The sun was shining, and the experiences of the night appeared a dubious nightmare. Surely she had dreamt it all?

With dread still burning in her heart she rang the bell. After a short interval of time the chamber-maid appeared. The girl's eyes were bright with some uncontrollable excitement. No, she had not been dreaming. This girl had heard something.

'Will you bring me some tea, please?'

'Certainly, madame.'

The maid drew back the curtains and fussed about the room. She was under a pledge of secrecy, but she could contain herself no longer. Suddenly she approached the bed and whispered excitedly:

'Oh, madame, I have promised not to tell . . . but a terrible thing has happened. A man, a dead man, has been found in room 117—a guest. Please not to say I tell you. But they have all been there, the gendarmes, the doctors, the inspectors. Oh, it is terrible . . . terrible.'

The little lady in the bed said nothing. There was indeed nothing to say. But Marie Louise Lancret was too full of emotional excitement to spare her.

'But the terrible thing is—— Do you know who he was, madame? They say it is Boldhu, the man wanted for the murder of Jeanne Carreton in the barn at Vincennes. They say he strangled her, and then cut her up in pieces and hid her in two barrels which he threw into the river. . . . Oh, but he was a bad man, madame, a terrible bad man . . . and he died in the room next door . . . suicide, they think; or was it an attack of the heart? . . . Remorse, some shock perhaps. . . . Did you say a *café complet*, madame?'

'No, thank you, my dear . . . just a cup of tea . . strong tea . . .'

'*Parfaitement*, madame.'

The girl retired, and a little later a waiter entered the room with a tray of tea. She could never get over her surprise at this. It seemed so—well, indecorous for a man—although only a waiter—to enter a lady's bedroom. There was no doubt a great deal in what the dear dean said. They were certainly very peculiar, these French people—they had most peculiar notions. It was not the way they behaved at Easingstoke. She got farther under the sheets, but the waiter appeared quite indifferent to the situation. He put the tray down and retired.

When he had gone she sat up and sipped her tea, which gradually warmed her. She was glad the sun was shining. She would have to get up soon. They said that her sister-in-law's boat was due to berth at one o'clock. That would give her time to dress comfortably, write to her brother, and then go down to the docks. Poor man! So he had been a murderer, a man who cut up the bodies of his victims . . . and she had spent the night in his bedroom! They were certainly a most—how could she describe it?—people. Nevertheless she felt a little glad that at the end she had been there to kneel and pray by his bedside. Probably nobody else had ever done that. It was very difficult to judge people. . . . Something at some time might have gone wrong. He might not have murdered the woman after all. People were often wrongly convicted. She herself . . . If the police had found her in that room at three o'clock that morning . . . It is that which takes place in the heart which counts. One learns and learns. Had she not learnt that one can pray just as effectively lying under a bed as kneeling beside it? . . . Poor man!

She washed and dressed herself and walked calmly down to the writing-room. There was no evidence of excitement among the other hotel guests. Probably none of them knew about the tragedy except herself. She went to a writing-table, and after profound meditation wrote as follows:

'My dear Brother,

'I arrived late last night after a very pleasant journey. Every one was very kind and attentive, the manager was sitting up for me. I nearly lost my spectacle case in the restaurant car! But a kind old gentleman found it and returned it to me. There was a most amusing American child on the train. I will tell you about her on my return. The people are very pleasant, but the food is peculiar, nothing *plain and wholesome*. I am going down to meet Annie at one o'clock. How have you been keeping, my dear? I hope you have not had any further return of the bronchial attacks.

'Please tell Lizzie that I remembered in the train on the way here that that large stone jar of marmalade that Mrs Hunt made is behind those empty tins in the top shelf of the cupboard next to the coach-house. I wonder whether Mrs Butler was able to come to evensong after all? This is a nice hotel, but I think Annie and I will stay at the 'Grand' to-night, as the bedrooms here are rather noisy. Well, my dear, nothing more till I return. Do take care of yourself.—Your loving sister,

'Millicent.'

Yes, she couldn't tell Peter about it, neither in the letter nor when she went back to him. It was her duty not to tell him. It would only distress him;

she felt convinced of it. In this curious foreign
atmosphere the thing appeared possible, but in
Easingstoke the mere recounting of the fantastic
situations would be positively . . . indelicate.
There was no escaping that broad general fact—she
had spent a night in a strange man's bedroom.
Whether he was a gentleman or a criminal, even
whether he was dead or alive, did not seem to
mitigate the jar upon her sensibilities, or rather it
would not mitigate the jar upon the peculiarly
sensitive relationship between her brother and herself. To say that she had been to the bathroom,
the knob of the door-handle came off in her hand,
she was too frightened to awaken the sleeper or
scream, she got under the bed—well, it was all
perfectly true. Peter would believe her, but—one
simply could not conceive such a situation in Easingstoke deanery. It would create a curious little
barrier between them, as though she had been
dipped in some mysterious solution which alienated
her. It was her duty not to tell.

She put on her hat, and went out to post the letter.
She distrusted an hotel letter-box. One never knew
who handled these letters. It was not a proper
official way of treating them. She walked to the
head post office in Bordeaux.

The sun was shining. It was very pleasant
walking about amongst these queer excitable people,
so foreign and different - looking — and the cafés
already crowded with chattering men and women,
and the flower stalls, and the strange odour of—
what was it? Salt? Brine? Charcoal? . . . A
military band was playing in the square . . . very

gay and moving. It was all life, and movement, and bustle . . . thrilling rather.

'I spent a night in a strange man's bedroom.'

Little Miss Bracegirdle hunched her shoulders, murmured to herself, and walked faster. She reached the post office and found the large metal plate with the slot for letters and 'R.F.' stamped above it. Something official at last! Her face was a little flushed—was it the warmth of the day or the contact of movement and life?—as she put her letter into the slot. After posting it she put her hand into the slot and flicked it round to see that there were no foreign contraptions to impede its safe delivery. No, the letter had dropped safely in. She sighed contentedly and walked off in the direction of the docks to meet her sister-in-law from Paraguay.

THE GARDEN PARTY

BY KATHERINE MANSFIELD

AND after all the weather was ideal. They could not have had a more perfect day for a garden party if they had ordered it. Windless, warm, the sky without a cloud. Only the blue was veiled with a haze of light gold, as it is sometimes in early summer.

The gardener had been up since dawn, mowing the lawns and sweeping them, until the grass and the dark flat rosettes where the daisy plants had been seemed to shine. As for the roses, you could not help feeling they understood that roses are the only flowers that impress people at garden parties; the only flowers that everybody is certain of knowing. Hundreds, yes, literally hundreds, had come out in a single night; the green bushes bowed down as though they had been visited by archangels.

Breakfast was not yet over before the men came to put up the marquee.

'Where do you want the marquee put, mother?'

'My dear child, it's no use asking me. I'm determined to leave everything to you children this year. Forget I am your mother. Treat me as an honoured guest.'

But Meg could not possibly go and supervise the men. She had washed her hair before breakfast, and she sat drinking her coffee in a green turban, with a dark wet curl stamped on each cheek.   Jose, the butterfly, always came down in a silk petticoat and a kimono jacket.

'You'll have to go, Laura; you're the artistic one.'

Away Laura flew, still holding her piece of bread-and-butter.   It's so delicious to have an excuse for eating out of doors, and besides, she loved having to arrange things; she always felt she could do it so much better than anybody else.

Four men in their shirt-sleeves stood grouped together on the garden path.   They carried staves covered with rolls of canvas, and they had big tool-bags slung on their backs.   They looked impressive. Laura wished now that she was not holding that piece of bread-and-butter, but there was nowhere to put it, and she couldn't possibly throw it away.   She blushed and tried to look severe and even a little bit short-sighted as she came up to them.

'Good morning,' she said, copying her mother's voice.   But that sounded so fearfully affected that she was ashamed, and stammered like a little girl, 'Oh—er—have you come—is it about the marquee?'

'That's right, miss,' said the tallest of the men, a lanky, freckled fellow, and he shifted his tool-bag, knocked back his straw hat, and smiled down at her. 'That's about it.'

His smile was so easy, so friendly, that Laura recovered.   What nice eyes he had, small, but such a dark blue!   And now she looked at the others, they were smiling too.   'Cheer up, we won't bite,' their smile seemed to say.   How very nice workmen were!   And what a beautiful morning!   She mustn't

mention the morning; she must be business-like.
The marquee.

'Well, what about the lily-lawn? Would that
do?'

And she pointed to the lily-lawn with the hand
that didn't hold the bread-and-butter. They turned,
they stared in the direction. A little fat chap thrust
out his under-lip, and the tall fellow frowned.

'I don't fancy it,' said he. 'Not conspicuous
enough. You see, with a thing like a marquee,'
and he turned to Laura in his easy way, 'you want to
put it somewhere where it 'll give you a bang slap in
the eye, if you follow me.'

Laura's upbringing made her wonder for a moment
whether it was quite respectful of a workman to talk
to her of bangs slap in the eye. But she did quite
follow him.

'A corner of the tennis-court,' she suggested.
'But the band 's going to be in one corner.'

'H'm, going to have a band, are you?' said another of the workmen. He was pale. He had a
haggard look as his dark eyes scanned the tennis-
court. What was he thinking?

'Only a very small band,' said Laura gently.
Perhaps he wouldn't mind so much if the band was
quite small. But the tall fellow interrupted.

'Look here, miss, that 's the place. Against those
trees. Over there. That 'll do fine.'

Against the karakas. Then the karaka-trees
would be hidden. And they were so lovely, with
their broad, gleaming leaves, and their clusters of
yellow fruit. They were like trees you imagined
growing on a desert island, proud, solitary, lifting

their leaves and fruits to the sun in a kind of silent splendour. Must they be hidden by a marquee?

They must. Already the men had shouldered their staves and were making for the place. Only the tall fellow was left. He bent down, pinched a sprig of lavender, put his thumb and forefinger to his nose and snuffed up the smell. When Laura saw that gesture she forgot all about the karakas in her wonder at him caring for things like that—caring for the smell of lavender. How many men that she knew would have done such a thing? Oh, how extraordinarily nice workmen were, she thought. Why couldn't she have workmen for friends rather than the silly boys she danced with and who came to Sunday night supper? She would get on much better with men like these.

It 's all the fault, she decided, as the tall fellow drew something on the back of an envelope, something that was to be looped up or left to hang, of these absurd class distinctions. Well, for her part, she didn't feel them. Not a bit, not an atom. . . . And now there came the chock-chock of wooden hammers. Someone whistled, someone sang out, 'Are you right there, matey?' 'Matey!' The friendliness of it, the—the—— Just to prove how happy she was, just to show the tall fellow how at home she felt, and how she despised stupid conventions, Laura took a big bite of her bread-and-butter as she stared at the little drawing. She felt just like a work-girl.

'Laura, Laura, where are you? Telephone, Laura!' a voice cried from the house.

'Coming!' Away she skimmed, over the lawn,

up the path, up the steps, across the veranda, and into the porch. In the hall her father and Laurie were brushing their hats ready to go to the office.

'I say, Laura,' said Laurie very fast, 'you might just give a squiz at my coat before this afternoon. See if it wants pressing.'

'I will,' said she. Suddenly she couldn't stop herself. She ran at Laurie and gave him a small, quick squeeze. 'Oh, I do love parties, don't you?' gasped Laura.

'Ra-ther,' said Laurie's warm, boyish voice, and he squeezed his sister too, and gave her a gentle push. 'Dash off to the telephone, old girl.'

The telephone. 'Yes, yes; oh, yes. Kitty? Good morning, dear. Come to lunch? Do, dear. Delighted of course. It will only be a very scratch meal — just the sandwich crusts and broken meringue-shells and what's left over. Yes, isn't it a perfect morning? Your white? Oh, I certainly should. One moment—hold the line. Mother's calling.' And Laura sat back. 'What, mother? Can't hear.'

Mrs Sheridan's voice floated down the stairs. 'Tell her to wear that sweet hat she had on last Sunday.'

'Mother says you're to wear that *sweet* hat you had on last Sunday. Good. One o'clock. Bye-bye.'

Laura put back the receiver, flung her arms over her head, took a deep breath, stretched and let them fall. 'Huh,' she sighed, and the moment after the sigh she sat up quickly. She was still, listening. All the doors in the house seemed to be open. The

house was alive with soft, quick steps and running
voices. The green baize door that led to the kitchen
regions swung open and shut with a muffled thud.
And now there came a long, chuckling, absurd sound.
It was the heavy piano being moved on its stiff
castors. But the air! If you stopped to notice,
was the air always like this? Little faint winds were
playing chase in at the tops of the windows, out at
the doors. And there were two tiny spots of sun,
one on the inkpot, one on a silver photograph frame,
playing too. Darling little spots. Especially the
one on the inkpot lid. It was quite warm. A warm
little silver star. She could have kissed it.

The front door bell pealed, and there sounded the
rustle of Sadie's print skirt on the stairs. A man's
voice murmured; Sadie answered, careless, 'I'm
sure I don't know. Wait. I'll ask Mrs Sheridan.'

'What is it, Sadie?' Laura came into the hall.

'It's the florist, Miss Laura.'

It was, indeed. There, just inside the door, stood
a wide, shallow tray full of pots of pink lilies. No
other kind. Nothing but lilies—canna lilies, big
pink flowers, wide open, radiant, almost frighten-
ingly alive on bright crimson stems.

'O-oh, Sadie!' said Laura, and the sound was like
a little moan. She crouched down as if to warm
herself at that blaze of lilies; she felt they were in her
fingers, on her lips, growing in her breast.

'It's some mistake,' she said faintly. 'Nobody
ever ordered so many. Sadie, go and find mother.'

But at that moment Mrs Sheridan joined them.

'It's quite right,' she said calmly. 'Yes, I
ordered them. Aren't they lovely?' She pressed

Laura's arm. 'I was passing the shop yesterday, and I saw them in the window. And I suddenly thought for once in my life I shall have enough canna lilies. The garden-party will be a good excuse.'

'But I thought you said you didn't mean to interfere,' said Laura. Sadie had gone. The florist's man was still outside at his van. She put her arm round her mother's neck and gently, very gently, she bit her mother's ear.

'My darling child, you wouldn't like a logical mother, would you? Don't do that. Here 's the man.'

He carried more lilies still, another whole tray.

'Bank them up, just inside the door, on both sides of the porch, please,' said Mrs Sheridan. 'Don't you agree, Laura?'

'Oh, I *do*, mother.'

In the drawing-room Meg, Jose, and good little Hans had at last succeeded in moving the piano.

'Now, if we put this chesterfield against the wall and move everything out of the room except the chairs, don't you think?'

'Quite.'

'Hans, move these tables into the smoking-room, and bring a sweeper to take these marks off the carpet and — one moment, Hans——' Jose loved giving orders to the servants, and they loved obeying her. She always made them feel they were taking part in some drama. 'Tell mother and Miss Laura to come here at once.'

'Very good, Miss Jose.'

She turned to Meg. 'I want to hear what the piano sounds like, just in case I 'm asked to sing this afternoon. Let's try over *This Life is Weary*.'

Pom! Ta-ta-ta *Tee*-ta! The piano burst out so passionately that Jose's face changed. She clasped her hands. She looked mournfully and enigmatically at her mother and Laura as they came in.

> 'This Life is *Wee*-ary,
> A Tear—a Sigh.
> A Love that *Chan*-ges,
> This Life is *Wee*-ary,
> A Tear—a Sigh.
> A Love that *Chan*-ges,
> And then . . . Good-bye!'

But at the word 'Good-bye,' and although the piano sounded more desperate than ever, her face broke into a brilliant, dreadfully unsympathetic smile.

'Aren't I in good voice, mummy?' she beamed.

> 'This Life is *Wee*-ary,
> Hope comes to Die.
> A Dream—a *Wa*-kening.'

But now Sadie interrupted them. 'What is it, Sadie?'

'If you please, m'm, cook says have you got the flags for the sandwiches?'

'The flags for the sandwiches, Sadie?' echoed Mrs Sheridan dreamily. And the children knew by her face that she hadn't got them. 'Let me see.' And she said to Sadie firmly, 'Tell cook I'll let her have them in ten minutes.'

Sadie went.

'Now, Laura,' said her mother quickly, 'come with me into the smoking-room. I've got the names somewhere on the back of an envelope. You'll

have to write them out for me. Meg, go upstairs
this minute and take that wet thing off your head.
Jose, run and finish dressing this instant. Do you
hear me, children, or shall I have to tell your father
when he comes home to-night? And—and, Jose,
pacify cook if you do go into the kitchen, will you?
I'm terrified of her this morning.'

The envelope was found at last behind the dining-
room clock, though how it had got there Mrs
Sheridan could not imagine.

'One of you children must have stolen it out of my
bag, because I remember vividly—— Cream-cheese
and lemon-curd. Have you done that?'

'Yes.'

'Egg and——' Mrs Sheridan held the envelope
away from her. 'It looks like mice. It can't be
mice, can it?'

'Olive, pet,' said Laura, looking over her shoulder.

'Yes, of course, olive. What a horrible combination it sounds. Egg and olive.'

They were finished at last, and Laura took them
off to the kitchen. She found Jose there pacifying
the cook, who did not look at all terrifying.

'I have never seen such exquisite sandwiches,'
said Jose's rapturous voice. 'How many kinds did
you say there were, cook? Fifteen?'

'Fifteen, Miss Jose.'

'Well, cook, I congratulate you.'

Cook swept up crusts with the long sandwich
knife, and smiled broadly.

'Godber's has come,' announced Sadie, issuing
out of the pantry. She had seen the man pass the
window.

That meant the cream puffs had come. Godber's were famous for their cream puffs. Nobody ever thought of making them at home.

'Bring them in and put them on the table, my girl,' ordered cook.

Sadie brought them in and went back to the door. Of course Laura and Jose were far too grown-up to really care about such things. All the same, they couldn't help agreeing that the puffs looked very attractive. Very. Cook began arranging them, shaking off the extra icing sugar.

'Don't they carry one back to all one's parties?' said Laura.

'I suppose they do,' said practical Jose, who never liked to be carried back. 'They look beautifully light and feathery, I must say.'

'Have one each, my dears,' said cook in her comfortable voice. 'Yer ma won't know.'

Oh, impossible. Fancy cream puffs so soon after breakfast. The very idea made one shudder. All the same, two minutes later Jose and Laura were licking their fingers with that absorbed inward look that only comes from whipped cream.

'Let 's go into the garden, out by the back way,' suggested Laura. 'I want to see how the men are getting on with the marquee. They 're such awfully nice men.'

But the back door was blocked by cook, Sadie, Godber's man and Hans.

Something had happened.

'Tuk-tuk-tuk,' clucked cook like an agitated hen. Sadie had her hand clapped to her cheek as though she had toothache. Hans's face was screwed up in the effort to understand. Only Godber's man seemed to be enjoying himself; it was his story.

'What 's the matter? What 's happened?'

'There 's been a horrible accident,' said cook. 'A man killed.'

'A man killed! Where? How? When?'

But Godber's man wasn't going to have his story snatched from under his very nose.

'Know those little cottages just below here, miss?' Know them? Of course, she knew them. 'Well, there 's a young chap living there, name of Scott, a carter. His horse shied at a traction-engine, corner of Hawke Street this morning, and he was thrown out on the back of his head. Killed.'

'Dead!' Laura stared at Godber's man.

'Dead when they picked him up,' said Godber's man with relish. 'They were taking the body home as I come up here.' And he said to the cook, 'He 's left a wife and five little ones.'

'Jose, come here.' Laura caught hold of her sister's sleeve and dragged her through the kitchen to the other side of the green baize door. There she paused and leaned against it. 'Jose!' she said, horrified, 'however are we going to stop everything?'

'Stop everything, Laura!' cried Jose in astonishment. 'What do you mean?'

'Stop the garden party, of course.' Why did Jose pretend?

But Jose was still more amazed. 'Stop the garden party? My dear Laura, don't be so absurd. Of course we can't do anything of the kind. Nobody expects us to. Don't be so extravagant.'

'But we can't possibly have a garden party with a man dead just outside the front gate.'

That really was extravagant, for the little cottages were in a lane to themselves at the very bottom of a steep rise that led up to the house. A broad road ran between. True, they were far too near. They were the greatest possible eyesore, and they had no right to be in that neighbourhood at all. They were little mean dwellings painted a chocolate brown. In the garden patches there was nothing but cabbage stalks, sick hens and tomato cans. The very smoke coming out of their chimneys was poverty-stricken. Little rags and shreds of smoke, so unlike the great silvery plumes that uncurled from the Sheridans' chimneys. Washerwomen lived in the lane and sweeps and a cobbler, and a man whose house-front was studded all over with minute bird-cages. Children swarmed. When the Sheridans were little they were forbidden to set foot there because of the revolting language and of what they might catch. But since they were grown up, Laura and Laurie on their prowls sometimes walked through. It was disgusting and sordid. They came out with a shudder. But still one must go everywhere; one must see everything. So through they went.

'And just think of what the band would sound like to that poor woman,' said Laura.

'Oh, Laura!' Jose began to be seriously annoyed. 'If you're going to stop a band playing every time someone has an accident, you'll lead a very strenuous life. I'm every bit as sorry about it as you. I feel just as sympathetic.' Her eyes hardened. She looked at her sister just as she used to when they were little and fighting together. 'You won't bring a drunken workman back to life by being sentimental,' she said softly.

'Drunk! Who said he was drunk?' Laura turned furiously on Jose. She said just as they had used to say on those occasions, 'I 'm going straight up to tell mother.'

'Do, dear,' cooed Jose.

'Mother, can I come into your room?' Laura turned the big glass door-knob.

'Of course, child. Why, what 's the matter? What 's given you such a colour?' And Mrs Sheridan turned round from her dressing-table. She was trying on a new hat.

'Mother, a man 's been killed,' began Laura.

'*Not* in the garden?' interrupted her mother.

'No, no!'

'Oh, what a fright you gave me!' Mrs Sheridan sighed with relief, and took off the big hat and held it on her knees.

'But listen, mother,' said Laura. Breathless, half-choking, she told the dreadful story. 'Of course, we can't have our party, can we?' she pleaded. 'The band and everybody arriving. They 'd hear us, mother; they 're nearly neighbours!'

To Laura's astonishment her mother behaved just like Jose; it was harder to bear because she seemed amused. She refused to take Laura seriously.

'But, my dear child, use your common sense. It 's only by accident we 've heard of it. If some one had died there normally—and I can't understand how they keep alive in those poky little holes—we should still be having our party, shouldn't we?'

Laura had to say 'yes' to that, but she felt it was all wrong. She sat down on her mother's sofa and pinched the cushion frill.

'Mother, isn't it really terribly heartless of us?' she asked.

'Darling!' Mrs Sheridan got up and came over to her, carrying the hat. Before Laura could stop her she had popped it on. 'My child!' said her mother, 'the hat is yours. It 's made for you. It 's much too young for me. I have never seen you look such a picture. Look at yourself!' And she held up her hand-mirror.

'But, mother,' Laura began again. She couldn't look at herself; she turned aside.

This time Mrs Sheridan lost patience just as Jose had done.

'You are being very absurd, Laura,' she said coldly. 'People like that don't expect sacrifices from us. And it 's not very sympathetic to spoil everybody's enjoyment as you 're doing now.'

'I don't understand,' said Laura, and she walked quickly out of the room into her own bedroom. There, quite by chance, the first thing she saw was this charming girl in the mirror, in her black hat trimmed with gold daisies, and a long black velvet ribbon. Never had she imagined she could look like that. Is mother right? she thought. And now she hoped her mother was right. Am I being extravagant? Perhaps it was extravagant. Just for a moment she had another glimpse of that poor woman and those little children, and the body being carried into the house. But it all seemed blurred, unreal, like a picture in the newspaper. I'll remember it again after the party's over, she decided. And somehow that seemed quite the best plan. . . .

Lunch was over by half-past one. By half-past two they were all ready for the fray. The green-coated band had arrived and was established in a corner of the tennis-court.

'My dear!' trilled Kitty Maitland, 'aren't they too like frogs for words? You ought to have arranged them round the pond with the conductor in the middle on a leaf.'

Laurie arrived and hailed them on his way to dress. At the sight of him Laura remembered the accident again. She wanted to tell him. If Laurie agreed with the others, then it was bound to be all right. And she followed him into the hall.

'Laurie!'

'Hallo!' He was half-way upstairs, but when he turned round and saw Laura he suddenly puffed out his cheeks and goggled his eyes at her. 'My word, Laura! You do look stunning,' said Laurie. 'What an absolutely topping hat!'

Laura said faintly 'Is it?' and smiled up at Laurie, and didn't tell him after all.

Soon after that people began coming in streams. The band struck up; the hired waiters ran from the house to the marquee. Wherever you looked there were couples, strolling, bending to the flowers, greeting, moving on over the lawn. They were like bright birds that had alighted in the Sheridans' garden for this one afternoon, on their way to—where? Ah, what happiness it is to be with people who all are happy, to press hands, press cheeks, smile into eyes.

'Darling Laura, how well you look!'

'What a becoming hat, child!'

'Laura, you look quite Spanish. I 've never seen you look so striking.'

And Laura, glowing, answered softly, 'Have you had tea? Won't you have an ice? The passion-fruit ices really are rather special.' She ran to her father and begged him. 'Daddy darling, can't the band have something to drink?'

And the perfect afternoon slowly ripened, slowly faded, slowly its petals closed.

'Never a more delightful garden party . . .' 'The greatest success . . .' 'Quite the most . . .'

Laura helped her mother with the good-byes. They stood side by side in the porch till it was all over.

'All over, all over, thank heaven,' said Mrs Sheridan. 'Round up the others, Laura. Let 's go and have some fresh coffee. I 'm exhausted. Yes, it 's been very successful. But oh, these parties, these parties! Why will you children insist on giving parties!' And they all of them sat down in the deserted marquee.

'Have a sandwich, daddy dear. I wrote the flag.'

'Thanks.' Mr Sheridan took a bite and the sandwich was gone. He took another. 'I suppose you didn't hear of a beastly accident that happened to-day?' he said.

'My dear,' said Mrs Sheridan, holding up her hand, 'we did. It nearly ruined the party. Laura insisted we should put it off.'

'Oh, mother!' Laura didn't want to be teased about it.

'It was a horrible affair all the same,' said Mr Sheridan. 'The chap was married too. Lived just below in the land, and leaves a wife and half a dozen kiddies, so they say.'

An awkward little silence fell. Mrs Sheridan fidgeted with her cup. Really, it was very tactless of father. . . .

Suddenly she looked up. There on the table were all those sandwiches, cakes, puffs, all uneaten, all going to be wasted. She had one of her brilliant ideas.

'I know,' she said. 'Let 's make up a basket. Let 's send that poor creature some of this perfectly good food. At any rate, it will be the greatest treat for the children. Don't you agree? And she 's sure to have neighbours calling in and so on. What a point to have it all ready prepared. Laura!' She jumped up. 'Get me the big basket out of the stairs cupboard.'

'But, mother, do you really think it 's a good idea?' said Laura.

Again, how curious, she seemed to be different from them all. To take scraps from their party. Would the poor woman really like that?

'Of course! What 's the matter with you to-day? An hour or two ago you were insisting on us being sympathetic, and now——'

Oh, well! Laura ran for the basket. It was filled, it was heaped by her mother.

'Take it yourself, darling,' said she. 'Run down just as you are. No, wait, take the arum lilies too.   People of that class are so impressed by arum lilies.'

'The stems will ruin her lace frock,' said practical Jose.

So they would.   Just in time.   'Only the basket, then.   And, Laura!'—her mother followed her out of the marquee—'don't on any account——'

'What mother?'

No, better not put such ideas into the child's head! 'Nothing!   Run along.'

It was just growing dusky as Laura shut their garden gates.   A big dog ran by like a shadow.   The road gleamed white, and down below in the hollow the little cottages were in deep shade.   How quiet it seemed after the afternoon.   Here she was going down the hill to somewhere where a man lay dead, and she couldn't realize it.   Why couldn't she?   She stopped a minute.   And it seemed to her that kisses, voices, tinkling spoons, laughter, the smell of crushed grass were somehow inside her.   She had no room for anything else.   How strange!   She looked up at the pale sky, and all she thought was, 'Yes, it was the most successful party.'

Now the broad road was crossed.   The lane began, smoky and dark.   Women in shawls and men's tweed caps hurried by.   Men hung over the palings; the children played in the doorways.   A low hum came from the mean little cottages.   In some of them there was a flicker of light, and a shadow, crab-like, moved across the window.   Laura bent her head and hurried on.   She wished now she had put on a coat.   How her frock shone!   And the big hat with the velvet streamer—if only it was another hat!

Were the people looking at her? They must be. It was a mistake to have come; she knew all along it was mistake. Should she go back even now?

No, too late. This was the house. It must be. A dark knot of people stood outside. Beside the gate an old, old woman with a crutch sat in a chair, watching. She had her feet on a newspaper. The voices stopped as Laura drew near. The group parted. It was as though she was expected, as though they had known she was coming here.

Laura was terribly nervous. Tossing the velvet ribbon over her shoulder, she said to a woman standing by, 'Is this Mrs Scott's house?' and the woman, smiling queerly, said, 'It is, my lass.'

Oh, to be away from this! She actually said, 'Help me, God,' as she walked up the tiny path and knocked. To be away from those staring eyes, or to be covered up in anything, one of those women's shawls even. I'll just leave the basket and go, she decided. I shan't even wait for it to be emptied.

Then the door opened. A little woman in black showed in the gloom.

Laura said, 'Are you Mrs Scott?' But to her horror the woman answered, 'Walk in, please, miss,' and she was shut in the passage.

'No,' said Laura, 'I don't want to come in. I only want to leave this basket. Mother sent——'

The little woman in the gloomy passage seemed not to have heard her. 'Step this way, please, miss,' she said in an oily voice, and Laura followed her.

She found herself in a wretched little low kitchen,

lighted by a smoky lamp. There was a woman
sitting before the fire.

'Em,' said the little creature who had let her in.
'Em! It's a young lady.' She turned to Laura.
She said meaningly, 'I'm 'er sister, miss. You'll
excuse 'er, won't you?'

'Oh, but of course!' said Laura. 'Please, please
don't disturb her. I—I only want to leave——'

But at that moment the woman at the fire turned
round. Her face, puffed up, red, with swollen eyes
and swollen lips, looked terrible. She seemed as
though she couldn't understand why Laura was
there. What did it mean? Why was this stranger
standing in the kitchen with a basket? What was
it all about? And the poor face puckered up
again.

'All right, my dear,' said the other. 'I'll thenk
the young lady.'

And again she began, 'You'll excuse her, miss,
I'm sure,' and her face, swollen too, tried an oily
smile.

Laura only wanted to get out, to get away. She
was back in the passage. The door opened. She
walked straight through into the bedroom, where
the dead man was lying.

'You'd like a look at 'im, wouldn't you?' said
Em's sister, and she brushed past Laura over to the
bed. 'Don't be afraid, my lass'—and now her voice
sounded fond and sly, and fondly she drew down the
sheet—''e looks a picture. There's nothing to
show. Come along, my dear.'

Laura came.

There lay a young man, fast asleep—sleeping so

soundly, so deeply, that he was far, far away from
them both. Oh, so remote, so peaceful. He was
dreaming. Never wake him up again. His head
was sunk in the pillow, his eyes were closed; they
were blind under the closed eyelids. He was given
up to his dream. What did garden parties and
baskets and lace frocks matter to him? He was far
from all those things. He was wonderful, beautiful.
While they were laughing and while the band was
playing, this marvel had come to the lane. Happy
. . . happy. . . . All is well, said that sleeping face.
This is just as it should be. I am content.

But all the same you had to cry, and she couldn't
go out of the room without saying something to him.
Laura gave a loud childish sob.

'Forgive my hat,' she said.

And this time she didn't wait for Em's sister. She
found her way out of the door, down the path, past
all those dark people. At the corner of the lane she
met Laurie.

He stepped out of the shadow. 'Is that you,
Laura?'

'Yes.'

'Mother was getting anxious. Was it all right?'

'Yes, quite. Oh, Laurie!' She took his arm,
she pressed up against him.

'I say, you 're not crying, are you?' asked her
brother.

Laura shook her head. She was.

Laurie put his arm round her shoulder. 'Don't
cry,' he said in his warm, loving voice. 'Was it
awful?'

'No,' sobbed Laura. 'It was simply marvellous.

But, Laurie——' She stopped, she looked at her
brother. 'Isn't life,' she stammered, isn't life——'
But what life was she couldn't explain. No matter.
He quite understood.

'*Isn't* it, darling?' said Laurie.

THE DESERT ISLANDER

By Stella Benson

CONSTANTINE hopefully followed the Chinese servant through the unknown house. He felt hopeful of success in his plan of begging this Englishman for help, for he knew that an Englishman, alone among people of a different colour (as this Englishman was alone in this South China town), treated the helping of stray white men almost as part of the White Man's Burden. But even without this claim of one lonely white man upon another, Constantine would have felt hopeful. He knew himself to be a man of compelling manner in spite of his ugly, too long face, and his ugly, too short legs.

As Constantine stumped in on his hobnailed soles, Mr White—who was evidently not a very tactful man—said, 'Oh, are you *another* deserter from the Foreign Legion?'

'I am Constantine Andreievitch Soloviev,' said Constantine, surprised. He spoke and understood English almost perfectly (his mother had been English), yet he could not remember ever having heard the word *another* applied to himself. In fact it did not—could not possibly—so apply. There was only one of him, he knew.

Of course, in a way there was some sense in what this stupid Englishman said. Constantine had certainly been a *légionnaire* in Tonkin up till last

Thursday—his narrow pipe-clayed helmet, stiff khaki greatcoat, shabby drill uniform, puttees, brass buttons, and inflexible boots were all the property of the French Government. But the core—the pearl inside this vulgar, horny shell—was Constantine Andreievitch Soloviev. That made all the difference.

Constantine saw that he must take this Didymus of an Englishman in hand at once and tell him a few exciting stories about his dangerous adventures between the Tonkin border and this Chinese city. Snakes, tigers, love-crazed Chinese princesses and brigands passed rapidly through his mind, and he chose the last, because he had previously planned several impressive things to do if he should be attacked by brigands. So now, though he had not actually met a brigand, those plans would come in useful. Constantine intended to write his autobiography some day when he should have married a rich wife and settled down. Not only did his actual life seem to him a very rare one but, also, lives were so interesting to make up.

Constantine was a desert islander—a spiritual Robinson Crusoe. He made up everything himself and he wasted nothing. *Robinson Crusoe* was his favourite book—in fact, almost the only book he had ever read—and he was proud to be, like his hero, a desert islander. He actually preferred clothing his spirit in the skins of wild thoughts that had been the prey of his wits and sheltering it from the world's weather in a leaky hut of his brain's own contriving, to enjoying the good tailoring and housing that dwellers on the mainland call experience and education. He enjoyed being barbarous, he enjoyed living alone on his island, accepting nothing, imitating nothing, believing nothing, adapting himself to nothing — implacably home - made. Even his tangible possessions were those of a marooned man rather than of a civilized citizen of this well-furnished world. At this moment his only luggage was a balalaika that he had made himself out of cigar-boxes, and to this he sang songs of his own composition—very imperfect songs. He would not have claimed that either his songs or his instrument were better than the songs and instruments made by song - makers and balalaika - makers; they were, however, much more rapturously *his* than any acquired music could have been and, indeed, in this as in almost all things, it simply never occurred to him to *take* rather than *make*. There was no mainland on the horizon of his desert island.

'I am not a beggar,' said Constantine. 'Until yesterday I had sixty piastres which I had saved by many sacrifices during my service in the Legion. But yesterday, passing through a dark forest of pines in the twilight, about twenty versts from here, I met——'

'You met a band of brigands,' said Mr White. 'Yes, I know . . . you all say that.'

Constantine stared at him. He had not lived, a desert islander, in a crowded and over - civilized world without meeting many rebuffs, so this one did not surprise him—did not even offend him. On the contrary, for a minute he almost loved the uncompromising Mr White, as a sportsman almost loves the chamois on a peculiarly inaccessible crag.

This was a friend worth a good deal of trouble to secure, Constantine saw. He realized at once that the desert islander's line here was to discard the brigands and to discard noble independence.

'Very well then,' said Constantine. 'I did *not* meet brigands. I *am* a beggar. I started without a penny and I still have no penny. I hope you will give me something. That is why I have come.' He paused, drawing long pleased breaths through his large nose. This, he felt, was a distinctly self-made line of talk; it set him apart from all previous deserting *légionnaires*.

Mr White evidently thought so too. He gave a short grunting laugh. 'That 's better,' he said.

'These English,' thought Constantine lovingly. 'They are the next best thing to *being* originals, for they *admire* originals.' 'I like you,' he added extravagantly, aloud. 'I like the English. I am so glad I found an Englishman to beg of instead of an American—though an American would have been much richer than you are, I expect. Still, to a beggar a little is enough. I dislike Americans; I dislike their women's wet finger-nails.'

'Wet finger-nails?' exclaimed Mr White. 'Oh, you mean their manicure polishes. Yes . . . they *do* always have wet finger-nails . . . ha, ha . . . so they do. I should never have thought of that myself.'

'Of course not,' said Constantine, genuinely surprised. '*I* thought of it. Why should *you* have thought of it?' After a moment he added, 'I am not a gramophone.'

Mr White thought that he had said, 'Have you

got a gramophone?' and replied at once with some
pleasure, 'Yes, I have—it is a very precious companion. Are you musical? But of course you are,
being Russian. I should be very lonely without my
daily ration of Chopin. Would you like some music
while the servants are getting you something to
eat?'

'I should like some music,' said Constantine,
'but I should not like to hear a gramophone. I will
play you some music—some unique and only music
on a unique and only instrument.'

'Thank you very much,' said Mr White, peering
doubtfully through his glasses at the cigar-box
balalaika. 'What good English you speak,' he
added, trying to divert his guest's attention from his
musical purpose. 'But all Russians, of course, are
wonderful linguists.'

'I will play you my music,' said Constantine.
'But first I must tell you that I do not like you to
say to me, "Being Russian you are musical" or "All
Russians speak good English." To me it seems so
stupid to see me as one of many.'

'Each one of us is one of many,' sighed Mr White
patiently.

'*You*, perhaps—but *I*, not,' said Constantine.
'When you notice my English words instead of my
thoughts it seems to me that you are listening
wrongly—you are listening to sounds only, in the
same way as you listen to your senseless gramophone——'

'But you haven't heard my gramophone,' interrupted Mr White, stung on his darling's behalf.

'What does it matter what sounds a man makes

—what words he uses? Words are common to all men; thoughts belong to one man only.'

Mr White considered telling his guest to go to hell, but he said instead, 'You're quite a philosopher, aren't you?'

'I am not *quite an* anything,' said Constantine abruptly. 'I am me. All people who like Chopin also say, 'You're quite a philosopher.''

'Now you're generalizing, yourself,' said Mr White, clinging to his good temper. 'Exactly what you've just complained of my doing.'

'Some people *are* general,' said Constantine. 'Now I will play you my music, and you will admit that is it not one of many musics.'

He sang a song with Russian words which Mr White did not understand. As a matter of fact, such was Constantine's horror of imitating that the words of his song were just a list of the names of the diseases of horses, learned while Constantine was a veterinary surgeon in the Ukraine. His voice was certainly peculiar to himself; it was hoarse — so hoarse that one felt as if a light cough or a discreet blowing of that long nose would clear the hoarseness away; it was veiled, as though heard from behind an intervening stillness; yet with all its hoarseness and insonorousness, it was flexible, alive, and exciting. His instrument had the same quality of quiet ugliness and oddity; it was almost enchanting. It was as if an animal—say, a goat—had found a way to control its voice into a crude goblin concord.

'That's my music,' said Constantine. 'Do you like it?'

'Frankly,' said Mr White, 'I prefer Chopin.'

'On the gramophone?'

'On the gramophone.'

'Yet one is a thing you never heard before and will never hear again—and the other is a machine that makes the same sound for millions.'

'I don't care.'

Constantine chewed his upper lip for a minute, thinking this over. Then he shook himself. 'Nevertheless, I like you,' he said insolently. 'You are almost a person. Would you like me to tell you about my life, or would you rather I explained to you my idea about Zigzags?'

'I would rather see you eat a good meal,' said Mr White, roused to a certain cordiality—as almost all Anglo-Saxons are—by the opportunity of dispensing food and drink.

'I can tell you my Zigzag idea while I eat,' said Constantine, leading the way towards the table at the other end of the room. 'Are you not eating too?'

'I'm not in the habit of eating a meat meal at ten o'clock at night.'

'Is "not being in the habit" a reason for not doing it now?'

'To me it is.'

'Oh—oh—*oh*—I wish I were like you,' said Constantine vehemently. 'It is so tiring being me—having no guide. I *do* like you.'

'Help yourself to spinach,' said Mr White crossly.

'Now shall I tell you my Zigzag idea?'

'If you can eat as well as talk.'

Constantine was exceedingly hungry; he bent low over his plate, though he sat sideways to the table, facing Mr White, ready to launch a frontal

H 954

attack of talk. His mouth was too full for a moment
to allow him to begin to speak, but quick, agonized
glances out of his black eyes implored his host to
be silent till his lips should be ready. 'You know,'
he said, swallowing hurriedly, 'I always think of a
zigzag as going *downwards*. I draw it in the air, *so*
. . . a straight honest line, then—see—a diagonal
subtle line cuts the air away from under it—so . . .
Do you see what I mean? I will call the *zig* a *to*,
and the *zag* a *from*. Now——'

'Why is one of your legs fatter than the other?'
asked Mr White.

'It is bandaged. Now, I think of this zigzag as
a diagram of human minds. Always human minds
are *zigs* or *zags*—a *to* or a *from*—the brave *zig* is
straight, *so* . . . the cleverer, crueller *zag* cuts away
below. So are men's——'

'But why is it bandaged?'

'It was kicked by a horse. Well, so are men's
understandings. Here I draw the simple, faith-
ful understanding—and here—*zag*—the easy, clever
understanding that sees through the simple faith.
Now below that—see—*zig* once more—the wise,
the serene, and now a *zag* contradicts once more;
this is the cynic who know all answers to serenity.
Then below, once more——'

'May I see your leg?' asked Mr White. 'I was
in an ambulance unit during the war.'

'Oh, what is this talk of legs?' cried Constantine.
'Legs are all the same; they belong to millions.
All legs are made of blood and bone and muscle—
all vulgar things. Your ambulance cuts off legs,
mends legs, fits bones together, corks up blood.

It treats men like bundles of bones and blood. This is so dull. Bodies are so dull. Minds are the only onliness in men.'

'Yes,' said Mr White. 'But minds have to have legs to walk about on. Let me see your leg.'

'Very well, then, let us talk of legs. We have at least legs in common, you and I.'

'Hadn't you got more sense than to put such a dirty rag round an open wound?'

'It is not dirty; it is simply of a grey colour. I washed it in a rice field.' Constantine spoke in a muffled voice from somewhere near his knee-cap, for he was now bent double, wholeheartedly interested in his leg. 'I washed the wound too, and three boils which are behind my knee. This blackness is not dirt; it is a blackness belonging to the injury.'

Mr White said nothing, but he rose to his feet as though he had heard a call. Constantine, leaving his puttee in limp coils about his foot like a dead snake, went on eating. He began to talk again about the zigzag while he stuffed food into his mouth, but he stopped talking soon, for Mr White was walking up and down the long room and not pretending to listen. Constantine, watching his host restively pacing the far end of the room, imagined that he himself perhaps smelled disagreeable, for this was a constant fear of his—that his body should play his rare personality this horrid trick. 'What is the matter?' he asked anxiously, with a shamed look. 'Why are you so far?'

Mr White's lazy, mild manner was quite changed. His voice seemed to burst out of seething irritation.

'It's a dam nuisance just now. It couldn't happen at a worse time. I've a great deal of work to do—and this fighting all over the province makes a journey so dam——'

'What is so dam?' asked Constantine, his bewilderment affecting his English.

'I'll tell you what,' said Mr White, standing in front of Constantine with his feet wide apart and speaking in an angry voice. 'You're going to bed now in my attic, and to-morrow at daylight you're going to be waked up and driven down in my car, by me (damn it!), to Lao-chow, to the hospital—a two days' drive—three hundred miles —over the worst roads you ever saw.'

Constantine's heart gave a sickening lurch. 'Why to hospital? You think my leg is dangerous?'

'If I know anything of legs,' said Mr White rather brutally, 'the doctor won't let you keep that one an hour longer than he has to.'

Constantine's mouth began instantly to tremble so much that he could scarcely speak. He thought, 'I shall die—I shall die like this—of a stupid black leg—this valuable lonely me will die.' He glared at Mr White, hungry for consolation. 'He isn't valuable—he's one of many . . . of course he could easily be brave.'

Mr White, once more indolent and indifferent, led the little Russian to the attic and left him there. As soon as Constantine saw the white sheets neatly folded back, the pleasant blue rugs squarely set upon the floor, the open wardrobe fringed with hangers, he doubted whether, after all, he did value himself so much. For in this neat room he felt betrayed by this body of his—this unwashed, unshaven, tired body, encased in coarse dirty clothes, propped on an offensive, festering leg. He decided to take all his clothes off, even though he had no other garment with him to put on; he would feel more appropriate to the shiny linen in his own shiny skin, he thought. He would have washed, but his attention was diverted as he pulled his clothes off by the wound on his leg. Though it was not very painful, it made him nearly sick with disgust now. Every nerve in his body seemed on tiptoe, alert to feel agony, as he studied the wound. He saw that a new sore place was beginning, well above the knee. With only his shirt on, he rushed downstairs, and in at the only lighted doorway. 'Look—look,' he cried. 'A new sore place. . . . Does this mean the danger is greater even than we thought?'

Mr White, in neat blue-and-white pyjamas, was carefully pressing a tie in a tie-press. Constantine had never felt so far away from a human being in his life as he felt on seeing the tie-press, those pyjamas, those monogrammed silver brushes, that elastic apparatus for reducing exercises that hung upon the door.

'Oh, go to bed,' said Mr White irascibly. 'For God's sake, show a little sense.'

Constantine was back in his attic before he thought, 'I ought to have said, "For God's sake, show a little *non*sense yourself." Sense is so vulgar.'

Sense, however, was to drive him three hundred miles to safety, next day.

All night the exhausted Constantine, sleeping only for a few minutes at a time, dreamed trivial, broken dreams about establishing his own superiority, finding, for instance, that he had after all managed to bring with him a suit-case full of clean, fashionable clothes, or noticing that his host was wearing a filthy bandage round his neck instead of a tie.

Constantine was asleep when Mr White, fully dressed, woke him next morning. A clear, steely light was slanting in at the window. Constantine was always fully conscious at the second of waking, and he was immediately horrified to see Mr White looking expressionlessly at the disorderly heap of dirty clothes that he had thrown in disgust on the floor the night before. Trying to divert his host's attention, Constantine put on a merry and courageous manner. 'Well, how is the weather for our motor car jaunt?'

'It could hardly be worse,' said Mr White placidly. 'Sheets of rain. God knows what the roads will be like.'

'Well, we are lucky to have roads at all, in this benighted China.'

'I don't know about that. If there weren't any roads we shouldn't be setting off on this beastly trip.'

'I shall be ready in two jiffies,' said Constantine, springing naked out of bed and shuffling his dreadful clothes out of Mr White's sight. 'But just tell me,' he added as his host went through the door, 'why do you drive three hundred miles on a horrible wet day just to take a perfect stranger—a beggar too—to hospital?' (He thought, 'Now he *must* say something showing that he recognizes my value.')

'Because I can't cut off your leg myself,' said

Mr White gloomily. Constantine did not press his question because this new reference to the cutting off of legs set his nerves jangling again; his hands trembled so that he could scarcely button his clothes. Service in the Foreign Legion, though it was certainly no suitable adventure for a rare and sensitive man, had never obliged him to face anything more frightening than non-appreciation, coarse food, and stupid treatment. None of these things could humiliate him—on the contrary, all confirmed him in his persuasion of his own value. Only the thought of being at the mercy of his body could humiliate the excited and glowing spirit of Constantine. Death was the final, most loathsome triumph of the body; death meant dumbness and decay—yet even death he could have faced courageously could he have been flattered to its very brink.

The car, a ramshackle Ford, stood in the rain on the bald gravel of the compound, as Constantine, white with excitement, limped out through the front door. His limp, though not consciously assumed, had developed only since last night. His whole leg now felt dangerous, its skin shrinking and tingling. Constantine looked into the car. In the back seat sat Mr White's coolie, clasping a conspicuously neat little white canvas kit-bag with leather straps. The kit-bag held Constantine's eye and attacked his self-respect as the tie-press had attacked and haunted him the night before. Every one of his host's possessions was like a perfectly well-balanced, indisputable statement in a world of fevered conjecture. 'And a camp-bed—so nicely rolled,' said Constantine, leaning into the car, fascinated and humiliated. 'But only one. . . .'

'I have only one,' said Mr White.

'And you are bringing it—for me?' said Constantine, looking at him ardently, overjoyed at this tribute.

'I am bringing it for myself,' said Mr White with his unamused and short-sighted smile. 'I am assuming that a *légionnaire* is used to sleeping rough. I'm not. I'm rather fixed in my habits and I have a horror of the arrangements in Chinese inns.'

'He is morally brave,' thought Constantine, though, for the first time, it occurred to him how satisfactory it would be to slap his host's face. 'A man less brave would have changed his plans about the camp-bed at once and said, "For you, my dear man, of course—why not?"' Constantine chattered nervously as he took his seat in the car next to his host, the driver. 'I feel such admiration for a man who can drive a motor car. I adore the machine when it does not—like the gramophone—trespass on matters outside its sphere. The machine's sphere is space, you see—it controls space—and that is so admirable—even when the machine is so very unimpressive as this one. Mr White, your motor car is *very* unimpressive indeed. Are you sure it will run three hundred miles?'

'It always seems to,' said Mr White. 'I never do anything to it except pour petrol, oil, and water into the proper openings. I am completely unmechanical.'

'You cannot be if you work a gramophone.'

'You seem to have my gramophone on your mind.

To me it doesn't answer the purpose of a machine—
it simply *is* Chopin, to me.'

Constantine stamped his foot in almost delighted
irritation, for this made him feel a god beside this
groundling.   After a few minutes of self-satisfaction,
however, a terrible thought invaded him.   He
became obsessed with an idea that he had left fleas
in his bed in Mr White's attic.   That smug, immaculate Chinese servant would see them when he
made the bed, and on Mr White's return would say,
'That foreign soldier left fleas in our attic bed.'
How bitterly did Constantine wish that he had
examined the bed carefully before leaving the room,
or alternatively, that he could invent some elaborate
lie that would prevent Mr White from believing
this revolting accusation.   Constantine's mind, already racked with the fear of pain and death and
with the agony of his impotence to impress his
companion, became overcast with the hopelessness
and remorselessness of everything.   Everything
despairing seemed a fact beyond dispute; everything
hopeful, a mere dream.   His growing certainty
about the fleas, the persistence of the rain, combined
with the leakiness of the car's side-curtains, the
skiddiness of the road, the festering of his leg, the
thought of the surgeon's saw, the perfection of that
complacent kit-bag in the back seat, with the poor
cigar-box balalaika tinkling beside it, the over-
stability and overrightness of his friend in need—
there was not one sweet or flattering thought to
which his poor trapped mind could turn.

The absurdly inadequate bullock-trail only just
served the purpose of a road for the Ford.   The

* H 954

wheels slid about, wrenching themselves from groove to groove. Constantine's comment on the difficulties of the road was silenced by a polite request on the part of Mr White. 'I can't talk while I 'm driving, if you don't mind. I 'm not a good driver, and I need all my attention, especially on such a bad road.'

'I will talk and you need not answer. That is my ideal plan of conversation. I will tell you why I joined the Foreign Legion. You must have been wondering about this. It will be a relief for me from my misfortunes, to talk.'

'I 'd rather not, if you don't mind,' said his host serenely.

'Mean old horse,' thought Constantine passionately, his heart contracting with offence. 'It is so English to give away nothing but the bare, bald, stony fact of help—no decorations of graciousnesses and smilings. A Russian would be a much poorer helper, but a how much better friend.'

The car ground on. Constantine turned over again and again in his mind the matter of the fleas. The wet ochre-and-green country of South China streamed unevenly past, the neat, complex shapes of rice fields altering, disintegrating and re-forming, like groups in a country dance. Abrupt horns of rock began piercing through the flat rain-striped valley, and these, it seemed, were the heralds of a mountain range that barred the path of the travellers, for soon cliffs towered above the road. A village which clung to a slope at the mouth of a gorge was occupied by soldiers. 'This is where our troubles begin,' said Mr White peacefully.

The soldiers were indolent, shabby, ineffectual-looking creatures, scarcely distinguishable from coolies, but their machine-guns, straddling mosquito-like about the forlorn village street, looked disagreeably wide awake and keen. Constantine felt as if his precious heart were the cynosure of all the machine-guns' waspish glances, as the car splashed between them. 'Is this safe?' he asked. 'Motoring through a Chinese war?'

'Not particularly,' smiled Mr White. 'But it's safer than neglecting that leg of yours.'

Constantine uttered a small, shrill, nervous exclamation—half a curse. 'Is a man nothing more than a leg to you?'

As he spoke, from one side of the gorge along which they were now driving, a rifle shot cracked, like the breaking of a taut wire. Its echoes were overtaken by the sputtering of more shots from a higher crag. Constantine had been tensely held for just such an attack on his courage as this—and yet he was not ready for it. His body moved instantly by itself, without consulting his self-respect; it flung its arms round Mr White. The car, thus immobilized at its source of energy, swerved, skidded, and stood still askew upon the trail. Constantine, sweating violently, recalled his pride and reassembled his sprawling arms. Mr White said nothing, but he looked with a cold benevolence into Constantine's face and shook his head slightly. Then he started the car again and drove on in silence. There was no more firing.

'Oh, *oh*, I do *wish* you had been a little bit frightened too,' said Constantine, clenching his fists. He was too much of a desert islander to deny his own fright, as a citizen of the tradition-ruled mainland might have denied it. Brave or afraid, Constantine was his own creation; he had made himself, he would stand or fall by this self that he had made. It was indeed, in a way, more interesting to have been afraid than to have been brave. Only, unfortunately, this exasperating benefactor of his did not think so.

The noon-light was scarcely brighter than the light of early morning. The unremitting rain slanted across the grey air. Trees, skies, valleys, mountains, seen through the rain-spotted windshield, were like a distorted, stippled landscape painted by a beginner who has not yet learned to wring living colour from his palette. However, sun or no sun, noontime it was at last, and Mr White, drawing his car conscientiously to the side of the bullock trail, as if a procession of Rolls-Royces might be expected to pass, unpacked a neat jigsaw puzzle of a sandwich-box.

'I brought a few caviare sandwiches for you,' he said gently. 'I know Russians like caviare.'

'Are your sandwiches then made of Old England's Rosbif?' asked Constantine crossly, for it seemed to him that this man used nothing but collective nouns.

'No; of bloater paste.'

They said nothing more but munched in a rather sullen silence. Constantine had lost his desire to tell Mr White why he had joined the Foreign Legion —or to tell him anything else, for that matter. There was something about Mr White that destroyed

the excitement of telling ingenious lies—or even
the common truth; and this *something* Constantine
resented more and more, though he was uncertain
how to define it. Mr White leaned over the steering-
wheel and covered his eyes with his hands, for driving
tired him. The caviare, and his host's evident
weariness, irritated Constantine more and more;
these things seemed like a crude insistence on his
increasing obligation. 'I suppose you are tired of
the very sight of me,' he felt impelled to say bitterly.

'No, no,' said Mr White politely but indifferently.
'Don't worry about me. It 'll all be the same a
hundred years hence.'

'Whether my leg is off or on—whether I die in
agony or live—it will all be the same a hundred
years hence, I suppose you would say,' said Constantine, morbidly goading his companion into
repeating this insult to the priceless mystery of
personality.

'My good man, I can't do more than I *am* doing
about your leg, can I?' said Mr White irritably, as
he restarted the car.

'A million times more—a million times more,'
thought Constantine hysterically, but with an effort
he said nothing.

As the wet evening light smouldered to an ashen
twilight, they drove into Mo-ming, which was to
be their night's stopping-place. Outside the city
wall they were stopped by soldiers; for Mo-ming
was being defended against the enemy's advance.
After twenty minutes' talk in the clanking Canton-
ese tongue, the two white men were allowed to go
through the city gate on foot, leaving the Ford

in a shed outside, in the care of Mr White's coolie.
Mr White carried his beautiful little kit-bag and
expected Constantine to carry the camp-bed.

'What—and leave my balalaika in the car?'
protested Constantine childishly.

'I think it would be safe,' said Mr White, only
faintly ironic. 'Hurry up. I must go at once and
call on the general in charge here. I don't want to
have my car commandeered.'

Constantine limped along behind him, the camp-
bed on one shoulder, the balalaika faintly tinkling
under his arm. They found the inn in the centre of
a tangle of looped, frayed, untidy streets—a box-
like gaunt house, one corner of which was partly
ruined, for the city had been bombarded that day.
The inn, which could never have been a comfortable
place, was wholly disorganized by its recent misfortune; most of the servants had fled, and the
innkeeper was entirely engrossed in counting and
piling up on the veranda his rescued possessions
from the wrecked rooms. An impudent little boy,
naked down to the waist—the only remaining
servant—showed Mr White and Constantine to
the only room the inn could offer.

'One room between us?' cried Constantine,
thinking of his shameful, possibly verminous, clothes
and his unwashed body. He felt unable to bear
the idea of unbuttoning even the greasy collar of
his tunic within sight of that virgin-new kit-bag.
Its luminous whiteness would seem in the night
like triumphant civilization's eye fixed upon the
barbarian—like the smug beam of a lighthouse
glowing from the mainland upon that uncouth

obstruction, a desert island. 'I 'm not consistent,' thought Constantine. 'That 's my trouble. I ought to be proud of being dirty. At least that is a home-made condition.'

'Yes—one room between us,' said Mr White tartly. 'We must do the best we can. You look after things here, will you, while I go and see the general and make the car safe.'

Left alone, Constantine decided not to take off any clothes at all—even his coarse greatcoat—but to say that he had fever and needed all the warmth he could get. No sooner had he come to this decision than he felt convinced that he actually was feverish; his head and his injured leg ached and throbbed as though all the hot blood in his body had concentrated in those two regions, while ice seemed to settle round his heart and loins. The room was dreary and very sparsely furnished with an ugly, too high table and rigid chairs to match. The beds were simply recesses in the wall, draped with dirty mud-brown mosquito-veils. Constantine, however, stepped more bravely into this hard, matted coffin than he had into Mr White's clean attic bed. As he lay down, his leg burned and throbbed more fiercely than ever, and he began to imagine the amputation—the blood, the yawning of the flesh, the scraping of the saw upon the bone. His imagination did not supply an anaesthetic. Fever came upon him now in good earnest; he shook so much that his body seemed to jump like a fish upon the unyielding matting, he seemed to breathe in heat, without being able to melt the ice in his bones. Yet he remained artistically conscious all the time of his plight, and even exaggerated the shivering spasms of his limbs. He was quite pleased to think that Mr White would presently return and find him in this condition, and so be obliged to be interested and compassionate. Yet as he heard Mr White's heavy step on the stair, poor Constantine's eye fell on the fastidious white kit-bag, and he suddenly remembered all his fancies and fears about vermin and smells. By the time Mr White was actually standing over him, Constantine was convinced that the deepest loathing was clearly shown on that superior, towering face.

'I can't help it—I can't help it,' cried Constantine, between his chattering teeth.

Mr White seemed to ignore the Russian's agitation. 'I think the car 'll be all right now,' he said. 'I left the coolie sleeping in it, to make sure. The general was quite civil and gave me a permit to get home; but it seems it's utterly impossible for us to drive on to Lao-chow. Fighting on the road is particularly hot, and the bridges are all destroyed. The enemy have reached the opposite side of the river, and they 've been bombarding the city all day. I told the general about your case; he suggests you go by river in a sampan down to Lao-chow to-morrow. You may be fired on just as you leave the city, but nothing to matter, I dare say. After that, you 'd be all right—the river makes a stiff bend south here, and gets right away from the country they 're fighting over. It would take you only about eighteen hours to Lao-chow, going down-stream. I 've already got a sampan for you. . . . Oh, Lord, isn't this disgusting?' he added, looking round the dreadful room and wrinkling his nose. 'How I loathe this kind of thing!'

'I can't help it. I can't help it.' Constantine began at first to moan and then to cry. He was by now in great pain, and he did not try to control his distress. It passed through his mind that crying was the last thing a stupid Englishman would expect of a *légionnaire*; so far so good, therefore— he was a desert islander even in his degradation. Yet he loathed himself; all his morbid fears of being offensive were upon him, and the unaccustomed exercise of crying, combined with the fever, nauseated him. Mr White, still wearing his expression of repugnance, came to his help, loosened that greasy collar, lent a handkerchief, ordered some refreshing hot Chinese tea.

'You should have known me in Odessa,' gasped Constantine in an interval between his paroxysms. 'Three of the prettiest women in the town were madly in love with me. You know me only at my worst.'

Mr White, soaking a folded silk handkerchief in cold water, before laying it on Constantine's burning forehead, did not answer. He unrolled the pillow from his camp-bed and put it under Constantine's head. As he did so, he recoiled a little, but after a second's hesitation, he pushed the immaculate little pillow into place with a heroic firmness.

'I wore only silk next to the skin then,' snuffled Constantine. The fever rose in a wave in his brain, and he shouted curses upon his cruelly perfect friend.

Mr White lay only intermittently on his camp-bed that night. He was kept busy making use of his past experience as a member of an ambulance unit.   Only at daylight he slept for an hour or so.

Constantine, awakened from a short sleep by the sound of firing outside, lay on his side and watched Mr White's relaxed, sleeping face.   The fever had left Constantine, and he was now sunk in cold, limp depression and fear.   Luckily, he thought, there was no need to stir, for certainly he could not be expected—a sick man—to set forth in a sampan through such dangers as the persistent firing suggested.   At least in this inn he knew the worst, he thought wearily, and his companion knew the worst too.   'I will not leave him,' Constantine vowed, 'until I have somehow cured him of these frightful memories of me — somehow amputated his memory of me. . . .'   He lay watching his companion's face—hating it—obscurely wishing that those eyes, which had seen the worst during this loathsome night, might remain for ever shut.

Mr White woke up quite suddenly.   'Good Lord!' he said, peering at his watch.   'Nearly seven. I told the sampan man to be at the foot of the steps at daylight.'

'Are you mad?' asked Constantine shrilly. 'Listen to the firing—quite near.   Besides—I'm a very sick man, as you should know by now.   I couldn't even walk—much less dodge through a crowd of Chinese assassins.'

Mr White, faintly whistling Chopin, laboriously keeping his temper, left the room, and could presently be heard hee-hawing in the Chinese language on the veranda to the hee-hawing innkeeper.

When he came back, he said, 'The sampaneer's

there, waiting—only too anxious to get away from the bombing they 're expecting to-day. He 's tied up only about a hundred yards away. You 'll be beyond the reach of the firing as soon as you 're round the bend. Hurry up, man; the sooner you get down to hospital, and I get off on the road home, the better for us both.'

Constantine, genuinely exhausted after his miserable night, did not speak, but lay with his eyes shut and his face obstinately turned to the wall. He certainly felt too ill to be brave or to face the crackling dangers of the battle-ridden streets, but he was conscious of no plan except a determination to be as obstructive as he could—to assert at least this ignoble power over his tyrant.

'Get up, you dam fool,' shouted Mr White, suddenly plucking the pillow from under the sick man's head, 'or I 'll drag you down to the river by the scruff of your dirty neck.'

Dirty neck! Instantly Constantine sat up—hopeless now of curing this man's contempt, full of an almost unendurable craving to be far away from him—to wipe him from his horizon—to be allowed to imagine him dead. Invigorated by this violent impulse, he rolled out of bed and sullenly watched Mr White settle up with the innkeeper and take a few packages out of that revoltingly refined kit-bag.

'A small tin of water-biscuits,' said Mr White, almost apologetically, 'and the remains of the bloater paste. It 's all I have with me, but it ought to keep you alive till you get to Lao-chow to-morrow morning. . . . I 'll see you down to the river first and then pick up these things.' He spoke as if he were trying to make little neat plans still against this disorderly and unwonted background. He brushed his splashed coat with a silver clothes-brush, wearing the eagerly safe expression Constantine had seen on his face as he bent over the tie-press the night before last. The orderly man was trying to maintain his quiet impersonal self-respect amid surroundings that humiliated him. Even Constantine understood vaguely that his attacker was himself being attacked. 'Well, I 've done my best,' added Mr White, straightening his back after buckling the last strap of the kit-bag, and looking at Constantine with an ambiguous, almost appealing look.

They left the inn. The steep street that led down to the river between mean, barricaded shops was deserted. The air of it was outraged by the whipping sound of rifle fire—echoes clanked sharply from wall to wall.

'It is not safe—it is not safe,' muttered Constantine, suddenly standing rooted, feeling that his next step must bring him into the path of a bullet.

'It 's safer than a gangrenous leg.' With his great hand, Mr White seized the little Russian's arm and dragged him almost gaily down the steps. Constantine was by now so hopelessly mired in humiliation that he did not even try to disguise his terror. He hung back like a rebellious child, but he was tweaked and twitched along, stumbling behind his rescuer. He was pressed into the little boat. 'Here, take the biscuits—good-bye—good luck,' shouted Mr White, and a smile of real gaiety broke out at last upon his face. The strip of rainy air and water widened between the two friends.

'Strike him dead, God!' said Constantine.

The smile did not fade at once from the Englishman's face, as his legs curiously crumpled into a
kneeling position. He seemed trying to kneel on
air; he clutched at his breast with one hand while
the other hand still waved good-bye; he turned
his alert, smiling face towards Constantine as though
he were going to say again—'Good-bye—good luck.'
Then he fell, head downward, on the steps, the bald
crown of his head just dipping into the water. Mud
was splashed over the coat he had brushed only five
minutes before.

There was a loud outcry from the sampan man
and his wife. They seemed to be calling Constantine's already riveted attention to the fallen
man—still only twenty yards away; they seemed
uncertain whether he would now let them row
yet more quickly away, as they desired, or insist on
returning to the help of his friend.

'Row on—row on,' cried Constantine in Russian
and, to show them what he meant, he snatched up
a spare pole and tried to increase the speed of the
boat as it swerved into the current. Spaces of
water were broadening all about the desert islander
—home on his desert island again at last. As Constantine swayed over the pole, he looked back over
his shoulder and flaunted his head, afraid no more
of the firing now that one blessed bullet had carried
away unpardonable memory out of the brain of
his friend.

WAX

By Gerald Bullett

It was understood in the Croop household that
Grandpa Boydel must be put away. The hour had
struck, and the family were making ready to conduct
the old man to his destiny. Alice, an undersized
child of eleven, bent over a basin half filled with
dirty water, sister Maudie at her elbow waiting with
dull-eyed patience to succeed her in the use of the
greasy flannel; Charles the younger, with an arm
round the shoulder of his twin-brother Alfie, stood
staring at the unwitting cause of this excitement;
and their mother, while giving suck to her two-year-
old baby-girl, kept a sharp eye on everything that
went forward. The room was bare of decoration,
the walls peeling, the floor covered with odd bits of
worn linoleum. It contained a large iron bedstead,
which at night accommodated half the family and
by day served as something to sit on; a deal table
crowded with saucepans, dishes, and dirty crockery;
and three rickety cane chairs. The atmosphere was
pungent with humanity.

Grandpa Boydel was old, older than his age. His
eyes had grown bigger, his nose sharper, his cheeks
more sunken. Rheumatism had gnarled and bent
him, working unseen, with subtle fingers, to make of
that cunning mechanism of bone and muscle and
sinew a conventional emblem of old age. But there

was still eighteen months to run before he would be
qualified for a state pension, and it had long been a
matter of anxious calculation for his daughter, Mrs
Croop, whether that 'little bit of extra' was worth
so much waiting for. The phrase was a euphemism
born of the fact that Liz Croop had seen better days,
days when an extra ten shillings a week had been not
quite the gigantic sum, the impossible affluence, that
it now seemed to her. Looking back on those days,
which she had owed in fact to this very father of hers,
she exaggerated her former dignity, especially in
conversation, until credulous neighbours might have
supposed that an exiled queen had come to dwell
among them. But since the day when a Covent
Garden porter had got her into trouble she had not
had much time for looking back, though enough for
the cultivation of an habitual self-pity. 'A narder-
working little woman you wouldn't find,' she told
the Social Worker who called to inquire after her
comfort. 'And he goes on at me something crool.'
No, she had not had much time for reflection; for
Charley Croop, having got her into trouble once,
and married her for his sins, had been getting her
into trouble (though she did not now call it that)
with appalling regularity ever since. She got out
of these troubles as best and as often as she could,
but eight stubborn souls had contrived, nevertheless,
to get themselves born of her, and five of these eight
—three girls and two gaunt little boys—had sur-
vived. With these pledges of Charley's affection,
with Grandpa, and with Charley himself when he
was not otherwise occupied, she lived in two rooms
of a large brick warren on the south side of Liberty

Street in Whitechapel. Two rooms, when, but for
Grandpa, they might perhaps have made do with
one. There was no chance of that now, for another
little Croop was kicking in her womb, and eight in
one room was more than the authorities permitted.
And Charley, too, was a difficulty. Charley liked
room to move in. 'Too 'andy with 'is 'ands, miss,'
she told the Social Worker. 'See what he done to
me larse night. And all because I got a new blouse
on. Take that thing orf, he says. Want to make
yourself pretty, do yer, he says. And then he
fetches me one on the side of the 'ead. And I 'm
sure,' Mrs Croop ended plaintively, 'I never done
nothing to deserve it. 'Ave a bit of pity, Charley, I
says. But would 'e? Not 'im. Take that bleeder
orf, he says, and sharp about it. And the things
he called me—I dursn't tell you arf. 'Tain't for
myself I mind, miss, but 'snot nice for the chooldren,
miss. Is it, miss? 'Tain't what *I* bin used to,
any'ow, sech foul-mouthed talk!' Mrs Croop was
accused, by her prouder and less expansive neighbours, of 'sucking up to the gentry.' She was a
woman who enjoyed sympathy and was ready to
get what she could in exchange for interesting
confidences. She did not, however, confide to any
stranger her plans for the disposal of Grandpa
Boydel. She had made up her mind about that;
Charley agreed with her; and it would be time enough
to talk when it was all over and done with.

It was clearly no use waiting any longer for that
wonderful little bit of extra. The odds were that
Grandpa, the old artful, would take good care to
eat his pension when he got it; more probable still he

would take and die before he became entitled to draw it; and anyhow it was impossible to wait any longer. For Grandpa himself had become impossible. Liz had done her duty by him. She had looked after him with daughterly devotion ever since—three years ago—he had become incapacitated for work. She had drudged and saved, a halfpenny here and a halfpenny there, to support this extra burden; Charley, who was easygoing enough when sober, had made no protest; and the poorhouse had never been so much as mentioned. She was fond of the old man, and a little in awe of him still; it was nice to have a bit of company of an evening; and, so long as he did what he was told and didn't try to interfere, she could put up with him well enough. If his uselessness got on her nerves, if his grumbling wearied her and his occasional flashes of contempt made her feel small and resentful like the child she had once been, she nevertheless bore with him patiently. But this last manifestation was too much. And now, moreover, was her chance to be rid of a nuisance. Even when eating her bread he had retained his masterful manners. He had never (she fancied) ceased to regard her as an unpromising child. And now the tables were turned. He was the child, and she was in authority. For weeks past he had sat moodily in his corner, lost in a dull dream. His large blue eyes were empty of recognition; his hands groped aimlessly in front of him; he dribbled and dropped his food, and seldom answered when spoken to, and then without intelligence. In short, Grandpa had lost his wits, declared Mrs Croop, and there was

no doing anything with him. He must be put
away. It was sad, but exciting; the children, in
their quiet way, enjoyed the sense of crisis; and
Mrs Croop thought eagerly of her coming release.

'He 'll be ever so nice and comfortable where
he 's going,' she assured her children. 'Crysake
stop that snivelling, Alfie, or I 'll skin the back orf
of yer!' She cuffed Alfie vigorously. 'Ever so
comfortable, he will. Won't you, Grandpa? Eh?
Now, Alice, my gal, be quick and get that face
washed if you want to come to the oresepital to see
your Grandpa orf. Don't stand there gaping, girl!
J'ear me? And you, Maudie, can take and give
'im a wipe down, see? Got your boots on, Grandpa?
Thass right.'

2

Muddled but not too unhappy, heedless of everything external and quite unaware of the fate in store
for him, Grandpa Boydel sat quiet in his corner.
For longer now than he could easily remember,
his private being, the city of himself, had been
strangely secluded from the outer world, walled
round with quietness. All sounds were agreeably
dimmed: he missed, and was glad to miss, the
scraping of the children's chairs on the floor, the
baby's howling, the strident voice of his daughter
enjoining good behaviour. The street noises that
had irked him for so long—the shouting and the
rumble—were now ended. It was as if those
hitherto snorting roaring vehicles were being moved
by magic over a road of silk; he watched them from

the window, and marvelled. Days were no longer wearisome; he had defeated weariness by surrendering to it, troubling no more to assert himself against a world insolently loud and young. Nights held no terrors; even the long hours of waking were quiet and drowsy and filled with dreams, and the snoring of Alfie and Charles, who shared his bed, could not disturb this new-found privacy. His sense of smell was also dulled—merciful dispensation to a man who must spend his last years cabined with the Croops.

At first these immunities had been unwelcome to him; their gradual approach had made him uneasy and short-tempered, and the shock of their sudden final completion had puzzled and frightened him. But he soon came to terms with the change, and learned to take a secret satisfaction in it. Deaf, that 's me. Deaf as a post. When he realized the comfort of it he began to think himself rather clever to be deaf. There was no one and nothing in the world worth listening to; so why worry? But even this gleam of vanity, this glancing reference to an outer world, became, as the silent days went on, muffled out of existence; and deafness, itself forgotten, was at last no more than a screen against which the drama of memory and dream incessantly moved. He forgot the world; he withdrew into himself, which was his past; images long lost came crowding upon him, so that, in time, not only were the surrounding voices mute, but the faces of his own people were strange in his sight. When Liz approached him with mouthing gestures, he averted his eyes distastefully, asking of memory: Who is this woman, and why am I here with her? And by emptying his sight of her he made her vanish, so that she had at last, she and her children with her, no more substance than the fancies with which he peopled the hospitable silence. Once or twice he went so far as to wonder if he were dead and disembodied, and with groping fingers he questioned the air about him; but the shooting pains in his head distracted him from such theories as that, and sent him grumbling to his accustomed corner. There, when the pains subsided, he could lapse back into the odd disjointed story of himself, a panorama of which he did not stop to ask the meaning. He was lost, lost to himself: he could not have told you so much as his name. But the clock of his life had become erratic, now reversing its movement, now jerking erratically from one point to another, so that vital moments were restored to him in a series of sharp bright musical sensations: a day in the country as a child; a summer's night; the touch of a girl's hair on his face; a thrashing from his father; ecstasy, anguish, a young woman lying marbled in her coffin; and a voice that kept saying again and again, quite unmeaningly: Saturday drill.

'Whatcher say, Grandpa?' screamed Liz, with sudden impatience. Arms akimbo she bent towards him menacingly, putting her face close to his. He turned his eyes away, muttering. 'Oh lumme,' said Liz, 'you and your blasted Saturday drill!' Remembering that he was to be put away, and this very morning, she yielded to a kindlier impulse and added with jocular humour: 'Want to go for a souljer, do yer? No, it's the Loony Bin for you, pore ole rudder!' Sad though it was, the prospect

cheered her. Her glance flashed round the room as
she made her final dispositions. 'Alfie and Charley
are to stay 'ere. Now 'old yer noise, Alfie, or I 'll
'it yer. Maudie comes with me. See, Maudie?
And Alice 'll come as fur as the tram with us and
that 's all. You 're to come back, Alice, and give
an eye to Baby. See? Thass right.'

Grandpa Boydel found himself being persuaded
to stand up. The woman was shouting at him.
The little girls looked excited and self-important:
they were ready for the outing. The little boys
could do nothing but stare. He could hear nothing
of what the woman said, and cared nothing. Not
troubling his head with questions and answers, he
suffered himself to be led out of the room, and down
the stairs, and into the sunlit squalor of Liberty.

3

It was a pleasant morning for a walk, but within
five minutes of the setting-out Grandpa Boydel was
wishing himself home again in his dingy corner.
The crisp April air stung him into a higher degree
of wakefulness than he had known for weeks, and
the unaccustomed exercise quickened his slow blood.
He began to be nettled by a suspicion, dimly formed,
that he was being led back, against his own desire,
to a life that he had been glad to leave. This shrill
woman and these large-eyed hungry children, they
would not let him rest, but must be for ever urging
him on with impatient or coaxing gestures. They
dragged at his arms; they shouted; he could see them

shouting. And when he wanted to sit down in the
road and forget everything, forget this new-minted
morning and return to his world within, they all
three pressed savagely upon him, and held him up,
and the woman's face became an angry grinning
mask. His bones ached. He longed to lie down
and be at rest. Fixing his eyes on the woman he
tried to send his thought to her across the chasm,
having, in this silent world, lost the habit and power
of voluntary speech. He saw her mouthing at him
and was intolerably puzzled. She drew back a step:
something hit him in the face, and he cowered away
from it. He surrendered; he submitted; his legs
were set in motion again, and after a weary treadmill
dream he found himself sitting in a tram. The
woman was at his side, and the elder of the two girls
stared accusingly at him from the opposite seat.
The woman was red-eyed; her cheeks were smeared.
Pore father, I didn't ought to 'ave 'it 'im, thought
Liz Croop. And she gave him a quick sidelong
glance, as though fearing that he might suddenly
change back into the masterful parent of whom she
had once stood in awe. But she was soon herself
again, and mistress of the situation. 'We want to
get orf at the orsepital,' she had told the conductor.
And now she rose, briskly practical. 'Kerm on,
Maudie! Give us an 'and wiv Grandpa, cantcher?'
She rebuked her children's offences before they were
committed: it saved time afterwards. 'Now, up
yer come, Grandpa! None of that nonsense this
time. J'ear me?'

He did not hear her, but it was all one. He had
no mind to resist her now, being busy with his

thoughts. Soon, moreover, he was allowed to sit down again. A small square room it was, crowded with sick people. At intervals a young man in a white overall put his red head round the edge of the inner door and said cheerfully: 'Who 's next?'

One by one the numbers diminished, and at last it was Grandpa Boydel's turn.

'Look lively!' said the red-haired young man. He was a cheerful fellow; he found life endlessly amusing. 'Bring him in here then.' Liz and her Maudie led their prisoner in to the surgery. 'Now, what 's wrong with the old gentleman? Rheumatism? Pains in the head? Speak up, uncle!'

Mrs Croop intervened. 'We want to put him away, sir. He 's loony, sir, pore old soul. That 's 'ow it is, sir.'

'Oh, so that 's it,' said the young man. He waited to hear more.

'He don't reckernize us, sir. Not none of us. And I 've been a good girl to him, as Gawd 's my judge. Don't answer when spoke to, and his 'abits ain't so nice either. 'Tisn't safe for my girls, that 's what I say. I 'm sure I done my best for 'im, but "Saturday drill" is all he 'll answer when spoke to—if you ever heard of sech a thing! It don't make sense to me and I can't do wiv 'im any longer, and that 's Gaw's troof. Not safe in our beds, we ain't!'

'You mean he 's violent?'

'Beg pardon, sir?'

'Has he been attacking you? Misbehaving himself?'

' 'E don't answer when spoke to, sir,' said Mrs

Croop, impatient of these sophistries. 'You can
see for yerself he don't answer,' she whined.

'Right you are,' said the young man, with extreme cheerfulness. 'Now just step into the other
room, you two. And I 'll call you when I want you.'

So Grandpa Boydel was left alone with his red-
headed young man, and his chance of a rest was
further off than ever. This did not much distress
him, for even his apathy was now in danger of
defeat. He frowned, averting his eyes; but this
new tormentor was not to be put off by tricks of that
kind. The patient was kept very busy. He was
made to sit down, made to stand up, made to sit
down again. Questions were bawled at him; he
shook his head. He became frightened, wondering
whether this young man, like Liz, would lose
patience with him and slap his face; but, except for
a smart blow above the knee-cap with the edge of
his hand, the young man offered him no violence.
Nor did he appear to be impatient: his slight frown
did not suggest anger. He approached his patient's
ears with an electric torch as small as a small pencil
. . . and three minutes later a second young man
appeared from nowhere, a curious little dish was
held against the side of Grandpa Boydel's neck, and
Red Head got to work with a syringe.

The patient bleated.

'A bit too warm for you?' said the operator.
'Sorry, uncle. But we 're breaking through.' He
refilled his syringe, whistling with satisfaction.

Grandpa Boydel sat alone in his silence. But
ruthless war was being waged on that sanctuary.
The roar of water in his ears became punctuated by

a tearing and a crackling; and then, suddenly, it was as if the whole earth went up in one hideous explosion. The world, with its trampling feet, its blare of trumpets, its multitudinous drums, rushed in upon him. His ears were open.

'Now for the other one,' said the young man. 'A bath wouldn't hurt you, uncle, if you keep yourself warm afterwards. I 'd try one if I were you. D' you know,' he added confidentially, 'there 's enough wax in these ears of yours to stock a beehive. Or was, a moment ago.'

Grandpa Boydel smiled vaguely, and shook his head. He was dazed after his long swift journey; dazed, like a man just emerged from a dark and quiet pit. The world was loud around him: it would take a little getting used to. 'How did I get here, sir?' he ventured to ask. The sound of his voice astonished him.

'Hi, you!—you can come in now,' shouted the red-headed young man, putting away his syringe. 'The old gentleman's asking for you.' A gasp, a sniff, and the two Croops came shuffling in. 'Here he is, right as a trivet,' cried the young man, greeting them boisterously. 'Undernourished, of course. But that goes without saying.' He laughed; for it was no use being mournful about it.

'Whadjer mean?' demanded Mrs Croop, with an ugly look. 'Jou mean to say——'

'He 's fine. He 'll do. You can take him home. That 's what I mean,' said the young man. 'Very difficult case,' he added, with a wink at his assistant. 'But I 've dealt with it, so off you go. Good-bye, uncle—don't forget about that bath.'

Mrs Croop stared at Grandpa Boydel, and the decision with which he returned the stare unnerved her. All too evidently a father had been restored to her. 'What, better again, Grandpa, are yer?' she said timidly. 'Fancy that now!' She glanced helplessly round the room. She was beaten: there was nothing for it but to wait for the little bit of extra. 'Well,' she concluded wearily, 'you 'd better come along home then, I s'pose.'

Unsteadily but unaided, Grandpa Boydel rose to his feet. 'I 'll come when I 'm ready, my gal,' he answered. 'And I could do with a bite of food, too.'

In single file, Liz leading, they emerged from the hospital. Maudie Croop, perplexed in the extreme by this drastic change of plan, could no longer withhold a question.

'Muvver!'

'What is it now?'

'Ain't Grandpa going in the Loony Bin, Muvver?'

'Eh?' said Grandpa sharply.

But he had heard the question imperfectly, and it was not repeated.

THE GHOST

By RICHARD HUGHES

HE killed me quite easily by crashing my head on
the cobbles. *Bang!* Lord, what a fool I was! All
my hate went out with that first bang: a fool to
have kicked up that fuss just because I had found
him with another woman. And now he was doing
this to me—*bang!* That was the second one, and
with it *everything* went out.

My sleek young soul must have glistened somewhat in the moonlight: for I saw him look up from
the body in a fixed sort of way. That gave me an
idea: I would haunt him. All my life I had been
scared of ghosts: now I was one myself, I would get
a bit of my own back. *He* never was: he said there
weren't such things as ghosts. Oh, weren't there!
I 'd soon teach him. John stood up, still staring
in front of him: I could see him plainly: gradually all
my hate came back. I thrust my face close up
against his: but he didn't seem to see it, he just
stared. Then he began to walk forward, as if to
walk through me: and I was afeard. Silly, for me—
a spirit—to be afeard of his solid flesh: but there
you are, fear doesn't act as you would expect, ever:
and I gave back before him, then slipped aside to let
him pass. Almost he was lost in the street-shadows
before I recovered myself and followed him.

And yet I don't think he could have given me

245

the slip: there was still something between us that drew me to him — willy - nilly, you might say, I followed him up to High Street, and down Lily Lane.

Lily Lane was all shadows: but yet I could still see him as clear as if it was daylight. Then my courage came back to me: I quickened my pace till I was ahead of him—turned round, flapping my hands and making a moaning sort of noise like the ghosts did I 'd read of. He began to smile a little, in a sort of satisfied way: but yet he didn't seem properly to see me. Could it be that his hard disbelief in ghosts made him so that he *couldn't* see me? '*Hoo!*' I whistled through my small teeth. '*Hoo! Murderer! Murderer!*'—Someone flung up a top window. 'Who 's that?' she called. 'What 's the matter?'—So other people could hear, at any rate. But I kept silent: I wouldn't give him away—not yet. And all the time he walked straight forward, smiling to himself. He never had any conscience, I said to myself: here he is with new murder on his mind, smiling as easy as if it was nothing. But there was a sort of hard look about him, *all* the same.

It was odd, my being a ghost so suddenly, when ten minutes ago I was a living woman: and now, walking on air, with the wind clear and wet between my shoulder - blades. Ha - ha! I gave a regular shriek and a screech of laughter, it all felt so funny . . . surely John must have heard *that*: but no, he just turned the corner into Pole Street.

All along Pole Street the plane-trees were shedding their leaves: and then I knew what I would do. I made those dead leaves rise up on their thin edges, as if the wind was doing it. All along Pole Street they followed him, pattering on the roadway with their five dry fingers. But John just stirred among them with his feet, and went on: and I followed him: for as I said, there was still some tie between us that drew me.

Once only he turned and seemed to see me: there was a sort of recognition in his face: but no fear, only triumph. 'You 're glad you 've killed me,' thought I, 'but I 'll make you sorry!'

And then all at once the fit left me. A nice sort of Christian, I, scarcely fifteen minutes dead and still thinking of revenge, instead of preparing to meet my Lord! Some sort of voice in me seemed to say: 'Leave him, Millie, leave him alone *before it is too late* !' Too late? Surely I could leave him when I wanted to? Ghosts haunt as they like, don't they? I 'd make just one more attempt at terrifying him: then I 'd give it up and think about going to heaven.

He stopped, and turned, and faced me full.

I pointed at him with both my hands.

'John!' I cried. 'John! It 's all very well for you to stand there, and smile, and stare with your great fish-eyes and think you 've won: but you haven't! I 'll do you. I 'll *finish* you! I 'll——'

I stopped, and laughed a little. Windows shot up. 'Who 's that? What 's the row?'—and so on. They had all heard: but he only turned and walked on.

'Leave him, Millie, before it is too late,' the voice said.

So that 's what the voice meant: leave him before I betrayed his secret, and had the crime of revenge

on my soul. Very well, I would: I 'd leave him.
I 'd go straight to heaven before any accident
happened. So I stretched up my two arms, and
tried to float into the air: but at once some force
seized me like a great gust, and I was swept away
after him down the street. There was something
stirring in me that still bound me to him.

Strange, that I should be so real to all those
people that they thought me still a living woman:
but he—who had most reason to fear me, why, it
seemed doubtful whether he even saw me. And
where was he going to, right up the desolate long
length of Pole Street?—He turned into Rope Street.
I saw a blue lamp: that was the police station.

'Oh, Lord,' I thought, 'I 've done it! Oh, Lord,
he 's going to give himself up!'

'You drove him to it,' the voice said. 'You fool,
did you think he didn't see you? What did you
expect? Did you think he 'd shriek, and gibber
with fear at you? Did you think your John was a
coward?—Now his death is on your head!'

'I didn't do it, I didn't!' I cried. 'I never wished
him any harm, never, not *really*! I wouldn't hurt
him, not for anything, I wouldn't. Oh, John, don't
stare like that. There 's still time . . . time!'

And all this while he stood in the door, looking
at me, while the policemen came out and stood
round him in a ring. He couldn't escape now.

'Oh, John,' I sobbed, 'forgive me! I didn't mean
to do it! It was jealousy, John, what did it . . .
because I loved you.'

Still the police took no notice of him.

'That 's her,' said one of them in a husky voice.

'Done it with a hammer, she done it . . . brained him. But, Lord, isn't her face ghastly? Haunted, like.'

'Look at her 'ead, poor girl. Looks as if she tried to do herself in with the 'ammer, after.'

Then the sergeant stepped forward.

'Anything you say will be taken down as evidence against you.'

'John!' I cried softly, and held out my arms—for at last his face had softened.

'Holy Mary!' said one policeman, crossing himself. 'She 's seeing him!'

'They 'll not hang her,' another whispered. 'Did you notice her condition, poor girl?'

SENSE OF HUMOUR

By V. S. PRITCHETT

IT started one Saturday. I was working new ground and I decided I 'd stay at the hotel the week-end and put in an appearance at church.

' All alone? ' asked the girl in the cash desk.

It had been raining since ten o'clock.

' Mr Good has gone,' she said. ' And Mr Straker. He usually stays with us. But he 's gone.'

' That 's where they make their mistake,' I said. ' They think they know everything because they 've been on the road all their lives.'

' You 're a stranger here, aren't you? ' she said.

' I am,' I said. ' And so are you.'

' How do you know that? '

' Obvious,' I said. ' Way you speak.'

' Let 's have a light,' she said.

' So 's I can see you,' I said.

That was how it started. The rain was pouring down on to the glass roof of the office.

She 'd a cup of tea steaming on the register. I said I 'd have one, too. ' What 's it going to be and I 'll tell them,' she said, but I said just a cup of tea.

' I 'm T.T.,' I said. ' Too many soakers on the road as it is.'

I was staying there the week-end so as to be sharp on the job on Monday morning. What 's more it pays in these small towns to turn up at church on

Sundays, Presbyterians in the morning, Methodists in the evening. Say 'Good morning' and 'Good evening' to them. 'Ah!' they say. 'Church-goer! Pleased to see that! T.T., too.' Makes them have a second look at your lines in the morning. 'Did you like our service, Mister—er—er?' 'Humphrey's my name.' 'Mr Humphrey.' See? It pays.

'Come into the office, Mr Humphrey,' she said, bringing me a cup. 'Listen to that rain.'

I went inside.

'Sugar?' she said.

'Three,' I said. We settled to a very pleasant chat. She told me all about herself, and we got on next to families.

'My father was on the railway,' she said.

'"The engine gave a squeal,"' I said. '"The driver took out his pocket-knife and scraped him off the wheel."'

'That 's it,' she said. 'And what is your father's business? You said he had a business.'

'Undertaker,' I said.

'Undertaker?' she said.

'Why not?' I said. 'Good business. Seasonable like everything else. High class undertaker,' I said.

She was looking at me all the time wondering what to say and suddenly she went into fits of laughter.

'Undertaker,' she said, covering her face with her hands and went on laughing.

'Here,' I said. 'What 's up?'

'Undertaker!' she laughed and laughed. Struck me as being a pretty thin joke.

'Don't mind me,' she said. 'I 'm Irish.'

'Oh, I see,' I said. 'That 's it, is it? Got a sense of humour.'

Then the bell rang and a woman called out 'Muriel! Muriel!' and there was a motor bike making a row at the front door.

'All right,' the girl called out. 'Excuse me a moment, Mr Humphrey,' she said. 'Don't think me rude. That 's my boy friend. He wants the bird turning up like this.'

She went out but there was her boy friend looking over the window ledge into the office. He had come in. He had a cape on, soaked with rain, and the rain was in beads in his hair. It was fair hair. It stood up on end. He 'd been economizing on the brilliantine. He didn't wear a hat. He gave me a look and I gave him a look. I didn't like the look of him. And he didn't like the look of me. A smell of oil and petrol and rain and mackintosh came off him. He had a big mouth with thick lips. They were very red. I recognized him at once as the son of the man who ran the Kounty Garage. I saw this chap when I put my car away. The firm's car. A lock-up, because of the samples. Took me ten minutes to ram the idea into his head. He looked as though he 'd never heard of samples. Slow—you know the way they are in the provinces. Slow on the job.

'Oh, Colin,' says she. 'What do you want?'

'Nothing,' the chap said. 'I came in to see you.'

'To see me?'

'Just to see you.'

'You came in this morning.'

'That 's right,' he said. He went red. 'You was busy,' he said.

'Well, I 'm busy now,' she said.

He bit his tongue, and licked his big lips over and took a look at me. Then he started grinning.

'I got the new bike, Muriel,' he said. 'I 've got it outside.

'It 's just come down from the works,' he said.

'The laddie wants you to look at his bike,' I said. So she went out and had a look at it.

When she came back she had got rid of him.

'Listen to that rain,' she said.

'Lord, I 'm fed up with this line,' she said.

'What line?' I said. 'The hotel line?'

'Yes,' she said. 'I 'm fed right up to the back teeth with it.'

'And you 've got good teeth,' I said.

'There 's not the class of person there used to be in it,' she said. 'All our family have got good teeth.'

'Not the class?'

'I 've been in it five years and there 's not the same class at all. You never meet any fellows.'

'Well,' said I. 'If they 're like that half-wit at the garage, they 're nothing to be struck on. And you 've met me.'

I said it to her like that.

'Oh,' says she. 'It isn't as bad as that yet.'

It was cold in the office. She used to sit all day in her overcoat. She was a smart girl with a big friendly chin and a second one coming and her forehead and nose were covered with freckles. She had copper-coloured hair too. She got her shoes through the trade from Duke's traveller and her clothes, too, off the Hollenborough mantle man. I told her I could do her better stockings than the ones she 'd got on. She got a good reduction on everything. Twenty-five or thirty-three and a third. She had her expenses cut right back. I took her to the pictures that night in the car. I made Colin get the car out for me.

'That boy wanted me to go on the back of his bike. On a night like this,' she said.

'Oh,' she said, when we got to the pictures. 'Two shillings's too much. Let's go into the one-and-sixes at the side and we can nip across into the two-shillings when the lights go down.'

'Fancy your father being an undertaker,' she said in the middle of the show. And she started laughing as she had laughed before.

She had her head screwed on all right. She said: 'Some girls have no pride once the lights go down.'

Every time I went to that town I took a box of something. Samples, mostly, they didn't cost me anything.

'Don't thank me,' I said. 'Thank the firm.'

Every time I took her out I pulled the blinds in the back seat of the car to hide the samples. That chap Colin used to give us oil and petrol. He used to give me a funny look. Fishy sort of small eyes he'd got. Always looking miserable. Then we would go off. Sunday was her free day. Not that driving's any holiday for me. And, of course, the firm paid. She used to take me down to see her family for the day. Start in the morning, and taking it you had dinner and tea there, a day's outing cost us nothing. Her father was something on the railway, retired. He had a long stocking, somewhere, but her sister, the one that was married, had had her share already.

He had a tumour after his wife died and they just played upon the old man's feelings. It wasn't right. She wouldn't go near her sister and I don't blame her, taking money like that. Just played upon the old man's feelings.

Every time I was up there Colin used to come in looking for her.

'Oh, Colin,' I used to say. 'Done my car yet?' He knew where he got off with me.

'No, now, I can't, Colin. I tell you I'm going out with Mr Humphrey,' she used to say to him. I heard her.

'He keeps on badgering me,' she said to me.

'You leave him to me,' I said.

'No, he's all right,' she said.

'You let me know if there's any trouble with Colin,' I said. 'Seems to be a harum-scarum sort of half-wit to me,' I said.

'And he spends every penny he makes,' she said.

Well, we know that sort of thing is all right while it lasts, I told her, but the trouble is that it doesn't last.

We were always meeting Colin on the road. I took no notice of it first of all and then I grew suspicious and awkward at always meeting him. He had a new motor bicycle. It was an Indian, a scarlet thing that he used to fly over the moor with, flat out. Muriel and I used to go out over the moor to Ingley Wood in the firm's Morris—I had a customer out that way.

'May as well do a bit of business while you're about it,' I said.

'About what?' she said.

'Ah ha!' I said.

'That's what Colin wants to know,' I said.

Sure enough, coming back we 'd hear him popping and backfiring close behind us, and I put out my hand to stop him and keep him following us, biting our dirt.

'I see his little game,' I said. 'Following us.'

So I saw to it that he did follow. We could hear him banging away behind us and the traffic is thick on the Ingley road in the afternoon.

'Oh, let him pass,' Muriel said. 'I can't stand those dirty things banging in my ears.'

I waved him on and past he flew with his scarf flying out, blazing red, into the traffic. 'We 're doing 58 ourselves,' she said, leaning across to look.

'Powerful buses those,' I said. 'Any fool can do it if he 's got the power. Watch me step on it.'

But we did not catch Colin. Half an hour later he passed us coming back. Cut right in between us and a lorry—I had to brake hard. I damn nearly killed him. His ears were red with the wind. He didn't wear a hat. I got after him as soon as I could but I couldn't touch him.

Nearly every week-end I was in that town seeing my girl, that fellow was hanging around. He came into the bar on Saturday nights, he poked his head into the office on Sunday mornings. It was a sure bet that if we went out in the car he would pass us on the road. Every time we would hear that scarlet thing roar by like a horse-stinger. It didn't matter where we were. He passed us on the main road, he met us down the side roads. There was a little cliff under oak-trees at May Ponds, she said, where the

view was pretty. And there, soon after we got
there, was Colin on the other side of the water,
watching us. Once we found him sitting on his
bike, just as though he were waiting for us.

'You been here in a car?' I said.

'No, motor bike,' she said and blushed. 'Cars
can't follow in these tracks.'

She knew a lot of places in that country. Some of
the roads weren't roads at all and were bad for tyres
and I didn't want the firm's car scratched by bushes,
but you would have thought Colin could read what
was in her mind. For nine times out of ten he was
there. It got on my nerves. It was a red, roaring,
powerful thing and he opened it full out.

'I'm going to speak to Colin,' I said. 'I won't
have him annoying you.'

'He's not annoying me,' she said. 'I've got a
sense of humour.'

'Here, Colin,' I said one evening when I put the
car away. 'What's the idea?'

He was taking off his overalls. He pretended he
did not know what I was talking about. He had a
way of rolling his eyeballs, as if they had got wet and
loose in his head, while he was speaking to me and
you never knew if it was sweat or oil on his face. It
was always pale, with high colour on his cheeks and
very red lips.

'Miss MacFarlane doesn't like being followed,' I
said.

He dropped his jaw and gaped at me. I could not
tell whether he was being very surprised or very sly.
I used to call him 'Marbles' because when he spoke
he seemed to have a lot of marbles in his mouth.

Then he said he never went to the places we went to, except by accident. He wasn't following us, he said, but we were following him. We never let him alone, he said. Everywhere he went, he said, we were there. Take last Saturday, he said, we were following him for miles down the by-pass, he said. 'But you passed us first and then sat down in front,' I said. 'I went to Ingley Wood,' he said. 'And you followed me there.' 'No, we didn't,' I said, 'Miss MacFarlane decided to go there.'

He said he did not want to complain but fair was fair. 'I suppose you know,' he said, 'that you have taken my girl off me. Well, you can leave *me* alone, can't you?'

'Here,' I said. 'One minute! Not so fast! You said I 've taken Miss MacFarlane from you. Well, she was never your girl. She only knew you in a friendly way.'

'She was my girl,' was all he said.

He was pouring oil into my engine. He had some cotton wool in one hand and the can in the other. He wiped up the green oil that had overflowed, screwed on the cap, pulled down the bonnet and whistled to himself.

I went back to Muriel and told her what Colin had said.

'I don't like trouble,' I said.

'Don't you worry,' she said. 'I had to have someone to go to all these places with before you came. Couldn't stick in here all day Sunday.'

'Ah,' I said. 'That 's it, is it? You 've been to all these places with him?'

'Yes,' she said. 'And he keeps on going to them. He 's sloppy about me.'

'Good God,' I said. 'Sentimental memories.'

I felt sorry for that fellow. He knew it was hopeless, but he loved her. I suppose he couldn't help himself. Well, it takes all sorts to make a world, as my old mother used to say. If we were all alike it wouldn't do. Some men can't save money. It just runs through their fingers. He couldn't save money so he lost her. I suppose all he thought of was love.

I could have been friends with that fellow. As it was I put a lot of business his way. I didn't want him to get the wrong idea about me. We're all human after all.

We didn't have any more trouble with Colin after this until Bank Holiday. I was going to take her down to see my family. The old man's getting a bit past it now and has given up living over the shop. He's living out on the Barnum Road, beyond the tram stop. We were going down in the firm's car, as per usual, but something went wrong with the mag. and Colin had not got it right for the holiday. I was wild about this. What's the use of a garage who can't do a rush job for the holidays! What's the use of being an old customer if they're going to let you down! I went for Colin bald-headed.

'You knew I wanted it,' I said. 'It's no use trying to put me off with a tale about the stuff not coming down from the works. I've heard that one before.'

I told him he'd got to let me have another car, because he'd let me down. I told him I wouldn't pay his account. I said I'd take my business away from him. But there wasn't a car to be had in the town because of the holiday. I could have knocked the fellow down. After the way I 'd sent business to him.

Then I saw through his little game. He knew Muriel and I were going to my people and he had done this to stop it. The moment I saw this I let him know that it would take more than him to stop me doing what I wanted.

I said:

'Right. I shall take the amount of Miss Mac-Farlane's train fare and my own from the account at the end of the month.'

I said:

'You may run a garage, but you don't run the railway service.'

I was damned angry going by train. I felt quite lost on the railway after having a car. It was crowd-ed with trippers too. It was slow—stopping at all the stations. The people come in, they tread all over your feet, they make you squeeze up till you 're crammed against the window, and the women stick out their elbows and fidget. And then the expense! A return for two runs you into just over a couple of quid. I could have murdered Colin.

We got there at last. We walked up from the tram stop. Mother was at the window and let us in.

'This is Miss MacFarlane,' I said.

And mother said:

'Oh, pleased to meet you. We 've heard a lot about you.'

'Oh,' mother said to me, giving me a kiss, 'are you tired? You haven't had your tea, have you? Sit down. Have this chair, dear. It 's more comfortable.'

'Well, my boy?' my father said.

'Want a wash?' my father said. 'We 've got a wash basin downstairs,' he said. 'I used not to mind about washing upstairs before. Now I couldn't do without it. Funny how your ideas change as you get older.'

'How 's business?' he said.

'Mustn't grumble,' I said. 'How's yours?'

'You knew,' he said, 'we took off the horses: except for one or two of the older families we have got motors now.'

But he 'd told me that the last time I was there. I 'd been at him for years about motor hearses.

'You 've forgotten I used to drive them,' I said.

'Bless me, so you did,' he said.

He took me up to my room. He showed me everything he had done to the house. 'Your mother likes it,' he said. 'The traffic 's company for her. You know what your mother is for company.'

Then he gives me a funny look.

'Who 's the girl?' he says.

My mother came in then and said:

'She 's pretty, Arthur.'

'Of course she 's pretty,' I said. 'She 's Irish.'

'Oh,' said the old man. 'Irish! Got a sense of humour, eh?'

'She wouldn't be marrying me if she hadn't,' I said. And then I gave *them* a look.

'Marrying her, did you say?' exclaimed my father.

'Any objection?' I said.

'Now, Ernest dear,' said my mother. 'Leave the boy alone. Come down while I pop the kettle on.'

She was terribly excited.

'Miss MacFarlane,' the old man said.

'No sugar, thank you, Mrs Humphrey. I beg your pardon, Mr Humphrey?'

'The Glen Hotel at Swansea, I don't suppose you know that?' my father said.

'I wondered if you did being in the catering line.'

'It doesn't follow she knows every hotel,' my mother said.

'Forty years ago,' the old man said, 'I was staying at the Glen in Swansea and the head waiter . . .'

'Oh, no, not that one. I 'm sure Miss MacFarlane doesn't want to hear that one,' my mother said.

'How 's business with you, Mr Humphrey?' said Muriel. 'We passed a large cemetery near the station.'

'Dad's Ledger,' I said.

'The whole business has changed so that you wouldn't know it, in my lifetime,' said my father. 'Silver fittings have gone clean out. Every one wants simplicity nowadays. Restraint. Dignity,' my father said.

'Prices did it,' my father said.

'The war,' he said.

'You couldn't get the wood,' he said.

'Take ordinary mahogany, just an ordinary piece of mahogany. Or teak,' he said. 'Take teak. Or walnut.'

'You can certainly see the world go by in this room,' I said to my mother.

'It never stops,' she said.

Now it was all bicycles over the new concrete road from the gun factory. Then traction engines and cars. They came up over the hill where the A.A.

man stands and choked up round the tram stop. It was mostly holiday traffic. Everything with a wheel on it was out.

'On this stretch,' my father told me, 'they get three accidents a week.' There was an ambulance station at the cross-roads.

We had hardly finished talking about this, in fact the old man was still saying that something ought to be done, when the telephone rang.

'Name of MacFarlane?' the voice said on the wire.

'No. Humphrey,' my father said. 'There is a Miss MacFarlane here.'

'There 's a man named Colin Mitchell lying seriously injured in an accident at the Cottage Hospital, gave me the name of MacFarlane as his nearest relative.'

That was the police. On to it at once. That fellow Colin had followed us down by road.

Cry, I never heard a girl cry, as Muriel cried, when we came back from the hospital. He had died in the ambulance. Cutting in, the old game he used to play on me. Clean off the saddle and under the Birmingham bus. The blood was everywhere, they said. People were still looking at it when we went by. Head on. What a mess! Don't let 's talk about it.

She wanted to see him but they said 'No.' There wasn't anything recognizable to see. She put her arms round my neck and cried 'Colin. Colin,' as if I were Colin, and clung to me. I was feeling sick myself. I held her tight and I kissed her and I thought, 'Holiday ruined.'

'Damn fool man,' I thought. 'Poor devil,' I thought.

'I knew he 'd do something like this.'

'There, there,' I said to her. 'Don't think about Colin.'

Didn't she love me, I said, and not Colin? Hadn't she got me? She said, yes, she had. And she loved me. But, 'Oh, Colin! Oh, Colin!' she cried. 'And Colin's mother,' she cried. 'Oh, it 's terrible.' She cried and cried.

We put her to bed and I sat with her and my mother kept coming in.

'Leave her to me,' I said. 'I understand her.'

Before they went to bed they both came in and looked at her. She lay sobbing with her head in the pillow.

I could quite understand her being upset. Colin was a decent fellow. He was always doing things for her. He mended her electric lamp and he riveted the stem of a wine-glass so that you couldn't see the break. He used to make things for her. He was very good with his hands.

She lay on her side with her face burning and feverish with misery and crying, scalded by the salt, and her lips shrivelled up. I put my arm under her neck and I stroked her forehead. She groaned. Sometimes she shivered and sometimes she clung to me, crying, 'Oh, Colin! Colin!'

My arm ached with the cramp and I had a crick in my back, sitting in the awkward way I was on the bed. It was late. There was nothing to do but to ache and sit watching her and thinking. It is funny the way your mind drifts. When I was kissing her and watching her I was thinking out who I 'd show our new autumn range to first. Her hand held my

wrist tight and when I kissed her I got her tears on
my lips. They burned and stung. Her neck and
shoulders were soft and I could feel her breath hot
out of her nostrils on the back of my hand. Ever
noticed how hot a woman's breath gets when she 's
crying? I drew out my hand and lay down beside
her and 'Oh, Colin, Colin,' she sobbed, turning over
and clinging to me. And so I lay there, listening
to the traffic, staring at the ceiling and shivering
whenever the picture of Colin shooting right off that
damned red thing into the bus came into my mind—
until I did not hear the traffic any more, or see the
ceiling any more, or think any more, but a change
happened—I don't know when. This Colin thing
seemed to have knocked the bottom out of everything and I had a funny feeling we were going down
and down and down in a lift. And the further we
went the hotter and softer she got. Perhaps it was
when I found with my hands that she had very big
breasts. But it was like being on the mail steamer
and feeling engines start up under your feet, thump-
ing louder and louder. You can feel it in every vein
of your body. Her mouth opened and her tears
dried. Her breath came through her open mouth
and her voice was blind and husky. 'Colin, Colin,
Colin,' she said, and her fingers were hooked into me.
I got out and turned the key in the door.

In the morning I left her sleeping. It did not
matter to me what my father might have heard in
the night, but still I wondered. She would hardly
let me touch her before that. I told her I was sorry
but she shut me up. I was afraid of her. I was
afraid of mentioning Colin. I wanted to go out of

the house there and then and tell someone everything. Did she love Colin all the time? Did she think I was Colin? And every time I thought of that poor devil covered over with a white sheet in the hospital mortuary, a kind of picture of her and me under the sheets with love came into my mind. I couldn't separate the two things. Just as though it had all come from Colin.

I 'd rather not talk any more about that. I never talked to Muriel about it. I waited for her to say something but she didn't. She didn't say a word.

The next day was a bad day. It was grey and hot and the air smelled of oil fumes from the road. There 's always a mess to clear up when things like this happen. I had to see to it. I had the job of ringing up the boy's mother. But I got round that, thank God, by ringing up the garage and getting them to go round and see the old lady. My father is useless when things are like this. I was the whole morning on the phone: to the hospital, the police, the coroner—and he stood fussing beside me, jerking up and down like a fat india-rubber ball. I found my mother washing up at the sink and she said:

'That poor boy's mother! I can't stop thinking of her.' Then my father comes in and says—just as though I was a customer:

'Of course if Mrs Mitchell desires it we can have the remains of the deceased conveyed to his house by one of our new specially sprung motor hearses and can, if necessary, make all the funeral arrangements.'

I could have hit him because Muriel came into the room when he was saying this. But she stood there as if nothing had happened.

'It 's the least we can do for poor Mrs Mitchell,' she said. There were small creases of shadow under her eyes which shone with a soft strong light I had never seen before. She walked as if she were really still in that room with me, asleep. God, I loved that girl! God, I wanted to get all over this, this damned Colin business that had come right into the middle of everything like this, and I wanted to get married right away. I wanted to be alone with her. That 's what Colin did for me.

'Yes,' I said. 'We must do the right thing by Colin.'

'We are sometimes asked for long-distance estimates,' my father said.

'It will be a little something,' my mother said.

'Dad and I will talk it over,' I said.

'Come into the office,' my father said. 'It occurred to me that it would be nice to do the right thing by this friend of yours.'

We talked it over. We went into the cost of it. There was the return journey to reckon. We worked it out that it would come no dearer to old Mrs Mitchell than if she took the train and buried the boy here. That is to say, my father said, if I drove it.

'It would look nice,' my father said.

'Saves money and it would look a bit friendly,' my father said. 'You 've done it before.'

'Well,' I said. 'I suppose I can get a refund on my return ticket from the railway.'

But it was not as simple as it looked, because Muriel wanted to come. She wanted to drive back with me and the hearse. My mother was very worried about this. It might upset Muriel, she thought. Father thought it might not look nice to see a young girl sitting by the coffin of a grown man.

'It must be dignified,' my father said. 'You see if she was there it might look as though she were just doing it for the ride—like these young women on bakers' vans.'

My father took me out into the hall to tell me this because he did not want her to hear. But she would not have it. She wanted to come back with Colin.

'Colin loved me. It is my duty to him,' she said.

'Besides,' she said, suddenly, in her full open voice —it had seeemed to be closed and carved and broken and small—'I 've never been in a hearse before.'

'And it will save her fare too,' I said to my father.

That night I went again to her room. She was awake. I said I was sorry to disturb her but I would go at once only I wanted to see if she was all right. She said, in the closed voice again, that she was all right.

'Are you sure?' I said.

She did not answer. I was worried. I went over to the bed.

'What is the matter? Tell me what is the matter,' I said.

For a long time she was silent. I held her hand, I stroked her head. She was lying stiff in the bed. She would not answer. I dropped my hand to her small white shoulder. She stirred and drew up her legs and half turned and said, 'I was thinking of Colin.'

'Where is he?' she asked.

'They 've brought him round. He 's lying down-stairs.'

'In the front room?'

'Yes, ready for the morning. Now be a sensible girl and go back by train.'

'No, no,' she said. 'I want to go with Colin. Poor Colin. He loved me and I didn't love him.' And she drew my hands down to her breasts.

'Colin loved me,' she whispered.

'Not like this,' I whispered.

It was a warm grey morning like all the others when we took Colin back. They had fixed the coffin in before Muriel came out. She came down wearing the bright blue hat she had got off Dormer's millinery man and she kissed my mother and father good-bye. They were very sorry for her. 'Look after her, Arthur,' my mother said. Muriel got in beside me without a glance behind her at the coffin. I started the engine. They smiled at us. My father raised his hat, but whether it was to Muriel and me or to Colin, or to the three of us, I do not know. He was not, you see, wearing his top hat. I 'll say this for the old boy, thirty years in the trade have taught him tact.

After leaving my father's house you have to go down to the tram terminus before you get on to the by-pass. There was always one or two drivers, conductors or inspectors there, doing up their tickets, or changing over the trolley arms. When we passed I saw two of them drop their jaws, stick their pencils in their ears, and raise their hats. I was so surprised by this that I nearly raised mine in acknowledgment, forgetting that we had the coffin behind. I had not driven one of my father's hearses for years.

Hearses are funny things to drive. They are well-sprung, smooth-running cars, with quiet engines, and, if you are used to driving a smaller car, before you know where you are, you are speeding. You know you ought to go slow, say 25 to 30 maximum, and it's hard to keep it down. You can return empty at 70 if you like. It's like driving a fire engine. Go fast out and come back slow—only the other way round. Open out in the country but slow down past houses. That's what it means. My father was very particular about this.

Muriel and I didn't speak very much at first. We sat listening to the engine and the occasional jerk of the coffin behind when we went over a pot-hole. We passed the place where poor Colin—but I didn't say anything to Muriel, and she, if she noticed—which I doubt—did not say anything to me. We went through Cox Hill, Wammering and Yodley Mount, flat country, don't care for it myself. 'There's a wonderful lot of building going on,' Muriel said at last.

'You won't know these places in five years,' I said.

But my mind kept drifting away from the road and the green fields and the dullness, and back to Colin—five days before he had come down this way. I expected to see that Indian coming flying straight out of every corner. But it was all bent and bust up properly now. I saw the damned thing.

He had been up to his old game, following us, and that had put the end to following. But not quite; he was following us now, behind us in the coffin. Then my mind drifted off that and I thought of those

nights at my parents' house, and Muriel. You
never know what a woman is going to be like. I
thought, too, that it had put my calculations out. I
mean, supposing she had a baby. You see I had
reckoned on waiting eighteen months or so. I would
have eight hundred then. But if we had to get
married at once, we should have to cut right down.
Then I kept thinking it was funny her saying 'Colin!'
like that in the night; it was funny it made her feel
that way with me, and how it made me feel when
she called me Colin. I 'd never thought of her in
that way, in what you might call the 'Colin' way.

I looked at her and she looked at me and she smiled
but still we did not say very much, but the smiles
kept coming to both of us. The light-railway bridge
at Dootheby took me by surprise and I thought the
coffin gave a jump as we took it.

'Colin 's still watching us,' I nearly said.

There were tears in her eyes.

'What was the matter with Colin?' I said. 'Nice
chap, I thought. Why didn't you marry him?'

'Yes,' she said. 'He was a nice boy. But he 'd
no sense of humour.

'And I wanted to get out of that town,' she said.

'I 'm not going to stay there, at that hotel,' she
said.

'I want to get away,' she said. 'I 've had
enough.'

She had a way of getting angry with the air, like
that. 'You 've got to take me away,' she said. We
were passing slowly into Muster, there was a tram
ahead and people thick on the narrow pavements,
dodging out into the road. But when we got into

the Market Square where they were standing around, they saw the coffin. They began to raise their hats. Suddenly she laughed. 'It 's like being the King and Queen,' she said.

'They 're raising their hats,' she said.

'Not all of them,' I said.

She squeezed my hand and I had to keep her from jumping about like a child on the seat as we went through.

'There they go.'

'Boys always do,' I said.

'And another.'

'Let 's see what the policeman does.'

She started to laugh but I shut her up. 'Keep your sense of humour to yourself,' I said.

Through all those towns that run into one another, as you might say, we caught it. We went through, as she said, like royalty. So many years since I drove a hearse, I 'd forgotten what it was like.

I was proud of her, I was proud of Colin, and I was proud of myself. And, after what had happened, I mean on the last two nights, it was like a wedding. And although we knew it was for Colin, it was for us too, because Colin was with both of us. It was like this all the way.

'Look at that man there. Why doesn't he raise his hat? People ought to show respect for the dead,' she said.

ALEXANDER

By H. E. BATES

I

EARLY one August morning a curious black cart on low springs, drawn by a little shaggy pony with a tail that swept about its legs like a skirt, jogged steadily off from a narrow street bordering the river, climbed in a leisurely manner through the town, and began travelling slowly and almost sleepily eastward towards open country.

In the cart, half concealed by piles of creaking baskets, sat a small, fair-haired boy of eleven or twelve, with drowsy blue eyes; and by his side a fat, sunburnt man with white hair, dressed in breeches and black leggings and a red waistcoat, evidently put on with special care and worn with special pride. All the buttons of this garment resembled fishes' eyes, and a good many cunning pockets were concealed in every part of it, inside and outside, back and front. A silver watch-chain dangled across it, bearing handsome engraved medals won for fishing and shooting. Something about the waistcoat, perhaps the medals themselves, seemed to attract the boy, for he sat very still, his head to one side, gazing at it. Sometimes he looked exactly as if about to drop off to sleep, his head nodding and his eyes shutting with a kind of thankful bliss. At these moments, as if regarding this as the pleasantest, most flattering thing in all the world, the man would turn on him a gaze mild with approbation and beatitude. He crouched as he drove, flapping the reins gently on the pony's back, and from time to time would raise his head and stare across the plain at the countless cornfields and orchards stretching away to an horizon darkened by misty woods lying upon it like sleeping giants.

For a mile or more the cart drove on in this fashion, the boy still half asleep, the man meditative, the pony never changing its pace. The sun rose up, at first like a fluffy yellow ball, then like a disk of polished brass. Trees, cornfields, farms, pastures, horses and workmen among the mown corn, all appeared instantly bathed in a soft transfiguring light. Objects a great distance off, little towers, smoking chimneys, village spires, became lightly pencilled into the scene. The sun ran swiftly over the plain, pursuing lines of black shadow. A covey of partridges scurried, screamed, then spread out like a black fan and vanished, the barley ears waving briefly and lightly where they came to earth. Slowly the woods resolved themselves; the trees stood in sharp, unbroken line; then the dew became visible in manifold, glittering drops, giving the parched grasses a look of fresh life, hanging upon the trees like ladies' ear-rings and covering each of the black and crimson berries on the hedge-side like a shell of glass. Soon everywhere was under a warm stillness; all the mist dispersed stealthily and silently, without wind, and the trees seemed to stoop with an invisible burden of heavy airs and the rich loveliness of the ripening year.

As the cart went on, a black shadow began to glide steadily by the horse's side, and a strong fresh scent, with something autumnal about it, began to blow swiftly into the nostrils of the boy, who could feel the sun growing warmer and warmer on his closed lids and on his cheeks and hands.

Presently the man took out his watch and remarked in a soft bass voice: 'Nearly nine.' The boy raised his head and yawned, but did not answer.

Little by little the nature of the country began to change. Gentle hills and a long shallow valley with a white stream appeared. Soon a vast and magnificent view unfolded like a picture.

Being long-sighted, the man would rest his eyes upon remote objects like windmills, water-towers, specks that were cattle or harvesters. All at once his eyes sparkled with eagerness and he began to nudge and pummel the boy into a state of wakefulness and attention. At last he tightened the reins and called excitedly, half standing up among the baskets:

'Alexander! Alexander! Boy, look, look! What is it? Can you see? Open your peepers, Alexander, and just look, look, look. What do you make of it?'

And the boy, excited also, sat upright.

'Herons!' the man whispered.

As the boy gazed up the word was repeated several times, more and more excitedly. Two large, beautiful birds appeared overhead, flapping their way with splendour towards the east, silently and impressively, with the sun shining golden upon them at sudden intervals. The cart had come for the first time to a standstill. The little horse stood quietly panting. Nothing else could be heard; only the strange, golden stillness seemed to ring like the dim echo of a bell over everything as they watched the birds, two diminishing shapes becoming swallowed in the depth of blue sky.

After a long interval, during which the boy emerged for the first time into unconfused wakefulness, the man flapped the reins and remarked:

'I used to know a man who stuffed birds, specially herons. If I 'd had a gun just now I might have knocked that pair down for him. He was a masterpiece. For all you knew they might as lief have been alive as dead.'

The cart moved forward again. The boy, on whom the herons had made a great impression, suddenly remarked:

'You shouldn't shoot birds, not even sparrows.'

'Sparrows are pests,' said the man. 'That 's law, Alexander. You can't get away from the law.'

'God might strike you, all the same,' said the boy.

'God what?' uttered the man, as if astonished or not catching the words. 'God what did you say?'

'It 's been known! Ursula told me about a man who had stolen a calf from a widow woman and while he was eating it afterwards, God struck him.'

'How? Struck him?'

'I don't know how. Ursula says——'

'Never mind what Ursula says! The woman 's all nonsense and popery. Never you mind what she says, the old fool. There 's no truth in it.'

The boy did not speak. To all this conversation he had listened gravely, taking everything to heart. Each time he looked at the man, his uncle, he was overcome with reverence and admiration. Nevertheless, there was a warm note of affection between them. Often something serious and mature lurked in Alexander's eyes; and frequently from the other's some child-like and naïve light shone down upon him.

The cart proceeded at the same unvarying pace as before. Now the boy sat upright. The hot morning sun began to burn him. Gradually the sky assumed a richer shade of blue and the grasses began to give off a little vapour. The boy began to take a great interest in what was going on, his mind dwelling on the day ahead—where they were going, what would take place, how much longer they must drive. He tried often to picture the great house to which he understood they were driving, the long avenues of plums and pears, the over-reaching apple-trees, the walls bearing peaches, apricots, and even quinces in great abundance, and the old, wizened, solitary creature who lived in this house surrounded by many brown-and-black dogs and a white cat which she never allowed out of sight. He pondered for a long time, but without enlightenment, on this strange creature who sold fruit to his uncle—'Because, Mr Bishop, you knew me when I was a girl and I can trust you not to break the trees and put the wrong measure in the basket for yourself,' and sometimes he pictured the garden with great success, almost smelling the warm ripeness given off by fruits and leaves.

'What time shall we be there?' he looked up and asked.

The man was lighting his pipe and to Alexander it seemed a long time before he answered:

'A little after ten if we don't stop anywhere. Are you hungry? Ursula put some cheese-cakes in the basket in case you were hungry.'

He was not hungry. In spite of this and though he considered Ursula's cheese-cakes very moderate indeed, he ate two and, while eating, loosened the collar of his shirt. The sun was hot on his face and neck. A little afterwards the road turned abruptly to the left, and from the hot stillness of the open country they passed suddenly into a cool wood of beeches, oaks, and firs, to the accompaniment of stirring leaves and branches, a fitful talking of birds, a gentle whispering of a thousand unknown mysterious voices.

'The house sits that way, on the far side of the wood,' said the man, pointing the whip.

Alexander looked into the wood, from which now and then broke strange scuffling noises. He saw nothing but a vast extent of trees with a glimpse of some fungi as large as pancakes and bright orange in colour. All the leaves, twigs, grasses were dripping with dew, setting up everywhere a kind of watery music, as if from a hidden spring. Drops fell from the overhanging branches and plopped on the cart and the baskets and even on his hands.

Something red appeared along the road. Before long it grew large and life-like and resolved into a woman in a red woollen jacket and a black skirt, carrying a basket. His uncle suddenly began whistling and gave the horse a playful flick as if he were very happy.

From that moment, until they drew level with the woman, the man stared hard at the black skirt, and when they came closer brought the little horse to a walk and tried to catch a glimpse of the woman's face, which was turned away from them. Suddenly she started violently at the sound of wheels, and turning sharply, almost, dropped her basket.

His uncle ceased whistling. 'I thought so! Annie Fell, my girl!' he shouted at once. 'It is you! Yes, it 's you right enough. Thinks I, coming all along the road, that 's Annie Fell's walk, it 's like her father's. God bless me! You look well. Mushrooms! So you got up before you went anywhere this morning. Well, God bless me, God bless me.'

While speaking he slapped one knee in astonishment. Alexander took in the woman's fresh, plump features, her sturdy body, and the immense yellow bunch of hair, too heavy to be held up, falling like fine wool about her neck and shoulders.

'Oh! it 's Eli. It 's so long since we saw you.'

'Yes! Seven or eight years. At Pollyanna's wedding. Ah, how 's Pollyanna?'

'Ah, she 's poorly. Her legs keep swelling. She ain't good for much.'

'That 's no good. A woman needs good legs. . . .' There was a pause, as if this statement had added to the sum of human knowledge or had a mysterious, subtle meaning. Alexander felt awkward and took his eyes away from the woman and was relieved when his uncle broke the silence again.

'How 's your father, my girl?'

She looked up and said in a weary, disillusioned voice, 'He ain't worth a hatful of crabs, either. He 's had an operation and every drop and tittle

he has Cilla and I have to put down him with a
spoon. We have a life with him.'

'So they cut him, did they?'

'There's cuts on him as long as a kidney bean,
and a bit longer, I'll swear,' she said.

'That's no good to a man. It's all knifing and
butchery with doctors. What do they care?
What's the like of me and you to one of them?
They want to see what's inside you, and so out
comes the knife and you're half-way to Kingdom
Come without a chance to say 'Our Father.' Ah!
. . . Are you going home? Give me your basket
then, and get up and we'll put you down at the
house. No, I don't hold with this butchery.'

He shook his head gravely and vehemently. The
woman climbed into the cart and sat between the
boy and his uncle. Alexander remained silent and
reserved. When they drove off he concentrated
his attention on the wood, looking for jays, squirrels,
and mushrooms. But often he glanced at the
woman furtively, attracted by something warm
about her, and the thought of the unfortunate man
with cuts as long as beans on his body would trouble
him strangely, until he felt that he would be glad
when they were alone once more, only his uncle and
himself and the little horse bearing them steadily
forward into the unfamiliar, golden country.

He observed with relief, a little later, a break in
the woodland and a small stone house with snug,
diamond-paned windows, tucked away in the clear
space. A number of hens and geese, with a white
goat, were bobbing hither and thither like scraps of
paper on the surrounding grass, and a warm smell

of animals and burning wood reached him. Uncle
Bishop brought the cart to a standstill and the
woman alighted.

Alexander felt as if he had been pressed in a little
box. His body seemed shrunken and he would have
been thankful to have driven off without delay.
But, looking up, the woman said:

'You must come in and say half a word to him——'

'I don't know about that,' said Eli, gazing at the
distance. 'We 've a long way to go.'

'Don't say you won't have a glass,' she went on,
as if pleading. 'You haven't so far but what it
might be a little farther.'

And to Alexander's disappointment and annoy-
ance his uncle began to alight also. The boy sat
still, holding the reins, glaring. His heart sank
lower. And in a not very convincing tone he
suddenly said:

'I 'll sit here.'

'Oh! but the horse can look after itself,' said the
woman.

They both looked at him. 'Make haste,' said his
uncle. 'It 's Fanny's boy; you know Fanny,' he
explained to the woman.

'Fanny's boy! So that 's Fanny's boy? Well,
well, I knew your mother years ago. You tell her
you saw Annie Fell.'

'Ah, that 's right, there 's something for you to
remember.'

So he followed them across the grass, through a
wicket-gate and into a garden flanked by trees. A
grey sheep-dog lay like a rug across the doorstep,
dozing. The door stood open. Uncle Bishop and

the woman entered, but Alexander lingered behind,
trying to look as if the sheep-dog interested him,
though secretly he was afraid of dogs.

'Cilla! Cilla!' the woman began to call upstairs.
'Cilla, here's a visitor. Ah! you couldn't guess in a
month of Sundays.

'Let's go up,' she said.

She removed her hat, and Uncle Bishop began to
follow her heavily up some narrow stairs. At their
departure the sheep-dog opened his eyes, got lazily
to his feet and pattered after them. Alexander
began to wonder if he too ought to go, but presently
feet resounded overhead and a murmur of voices
floated down, and he felt that he had been forgotten.

A little time passed. The sun was hot on his face,
and the wooden lintel burned against his hand.
Nothing stirred. In the dense sheltered growth of
the garden there was not a breath, not a petal or
leaf in motion. Bees would appear and spend a
little time among some yellow dahlias and then
surge away.

Absolute silence seized all things. Alexander
began to look for something to occupy his mind,
and, turning to the house, he caught sight of a
double-barrel sporting gun standing by the wall.
The gun was very handsome and fascinating, and
though he dare not touch it, he remained gazing
at it for a long time, imagining himself taking aim.
Presently, tiring of the gun, he looked about the
room. It had a low, curious aspect and an appearance of being very old. Some tall geraniums, pink
and milk in colour, bloomed in the window, their
pretty silken petals falling on a lace-cushion, hung

with bunches of bobbins, standing beneath. A chain of birds' eggs was looped over a looking-glass, and a blue enamel bowl of small dark plums stood on the floor.

Presently, as he was scrutinizing a photograph of some soldiers and wondering if they had ever fought with Zulus, a curious, rhythmical noise, like that of a purring cat, startled him. It seemed to him to issue from a door standing half-open by the stairs.

He tiptoed towards the door, stood for a moment very still, and then poked in his head. He recoiled with great haste immediately, trembling.

In the room an old woman, an incredibly astoundingly old woman, with a face like a dried lemon and scarcely any hairs on her head, sat asleep with her hands locked together in her lap, clasping a yellow comb. Her mouth opened regularly the smallest fraction, and emitted a strange half-whistling, half-purring sound. His startled mind refused to think who she might be, or what she was doing there, but retained only the awful, haunting impression that her closed eyes were staring at him through their bluish lids.

He turned and retreated hurriedly. As he reached the garden something stirred there also and the hot stillness was broken by the noise of footsteps coming. He waited, a little nervously, and then, without any other hint or warning, he found himself face to face with a young girl. He looked at her, but did not move, and again nothing seemed to take place in his mind. Only his eyes did their work, drinking in the impression of her pretty, delicate face, her soft

neck, and her light hair almost the colour of barley.
Each impression smote him sharply, until his breast
seemed as if about to burst with its own throbbing.
In a strange way, without deliberation, he idealized
her at once, thinking that he must be careful how
he spoke to her and how he acted before her, and he
felt acutely conscious of his physical self and was
filled with the impression that everything about her,
her large profound blue eyes, the yellow pansy tucked
in her hair, the little printed flowerets on her dress,
and also the plums in her basket, were all staring at
him, astonished and unflinching.

After a little silence she began to move in his
direction. As she came nearer the look of dumb
astonishment on her face increased.

Not knowing what to do, Alexander muttered
stupidly:

'I 'm waiting for someone.'

In rather a soft, drawling voice, and looking first
towards the road and then at him, she said slowly
in reply:

'Did you come in that cart?'

'Yes, that 's our cart,' he said quickly. Then,
as if to appear at ease, he added:

'You didn't notice if the horse had moved on, I
expect, did you?'

'No, he hadn't moved.'

'That 's all right,' he said. 'I only wondered,
because he 's a bit restless in summer.'

She remained silent, and feeling this silence acutely
he remarked:

'They 're nice plums,' not daring to look into her
face, but simply gazing at the dark blue fruit instead.

'They fall off and I have to pick them up every morning,' she told him. 'Look at my hands.'

He cast a brief glance at her stained fingers and felt immediately in some way flattered because she had asked him to do so.

'They 're eating plums, I suppose,' he remarked.

Suddenly, without answering, she moved past him, and thinking that he had perhaps offended her and that she was about to disappear irrevocably, he called rather timidly after her:

'I suppose I could have a look at the garden?'

She called back at once:

'Wait a moment, I 'll take you down.'

Almost simultaneously with this she reappeared, now with an empty basket.

'Perhaps I 'd better make certain about the horse; he won't stand in hot weather,' remarked Alexander.

He satisfied himself by staring over the wicket at the little horse grazing peacefully by the woodside. As he rejoined the girl he tried to walk slowly and naturally, without eagerness and without excitement. Nevertheless, he was conscious of being filled and overcome by a sensation which in its novelty and wonder seemed to deprive him of something with every step he took with the girl deeper into the the garden. And in place of what he lost came a host of strange, unbelievable emotions of which hitherto he had suspected nothing, a sense of pleasure which filled his mind like a sweet smell.

It was a long garden, with not many flowers, but a great number of fruit-trees set very thick and close, so that they appeared to be strangling each other.

White beehives stood here and there in open spaces.
Under the trees the same hot, overpowering stillness
as ever stifled everything. All the time Alexander
longed to make some sensible or amusing remark to
the girl, who walked a little ahead of him, bumping
the empty basket softly on her knees at each step,
but something prevented him, and he became en-
tranced merely by watching her.

He walked behind her as if dreaming. Presently
the path turned to the right, and he caught a faint,
brackish odour of water and saw a small pond.

The water was shallow and dingy-looking, the
surface sprinkled with countless little yellow sloe
leaves and the edge fringed with coarse grasses.
When the girl ran on, however, and reached the far
side, it seemed to Alexander as clear as a mirror,
reflecting her white figure with strange purity, and
he felt an odd desire to jump across the pond in a
very romantic fashion and land at her feet.

But suddenly the girl called:

'Can you climb trees?'

How best to answer this he did not know. But
after a second he said:

'What trees are there to climb?'

'Only the sloe-tree!' she cried.

She ran towards a large sloe-bush overhanging
the pond. Climbing trees was an accomplishment
of Alexander's, but the sloe-bush seemed to him
dense, prickly, and not quite assailable.

'Do you think the sloes are quite ripe?' he remarked in a hesitant voice.

'Don't you want to climb?' the girl flashed out
at once.

'Yes, of course.'

'Then shall I climb first or will you?' she asked, while he hesitated.

'Oh, you first, you go,' he said.

She immediately made a light spring and climbed easily and quickly to a fork in the trunk, and, squatting there, gave the tree a sudden violent shake which brought sloes pelting down on the grass, in the pond, and on Alexander's head.

'Bite one, bite one!' she called in extreme excitement.

But Alexander only shook his head, and dropping into the grass, broke into a slow, almost diplomatic smile, without a word.

All this gave him confidence and he looked up at her light form. In these moments he forgot his uncle, the little horse and the journey which meant so much to him, and felt that his whole existence was bound up in the girl, who never ceased attracting him. Seeing her suddenly leave the tree and take a bound through the grass to his side overcame him with a strange faintness. When she sat down he tried at once to look as if interested in some object in the pond. His quick glance arrested her. She followed his gaze, a silence deepening and falling upon them immediately, a silence he found hard to endure again.

But he could say nothing. He half-closed his eyes against the brilliant sunshine. The thoughts he conceived were unbalanced and spasmodic and he could never work them out. An incredible length of time seemed to pass. . . . At last a pair of pigeons broke from just beyond the sloe-bush, and flew over the house. The girl gazed up at them. In a flash, his heart clamouring in his throat, he turned and looked at her face, upturned to the sunshine, her bright hair and her long sunburnt neck uncovered almost to the delicate bosom having its source in a little shadow. He was carried utterly away. It seemed to him that he must lie flat on his face, without speaking or moving, lest he should choke with joy.

'Pigeons . . .' Her voice floated off, tranquilly. Then in the distance rose suddenly a sound and Alexander imagined he heard voices.

They both sprang to their feet and began instinctively to walk in the direction of the house.

'I can hear my mother,' said the girl.

He felt it would be somehow nice and courteous if he said:

'Is that your mother in the red blouse?'

'Yes . . . only that 's not a blouse,' she answered in a rather deprecating tone. 'Are you going a long way?'

'I don't know how far it is.'

'What are all those baskets for?'

And feeling rather important, he answered:

'They 're fruit-baskets. Every one has to be filled before we come back again.'

But although he spoke in a very bold way his excitement never ceased.

When they reached the house his uncle, the girl's mother, and another woman with fair hair and a pale pink dress and a rather cheerful, pretty face, whom he had not seen before, all stood about a well, the woman peering into the well—while his uncle turned the windlass. As he approached the bucket rose, swaying and spilling water.

He stood still and watched, trying to assume a very careless appearance, as if nothing had happened and he had never moved from that spot.

Then, rather than have his presence noticed with surprise, he said:

'Are you going to start?'

The two women and his uncle turned sharply and looked at him.

'Where in thunder have you sprung from?'

'He's been after the plums . . . that's it. I'll be bound that's about the drift . . .' and such remarks came from the smiling women.

He only broke into the same slow, almost diplomatic smile as before, without a word.

When he turned the girl had vanished. He felt at once a sickening sensation and a desire, regardless of what his uncle and the women might say, to run and look for her. Uncle Bishop and the two women made off in the direction of the wicket, taking the water for the little horse. Casting hurried glances about him, but without reward, he sauntered after them.

While the horse was drinking, the woman in the pink dress, whom he rather liked, said in such a way that it was difficult to understand if she referred to him or to the horse:

'Would he like a curd tart, do you think?'

Alexander did not answer. The horse ceased drinking. Suddenly his uncle bellowed in a stentorian voice in his ear:

'Do you hear? Would you like a curd tart?'

'Please,' said Alexander at once, starting.

'Well then, fathead, listen! Go along with you.'

Alexander followed the pink dress. All the time he was conscious of a vagueness, an unreality in everything. As he stood in the kitchen waiting for the woman to return with the tart he darted glances this way and that, in pursuit of the vanished girl, and even took three steps towards the other door, thinking himself alone, in order to search further for her.

Again a sound startled him. Glancing round, he found himself for the second time face to face with the old, dried-up woman. This time her eyes, wide open, looked at him like two black balls of peppermint. They stared horribly, and all of her little black figure huddled soundlessly in the corner seemed to him sinister in its watchfulness and lack of life.

He felt hypnotized and yet revolted, and dared not move until the woman in the pink dress returned. And then he turned away quickly, eating with difficulty and conscious of a lump in his throat.

'Perhaps you 'll remember me to your mother,' the woman said behind him. 'Say you saw Cilla . . . just Cilla. Then she 'll know. Don't you forget.'

He made an obedient murmur, and cast a last hasty glance into the garden, hotter and stiller it seemed than ever. But nothing stirred, nothing broke the stillness there.

He climbed into the cart and sat motionless. Uncle Bishop looked at his watch and said, 'God

bless me!' four or five times over, and after climbing
into the cart too, he began to say farewell.

'Good day, good day,' he kept repeating. 'You
ought to rub Pollyanna's legs every day with hound's-
tongue ointment three or four times. Tell her
they 're Bishop's very words, and she knows I 'm
right. You can't go wrong with hound's-tongue,
it 's a cure-all. What? . . . Doctors? . . . They
might as well be in Bedlam, with the poor thing's
legs rotting off with pain. What 's that? Ha, ha!
God bless me, that 's a fact!' he burst out, trying
to give the girl's mother a playful poke with the whip.
'You 're fat enough, too, and no mistake, but I
remember what my mother said about you the day
you were married. There 's no flesh on her, she
says, she 's got neither bosom not backside. They're
nothing but little apples.'

The women laughed and Uncle Bishop, in great
spirits, suddenly began to shout a great many
indiscreet things, saying farewell over and over
again, alternately flicking the little horse and reining
it tight again.

They began to move off at last. Alexander tried
to smile. The wheels turned, a little faster every
second. He was overcome by a sensation of being
dragged somewhere against his will.

Then all at once, in a most subtle way, he was
aware that the girl was watching him. He felt this
as certainly as if she had held her finger-tips very
close to his cheek. He turned impulsively, and
beheld her with her chin resting on her hands
and her hands resting on the top of the little gate,
staring at him. The blood rushed to his cheeks, and

filled with all his former joy, he kept turning and seeing her in the same careless, lovely watchful pose, while the cart drew steadily farther and farther away.

Finally he saw her no more. The house, the goat, the hens, and at last the wood itself slipped into the distance. An unfamiliar, beautiful valley unfolded itself before his gaze. The dew had vanished and there was a hard brilliance about the sky as if it were a gem.

A clock chimed eleven. Uncle Bishop's breath smelt sweetly of wine. Alexander fixed his eyes on the distance, hardly knowing what he did, dreaming endlessly.

II

When they had driven a little longer the road made a sudden curve like a sickle, and while his thoughts were still of the girl and all that had taken place in the wood, a square stone house standing alone among dark clumps of trees came suddenly into sight. All other thoughts momentarily at an end, he gazed and asked:

'Is this where she lives?'

'Hold hard,' said his uncle. 'You'll see her if you wait a moment. Go along with you and open the gate. Hullo! the damned dogs already! Go along and don't be frightened.'

As Alexander alighted and began to push back the massive iron gates a furious chorus of barking dogs greeted him, and suddenly six or seven bitches, all of the same black-and-brown breed and each very corpulent, rushed out at him from nowhere, yelping and snapping about his heels and striking terror into him. He hated dogs, and standing stock-still, cast one despairing look at his uncle, who at once leapt up like a fat old jack-in-the-box and began wildly brandishing his whip and shouting:

'Damn the dogs, get back! Damn the dogs!'

He jerked the reins excitedly. 'Get out, you scallywags!' he shouted afresh as the cart moved forward. 'God bless me, what does a woman want with seven dogs? Get back!'

The cart drove in and the yelping bitches were scattered in all directions. Partly to protect himself, and partly to show that he was not wholly afraid, Alexander seized the little horse's bridle and led it towards the house. Green lawns and a superb orchard lay before him. His gaze fell fascinated on scores and scores of trees stretching infinitely ahead.

Suddenly his uncle whispered a little excitedly:

'There's the old tit herself, yes, there she is. Coming towards us. See her?'

And looking up, Alexander saw approaching him a small, frail woman in black, wearing a snuff-brown bonnet and carrying a silver-knobbed walking-stick in her hands. She looked as if got up to match her dogs, who all instantly ceased barking and waddled towards her in a curious apathetic way, snuffing about her skirts. She walked as though on ice, hardly progressing at all, with her head and hands quivering in agitation, as if for ever dispatching little signals of terror and distress. Behind her came a white cat and yet another dog, an aged, weary creature who moved even more slowly than its mistress.

His uncle began to hobble across the lawn to meet

her, muttering again, 'The old tit, the old tit!' at every step he took.

When he reached the old lady he formed an enormous trumpet with his hands, and bellowed into her ears like thunder:

'Glad to see you. Nice weather, God bless me. Not very lucky with the dogs again, I see.'

A little plaintive voice piped out, hardly audible, in reply:

'So you've come. No, no . . . it's awful. What with the boys stealing the fruit, and then the dogs having litters all the time. . . . The boys have broken the wall again. It's dreadful. I don't know what to do, people rob me right and left. What's it coming to?'

She turned her doleful, shaking head first to the garden, then to the dogs, half of which were heavy with puppies, and lastly to Uncle Bishop.

'Damn brutes!' he began. 'Not the dogs, I've nothing against the dogs. The boys I mean. . . . Not the dogs. Why don't you do something?'

'What can I do?'

'Say your prayers . . .' muttered Uncle Bishop in an undertone. 'The old tit. Say your prayers.'

'Wha-a-at? . . . Whose boy is that?'

'My nephew; Fanny's boy. Alexander, come and shake hands. He's twelve. Strong lad, isn't he?' he bellowed.

And Alexander, trying to bear out this statement, yet afraid of hurting the old woman, shook hands, and her hand seemed to him like a piece of cold fish and her eyes seemed ready to stream with tears as she looked at him.

'Would he like a piece of cake, do you think?' she said.

Alexander, not daring to refuse, although again not hungry, at once said 'Please.'

'Please!' repeated his uncle in a staggering voice.

Nodding and quaking, the old lady turned and slowly retreated, all the dogs following her like mourners at a funeral. While she had gone Uncle Bishop gave the little horse its nose-bag and Alexander unpacked the fruit-baskets and set them on the grass.

After a long interval the procession returned. Alexander's uncle at once began a secretive whisper:

'She 's rich, the old teaser. Her husband invented a patent candlestick and made a fortune, but he broke his neck on horseback. She had a son, but he 's a lunatic and no one knows where he is, and so it 's all hers, all the blessed money and this orchard, everything. Fetch the piece of cake, fetch it, fetch it—be on the right side of her, my boy, go along, fetch it.'

Alexander was forced to go and take from the old lady's quivering fingers a large triangle of bright yellow cake, which looked distasteful and sickly.

'It 's saffron cake,' she said to him, in a trembling little voice.

What saffron cake was he did not know, but he tried to look as if he did know and as if he were very grateful. Then his uncle and the old woman began to discuss the fruit-gathering and he was left unnoticed, feeling awkward as he lingered about with the cake he did not want.

'The little golden plums on the bank are ripe, two

trees of them,' he heard her say. 'Get them . . .
get them all. The boys and the wasps are after them.
And then there's a tree of pearmains: that's
loaded, and there'll be none left if you leave them.
Pears, there's two trees of pears, the big early ones
at the end of the garden, and the little sweet pears.
You know where they are. There's a ladder stands
by the wall. You know where everything is, don't
you? It's a poor year. Some of the trees are
blighted, but you do as you think fit.'

'You know you can trust us,' bellowed Uncle
Bishop. 'You know that you always have trusted
us.'

'Yes, I trust you.'

But while they were taking hooks and baskets
and all the time they were walking down the long
avenue of apples into the depths of the garden,
Alexander was conscious of her eyes pursuing all
their movements, as if she did not trust them. Her
eyes reminded him of gooseberries, and he also felt
that though she was so very deaf this deafness did
not matter, since her sight was so uncanny and
remarkable. And as he turned and shot a last
furtive look along the avenue all the seven dogs and
the white cat appeared to be watching him too.

'It's a garden, if you like, isn't it?' his old uncle
kept whispering, as though the intricacy of the
avenues and the never-ending branches stooping
under a weight of red, yellow and green globes awed
him. 'There's a peach, on the wall, and next to
it's an apricot, but there's never a finger allowed
on them, the old tit, not a finger. Don't you touch
them, do you hear that? Eat what you like and

fill your pockets, but she 'll know almost if you look on that wall. God bless me if she won't.'

But Alexander, so much attracted by the garden, scarcely listened. Everywhere heavily laden trees stood, and as in the little garden in the wood, not a breath or leaf stirred itself, and the sunshine seemed to burn the stillness and came through the leaves with a soft liquid light. In odd places under the trees there were vegetable marrows, which he thought looked like fat sucking pigs asleep in the sunshine. In the distance some pigeons were cooing, and a flock of starlings flew up from an apple-tree and soared away like black dust. They walked on and on. 'Did you ever see the like?' the old man kept saying. And then suddenly they came to a point where this level, tranquil order of things changed, and the garden dipped abruptly. They halted. Before them lay a kind of oval basin which it seemed to Alexander might have been a stone-pit in some bygone time. Here the trees hung from ledges and precipices and flourished in a toy green valley. 'Cunning,' he heard his uncle say. Very cunning and very wonderful indeed he thought it also as he stood there gazing with large eyes at the little golden plums in the grass, with a sensation as if the outer world had been left aside for ever.

'Get a basket. Let 's begin,' said his uncle suddenly. 'The little yellow tree first of all.'

Alexander, rather dazed, took the basket in which lay the saffron cake, and though not hungry, he longed to taste the cake and the tempting, sweet-looking plums. And so he took first a bite at the strange-coloured cake and then at the fruit. The

cake he concluded at once was poisonous, but the
plums were like honey, and he went on eating them,
hardly filling up the basket at all. And shortly,
without fuss, and with an expression of sleepy
indifference, he put some of the ripest plums in his
pockets and dropped the saffron cake into long grass,
like a stone.

As the work went on, Uncle Bishop at times
murmured in a cracked bass some old song Alexander had heard already a hundred times, but which
possessed for him still the same enchantment and
surprise, and at others related all he knew of some
old murder, very cold-blooded and gruesome, telling
it all so skilfully and with such cunning pauses that
Alexander would cease all movement, and sit on a
branch or stand in the grass as if paralysed, not
breathing, wondering if the climax would ever come.
At times they were very silent. In these pauses
the boy wished only that he might lie still in the
shady grass, to sleep, or to watch with sleepy eyes
the rabbits feeding in the green hollow. But each
time a curious sense of pride prevented his doing this.
And conscientiously he went on filling and refilling
his basket with plums.

When the plum-tree had been stripped the man
sighed, and as if for reward, ate the first plum
Alexander had seen pass his lips, and blew out his
cheeks and spat the stone to an extraordinary height
in the air. Then he seized his jacket and opened
his watch and looked at the sun.

'Oh, Lord!' he muttered, scratching himself. 'It's
nearly one. Fetch the basket.'

A sudden feeling of joy and relief filled Alexander,

who felt as if he had been locked in a room and
released.

When he returned with the basket Uncle Bishop
was already seated under a large pear-tree, stropping
a magnificent clasp-knife on his trousers-knee in
readiness.

'What have they put in for us?' he kept saying.
'What? Cold pie? What sort of a pie? What
. . . Rabbit? Never! God bless my buttons, but
it must be. It can't be pigeon. It must be the
rabbit Ursula bought from the gipsy. And what
else? Give me the pie. God bless me, it's heavy,
it must have been a hare. What else, my son?'

'Potatoes, cold beans, bread . . . cheese,' recited
Alexander, 'and here's another pie, a fruit pie, yes,
that's fruit, and here's something else. Bottles.'

'Bottles?'

After saying this, his mouth remained open and
Alexander saw a look of sly astonishment creep into
his face. Then he stretched out his hands and took
the bottles from Alexander and slowly held them
up to the sunshine, closing one eye deliberately.
Presently he remarked:

'That's for you.'

'What is it?'

'Drink! Never mind what. Never ask what a
drink is, it's not manners.'

And leaning backwards, Alexander drank slowly
and deeply, scarcely tasting what he drank, but
aware only of the satisfaction and coolness of drinking, until he felt as if the breath were being squeezed
from his body and he could drink no longer. Suddenly, with a great burst for breath, he ceased and

sat upright. His uncle was still drinking, with his
head also thrown back, so that he looked to Alexander very like a man blowing a black trumpet from
which no sound ever came. And as he watched,
wondering how long this could last, the half-sweet,
half-bitter taste of what he had drunk awoke in his
mouth.

'Is yours herb beer too?' he leaned forward and
asked.

His uncle did not answer, however, but suddenly
smacking his lips and corking up the bottle, took
his clasp-knife and cut the pie. Alexander received
the leg of a rabbit, and immediately felt strangely
important, as if he had been given a prize or had
said something very witty and clever. He sat with
his mouth open, staring.

'Eat, sonny, eat,' urged his uncle at once. 'There's
beans too, and potatoes. Eat!' He waved his long
arms about him to the trees and the sky. 'All the
pears and the little red apples have to be gathered
before we go, and it's a long journey.'

He himself cut two thick slices of bread and began
to spear pieces of rabbit with the point of his knife,
eating ravenously. A knife and fork had been
packed up for the boy, but he felt it would be almost
degrading and a little childish to use them, and
rather furtively he took out a small tortoise-shell
penknife and began spearing fragments of rabbit's
flesh too. There was no time for conversation.
And gradually everywhere grew silent. Hardly a
bird spoke, and the thick wall of trees about them
stood still and breathless. The sun lay directly
overhead and Alexander could see the heat shim-

mering in waves beyond the baskets lying in squares
and rings of yellow in the grass.

Soon he felt his thoughts fly back again to all that
had happened in the wood. The same overbearing
silence, the same heat, the same uncanny sense of
utter stillness, without a quiver or breath! The
picturesque little house, the old woman sitting
staring like death, with a comb clasped in her hands,
the pond, the sloe-tree, and most vivid of all, the
flowerets on the young girl's dress reflected in the
shining dark water! He ceased eating and the
faint sickness and shock of unexpected joy obsessed
him.

'Come, eat your leg, eat your leg, boy!'

He started and responded mechanically, lifting
the rabbit-leg in his fingers, and then sank into
thought again.

As he sat there, alternately eating and dreaming,
he could only wonder what she was doing, where
she could be.

'If you don't want the leg, don't waste it. Have
a little of this pie instead. Look, see the crust.'

He took a slice of pie, which had been made with
late raspberries, gooseberries, damsons, and a sprink-
ling of dewberries. As he ate he looked up and
asked:

'That man in the little house over there, he's
very ill, isn't he?'

'Yes, God bless him; he won't live, poor fellow.'

'Shall you go back to see him?'

'We might and we might not. I don't know,' he
said, shaking his head, and the boy felt driven back
to silence.

During the remainder of that meal he did not speak again; only his uncle's answer, 'We might and we might not,' careered repeatedly through his head, troubling him.

Not long later the man, with a sleepy 'Don't you fidget, my son,' stretched back on the grass and closed his eyes. In obedience the boy sat for some moments very still, feeling as if he were the only creature alive in the still, drowsy noonday.

He rose presently and walked idly away. . . . The house appeared, its white stone exterior looking forbidding in the sunshine. He stood for some moments staring at it, and then turned abruptly down a little sloping path leading towards a group of firs. A grasshopper began chirring, and a low hum of wasps rose from the plum-trees. Suddenly Alexander stared, slackened his pace, and then, gazing still harder at the object he saw under an apple-tree just ahead, ceased walking altogether. Two small eyes like black beans returned his stare, and an intense sensation of guilt and nervousness refused to let him go forward or run away.

Before him sat a man, a very small person in a blue-striped shirt, a black cap, and stone-coloured trousers fastened with a most handsome belt of plaited and twisted leather decorated with pieces of brass. His shirt-sleeves were rolled up, and on his right fore-arm a purple dragon had been tattooed and on his left there was a crimson bird, like a swallow, designed as if it were flying towards his shoulder. Alexander could not surmise if this man were old or young. He only felt that his thin face with its sharp nose, black little eyes, and bony forehead was very, very cunning. And after a long silence, during which the eyes never flickered, he said falteringly in an apologetic voice:

'We're picking the fruit.'

'What's your name?' asked the man, with a very cunning squint and in a sharp arresting voice.

'I'm Mr Bishop's nephew.'

The man thought a minute, then asked: 'Did you come in that cart with that little nag?'

'Yes.'

'Well, that's all about of a nag, that is. I wouldn't be seen dead with a nag like that. It's a midget!' he went on derisively. 'Don't you feed it?'

Alexander, who was devoted to the little horse, was too outraged to speak, and only nodded several times, staring at the other's thin, cunning face until he detested it. And then suddenly the man remarked:

'I've got a boy about your clip. How old are you?'

'Twelve,' said Alexander.

'Yes, he's about that. Perhaps he's older, though. I don't know, it's a job to tell.' And he informed Alexander abruptly: 'I've got fourteen children; you wouldn't believe that perhaps, would you?'

'Yes,' said Alexander at once, though he felt he couldn't believe a word.

'He was the first to be born after I came home from Turkey, he was. Seven came before Turkey, and seven after, and there's no doubt the first are the strongest. There's no doubt they are. Fine, strong women and men all of them, and two with children of their own. Only yesterday my eldest came to see me. He 's with a duke—yes, he 's a duke's servant—a duke with a name as long as your legs. I can't pronounce his name, no more could you. And this duke says to him, "Baxter," he says, "if there 's any mortal thing you want while I 'm away from home, you take it. Take it!' He was drunk—he drinks a lot, this duke—but it didn't matter, and no sooner 's his back turned than Wag —that 's my son—orders another servant to kill a turkey and gets a leg of mutton and a little barrel of beer, besides a lot of waistcoats and a pair of gaiters —doeskin gaiters, mark you—gentlefolk don't know what they have got, they don't wear things out— and a pair of pants worn once and never a second more, and shoes and God knows what besides he didn't get—and I 'll slit my throat if he didn't hire a conveyance and bring them home and say to me, "Dad, what with having fourteen of us and times hard, you could do with the duke's trousers!' Oh, my God! I laughed till the tears rolled down my cheeks. Why I laughed I don't know, but there you are, he 's my son, and he 's a chip off the old block, and I 'm proud of him. And money! Before he goes he says to me, "Dad, here 's a quid," and he opens his pocket for me to look. And there they lay, hundreds of them, hundreds and hundreds of pounds like packs of playing cards, hundreds and hundreds. . . .'

During all this discourse Alexander grew more and more incredulous and yet more and more fascinated. He felt all the time that he was being told wonderful enormous lies. Everything he could do towards believing these lies he did, yet the thought of so much money, so many children, and the look of constant craftiness on the man's face defeated him.

He stood as if spellbound.

'Haven't seen the old lady about, I suppose?' asked the man suddenly, completely closing one eye and squinting up at Alexander with the other.

The boy shook his head.

'Good,' remarked the other, and took out a small clay pipe, very stained and dirty. 'She's a tough customer. No smoking in this garden — perhaps you don't believe that? Well, believe it or not, it 's true. She 's afraid she 'll be burnt in her bed. Her husband, when he was alive, did nothing but experiment and experiment with things all day and all night long. And one night he set the house afire. . . . That 's the reason. "Baxter," she says every morning, "don't you dare strike a match."' Just at this moment the man did strike a match and began smoking. 'She's like some little cheese-mouse, twittering and trembling about her money. Not like a man I worked for once. He had money. God strike me, he had some money! "Baxter," he used to say to me, "if you want a glass of beer there 's a bucket." A bucket! And I used to draw a bucket of beer as you might draw a bucket of water for your little old nag. . . . But he killed himself. Money! That 's what money did for that man. Money ain't no good. The old lady, what 's all her money bring? What 's she got? Her only son in an asylum, and nobody, not a soul, to live with her—all alone—might as well be under the ground.'

This time Alexander followed the discourse without a thought for its truth, only fascinated profoundly, and as the man went on to tell more and more fantastic episodes he crept nearer and at last sat down at his feet.

While listening he caught sight of an object lying partially concealed by the man's jacket. After some time he made out the fur, then the ears and whiskers of a dead rabbit. From its snout hung a globule of bright red.

'Did you catch that?' he asked, pointing at the dead animal.

'Not so loud. Did I catch what?' the man asked sharply, and pretended suddenly to be extremely stupid, looking everywhere except where Alexander was pointing.

'That!' repeated the boy.

'Where? What is it you 're after? What you mean—"catch"? There 's nothing but slugs to catch here.'

To judge from his puzzled, apathetic movements the man looked as if he had just woken up. Nothing of his slyness remained. And yet Alexander felt that under this mask of stupidity the cunning was growing deeper.

He became silent, and the man took advantage of the silence to relight his pipe, while Alexander, nonplussed by this last change of attitude, wondered if he dare ask another question. After a long silence he did ask it.

'Do you live here?' he said.

'Over yonder, by the wood,' said the man.

'What 's your name?' he ventured to ask, timidly.

'Smack. . . .'

As he uttered this, his mouth snapped shut as sharply as a mouse-trap, and with a sound very like a smack. This produced a great effect on Alexander, who sat open-mouthed for some moments before daring to say:

'Were you christened that?'

'Christened? . . . Lord God, my mother ran off all of a sudden, feeling a bit of a pain in the fields one day, and delivered me under a haystack. I wasn't christened.'

'Don't you go to church, either?'

His face screwed itself up with contempt.

'Church?' he said.

Alexander was impressed by this also, and would have been glad to say how he too hated church, and that he did not understand the psalms or the sermon and could never remember the responses, and how he agreed with his Uncle Bishop that it was all popery and humbug, but suddenly the man drew out a bottle from somewhere and took an immense drink, a drink so long that it seemed to the boy that the bottle must have been emptied over and over again. When it ended the man stretched himself, licked his lips several times, and said suddenly:

'You look as if you 've never seen a man drink. Why, my dad, if he were alive, poor old devil that I should ever say so, he 'd tell you how he used to drink ten pints of a morning, mowing grass. . . .' He squinted and nodded with all his cunning, and then got nimbly to his feet.

Something at frequent intervals had been troubling Alexander, and now as the man prepared to leave him he felt an overwhelming desire to ask another question. And almost against his will he said:

'Do you know the people over there in the wood?'

'Which wood?' said the man.

'There 's a little house,' began Alexander, and suddenly he felt a strange ache as he visualized it all, 'you can hardly see it, the trees are so thick. There 's an old woman there and someone used to live there named Pollyanna, only she 's married and bedridden now, because of her legs. And there 's an old man— he 's had an operation. It 's over there, not very far. We passed it as we came this morning.'

All through this the boy's voice trembled and there lurked in his mind a picture of the young girl. Overcome by a suspicion that every word he spoke must reveal his inner feelings he began to stammer also. Anxiety and joy set up a conflict within him.

'In the wood, you say? The wood . . . but which wood?' said the man. 'There 's so many woods.'

'Over there,' said Alexander, almost desperately.

'No, I can't say. Lord Almighty, there 's a good many people I don't know—thousands!'

Suddenly he cocked his eyes for the last time at Alexander, and walking very sharp like a sharp little dog down the narrow path, passed from sight.

When Alexander returned to the high bank overlooking the disused stone-pit his Uncle Bishop was stretching himself after his sleep.

'Cover the plums with a sack or two,' he began saying. 'That's it, that's it. The basket we'd better take down with us. Drink before you put the bottle away, drink, drink!'

'Where are we going?' asked the boy after drinking some herb beer.

'You take the baskets while I bring the ladder. Make straight for the big pear-tree. Straight on, you couldn't miss it.'

Under an immense pear-tree, on which the fruit hung almost like ropes of onions, the boy presently set down the baskets. A thick, angry hum of wasps met him, and some birds flew up with startled cries from among the branches. Half-rotted pears lay about in the grass under the tree, bored by wasps and pecked at by birds, and a faint odour of what he thought was like wine or balm met him as he walked round and round the tree, crushing pears with his boots and disturbing wasps in his anxiety to find a pear to taste.

'Try one, try one,' suddenly urged his uncle, who had come up behind, a little breathless, with the ladder.

Gaining courage from this, Alexander snatched a fine yellow pear from the tree and crushed his teeth into its unblemished skin. For ever afterwards a recollection of the rare flavour, the strange, wine-like odour and honeyed juice of this pear remained with him. His uncle had seized a pear also and was sucking it with quick gasps of pleasure. Even more excited than Alexander about the fruit he kept opening his eyes extremely wide, until they shone like blue glass marbles.

Neither the man nor the boy for some time uttered a word. At last Uncle Bishop said:

'You must put a few in a bag for yourself. Not yet, later on. And don't let the old tit see you do it.'

Alexander neither did nor said anything in answer to this, but remained spellbound for some moments under a sudden notion which had flashed into his head.

And throughout the afternoon this same idea of taking something, perhaps a plum or a pear, as a gift to the girl never ceased to attract and trouble him. Screened by the thick leaves from view, he would sometimes gather a pear, rub it to a polish on his shirt and put it aside very religiously and tenderly. If however a bruise or crack appeared, he would drop it, feeling a sense of acute loss, into the basket. The afternoon slipped by. Once as he was gathering a pear from a high branch he heard a rustling in the grass beneath him. He started and looked down to see four or five dogs snuffing about the baskets. He heard the old woman coming too. Her snail-like approach and the remembrance of her keen sight made it agonizing for him to sit in the tree without movement or sound.

Then she carried on a conversation with his uncle which seemed to him to go on and on, everlastingly.

'Oh! the wasps, you see the destruction they cause,' she wailed. 'The fruit all eaten away! If it goes on like this I shall have nothing. Dear, dear, just look at it. Just look. It drives me out of my mind to think about it. What shall I do? Come away, Pretty, come away, naughty creature. There's nothing for you. Oh, dear, dear! If it weren't for

the labour I 'd have all the trees down, I 'd have
them all down to-morrow, and there 'd be an end
of it all.'

All her troubles and griefs had to be poured into
Uncle Bishop's ear. Over and over again she complained and sighed, until Alexander felt that he
must drop off the branch with exhaustion and
suspense.

Worst of all, she at last looked round and asked
in a quaking, suspicious voice:

'Where 's the little boy?'

'Oh! he 's gone off,' bellowed Uncle Bishop.
'Lord knows where, but he 's not far away. Down
among the rabbits, I shouldn't wonder.'

'Look after him,' she implored. 'Don't let him
touch them. I wouldn't have them touched, not
for anything. No one 's ever killed one, and no
one ever shall, I can't bear it.'

'They 'll eat you out of your bed before very
long!' muttered Uncle Bishop brutally, not loud
enough for her to hear.

'Don't let him touch them, don't let him touch
them,' was all she said.

A moment later she had begun to shuffle away,
all the dogs trailing in a waddling, abject string
behind her skirts. A long time elapsed before she
passed out of sight and the boy had courage to move
again. When he descended at last and looked about
him it seemed as if the sun were already lower in
the sky.

III

When evening began to come on at last, Alexander and his uncle carried back to the house all the fruit they had gathered, and under the supervision of the old lady, who stood tottering a little distance off, weighed and measured it, Alexander writing down the figures with extreme care on a sheet of paper. All the dogs and the white cat were also there, staring like wooden things or dragging themselves about the grass on their bellies, never running or barking. The little horse seemed to have grown impatient and stood restlessly stamping and frisking against the evening flies. The boy shared this impatience, fixing his mind constantly on the time when they must pass through the wood, longing desperately to depart.

'Does the little boy understand figures?' the old lady wanted to know. 'He won't make mistakes?'

'Bless you, he goes to school!' shouted Uncle Bishop, with pride and force. 'What he doesn't know isn't worth knowing. Nowadays things are different. They 're taught everything, every mortal thing you can wish. Why, he learns Latin now— Latin! God bless your heart, he could write all the names of these apples and pears down for you in Latin.'

'What good would that do?'

'A good deal, you bet your life, a good deal. The boy wouldn't do it for nothing. He 's got a head on him—you see for yourself. Turn round, my boy.

There, you can see now — his head 's as big as a pumpkin.'

Uncle Bishop never lost an opportunity of showing how proud he was of Alexander, and to complete the force of this pride he often exaggerated and frequently told lies. And as he turned round in order to display his head, Alexander felt extremely foolish and half-scowled in vexation. He longed for his uncle to pay his accounts and ached for the sound of wheels again. But his uncle dallied a little longer, and patting the boy's head, at last said to him:

'Now, you go over and show the lady what you 've written. Go along.'

Alexander held out the paper in silence.

'I see, I see,' she said, squinting and trembling more than ever. 'Good lad, he writes well.' And for a long time he had to stand at her side, writing down all the figures his uncle shouted, vexed and uneasy. During this time he discovered that a strange smell hung about her, compound of preserved cloth, dogs, camphor, horse-beans and something dry and musty. And so much fruit had to be weighed and accounted for that he felt at last as if he had breathed this queer odour all his life.

The sun had plunged behind the largest tree before his uncle and the old woman vanished into the house to settle the accounts. All the dogs disappearing also, he was left alone and sat on a little wooden bench with great relief, wondering what time it could be and how soon a start would be made. Then shortly his face assumed an intense, meditative expression.

'Shall I get the apricot?' he thought. 'Could I go back into the garden without being seen?'

And presently, followed by the indistinct voices of his uncle and the old woman, he edged away and strolled in an indifferent manner down the path under the trees. His heart seemed to swell, beating with ponderous thumps. All things were flagged and hushed. An army of shadows advanced to meet him. His footsteps awoke echoes infinitely, making him turn round in fear, as if other footsteps were following him. Mysterious objects under the trees made him start and hasten too.

Suddenly he became aware of footsteps coming not from behind, but before. His impulse was to turn and run, but for some strange reason he ceased walking.

Then a figure appeared. It was Smack. Approaching very slowly, he began to say as soon as he saw Alexander:

'Oh, it's you, it's you, is it? God strike me, it looked like the old woman.' The boy remained dumb, simply gazing at the sack of either apples or potatoes that the man was carrying.

'You're like my son Squint, you are,' Smack went on, 'he creeps about on hands and knees and gets atop of you before you hear a sound. Why, I've seen him drop on a hare like you might drop on a beetle. Perhaps you wouldn't believe that? Well, believe it or not, but there it is. He's a miracle. . . . "Squint," I says to him one day, "you can drop on hares, but could you drop on a fox?" He looks at me and says "Could I drop on a fox?"—just like that. That's all. He's like that. But next day there was a meet. Full cry they

came across from these woods, all the pinks and the
ladies thinking they would be in at the kill, and the
dogs running like mad. I was there, with Squint,
behind a hedge. All of a sudden there's a gallows
of a row, and God bless my poor old mother, the
fox walked through the hedge. Dainty! I never
saw a wedding where there was anything so dainty.
And there she stood. She never moved. She just
looked at Squint, and Squint—what did he do?
God strike me, but he dropped on her, he dropped
on her. And when the hunt came up, there he
stood, there stood our Squint with his arms round
the fox's neck.'

And once again Alexander was carried away by
the cunning of it all. Almost hypnotized by nods
and winks he did not know what to say. But
suddenly Smack asked him sharply:

'Where's the old woman, eh?'

'She's in the house, settling the accounts up,'
stammered Alexander.

'In the house, eh?'

'They've just gone in.' And abruptly he gathered courage to ask: 'You didn't remember the name
of the people in the wood, did you, after all?'

'Name of the people in the wood?'

'There's an old man, and two women . . .'
began the boy.

But Smack shook his head, this time almost
sorrowfully, as if he hated not being able to conjure
up some answer.

'Perhaps I know them,' he said at last. 'There's
thousands of people I do know, thousands. I dare
say I know them.'

'There 's a girl,' persisted Alexander.

'A girl?' the other repeated. 'A girl?' And suddenly he managed to attach to that word something incredulous, cynical, mocking, and his thin lips and eyes squeezed themselves into a repellent smile.

Directly afterwards he laughed and sidled off, and Alexander found himself walking rapidly towards the wall bearing the apricot-tree, no longer afraid, but driven by a feeling of desperation and wretchedness. All his sweetest, most tender emotions felt wounded. It seemed to him monstrous that what aroused in him elation and joy should have struck Smack as contemptible and pretty. He did not understand and felt that it was all horrible, that in some strange way he had betrayed a mysterious and precious trust. Only the intensity of his own beliefs comforted him.

He hurried on. He resolved suddenly to snatch the apricot quickly, and, regardless of everything, run as fast as possible back to the house again.

In the dying sunlight the apricot-trees had a rich, luxuriant, exclusive look about them. On the third tree hung a very special apricot he had noted several times. He plucked it, quickly and gently, and began to run.

He emerged from among the trees just in time to hear the voice of his uncle begin impatiently shouting:

'Where are you? Where are you? Boy! Where have you been? Here, here . . . tell us what ninety-three pence make. Ninety-three pence . . . what? Come here, you 'd better come inside. Take

your cap off. And remember if the old tit asks
you anything shout in her ear. Shout! Now make
haste, go along the passage.'

Alexander was hurried into a gloomy passage,
where he noted a strong odour of damp and mice and
saw several pairs of antlers branched from the walls
and a stuffed white owl staring down at him. When
at a furtive whisper from his uncle he entered a door
on the right, he saw the old lady, now with spectacles
on, sitting alone at a shining oval table. A good
deal of money, with three or four dark red leather
bags and heaps of bills, were strewn about. Again
the odour of damp and mice met him. All the
furniture was of pale yellow wood, with faded blue
damask upholstery and many cushions. Little
pairs of milky green and pink glass vases stood on a
white mantelpiece, like small dolls preening themselves in the large mirror behind. Something dead,
old-fashioned, and sad lurked about the room, and
to the boy it seemed full of memories, of the lingering
presences of men and women who had once lived,
talked, and perhaps sung and danced there. He
noticed that the walls were covered with old portraits,
every other portrait looking like a picture of the
Saviour, except that all the figures were wearing
bowler hats and deerstalkers and white silk neck-
ties.

'Go in, go in,' urged his uncle, giving him little
impatient punches from behind.

He advanced and stood silently before the table,
staring at the heaps of money.

Suddenly his uncle began to say at the top of his
voice:

'Here 's the boy. He 'll manage it. It 'll be put right before you can wink.'

The old lady turned and searched Alexander's face with sharp squints. 'Mind you do, and don't make mistakes,' she said.

'That 's all right, you trust him,' bawled his uncle. 'Now, my son, tell the lady what ninety-three pence are.'

Alexander, a little bewildered, had to think a moment before replying. 'Seven and ninepence,' he said at last.

'Shout!'

'Seven and ninepence,' he shouted.

'Seven and ninepence?' she repeated. 'Are you sure? You haven't made a mistake, have you? If you think you haven't made a mistake, write it down . . . just there . . . write it down.'

Alexander took from her shaking fingers a small black pen, with which he wrote down the figures seven and nine with laborious care in an old, dirty book. As he wrote, her stiff sleeves brushed against him and he was continually afraid that she would feel or smell or in some other way divine that he had the apricot about him. All the little tremors and starts of her body alarmed him.

'Has he written it?' she croaked suspiciously after a silence. 'I can't see.'

'Yes, he 's written it!' proclaimed his uncle. 'You can trust him. What you want is a light.' Twilight was rapidly creeping through the room. 'You 're not likely to see. Haven't you got some sort of a lamp?' he asked.

'Wha-a-t?'

'A lamp! You want some sort of a light on the subject or else you won't know shillings from ha'pence.'

'What does he say?' she turned and asked Alexander in a puzzled voice.

But this was never answered, for suddenly his Uncle Bishop snatched out his matches and struck a light, letting it flare up in his fingers. The old woman stood at once petrified, all her features white and stiff with horror. Then she began to struggle, as if choking, her eyes bulged, her hands waved hither and thither, she tried to stand up, her head looked as if it must totter off with rage, and then at last she croaked out in a terrible voice:

'What are you doing, what are you doing? Put it out at once! Oh, you wicked man, you wicked man! You mustn't do it, I won't have it! Put it out at once!'

Her voice was thin and rasping. 'Put it out, you wicked man! Put it out!' she kept saying in fury.

Uncle Bishop's mouth fell open, and without a word he pinched out the flame with his fingers. There was silence. The boy dared not stir.

Then the old lady began another struggle: she tried to calm herself, to sit down, to administer reprimands, but only infuriated trembling went on accompanied by a strange half-hissing, half-rattling sound. Gradually she coiled herself up, trembling less and less, like a spring, until she sank into the chair again. As she became quieter the silence seemed to become more and more intense. A little smoke wandered through the air and the pungent odour of it spread about the room. But the boy hardly dared to look or smell.

After what seemed an interminable silence, the old woman held up one finger and shook it admonishingly at Uncle Bishop for a long time. 'You must never do that,' she said. 'I never allow that—I never allow a naked light, not even in the garden, not anywhere. Did you want to frighten my life out?'

'Let me pay you what I owe. That's enough. God damn it, what next, what else?' he muttered. 'Let me pay you!'

'You might have been the death of me!' she quavered.

He did not heed, however, and began to shout with increased impatience:

'Never mind that, let's pay you and be off; we shall have dark on us.'

Still she remained unenlightened, muttering constantly about life, fire, and death, until the man mustered suddenly a thunderous shout:

'Let me pay you, do you hear, let me pay you!'

When she heard at last, there was a change in her demeanour. After an abrupt jerk of her head towards the table and a rapid fluttering of her hands about the bills and leather money-bags, an excited, almost skilful motion, as if she were working on a lace-pillow, she suddenly looked up at Alexander almost gratefully and asked him to add up a little column of figures.

'Add them carefully,' she warned him, however. 'Be very careful, your uncle's money isn't to be thrown away.'

'Never mind her. Add them up quickly,' urged his uncle. 'She's scared out of her life because we might cheat her. But it 's all right, never mind, you just tell her what amounts to.'

'Three pounds, seven and a penny,' said Alexander after a feverish interval.

'Tell her. Shout!'

Urged on by his uncle, he found something delightful in shouting, deliberately:

'Three pounds, seven shillings and a penny,' several times over.

His uncle began to count out the money, the woman nodding her head with a sort of feverish anticipation. When the three notes, the silver, and the odd penny were being passed across the table, he kept shouting:

'Are you satisfied? Are you satisfied?'

'If you are,' she said. 'I am if you are.'

'Thank God for that!'

'Shall I get the reins untied?' asked Alexander.

'Yes, off you go! I 'll be there before very long!'

As he left the room and hurried along the gloomy passage he was overcome by a sense of great relief, followed by elation. Reaching the yard, he heard a sound and turned to see all the seven fat dogs following him. He clapped his hands loudly, hastening them into retreat. He felt he was sick of dogs, money, the dark house, and the rasping voice and ever-quivering head and fingers of the old woman. He touched the apricot in his pocket repeatedly, feeling very happy. Aroused by his approach, the little horse began to show signs of joy too, stamping one foot, tossing its head and tinkling the harness. Alexander stroked the horse's nose and then untied the reins and climbed into the cart.

Five minutes later all was ready. Surrounded by the seven dogs, who crawled about like huge beetles in the approaching twilight, the old woman muttered a few departing words.

'You must come again,' she said, and it almost seemed as if she regretted their departure. 'It's a bad year, and there's no peace from the boys, but there's a few black plums, and if any one does have them it shall be you. They're very good. Shall I expect you?'

'Yes, you can expect us!' shouted the man, impatient to flick the whip.

'Here, little one,' she then said.

And into the boy's outstretched hands she reached up and put first a small apple, on which already birds had been feeding, then a piece of cake, this time made with fruit and baked very hard, and lastly a penny. Then she looked up at him softly and said:

'God bless you.'

And these words seemed to transport him into a rare, trance-like frame of mind, so that he was hardly conscious of her face, the grey house, and the seven stupid faces of the dogs slipping gradually away from him, and of the cart beginning to move forward smoothly and steadily into the summer twilight.

IV

They drove forward at an even more leisurely pace than that of the morning. Frequently the little horse walked, the man not using the whip except to flick the air. The baskets creaked under their great weight and the wheels made a monotonous grinding sound. Elsewhere the same tranquil, almost sleepy hush prevailed as in the early morning and at noon, and the same summer odours remained and the same sense of rich and lovely fruitfulness; only outlines and colours were changed; everything shaped itself by degrees of shadow and not light, and it seemed as if flowers and leaves were resting after intense toil, colourless and drooping, simply releasing breaths of heavy perfume.

Ever since morning the boy had been conscious of casting his thoughts forward to this time. Now, as he began to arrive near the fulfilment of them, he felt a desire to travel as swiftly as they had done. To sit still and not surge recklessly on at the pace of thought was an agony. And before long he could not resist asking:

'Let me drive.'

'You! It 's too dark. You sit still and eat the old tit's cake.'

'Shall we be long?'

'We 're almost in the wood.'

There was something calm and reassuring about these words. He saw the dark belt of trees grow closer and vaster, as though it would reassure and protect him. The singing season was almost past, and owls and jays alone would call in the twilight, but there seemed to him something singing and jubilant in the silence and half-darkness, and gradually his mind filled itself with thoughts and images of a singing, dream-like quality also. And so the distance was obscured, the fading sky retreated and solitary trees standing like dark ghosts seemed to creep away or dissolve where they stood, and nothing remained but the wood standing ready to receive them into its bosom. The little horse slowed to a walk, its feet padding the dust as softly as if shod with leather. The wheels scarcely turned. Nothing called, nothing seemed to happen. . . . Alexander's hand crept to his pocket and closed about the apricot. And then, simultaneously, to the accompaniment of myriads of echoes rising like a confusion of voices, the wood closed about him, and the air he breathed became cooler, sharply sweet with a scent of damp leaves and of evening time and decay.

They drove on and on. Sounds became more numerous, and the wood seemed to be quivering with life. In the echoes of hoofs and wheels, in the stirring branches, in the rustle of invisible creatures over dead leaves, in passing moths, in the cries of birds, in his own breathing, there was something urgent and vital. Sounds seemed to run on before him, heralding his coming.

More and more, however, he became troubled by the thought that this coming might signify nothing. He was oppressed by uncertainty, and he dared not ask if they might stop in the wood.

All he dared to say, in a casual tone as if he had half-forgotten its existence, was:

'Isn't this where we stopped at a house?'

But there was no answer. He waited, and not daring to repeat his question, looked cautiously at his uncle's face, and seeing something passive and preoccupied about it, looked away quickly without a word, lapsing into a mood of half-painful, half-joyful expectancy.

He was astonished a moment later by feeling the cart suddenly come to a standstill. No house was visible, and he did not understand the reason of it all until his uncle climbed out and began striking matches for the lamps.

In order to relieve his wonder completely, he half-whispered, however:

'What's the matter?'

There was a low grunt in answer. Then, as he watched the lamplight swell into a soft circle in the surrounding darkness, he felt unresistingly borne upon him an image of the girl's young, sweet face, filling him with an exuberance of happiness mingled with pain and longing, all the sublime emotion of first ecstasy transforming him, filling his soul with something so fresh, so joyous and amazing that he felt he could not have spoken or that he could scarcely have looked at her even had she suddenly appeared in the lamplight. He felt that he would suffer deeply if he never saw her again, knowing at last, and for the first time in his life, the meaning of suffering as he already knew the meaning of joy.

He was scarcely conscious of the cart moving forward again, the lamplight floating constantly before them like a yellow cloud, the air growing cooler under the trees. His mood of ecstasy resembled a tide, flowing in upon him wave after wave, and his thoughts became tangled and he gained only an impression of trees, very dark and monarchal, endlessly passing and passing.

A light appeared in the wood at last, and startled him abruptly from this mood of entrancement. He became alert and conscious of realities, sitting upright and tense. As he saw the light approaching and enlarging, he felt himself seized with sudden courage, and he said quickly and almost sharply, as if afraid his voice would break:

'Are we going to stop here?'

'Good Lord, what should we stop for?' came the answer. 'At this time of night? God bless me, we 've nothing to stop for; we 've long enough to go without that. What 's the matter? Eat the cake she gave you if you 're hungry. Fill your belly a bit. It 's a long way, my lad, out of the wood and through the valley. A long way yet.'

It seemed as if he did not listen to these words. He became aware of them instead as one becomes aware of a flock of birds flying from an horizon. The character of each word is lost in the whole as the individuality of each bird is lost in the flock; only about their meaning, as of the species of bird, there remains no doubt. And he did not answer, feeling once again that he could not trust himself to speak, and also that perhaps he would have cried if he had begun to speak. A white moth flew past, and he felt that just as swiftly and irrevocably had the light of the house flown by before he could raise a hand to catch it. A great oak stumbled towards them like a malformed creature and lurched into darkness.

All things retreated or moved endlessly on and on.
Only he himself, clinging to his precious thoughts,
remained unmoving, not able to resist the wretchedness overpowering him.

Again the little horse fell into the same unbroken
leisurely pace as in the early morning. Soon they
passed out of the wood, reaching open fields under a
calm deep-blue sky sown with stars. A smell of
harvest would come, pass away, and be renewed,
stronger and stronger.

His uncle began to murmur some old song, as he
had done under the plum-trees.

His wretchedness became complete, and his
thoughts raced backward to the morning. With
strange sharpness he saw the sunshine begin to
beautify everything again, the golden, unfamiliar
countryside, the harvesters, the distant woods, the
dew clinging to the leaves—and at last the house,
the hot, sweet garden, the unbroken stillness into
which the girl had come like a vision, silently too.

The song went on. And to the boy it seemed that
nothing so beautiful or memorable had ever taken
place in his life, and as he recalled the moments by
the pond, under the sloe-tree, his unhappiness was
mingled suddenly with an ecstatic joy. He felt that
there was a strange sharp pleasure even in disappointment, even in the pain of not seeing her
again.

The sleepy voice of his uncle sang drowsily on for
long afterwards. Something in it alternately pained
and fortified him. Then he would feel half ashamed,
half foolish as he remembered all his secret thoughts,
all his idealizing of the girl throughout the long day.

Once he caught an image of her face, beautifully
fresh and enchanting in all its detail, and filled with
an agony of bliss he asked himself over and over
again:

'Why didn't we stop there? Shall I ever see her
again? Will she remember me?'

When this mood, like all others, had exhausted
itself, he passed into a long tranquillity. Familiar
fields and trees appeared in the darkness, and the
horse began travelling a little faster, as if sensing
home. He brooded quietly now on the day that
had passed, turning it over and over in his mind
like some legend almost too wonderful to believe,
mingling with it strange tales he had heard, things
he had treasured up in his soul long, long ago, and
he thought with special pleasure of the little house,
the woman whose name was Cilla, the great fruit
garden, the dogs, the little sharp man who had told
him wonderful lies, and the old woman saying 'God
bless you' as they drove away, his mind filling
moment by moment with a mysterious elation and
joy.

Soon they drove into a street by the river and so
into a little yard. He saw the familiar sycamore-
tree, obscure sheds, low black stables, and then the
house, throwing a stream of light on the tree.

At the sound of their approach a door opened, and
there appeared first an old fat woman with a shawl
over her head, then his aunt, a little shrewd, quick
person who ran hither and thither like an ant, and
lastly his mother, plump, rosy-faced, and looking
rather like a kind, soft-hearted nurse.

They began to pour out a stream of arguments

and questions and to remonstrate severely with his uncle, who did not once reply.

'Where have you been, what 's been happening to you? Oh, dear! keeping the boy out in that cart, I wonder you don't die of shame. What 's been happening, Alexander? Aren't you cold riding in the cart? I wonder he isn't perished. Hot, did you say? Yes, in day-time I 'll own, but the dews are so heavy. It 's not sense—I 'd be ashamed. Jump you down, my lamb. Lord, there 's dew on the cart, bless me if there isn't. Jump you down and come indoors. Lord love us!'

To all this he said nothing. He felt that the three women, particularly Ursula and even his mother, were being foolish. In the cart it had been peaceful and he had dreamed. Not to relinquish this peace or these dreams seemed everything to him. He turned slowly and walked away.

Ursula hobbled after him to the house. As he reached the door and she ushered him into the light she broke out again:

'What happened, my lamb? Did you stop anywhere?'

He shook his head; a sharp feeling half of wretchedness, half of aching joy, swept over him; with difficulty he murmured: 'No, we didn't stop anywhere.'

With these words he heard the little horse walking away to its stable and the last tinkle of chains, and with the cry of an owl, with the closing of a door somewhere, with his uncle's voice asking if all were locked for the night, he felt that the strange long eventfulness of the day was closing, was being shut away from him like a book. He sat motionless, not knowing whether to laugh or cry with overwhelming happiness and pain.

And suddenly, his heart very full, he felt that everything which had filled and beautified the day had at last slipped away into the past, and lay in his mind like a clearly remembered dream.

He could only sit silent in wonder. The day had passed, the journey was at an end.

When would another begin?

EVER FALL IN LOVE WITH A
MIDGET?

By WILLIAM SAROYAN

'I don't suppose you ever fell in love with a midget
weighing thirty-nine pounds, did you?'

'No,' I said, 'but have another beer.'

'Down in Gallup,' he said, 'twenty years ago.
Fellow by the name of Rufus Jenkins came to town
with six white horses and two black ones. Said he
wanted a man to break the horses for him because
his left leg was wood and he couldn't do it. Had a
meeting at Parker's Mercantile Store and finally
came to blows, me and Henry Walpal. Bashed his
head with a brass cuspidor and ran away to Mexico,
but he didn't die.

'Couldn't speak a word. Took up with a cattle-
breeder named Diego, educated in California.
Spoke the language better than you and me. Said,
"Your job, Murph, is to feed them prize bulls." I
said, "Fine; what 'll I feed them?" He said, "Hay,
lettuce, salt, and beer." I said, "Fine; they 're
your bulls."

'Came to blows two days later over an accordion
he claimed I stole. I borrowed it and during the
fight busted it over his head; ruined one of the
finest accordions I ever saw. Grabbed a horse
and rode back across the border. Texas. Got to
talking with a fellow who looked honest. Turned
out to be a Ranger who was looking for me.'

'Yeah,' I said.   'You were saying, a thirty-nine pound midget.'

'Will I ever forget that lady?' he said.   'Will I ever get over that amazon of small proportions?'

'Will you?' I said.

'If I live to be sixty,' he said.

'Sixty?' I said.   'You look more than sixty now.'

'That's trouble showing in my face.   Trouble and complications.   I was fifty-six three months ago.'

'Oh.'

'Told the Texas Ranger my name was Rothstein, mining engineer from Pennsylvania, looking for something worth while.   Mentioned two places in Houston.   Nearly lost an eye early one morning, going down the stairs.   Ran into a six-footer with an iron-claw where his right hand was supposed to be.   Said, "You broke up my home."   Told him I was a stranger in Houston.   The girls gathered at the top of the stairs to see a fight.   Seven of them.   Six feet and an iron-claw.   That's bad on the nerves.   Kicked him in the mouth when he swung for my head with the claw.   Would have lost an eye except for quick thinking.   Rolled into the gutter and pulled a gun.   Fired seven times, but I was back upstairs.   Left the place an hour later, dressed in silk and feathers, with a hat swung around over my face.   Saw him standing on the corner, waiting.   Said, "Care for a wiggle?"   Said he didn't.   Went on down the street, left town.'

'I don't suppose you ever had to put on a dress to save your skin, did you?'

'No,' I said, 'and I never fell in love with a midget weighing thirty-nine pounds. Have another beer.'

'Thanks. Ever try to herd cattle on a bicycle?'

'No,' I said.

'Left Houston with sixty cents in my pocket, gift of a girl named Lucinda. Walked fourteen miles in fourteen hours. Big house with barb-wire all around, and big dogs. One thing I never could get around. Walked past the gate, anyway, from hunger and thirst. Dogs jumped up and came for me. Walked right into them, growing older every second. Went up to the door and knocked. Big negress opened the door, closed it quick. Said, "On your way, white trash."

'Knocked again. Said, "On your way." Again. "On your way." Again. This time the old man himself opened the door, ninety if he was a day. Sawed-off shotgun too.

'Said, "I ain't looking for trouble, father. I'm hungry and thirsty, name's Cavanaugh."

'Took me in and made mint juleps for the two of us.

'Said, "Living here alone, father?"

'Said, "Drink and ask no questions; maybe I am and maybe I ain't. You saw the negress. Draw your own conclusions."

'I'd heard of that, but didn't wink out of tact.

'Called out, "Elvira, bring this gentleman sandwiches."

'Young enough for a man of seventy, probably no more than forty, and big.

'Said, "Any good at cards?" Said, "No."

'Said, "Fine, Cavanaugh, take a hand of poker."

'Played all night.

'If I told you that old Southern gentleman was my grandfather, you wouldn't believe me, would you?'

'No.'

'Well, it so happens he wasn't, although it would have been remarkable if he had been.'

'Where did you herd cattle on a bicycle?'

'Toledo, Ohio, 1918.'

'Toledo, Ohio?' I said. 'They don't herd cattle up there.'

'They don't any more. 'They did in 1918. One fellow did, leastways. Book-keeper named Sam Gold. Only Jewish cowboy I ever saw. Straight from the East-Side New York. Sombrero, lariats, Bull Durham, two head of cattle, and two bicycles. Called his place Gold Bar Ranch, two acres, just outside the city limits.

'That was the year of the War, you 'll remember.'

'Yeah,' I said.

'Remember a picture called *Shoulder Arms*?'

'Sure. Saw it five times.'

'Remember when Charlie Chaplin thought he was washing *his* foot, and the foot turned out to be another man's?'

'Sure.'

'You may not believe me, but I was the man whose foot was washed by Chaplin in that picture.'

'It 's possible,' I said, 'but how about herding them two cows on a bicycle? How 'd you do it?'

'Easiest thing in the world. Rode no hands. Had to, otherwise couldn't lasso the cows. Worked for Sam Gold till the cows ran away. Bicycles scared them. They went into Toledo and we never saw hide or hair of them again. Advertised in every paper, but never got them back. Broke his heart. Sold both bikes and returned to New York.

'Took four aces from a deck of red cards and walked to town. Poker. Fellow in the game named Chuck Collins, liked to gamble. Told him with a smile I didn't suppose he 'd care to bet a hundred dollars I wouldn't hold four aces the next hand. Called it. My cards were red on the blank side. The other cards were blue. Plumb forgot all about it. Showed him four aces. Ace of spades, ace of clubs, ace of diamonds, ace of hearts. I 'll remember them four cards if I live to be sixty. Would have been killed on the spot except for the hurricane that year.'

'Hurricane?'

'You haven't forgotten the Toledo hurricane of 1918, have you?'

'No,' I said. 'There was no hurricane in Toledo, in 1918, or any other year.'

'For the love of God, then, what do you suppose that commotion was? And how come I came to in Chicago? Dream-walking down State Street?'

'I guess they scared you.'

'No, that wasn't it. You go back to the papers of November 1918 and I think you 'll find there was a hurricane in Toledo. I remember sitting on the roof of a two-story house, floating north-west.'

'North-west?'

'Sure.'

'Okay, have another beer.'

'Thanks,' he said, 'thaaaaanks.'

'I don't suppose *you* ever fell in love with a midget weighing thirty-nine pounds, did you?' I said.

'Who?' he said.

'You,' I said.

'No,' he said, 'can't say I have.'

'Well,' I said, 'let *me* tell *you* about it.'

Made At The
Temple Press
Letchworth
in
Great Britain

EVERYMAN'S
LIBRARY

EDITED BY ERNEST RHYS

A CLASSIFIED LIST
OF THE FIRST 944 VOLUMES

In Cloth Binding
In Special Library Binding
Also Selected Volumes in Leather

EVERYMAN'S LIBRARY
CLASSIFIED LIST of 944 VOLS. in 13 SECTIONS

> *In each section of this list the volumes are arranged, as a general rule, alphabetically under the authors' names. Where authors appear in more than one section, a reference is given, viz.: (See also* FICTION*). The number at the end of each item is the number of the volume in the series.*
> *Volumes obtainable in Leather are marked* L

BIOGRAPHY

Audubon the Naturalist, Life and Adventures of. By R. Buchanan. 601

Baxter (Richard), Autobiography of. Edited by Rev. J. M. Lloyd Thomas. 868

Beaconsfield (Lord), Life of. By J. A. Froude. 666

Berlioz (Hector), Life of. Translated by Katherine F. Boult. 602

Blackwell (Dr Elizabeth): Pioneer Work for Women. With an Introduction by Mrs Fawcett. 667

L Boswell's Life of Johnson. 2 vols. 1–2
    (*See also* TRAVEL)

Browning (Robert), Life of. By E. Dowden. 701

Buxton (Sir Thomas Fowell), Memoirs of. Edited by Charles Buxton. Introduction by Lord Buxton. 773

L Byron's Letters. Introduction by André Maurois. 931

Carey (William), Life of: Shoemaker and Missionary. 395

Carlyle's Letters, and Speeches of Cromwell. 3 vols. 266–8
    ,,   Reminiscences. 875
    (*See also* ESSAYS *and* HISTORY)

L Cellini's (Benvenuto) Autobiography. 51

Cibber's (Colley) An Apology for his Life. 668

Constable (John), Memoirs of. By C. R. Leslie, R.A. 563

Cowper (William), Selected Letters of. Intro. by W. Hadley, M.A. 774
    (*See also* POETRY AND DRAMA)

De Quincey's Reminiscences of the Lake Poets. Intro. by E. Rhys. 163
    (*See also* ESSAYS)

De Retz (Cardinal): Memoirs. By Himself. 2 vols. 735–6

Evelyn's Diary. 2 vols. Introduction by G. W. E. Russell. 220–1

Forster's Life of Dickens. Intro. by G. K. Chesterton. 2 vols. 781–2
    (*See also* FICTION)

Fox (George), Journal of. Text revised by Norman Penney, F.S.A. Introduction by Rufus M. Jones, LL.D. 754

Franklin's (Benjamin) Autobiography. 316

Froude's Life of Benjamin Disraeli, Earl of Beaconsfield. 666

L Gaskell's (Mrs) Life of Charlotte Brontë. Intro. by May Sinclair. 318

Gibbon (Edward), Autobiography of. Intro. by Oliphant Smeaton. 511
    (*See also* HISTORY)

Gladstone, Life of. By G. W. E. Russell ('Onlooker'). 661

Hastings (Warren), Life of. By Capt. L. J. Trotter. 452

Helps' (Sir Arthur) Life of Columbus. 332

Hodson, of Hodson's Horse. By Capt. L. J. Trotter. 401

Holmes' Life of Mozart. Introduction by Ernest Newman. 564

Houghton's Life and Letters of Keats. Introduction by Robert Lynd. 801

Hutchinson (Col.) Memoirs of. Intro. Monograph by F. P. G. Guizot. 317

Irving's Life of Mahomet. Introduction by Professor E. V. Arnold. 513

Johnson's Lives of the Poets. Intro. by Mrs Archer-Hind, M.A. 770–1

Lamb (Charles), Letters of. 2 vols. 342–3
    (*See also* ESSAYS *and* FOR YOUNG PEOPLE)

Lewes' Life of Goethe. Introduction by Havelock Ellis. 269

Lincoln (Abraham), Life of. By Henry Bryan Binns. 783
    (*See also* ORATORY)

Lockhart's Life of Robert Burns. Introduction by E. Rhys. 156

L   ,,   Life of Napoleon. 3

    ,,   Life of Sir Walter Scott (abridged). 55

Mazzini, Life of. By Bolton King, M.A. 562   [Newcastle. 722

Newcastle (First Duke of), Life of, and other writings by the Duchess of Outram (Sir J.), The Bayard of India. By Capt. L. J. Trotter. 396

BIOGRAPHY—*continued*

FICTION—continued

FICTION—*continued*

FICTION—*continued*

FICTION—continued

HISTORY

HISTORY—*continued*

ORATORY

PHILOSOPHY AND THEOLOGY

PHILOSOPHY AND THEOLOGY—*continued*

POETRY AND DRAMA

REFERENCE

ROMANCE

SCIENCE

SCIENCE—*continued*

TRAVEL AND TOPOGRAPHY

FOR YOUNG PEOPLE

PUBLISHERS:

J. M. DENT & SONS LTD
ALDINE HOUSE · BEDFORD STREET
LONDON W.C.2

E. P. DUTTON & COMPANY INC.
286–302 FOURTH AVENUE
NEW YORK

Made in Great Britain at The Temple Press, Letchworth, Herts (M 56)